The Walk

First published in English in 2017 by
New Internationalist Publications Ltd
The Old Music Hall
106-108 Cowley Road
Oxford
OX4 1JE, UK
newint.org

© Peter Barry

Edited by Chris Brazier

Front cover design: Rawshock design

Design: New Internationalist

Printed by TJ International Limited, Cornwall, UK
who hold environmental accreditation ISO 14001.

MIX
Paper from
responsible sources
FSC® C013056
www.fsc.org

British Library Cataloguing-in-Publication Data.
A catalogue record for this book is available from the British Library.

Library of Congress Cataloging-in-Publication Data.
A catalog for this book is available from the Library of Congress.

ISBN 978-1-78026-394-6
(ISBN ebook 978-1-78026-395-3)

THE WALK

PETER BARRY

New Internationalist

For Elizabeth

Before

*A*drian Burles believed himself to be a good man. He also insisted that the events he organized in the summer of 1987 were done with the best of intentions and were of benefit to millions of people. But that didn't stop his many critics from condemning his actions as being nothing short of unforgivable – murderous, some even whispered.

He was struck with the idea in the middle of the night after his visit to the health clinic at Korem in the Northern Highlands. It was his first visit to Ethiopia, and the nurse, Anne Chaffey, had said something to him earlier that day that meant little to him at the time – in fact had barely registered in his consciousness. This was most likely because he'd been too upset, as well as embarrassed, by his own sudden, very public and totally uncharacteristic display of emotion.

They'd been standing outside the clinic, and she'd been speaking to him – about what he had little idea, or certainly couldn't remember later. Perhaps, almost certainly, she'd been firing statistics at him, statistics so outrageous, incessant and ubiquitous that it resulted in a seeming inability on his part to absorb them all. In the few days he'd spent in Ethiopia, such statistics had become almost meaningless, and he'd been asking himself why everyone was so obsessed with them (the latest to find a permanent lodging in his head was that, at the height of the famine two years earlier, 16,000 people had been dying of starvation every week), when their case or whatever it was they were proposing would have been won more speedily by simply telling their audience to look at what was under their noses. Forget the statistics, those cold-blooded facts and numbers, just look at what's around you! The mathematics are weak in comparison to the spectacle. And it was exactly that – what was directly in front of him – that had distracted him from what the nurse was saying.

At his feet were hundreds of refugees. They were the overflow from the health clinic itself, but also from the camp a couple of miles to the north. They were sitting motionless around Adrian and Anne, packed so closely together that he wasn't quite sure how the two of them had managed to reach the point where they were then standing. He felt hemmed in on every side, and even though he was outdoors, could scarcely breathe. Knowing there was no place for him to escape to, nowhere that would make him feel any better, made his situation almost unbearable. The only escape would be to get on a plane and leave the country. He was imprisoned in a monochromatic sepia nightmare, with everyone – men and women, young and old, infants – coated in desert dust, the rags on their backs and the pathetic bundles in their arms all covered in a fine film, as if they'd been left untouched for hundreds of years in an Elizabethan attic. They paid absolutely no attention to the two white people in their midst, even to their benefactor, the nurse now addressing Adrian. No one in the crowd spoke. Instead of words there was an incessant hum, a low, hopeless moaning mixed in with a high-pitched, pain-filled keening. Lethargy was too weak a word to describe the inaction of these people; what they exuded was a forceful indifference. They waited at Adrian's feet with the patience of death.

And it was then that it happened.

As in a nightmare, he suddenly and quite unexpectedly became aware that he was standing directly over a motionless and obviously uninterested mother. She was sitting on the barren earth with a baby at her withered breast, a young child leaning against her on one side, and a dead infant, lying like a discarded rag, on the other. At the very moment Adrian became aware of this horrifying spectacle, one of Anne Chaffey's assistants suddenly appeared at their side, bent quickly over the infant, and then picked the tiny body up to carry it into the clinic. It was obviously dead. The resemblance to an early-morning refuse collection in a suburban street back home was both startling and unsettling. A dense cloud of flies was covering each of the spectral figures in the scene, and had the effect of momentarily making the infant's corpse look as if it were moving. Adrian wanted to shout out, to tell the assistant to check the baby's pulse – just in case – or for Anne Chaffey to intervene, even though he had no idea to what purpose. But he did nothing. He told himself they must surely know what they were doing, that it was not his place... And then, as he watched the assistant disappear inside the clinic with her pitiful burden, he started to weep.

Ethiopia made him feel like this: to feel suffocated and oppressed, to have scarcely the strength to move. He was as ashamed of these feelings as he was startled by the tears that now escaped from beneath his shut eyelids. The nurse stopped talking, and he wondered if it was his tears that had so suddenly and successfully dammed the unending flow of statistics. He opened his eyes to see her quickly turn away and look into the distance, over the heads of the waiting crowd. He supposed it was either to give him time to recover, or because she didn't know what to say. Finally, she glanced in his direction. It was a shrewd, appraising look, both unselfconscious and uncritical.

'I'm sorry,' he said, 'I don't usually...' He was mortified, and had to make an effort to stifle the urge to tell her that he never cried. He wasn't one for public displays of emotion, especially in circumstances like these. Here he would have regarded them as a futile, self-serving gesture.

She looked sympathetic, but said nothing. She did, briefly, put a hand on his arm, however, and give it a small squeeze before turning away to scan the people encamped in front of her clinic. 'I just have to deal with something inside, Mr Burles', she said a moment later. 'A crisis – another one.' She shook her head ruefully. 'I shan't be too long,' and, stepping carefully between the refugees, she disappeared through the door – the same door that the assistant carrying the dead baby had walked through a few minutes earlier. Adrian suspected she was being diplomatic, and wanted to give him a moment or two by himself to gather his thoughts.

He felt not just out of place but out of uniform, like a

twitchy middle-aged business executive unused to wearing the informal clothes he now found himself in: neatly pressed shorts that went down to the knees, and a baggy T-shirt whose sole purpose – although he would have denied it – was an attempt to hide his bulky frame. Streaks of sunblock were visible on his forearms, legs and the back of his neck, but his face, especially his forehead, beneath the thick crew cut of his salt-and-pepper hair, was already burning red. He was aware, painfully aware, of being a Westerner – pampered, clean, prosperous, heavily perspiring – but most of all, white. Screamingly, obviously white. And screamingly, obviously well fed. Not just cuddly (as he would have described himself), but overweight. He wouldn't have stuck out more if he'd been stark naked.

Around him were strangers – aliens, skeletons covered in skin. Skin that was translucent and taut, lying over bones like the varnished tissue paper on a child's model airplane. Heads more like skulls, eyes sunken, hands and feet merely skin and bones. He fought to block the obscenely uncomfortable thought that kept presenting itself to him, the startling similarity to the black-and-white photographs he'd seen of Jewish inmates at Belsen and Auschwitz after liberation. The only difference was that the people around him now were an inky, midnight, coal-like black. Screamingly, obviously black. And screamingly, obviously underfed.

He tried to avoid everyone's eye. What was the point in trying to engage with anyone? he asked himself. To bridge such gulfs, of colour and nutrition, was an impossibility, and, anyway, he didn't speak their language. Even a smile in such circumstances would be meaningless. It would most likely be interpreted as an insult, or as a sign of indifference. Fortunately, no one seemed in the slightest bit interested in him; even the children barely glanced in his direction. Everyone was paralysed by torpor. So he stood there – in the dust, out of place, like a cuckoo in a nest of sparrows – and wallowed in a feeling he'd never before experienced: inadequacy.

He was eventually rescued by Anne Chaffey emerging from the clinic. 'People who visit us are always so moved.' She was obviously referring to the tears he'd shed a few minutes earlier. These had already dried on his face, leaving his skin feeling uncomfortably taut.

'Is it possible not to be?'

'Sometimes, Mr Burles. People's responses can be surprising. But I always say to visitors, if only those at home could see what you're seeing. If they could see what's right in front of us now, and what I see every day, I know they would also be moved. Then they'd be only too happy to help us. Witnessing makes people generous.'

At the time, those words meant little to him, and he'd simply shrugged as if to say, what can you do? 'We do our best to explain to people... You know... So that they can experience... It's my job, of course, to...' His sentences, like rivulets of water on the fringes of a desert, petered out in the heat. He found it almost too great an effort to speak. When he opened his mouth, the hot air made him gasp. He wanted to retreat into the clinic, but knew it was almost as hot in there, possibly hotter.

Later that afternoon, he said goodbye to the old nurse, thanked her for showing him around the health clinic, and flew back to Addis Ababa with the Australian Tim Haden, owner of the private charter business, Abyssinia Air. He felt dissatisfied leaving Korem. Apart from having reached a clearer understanding of the scale of the problem facing charities like Africa Assist, he felt he'd achieved little. It was as if he'd seen a play, been a member of a theatre audience, no more than a spectator – removed, despite having been moved.

'Learn anything useful?' the pilot shouted over the roar of the Cessna as the plane climbed over the refugee camp. From above, it resembled a pustular growth on the face of the small town, a mishmash of canvas and cardboard on dead, flattened soil. It was barren, dull and grey, little different from the desert that lay at the foot of the escarpment to the east. A pall of smoke hung above the camp from the countless fires that littered the area, making the sky the same smudgy umber that wraps itself around the industrial towns of the English Midlands. Adrian felt he might be looking down into the ninth circle of Dante's inferno: all that was missing was the screaming and the wailing. To the south of the camp he could just make out Anne Chaffey's health clinic.

'The problem seems intractable, almost too large to comprehend or deal with. I think that's what I've learnt.'

'Believe it or not, mate, it's better than it was a couple of years back. Although there are still too many people dying of malnutrition – but then I guess you know that.'

'Despite Band Aid and Live Aid?'

'They need a few good harvests rather than money, that's what many people don't understand.'

They flew on in silence.

'If you like, I'll take you over the desert. It's scarcely out of the way, and it's worth seeing.'

A moment later the single-engined Cessna banked towards the east in a broad arc, and it was as if the plane, already airborne, abruptly took off over the edge of the escarpment. The land beneath them simply disappeared. Adrian felt the sudden updraught of air almost throw the small plane back over the clifftop, but then they were descending, the noise of the engine rising in pitch as the plane fell. They finally levelled out, to Adrian's relief, a couple of hundred feet above the sand.

The emptiness of the environment filled him with foreboding. He felt out of his depth. Such surroundings couldn't be contained. There were no familiar hedgerows here, no wire fences or dry stone walls to mark off boundaries alongside winding country lanes, nothing to separate one person's property from another's, nothing to say this is mine and that is yours – no *civilization*. This place, which ran wild and unpossessed into the distance, belonged to no one, and Adrian found himself oppressed by the weight of its emptiness. As he stared out, almost mesmerized by its strangeness, he recalled, from school, how Nature hates a vacuum, yet it had left one here. Below them there was nothing, and this nothingness spread as far as the eye could see, to the gentle, barely discernible curve at the very edge of the world. There it doubtless fell away into another void. Certainly there were daubs of coarse grass to be seen here and there, a meagreness of black volcanic rocks, even the rare shrub, but the overall effect was of an immense infinity of sand, like the edge of some huge canvas which the artist has yet to get around to working on. It was as if the subject of the painting were far away in the centre of the canvas, possibly in Europe, while here in a corner of Africa the artist had only found time to apply, in hurried, careless strokes, broad slashes of undercoat. It was the dried-out, burnt-up, barely formed edge of a continent.

Their matchbox plane was being thrown around by the hot air rising off the desert as if in the hands of an incompetent puppeteer. Adrian's stomach rose and fell in a matching rhythm, but always slightly out of sync, always a split second later. He wondered if he was going to be sick.

'See them over there?'

He peered through the small, distorted and scratched plastic window at his side, and at first was unable to see what had caught the pilot's eye, but then he spotted an ectopic human shape, a speck in the enormity of the sun-blackened lava desert below, insect-like in its insignificance. And then his eyes focused on others, groups and individuals, strung out in a meandering, far-flung thread.

'They're heading for Weldiya,' Tim shouted over the noise of the engine. 'That's the track they're on.' He was twisted round in his seat, and Adrian wished he wouldn't ignore the controls for such long periods of time. 'They say there are still 500 refugees arriving there every day.'

More statistics, Adrian thought, more meaningless numbers, but he said nothing. The pilot seemed determined to talk (so much for Australians being laconic, Adrian thought). 'The country's always going to have problems while there's fighting.'

'I wouldn't argue with that.'

'But none of the factions in the civil war will allow peace unless it's on their own terms.'

Adrian nodded, reluctant to be drawn in.

'Reason I'm telling you this, it's generally reckoned most of the food you lot fly in goes straight into the pockets of the military, and it's their relocation policy that's largely to blame for the famine in the first place. The fact they steal most of the relief food just adds insult to injury.'

'It's impossible to prevent it. That's how it is: armies always do well in famines.'

The pilot grunted, and the two men sank back into the close embrace of another sticky silence. They both, separately, contemplated the enormity of the task facing Ethiopia, a task personified in the figures barely visible in the desert landscape beneath them.

Adrian asked: 'What's the idea behind the resettlements?' When Tim looked surprised, he added: 'I'm a little new to this; never been in Ethiopia before.'

'What do you do?'

'Public relations. Africa Assist is a client of ours.'

The pilot nodded, staring at him, a little mystified, before saying: 'The government moves people from areas where there's little food to areas where it's more plentiful. Claims their motives are humanitarian, but what they're really doing is isolating the rebels by taking away their bases. They also want cheap labour for their agricultural enterprises in the south of the country.'

Without turning his head, Adrian said, 'You can do that kind of thing when you're a dictator.' He'd never understood why dictators received such a bad press. If people were determined to prove they couldn't run their own lives, then someone needed to do it for them; it was as simple as that. An individual was better at solving problems than any government. 'At least it's their own government they have to contend with.'

'Meaning?'

'At least it's not a colonial power, the Italians, the British or the French that they're dealing with now.' This is exhausting, he thought. I'm too tired. And he decided there and then to be less forthcoming, and hope to discourage the pilot from further conversation.

'The Ethiopians have never been colonized – or so they claim.'

'What about the Italians?'

'Like to pretend they were never here. Selective amnesia, I'd call it. But they've been colonized now – since 1985.'

Adrian frowned, not understanding.

'By you lot – by the aid agencies. Since Live Aid, you've become the country's new masters.'

Adrian wondered if he was being criticized, but rather than attempt to come to any conclusion, he said, with the slightest of smiles, 'If you ask me, the only answer for Ethiopia – *and* every other country in Africa – is to be recolonized.'

The pilot blew through his lips, almost as if he'd been punched in the solar plexus. He looked momentarily puzzled, perhaps unsure as to whether his companion meant what he was saying. 'You being serious?'

'It's the only solution I know that would sort out this mess.'

'Doubt it would go down well in Cape Town – to pick one city at random.'

'Even the South Africans are incapable of getting their affairs in order. As for the rest of the continent, it's a disaster. Take Somalia as a case in point. Or Sudan, Kenya, the Congo, Namibia, Rwanda, Uganda, Liberia, Zimbabwe – you name it. Africa has everything, except the people to rule it. At least when the British were here, the place was run efficiently.'

Tim stared out of the cockpit. Whether he was examining the distant horizon or the outrageousness of Adrian's last statement, it was hard to tell. Perhaps he was reluctant to argue with a client. Then, as if deciding an oblique rejoinder might be the best approach, he said with a grin: 'You Brits can never face up to the fact that the only successful colony you ever established was Australia. And that was by mistake.'

Adrian ignored the provocation. He stared at the large, solid man in the pilot's seat, with his long, thick blond hair swept back from his forehead and his eyes deep set like the embrasures of a coastal fortification (probably used to scanning some outback scene, far inland from any sea), and was suddenly uncomfortably aware of how he himself must come across to this self-sufficient Antipodean. Tim was likely seeing the face of someone for whom life has been a little too easy, a face that was a little too plump and soft, a little too round and unlined. He'd think it was the face of someone who wouldn't survive long in the wild.

The pilot was pointing down to where the flat plains of eastern Ethiopia are funnelled into a deep gorge by the mountains that surround Addis Ababa. The towering, three-and-a-half-thousand feet red cliffs resembled fortress walls protecting the city against the onslaught of the desert. Elegant spurs and solitary summits, bluish in the afternoon sun, paraded their majesty and fertility over the flat sterility of the Danakil Desert far below. 'That's the Great Rift Valley and the Awash River down there. Reckon that's where humans first appeared in the world, the cradle of civilization. Twelve years or so ago – in 1974 I think it was – anthropologists discovered Lucy there, a fossilized skeleton that was about three or four million years old.'

Adrian was more interested in the fact that a pilot – an Australian pilot, what's more – should know so much about a country that wasn't his own.

'That's where it all started,' Tim said, almost to himself, shaking his head with wonder. 'That's where *we* all started.'

Ten minutes later they were talking to traffic control at the international airport, on the outskirts of Addis Ababa. Almost immediately they were given the all clear to land. They flew low over a World War Two Russian transport plane rusting at the end of the runway. After they touched down, they taxied to the terminal building.

At two in the morning, Adrian woke up in his Addis Ababa hotel room, and was unable to get back to sleep. Perhaps it was sleeping in a strange bed, or that he was upset by all that he'd seen at Korem, or that he was too wound up, but he lay for a long time with thoughts teeming through his brain: the refugee camp, work, Judith and Emma, the famine, Anne Chaffey... Round and round they went, in no particular order and with little sense of logic, a whirlpool he was unable to escape from. And then, in the middle of all this, quite out of the blue, without any conscious effort on his part, the nurse's statement hit him. And at exactly the same time, so did the solution. He turned on the light, reached for the notepad and pen he always kept at his bedside for moments like this, and began scribbling, He was terrified to lose any of his inspiration. After that, he began to think, to take the idea that had come to him in a subconscious flash a few minutes earlier, and worked on it, applied logic to it, picked and nagged at it until it revealed so much more, details that opened up a whole world of possibilities.

He was so excited that he wanted to phone someone and share his discovery, but he knew Judith would be fast asleep. Anyway, she was likely to have been slumberously dismissive, as she was with any of her husband's ideas that were to do with work. Nor could he wake Emma – like most 14-year-olds, she slept like a log. Everyone else in the UK, including his business partner, would also be asleep. Even for this revelation, he couldn't presume to wake someone up in the small hours. Eventually, he turned out the light, and tried to get some sleep, but not before having decided to postpone his flight back to London, and to call Tim first thing and get him to fly back to Korem. He had to talk to Anne Chaffey immediately.

Soon after ten the next day, he was back in the Cessna, flying north. Anne Chaffey was taken aback to see him again so soon, but when they sat down in her tiny office at the back of the clinic, she soon became engrossed in what he had to say. Adrian kept calm, and explained – or sold – his idea as simply as possible. As well as attempting to foresee any worries she might have, he also emphasized the fact that it had been her words that had inspired him in the first place.

Her only real worry – apart from the logistics of the project – turned out to be with its ethical aspects. But, to Adrian's surprise, she proceeded to argue against each of these as soon as she raised them. He simply had to sit there, nod his head vigorously and say every now and again, Yes, Anne… Absolutely… Quite right… I agree…

'I imagine you're looking for a young person, Mr Burles.'

'You must call me Adrian.'

'I feel more comfortable…'

'I insist. We can't be so formal when we'll be living on top of each other for several weeks if this goes ahead.'

15

She nodded, so reluctantly she could almost have been shaking her head.

'I think, ideally, someone in their late teens or early twenties.'

'And male?'

'I'll leave that to you. What do you think?'

'It's very much a male-orientated society, and although it pains me to do anything that might perpetuate that inequality, I'm not sure it would be acceptable to ask a woman to undertake such a task.'

Adrian was pleased she was thinking things through as carefully as he himself had done. It gave him faith in her.

'There's no one suitable in the clinic at the moment. As for the camp, I'd prefer not to involve them if at all possible.'

'Why's that?'

She sat straight-backed before him, her lined, suntanned face, although austere, looking emphatically granny-like. There was a gently humorous warmth in the eyes that he hadn't noticed before. They sparkled with life, and there was a softness in her hair, which was delicately curled and white.

'In the Korem camp, and also in the seven camps around Mek'ele, there's a bureaucracy that can be quite overwhelming. I've heard stories,' she added, smiling suddenly, leaving the three words alone to tell those stories.

'What kind of stories?'

'Oh, that's not so important,' she said dismissively. 'It's their attitude that will be a problem, especially with a request as unusual as this one. The camps are full of young aid workers, and, heaven forbid there's anything wrong with that – far from it, but they can be, well, how shall I put this…? Maybe I have spent too long working on my own, but I feel they can be a little earnest and idealistic at times – too hesitant and overly suspicious.' She smiled. '"It can't be done, it can't be done," they tell me over and over again – even about the most trivial request – and they demand the filling in of countless forms, and emphasize the necessity of consulting with Paris or Geneva or New York rather than making any kind of decision themselves. You could be waiting for months, possibly years, before you receive an answer.

And, to tell you the truth, I don't think they'll be happy to co-operate, anyway.'

'But we only need one person, for heaven's sake, to borrow one person, that's all we're looking for.' And even though this imagined youthful slayer of dreams was not before him now, he supposed Anne Chaffey was right. If such people, with their do-gooding, pious sentiments and their tunnel-vision minds could try even the patience of an old nurse, he was unlikely to get far with them.

'"We can't just let you walk out of here with someone who's in our care,"' the nurse parroted, '"it would be irresponsible, even immoral." That would be their justification.' She giggled. 'But I'm being most uncharitable.'

'How can they talk about morality and responsibility in this chaos, in this hell where people, despite all the food and medicine, are still dying? Are you saying Korem would also be like that?'

She hesitated. 'I've been here a long time, Adrian, long before Korem and the other camps were set up to cope with the latest famine. My primary concern has always been the long-term health of the locals, whereas their primary concern is to feed people.' She picked up a folder lying on top of the small table, and carried it across to the filing cabinet in the corner of the room. It was as if she were saying she couldn't spare any more time simply sitting and chatting to Adrian. 'There's some crossover between us, and with so much food now being flown in from the West, the camp is able to keep us supplied too. This is necessary because many refugees from the Tigray and Wollo districts still come here, to the clinic. They've known about us for many years, and see no difference between us and a refugee camp; to them we're both sources of relief.'

She closed the cabinet door and returned to sit at the table. 'So, although we work closely with their aid workers, I wouldn't be happy involving them in this.'

Adrian shrugged. 'Well, you should know.'

'There's also a problem with refugees *not* wanting to leave the camps.'

'Why's that?'

'Why would you leave when you have food and shelter, when there are soldiers outside the camp who may kill you? The civil war is still being fought. It's much safer to live in a camp.'

'I've heard there are many who'd be more than happy to leave the camps. I understood they regard them as a last resort, almost as an admission of defeat. A nurse I met in London, someone who worked in Ethiopia in 1985, told me she never had it in her to send anyone to the camps. It didn't matter if they were starving, her conscience wouldn't allow it. "It's a death sentence" was how she put it to me.'

Anne moved her head from side to side, as if weighing up the options. 'I think that's a little exaggerated, even for then. They do their best in an impossible situation. It's the local officials who are to blame for making the camps difficult to run. There's theft, corruption and, worst of all, incompetence.'

By early afternoon, everything had been agreed. Anne would find a suitable person, and Adrian would return to London and make as many arrangements as he could in the meantime. 'But we must do it this year, and preferably this summer. August would be perfect, Anne. It still gives us time to organize everything. Do you think you can find someone in that time?'

'I'll try.'

Anne struck Adrian as being trustworthy and efficient and, best of all, someone who had invaluable experience with Ethiopians, yet he still worried. It was such an amazing PR stunt, it just had to succeed, no matter how crazy the rest of the world might think it. But he understood that if the nurse couldn't organize things in Korem in his absence, then his dream was in serious danger. Everything hinged on her finding the right person.

'And, of course, you'll come to London as well?'

She looked doubtful, almost panicked. 'It will be hard for me to get away.'

'But, Anne, you have to. We couldn't do this without you.' It was a huge admission for Adrian to make. He was a man who considered anything was possible so long as he himself was involved; other people did not usually feature.

'Well, I do have a sister in Yorkshire whom I haven't seen for over 20 years, so it would be nice to visit her.'

'There you go then. It's settled.' But he sensed her hesitation.

He returned to London to sell his idea to James Balcombe. He didn't foresee any problems in that area; the executive director of Africa Assist was an ineffectual, even weak man, who was more interested in the social introductions that arose from working for a well-known charity than in any good it might achieve for strangers barely existing on some far-off continent. He did have a heart, but in the main his feelings were a little abstract and easily ambushed when not directly involving himself.

At the end of his first day back at work, however, before discussing the matter with anyone else, Adrian spoke to his partner at Talcott & Burles.

He explained to Jack Talcott how greatly affected he had been by his visit to Ethiopia, never before having understood either the scale or the horror of the famine. 'Neither Live Aid nor Band Aid really brought home to me the sheer size of this humanitarian disaster. And that's important, Jack, that word, *humanitarian*. Remember, we're talking human beings here; that old cliché, about people not being statistics. It's too easily forgotten by all of us, myself included.'

Jack Talcott respected his partner too much either to interrupt him or to argue with him – at least not before he'd had the opportunity to put his case. He nodded, said nothing, and topped up both glasses of wine.

'I was genuinely moved by what I saw – and you of all people know what a cynic I am.'

'I certainly do.'

Adrian told his partner about Anne Chaffey, and what she'd told him, and the impact of her words. 'At first I didn't take in what she said, but it obviously sank in somewhere.' He changed the subject suddenly. 'Remember how we were talking about the Tobu World Square theme park a few months ago?'

'That place in Japan where they're going to have more than 40 World Heritage sites, and over 100 perfect replicas of world-famous architectural works and ancient monuments?'

'That's right. All on a scale of 1/25. The Eiffel Tower, the Statue of Liberty, the Leaning Tower of Pisa and the Taj Mahal, Big Ben and the Great Wall of China, the Pyramids and the Parthenon, St Peter's Basilica and the White House – they'll all be there, in the park, when it opens in the 1990s.'

'And the sites are going to be populated by around 140,000 miniature people, each just three inches high.'

'Correct.'

The Lilliputian figurines especially appealed to Adrian because of the way they'd bring an instantly understandable scale to the project. 'The theme park means that, instead of travelling around the world to see these marvels, the Japanese will be able to drive a few miles out of Tokyo and photograph themselves against each of them, all on the same day. It'll be easier, quicker and less expensive than visiting the originals. Which is quite something – if,' he added with a smile, 'you're into that kind of thing.'

He stopped pacing the room and, standing directly in front of his partner, said: 'Imagine if we could do the same as the Tobu World Square Park for Africa Assist?'

Jack looked blank. 'I don't follow.'

'What if we brought a starving person to London? If we placed the reality of Africa right on our own front doorstep? Instead of Londoners going to Africa, which only a few people ever even consider, why not bring Africa to London? Just as the Japanese will be doing with all of the world's great tourism icons. That would really make people sit up and take notice.'

Jack became enthusiastic. And Adrian thought, this is a great idea if only because everyone believes it's a great idea. Even though he'd only explained it to Anne and Jack so far, both of them had immediately seen its potential. He then made a request of his partner that he didn't expect to be a problem, but it had to be asked. 'I want to take a month off. I want to become a full time consultant with Africa Assist. I want to run this operation from within their organization. Can you do without me for that amount of time?'

His partner laughed. 'You'll hardly be missed. We probably won't even notice your absence.'

'Thanks, Jack.'

'But has James Balcombe agreed to you doing this?' Jack knew how easily his partner was carried away by sudden enthusiasms.

'Not as yet. I wanted to speak to you first. That's my next task.'

Adrian wasn't at all surprised when James Balcombe struggled to get his head around the idea; the thinking was too outside the box. He watched him puzzle over the implications of what he'd been told, like a child listening to a teacher explaining the principles of algebra for the first time. When he spoke, eventually, it was with his usual ponderous, almost carping tone of voice. James didn't do enthusiasm; he preferred looking for problems.

'I'm being totally honest when I say this: it worries me sick.' (Adrian knew of his client's inclination to speak in hyperbole.) 'I'm not sure you understand the implications of what we could be letting ourselves in for here.' (Adrian also knew of his client's inclination to miss the whole point of an argument.) 'This could all go horribly wrong, Adrian. We can't afford to damage our reputation, you know. Africa Assist is highly regarded amongst the people who count. There's never been even a whiff of scandal attached to our name.'

Adrian did his best to reassure. 'Everything will be all right. Trust me, James. This is going to be the biggest thing you've ever done. It could be bigger than Live Aid.'

'That's absurd. I'd remind you Geldof raised millions of pounds.'

'I still think we could be bigger.' As he said it, Adrian wondered if he wasn't being wildly optimistic. But he knew that only if he appeared to be without a scintilla of doubt would he receive the necessary backing from James. 'On top of which, I want to run the show. One advantage of this is that you can keep the whole thing at arm's length. If it's a failure, I'll be the one who cops all the flak; if it's a success – as I'm sure it will be – I'm more than happy for you to step forward and receive the plaudits.'

'That's all very well…' There was a 'but' in there somewhere, but Balcombe never managed to reach it. Instead he stood up and moved from behind his desk to sit down, with a weak groan, on the sofa next to Adrian. It was an unconscious attempt to show Adrian that although James considered himself to be on a different, as in higher, level from him, he had the generosity of spirit to play the egalitarian card, to bring himself down to Adrian's level. His PR consultant could see this quite clearly; James couldn't. 'It's a crazy idea,' he said, 'quite mad, and I don't believe we should do it.'

'Crazy or not, the idea is everything. And that's why you employed Talcott & Burles, remember? You wanted us to make you famous. That was your brief, James, and that's what this idea will achieve.'

Balcombe perked up a little at this remark, but only momentarily. Like many weak people, he could be stubborn. 'I could forbid it, you know.' It was a feeble rejoinder.

'Of course you could, but you won't, will you? That would be stupid, and you know it. You missed out on Live Aid and Band Aid, with most of the money going to the big charities like Oxfam, Save the Children and World Vision. You don't want that to happen again, and this will make sure it doesn't. Believe me, you'll have the other charities, even the juggernauts, knocking on your door, begging for a slice of the action. They'll go crazy with jealousy.'

James smiled at this possibility, but persisted with a final, weak, 'I still have grave doubts about such a project'. But he had already begun to sound as if he was exhausted by their disagreement.

At that point, Adrian knew he'd won. He didn't relent though. 'I'll say it again, James, this is why you employed us, to raise your profile. It's our area of expertise, it's the only reason we took on your business in the first place – on a pro bono basis, I have to remind you.' The executive director looked pained by this reminder. It perhaps made him conscious of having a somewhat lowly status in the corporate world. 'You need this kind of publicity; it's the only way Africa Assist can survive.'

'I'd remind you that we've been doing all right for a few years now.'

'All right isn't good enough. The world is changing. You have to stay ahead of the game, otherwise you're finished.'

Finally, James Balcombe gave the project his very half-hearted support, but only on condition that his trusted assistant, Dave Parker, worked closely with Adrian on its planning and implementation. Adrian had little time for Dave, considering him an ineffectual and sycophantic nobody, too busy agreeing with everything his boss said to ever be capable of doing anything worthwhile by himself. But he didn't see any problem working alongside him; he'd be harmless.

Three weeks later he received a call from Anne. She'd found someone. She described him to Adrian over the phone, her voice fading in and out as if she were speaking to him outdoors in the middle of a snowstorm. The static was dreadful.

Two days later, he flew out of London.

Sunday

*E*arly in the morning, the sun just rising above the horizon, Adrian flew with Tim back to Korem. One of the staff at the airstrip drove the two men the short distance to the clinic.

Anne Chaffey stood with them on the verandah and pointed out the young man in the distance. He stood well away from the clinic, against the perimeter fence, as if he wished to separate himself from those camped in its immediate vicinity. 'He likes to keep to himself,' she said, placing a wide-brimmed straw hat on her head. 'Perhaps it's because he came here by himself. Bit of a wanderer, too,' she added, as if they were lucky to find him still there.

'Goes walkabout, does he?' laughed Tim. 'We have fellas like that in Australia; always heading off into the back of beyond.'

The lone figure stood immobile, oscillating in the harsh light, as black and insubstantial as a Giacometti ink drawing, almost transparent in the waves of rising heat, like a wisp of blackened paper dancing above the heat of a bonfire. He was so fragile, he looked to Adrian as if he might suddenly waft upwards into the sky.

'Stay here, please,' said Anne, and she set off towards the distant figure, picking her way carefully between those who were sitting and lying in front of the clinic, then marching with a speed that belied her age across the open ground. She spoke to the young man for a minute or two. Finally, they started to walk back towards Adrian and Tim where they waited in the shade of the building. Adrian was reminded of an old couple in an English country garden, walking side by side, taking a quiet afternoon stroll around the grounds after an extended lunch.

The nurse's companion was soon almost close enough to

be properly seen. Adrian studied him with a rising sense of excitement. He had that economy of movement characteristic of those who are starving, as if intent on saving what little energy he had left. One arm hung loosely by his side, while in his other hand he was grasping a long wooden pole, a rough walking staff. He towered over the nurse, his tightly curled black hair making him appear even taller. She barely came up to his chest.

Adrian wondered what he should do. Should he advance and greet them? Should he start talking to Tim, who was now sitting on the edge of the verandah smoking a cigarette? Should he behave as if the stranger were barely of interest to him? Should he look at him, or was it more polite to turn away? He wanted to do the right thing, but out here, in these surroundings, what was the right thing? He had no idea, so he stood there, undecided, with the air of a schoolteacher watching the approach of two naughty children.

Tim moved to his side. 'Looks little more than a kid.' Some cigarette smoke drifted in Adrian's direction, and he flapped a hand irritably.

'Sorry, mate' – said more with amusement than apology. 'Want one?'

Adrian grunted, and briefly shook his head. He detested being called mate, the warm, antipodean familiarity not just enveloping him in its damp embrace, but dragging him down to uncouth colonial levels, and making the heat of their surroundings even more unbearable.

The Ethiopian had his head down as he walked, as if he didn't want to look at them. Or is it deference? Adrian asked himself. His legs were long, more than half his height. They were the legs of a leopard, almost out of proportion to the rest of his body. He loped across the ground, seemingly without effort, making Anne look slow and ponderous.

The nurse stopped in front of them, and the stranger copied her. 'Adrian, Tim, this is Mujtabaa.'

'G'day, mate.'

Adrian muttered something about being pleased to meet him, but realized that his words were unlikely to be understood. He considered shaking hands, but decided against it – probably too English, he told himself. The young man bowed his head three times, slowly and solemnly, and the four of them stood in silence facing each other on the very edge of the desolate crowd outside the whitewashed clinic, incongruous, thrown together by one man's outrageous and improbable dream.

The Ethiopian was wearing a large, shroud-like, thin cotton cloth around his body like a dress. A smaller piece of the same material half-covered his head, like a hood. Round his waist was a garment like a skirt, tied at the right hip and reaching to his calves. A double-edged dagger, with a blade that must have been about 16 inches in length, hung from his waist, across the front of his body, in an ornate scabbard. He wore several amulets around his neck, and had a goatskin waterbag slung from his left shoulder. His skin and clothes were both tinged with salt, like a fine, white dust.

As if reading Adrian's thoughts, Anne said: 'This is how he arrived here from the Danakil. As instructed by you, I haven't washed him and haven't changed his clothes. All I've done is feed him a little food.'

He didn't thank her. 'How thin is he? It's hard to tell in that thing.'

The nurse looked surprised. 'His main garment is a *shämma*.' After the briefest of pauses, she added: 'And you don't have to worry about that, Adrian – he's very thin. You can see that from his face, his legs, his hands...'

'Does he wear anything under that?'

'Under his *shämma*? Only the *sanafil*, that skirt-like garment you can see. The *sanafil* would be his normal attire – that alone, but he's travelling now. Hence his *shämma*.' She sounded like an expat, both formal and rather out of date.

The young man stood before them, tall, straight and unmoving, a little separate from the three Westerners, anchored to the sandy soil, joined to it down the length of his body, so unlike the way the foreigners simply skittered, barely touching, across its surface, like mayflies across a pond on a summer's evening. He towered over them, his large feet, square and bony, cracked and filthy, rooting him to the earth.

'Please ask him to take off his *shämma*.' He made little effort to hide the impatience in his voice.

'I can't do that, Adrian.'

'In heaven's name, why not?'

'We don't know him. He'd be insulted.'

'But he's practically a child.'

'You have to take my word on this: under that *shämma*, he'll be very thin.'

'He'll have to take it off some time. He's no use to us like that.'

There was a heavy silence. Adrian was aware of Tim reaching into his shirt pocket and pulling out a packet of tobacco and some cigarette papers. He started to roll himself another cigarette, leaning nonchalantly against one of the uprights supporting the verandah roof, politely disengaging himself from the conversation.

It struck Adrian that the heat wouldn't be unusual for him. No wonder he looks so comfortable, he thought. In fact he looked loose, as if he were hanging from a coat-hanger in the cool shadows of a wardrobe. Adrian, tense and awkward, tried to emulate the Australian, to relax and think cool, but it was difficult when his T-shirt was already saturated. It stuck to his body and was dark with sweat beneath his armpits and down his back.

'How old would you say he is?' he asked the nurse.

'It's hard to tell when someone's so malnourished, but I'd guess he's about 16 or 17, possibly younger. He could be 15. People look older when they're starving.' She ended their short conversation by turning away and studying those who were sitting and lying on the ground.

Adrian told himself that a 15- or 16-year-old was perfect. 'So what have you said to him?'

She turned back towards him, regarding him calmly from beneath the shade of her hat, patiently respectful. 'What you told me to tell him.'

'Which was?' Trying to coax it out of her.

'That we will help his people with food and money if he accompanies us.'

'And will he?'

'It's hard to tell. He doesn't say much. If you push him he nods his head. But I'm certain he has agreed to help us.'

'You don't sound very sure, if you don't mind my saying so, Anne. I'd hate to have come all the way from London just to have him refuse to come with us.'

'I know these people, Adrian. His silence is acquiescence. You have to trust me on this.'

Adrian had always had a problem with delegating. If anyone ever confronted him on the issue, he'd defend himself by admitting that he wasn't happy delegating because no one else could be trusted. He was feeling this now: he knew Anne was essential to the successful implementation of his idea, and that he had to trust her, but everything inside him was screaming at him to intervene. That would be a mistake; he knew that. The idea was important, it was sacrosanct, but he needed people around him to make it happen.

'What language does he speak?'

'Afar. That's what the Afar speak.' Said as if he should know that.

'And do you speak Afar?'

'I speak Amharic, the country's official language and the main language around here. But I have an adequate understanding of Afar. In the Danakil, it's the main language.'

Looking at the Ethiopian: 'And does he speak Amharic?'

'He doesn't seem to. But I'm making myself understood in his language.'

'Well, let's hope so. We need to communicate with each other somehow if he's going to come with us.'

The pilot stood watching the two of them. They were nitpicking like a married couple; the sixty-something, straight-backed, expat nurse and the slightly overweight, heavily perspiring and twitchy middle-aged executive. Each wore neatly pressed shorts that went down to the knees. She also had on a short-sleeved check shirt, buttoned almost to the chin. Her skin was brown, his shockingly white. The two of them stood facing each other: he, ill-tempered and out of his depth; she, self-possessed and quietly in control. The sun beat down, without discrimination – on Adrian and Anne, on the two bystanders, Tim and Mujtabaa, and on the gathering of refugees who seemed to have been stupefied by it.

'You've told him where we're planning to take him?'

The young man stood next to Anne, staring fixedly at his feet, as if determined to take no part in the discussion – even if he'd been able to. He looked no different from a child being forced to listen to a scene between his parents and wishing he could leave the room.

'Yes, I've told him where we want to take him – of course. It's just that I can't be certain he understood.'

Adrian thought, why have I ended up with someone like this? Surely there must have been someone else available? A good account man, someone like Simon Twining, that's who I need now. Someone whom I can absolutely trust, someone I barely need to give instructions to. He closed his eyes. 'And what makes you think he may not have understood you, Anne?'

'It's nothing to do with interpretation difficulties. It's to do with the fact that these people usually stay within the same locality all of their lives. Although they're nomadic, they rarely wander great distances.'

'But you can still explain to him that we're taking him to another country, to the UK, can't you?'

'He won't understand what I'm talking about. The UK could be on the other side of the Danakil for all he knows. I may as well tell him we're taking him to the moon. That would probably make more sense to him; at least he can see the moon.' She was clasping and unclasping her hands, suddenly looking agitated and ill at ease amongst the three men.

The PR consultant and the nurse scowled at each other. Then, possibly in an attempt to be more placatory, she said: 'I told him we're taking him to visit another tribe. I think he understood that.'

'Another tribe?' Adrian was incredulous. He wiped the back of his neck with his handkerchief, and thought how his plans always tended to fall apart whenever other people became involved.

The pilot stepped in. 'Can I make a suggestion, you guys?' They both turned to him. 'As pleasant as it is out here, maybe we should leave for Addis before our brains fry, and before you miss your London flight. Explain everything to him on the way.'

Adrian turned his back on the pilot, saying to the nurse: 'I'm taking your word for it, Anne, that he's happy to come with us. So we'll leave as soon as you're ready.'

They were farewelled by the replacement nurse on loan from the sister clinic at Weldiya, and three of the local girls who helped out.

Back at the Korem airstrip, Tim opened the Cessna's cockpit door, saying over his shoulder, 'Don't worry, Anne, he'll definitely be better off coming with us than remaining here.'

She didn't reply to this attempted reassurance. Instead, giving the Ethiopian a quick smile of encouragement, she climbed into the plane. When Adrian indicated that the young man should follow her, a look of sheer panic appeared on his face. His eyes opened wide, making his head look even more skull-like. He stepped backwards, his hand hovering above the hilt of his *jile*.

Oh my God, thought Adrian, this is all we need. Even if we get him into the plane, we'll be up on kidnapping charges. He obviously has no idea what's going on.

'It's all right,' he said, giving a strained smile, 'keep calm. We're not going to harm you. We're doing this to help you. Help?' he added loudly, questioningly, throwing the one word directly into the stranger's face as if on the off-chance it might lodge there, on his skull, on the shell of his brain. There was a mixture of sweat and sunblock in Adrian's eyes and he was doing his best not to screw them up, but the stinging was making him blink furiously. Although the young man had his head down, he was watching Adrian intently from beneath his white, salt-crusted eyebrows, his right hand now firmly gripping the hilt of the *jile*.

Adrian put his head in the plane to speak to Anne. 'I don't think he's been in a plane before.'

There was a roar of laughter behind him. 'You're joking,

30

mate?' Tim said. 'Been in one? It's quite likely he's never bloody seen one before.'

Adrian swore into the cockpit and closed his eyes with exasperation and frustration. Was his dream finished before it had even started? 'I don't care how you do it, Anne, but we have to get him into the plane. We have to! We're trying to help him – and his people. Does he not understand that?'

Anne, possibly startled by the vehemence with which he spoke, reached out and put a hand on his arm. 'I'll talk to him again.' She climbed out of the plane and addressed the young man in a low, earnest voice. His head and eyes remained down, and his face expressionless, so it was difficult to tell whether he was either listening to, or understanding, what she was saying. She held out her hand, speaking quietly, without pause, her voice soothing and encouraging. She then took his hand, the one resting on his *jile*, and turned and stepped back towards the plane. Adrian and Tim watched, both men looking as if they might be betting on how far she'd get, the diminutive woman leading the giant, like a child trying to lure a stallion into a horsebox. The Ethiopian followed her, his head still down, one arm at full stretch, being dragged like a child unwillingly to school.

Anne climbed into the plane, crouching down in the doorway, still holding the young man's hand. Adrian moved in behind him, as if to cut off his escape. The nurse continued talking, almost whispering, trying to reassure. The Ethiopian attempted to grasp the side of the door with the hand that was already holding his long, polished walking staff, but couldn't manage it. His eyes were almost popping out of his head. Anne gently prised the staff from his hand and lay it on the floor of the plane.

Adrian reached out to support the young man's arm. It was dry and dusty, and felt like bone, hard and brittle. He was scared of breaking something. He felt big and clumsy next to his skeletal neighbour, like a heavyweight boxer handling fine porcelain china. With a little pulling from Anne and some pushing by Adrian, they managed to manoeuvre him into the fuselage. There was then the problem of getting him off the floor of the plane and into a seat. It was a while before they succeeded. Anne put the safety belt round his waist, and even after tightening it as far as it would go, it still lay loosely across his lap.

Adrian struggled into the front seat of the plane next to the pilot. As Tim slammed the cockpit door closed, Adrian turned round and said: 'Might be a good idea to warn him about the noise, Anne.'

She spoke to the young man, placing her hand on his. She nodded to Tim. He started the engine, and the propeller whirred to life. Immediately the Ethiopian threw himself against the window, scrabbling to get out. She took both of his hands in hers, clasping them, talking all the time, trying to pull him back from the window.

Tim looked across at Adrian. 'Reckon this is still such a good idea?' Because of the noise, Adrian didn't hear the question. The pilot raised his eyes skywards, turned back to the controls and, almost with reluctance, released the brake. The engine revved louder and the aircraft started taxiing towards the end of the landing strip. The Ethiopian had closed his eyes and was now gabbling away in a panic-stricken voice. Adrian looked at Anne, questioning.

'I believe he's praying,' she said. 'To Wak.'

'Who's Wak?'

'He's their Sky God.'

Tim laughed. 'That's kind of appropriate. Maybe I should pray to him too.'

The aircraft bumped along the packed earth, quickly picking up speed, before lifting into the air. The young man opened his eyes. What had happened? He turned, almost as an afterthought, and looked out of the window. As the small township rapidly disappeared beneath them, he started to wail as if his death was now imminent and some evil spirit was already calling out his name. Anne spoke to him, patting his hands, trying to reassure him with smiles and words, until finally, in despair and totally spent, he sank forward in his seat, his chin on his chest and, looking as if it was all too much for him and he no longer had the strength to care what happened, he closed his eyes. He didn't move for the rest of the flight.

The plane headed south, and for a while the only sound was the steady drone of the engine. There was a feeling of relief in the cockpit now that the young man had quietened down. Adrian twisted round in his seat and spoke to Anne: 'Is he asleep?'

'I think he may be.'

'Does he need a blanket?'

She raised her eyebrows, as if surprised by his concern. 'I think he's all right, Adrian. Thank you.'

Turning further round, and putting an arm up on the back of his seat, he said: 'You know I don't expect anything of you, Anne, except to keep – what's his name?'

'Mujtabaa.'

'That's right, Mujtabaa. Just to keep him alive. That's all.' He stared at her for slightly longer than was necessary.

She looked small in the back of the plane next to her tall neighbour, like a schoolgirl. Adrian thought she could almost have been one of Emma's friends if it weren't for the white hair and the fine lines on the tanned face.

'Yes, that's quite clear.'

And it went through his mind that in fact no one was going to give a damn if the young man died. Two thousand deaths or two thousand and one deaths. Four thousand deaths, or four thousand and one deaths. If you were honest with yourself, if you weren't a hypocrite, it was surely immaterial. But he had sufficient sense to keep this thought to himself.

The nurse looked away, and gazed out of the window. Her face betrayed no emotion. Adrian looked briefly at Tim, maybe hoping for support, but the pilot's face remained determinedly expressionless.

His eyes wandered, but there was nothing on which they could settle. Nature had split its canvas in two, the desert and the sky. Each reverberated in the heat, gleaming white where they met, then changing to a cobalt blue overhead and a drab yellow at their feet. He knew that, thousands of years ago, the landscape beneath them had been covered by forests, but now, after centuries of human abuse, it had been worn out, ravaged and discarded. It had the air of a deserted campsite. A small

33

group of refugees was heading along a deeply furrowed track in the direction of the mountains. He wondered if any of them would know Mujtabaa and what they would think if they realized he was now flying through the sky, hundreds of feet above their heads, in the company of three white people.

Seeing him look out of the window, Tim said, 'Wouldn't think it was the wet season, would you?'

'Is it?'

'From June to September, that's when the long rains fall – the *meher*. It's also called the hungry season, because everyone is waiting for the harvest to come. The short rains are in March and April – the *belg* – but we haven't had those for three or four years now. That's half the problem – the lack of rain. The other half is the civil war. There's little or no grass left for their herds, and they say next year will be even worse.'

The pilot broke the long silence that followed. 'So what are you going to do with this bloke in London?'

'Keeping that to ourselves for the moment.'

'Sure.'

Adrian relented a little. 'He's helping us with our fundraising efforts. We're hoping to capitalize on the success and publicity of Live Aid.' He didn't want to reveal too much. He remembered Anne telling him Tim also did flights for the other charities – it would be a disaster if they found out what he was up to before it got under way. 'Fact is, its influence is waning, and people need to be reminded of what's happening here.'

'So long as you're not going to inflict another *Do they know it's Christmas?* on us. If I hear that song one more time, think I'll go barmy as a bandicoot.'

'What we're trying to do will make a real difference. I'm sure of it.'

Tim changed the subject. 'We should be back in Addis in under two hours.'

Adrian nodded. Again, he glanced back to study the features of the young man. He was now leaning against the side of the cockpit, his head, with its chaotic mass of tightly curled hair, resting on the window, his skeletal frame almost enveloped in dusty robes. If he'd been holding a scythe, he'd have made a good Grim Reaper at a fancy-dress party. Adrian smelt a distinctive mixture of sweat, dirt and illness. He wondered if it was the smell of death, the young man decomposing before their eyes. Concerned, he shouted back to Anne: 'Do you think he'll be OK?'

She leant forward so she didn't have to shout. 'This would be a nasty shock to anyone's immune system, but especially someone who isn't well.'

Adrian suspected she was avoiding answering his question. 'But do you think he'll survive?' he insisted. 'Is he healthy?'

'I wouldn't have agreed to this if I didn't think he'd survive, Adrian.' She sounded quite frosty. 'As to whether or not he's healthy, I find that almost impossible to answer. Being the weight he is, he's scarcely healthy, yet I wouldn't necessarily describe him as unhealthy. He doesn't look well, obviously, but then he's young, so...' She left her sentence unfinished, before adding: 'So far as I can tell, he's not ill. If he had malaria it would be obvious enough, or TB, which is the main killer amongst these people. But there are other diseases which are harder to detect in the early stages.'

Despite Adrian's worries about the young man attracting undue attention at Addis Ababa airport, no one gave him more than a cursory glance. Since the famine had attracted worldwide attention two years earlier, the capital had been besieged by relief-agency workers, government officials, and the well-educated, well-fed, well-off and well-meaning middle classes of the Western world. Famine was a booming business. Even celebrities and Hollywood film stars, looking appropriately gloomy, earnest and sympathetic, could be spotted at regular intervals flying in or out of the country. To see an actual victim of the famine was far less interesting.

Inside the terminal, a noisy air-conditioning system was trying, unsuccessfully, to cope with the heat. The paint on the ceiling was flaking, and mould was creeping up the walls. A bored and listless throng shuffled aimlessly around the building as if they had no plans to go anywhere, but were more intent on finding a place to lie down and have a quiet doze.

Tim's office was in a Nissan hut at the back of the terminal. The raised floor was covered in linoleum, badly worn where the traffic in the room had been heaviest. The desk, filing cabinets and chairs looked as if they'd come straight from a surplus store, and the piles of paperwork appeared to have settled permanently beneath a thin patina of dust. There was a window, which Tim now opened, and a fan, which he now switched on. Anne made Mujtabaa lie down on an old, worn sofa, its plastic covering split in several places, like a patient undergoing surgery, revealing seeping, rubbery, yellowed guts.

Tim told Adrian he could use the phone to call London – 'though you'll be lucky to get through' – then showed Anne where the kitchen was. After that, he shook hands with both of them and left, saying he probably wouldn't be back before they left for London.

Adrian made himself at home, already visualizing the small, cramped office as his command centre, a place where he could manage his small team – only four, but enough people to feed his fantasy. Rory, who worked for Africa Assist in the capital, had just arrived to help out with the 'top secret project'. He was a tall, sinewy and unexpectedly white individual, despite his years in Africa, who offered his services in a rather laid-back and supercilious manner. As well as Anne and Mujtabaa, Adrian mentally included Tim amongst his team, even though it was unlikely they'd see him again. Numbers were important to him.

As he arranged the contents of his briefcase on the desk, he instructed Rory to confirm their tickets on the 2.15 Ethiopian Airlines flight to London.

'What about Mujtabaa's national ID card and visa?'

'Already done. Anne arranged it.'

'And Anne?'

'She still has her British passport.'

He turned to the nurse sitting patiently on a chair between his desk and the sofa on which the young man was lying. 'What about our friend? Does he need anything?'

'I think he needs to eat something.'

She saw the concern on his face. 'Since he reached the clinic,

36

I've just been giving him some zinc and vitamin A mixed in with a little milk and cereal. It's not enough for him to put on any weight, certainly not enough to be noticeable.'

'It's important he doesn't. I want to keep him lean and hungry. But that doesn't mean I want to starve him,' he added hastily.

'I'd remind you, Adrian, that I have the final say on what Mujtabaa does or does not eat. I won't compromise on that. We must be clear on that from the start.'

He nodded, smiling briefly, feeling more conciliatory now that things were going his way.

'Once I've prepared the milk, I suggest you give it to Mujtabaa.'

'Yes?'

'Amongst nomads, accepting food, even a drink of milk, means the forming of a bond between the giver and the receiver, between the host and the guest. It shows you're willing to take on the responsibility of protecting Mujtabaa should there be any trouble in the future.'

Rory interrupted. 'It also means you have to avenge his death if he's killed.'

'Maybe it would be better coming from you, Anne.'

'I don't think so. I've already fed him, obviously, but in his eyes at least, I'm only a woman.' She was adamant, as if daring Adrian to make the same mistake as the Ethiopian.

He didn't want the responsibility, but told himself it was simply some peasant belief and he should go along with it.

He got through to London with surprising ease. First he spoke to Dave Parker, the new assistant foisted on him by James Balcombe. Adrian ordered him to set everything in motion now, to organize the army of volunteer collectors, the placards and advertising placements, the police and council clearances, and anything else that needed to be put in place before their arrival. Some of these were already under way and had just been awaiting the final go-ahead once they'd found their Ethiopian.

Next, Adrian spoke to the executive director of Africa Assist. 'All going well, James, we'll be in London soon after eight o'clock your time this evening. The only flight out of Addis is via Rome.'

'How many of you are there?'

'Three. Myself, Anne Chaffey – the nurse I was telling you about – and the Ethiopian fellow.'

'Tell me about him.' He sounded peremptory.

'He's perfect.' He read from the piece of paper Anne had placed on the side of his desk. 'Name: Mujtabaa bin Qurban-Ali. Approximately 16 years old. Height, six foot three. No distinguishing marks, except that he's incredibly thin.'

'I doubt that's a distinguishing mark in Ethiopia.'

'I don't suppose it is.' He looked across at the young man sitting on the couch. 'We couldn't have hoped for better.'

There was a long silence, during which Adrian stared at Mujtabaa, who sat listlessly, almost like a rag doll, his eyes open but unseeing, seemingly indifferent to what was going on around him.

Adrian was imagining James Balcombe in his big house in Esher. He was probably enjoying drinks on the terrace, overlooking the extensive, lovingly tended gardens, discussing with his wife their social engagements for the week ahead. Maybe they had weekend guests down from the city, listening, with furrowed brows, to their host relaying his concerns to some troublesome minion on a faraway continent.

'I have to make certain this is absolutely clear to you' – he's probably casting a meaningful glance at his guests right now, thought Adrian – 'If anything goes wrong – you hear what I'm saying? – anything at all, it will be your responsibility, Adrian. I've been against this escapade from day one. Don't forget that.' There was a brief pause, both men listening to what sounded like a loud humming from some distant ocean bed. 'Do I make myself clear?'

'Perfectly. I understand exactly where you're coming from.' You fence-sitter, he thought, you weak-minded, bureaucratic idiot; covering your backside as usual. But he said, 'Your concerns have been noted, James. I'm more than happy to take responsibility.' As an afterthought, he added: 'We don't want any publicity by the way. Not yet.'

'No?'

'Just in case.'

'I don't understand.'

'In case something does go wrong.'

'You mean should he die? Is that what you mean, Adrian – if the young man should die?'

He could hear the panic in the man's voice. 'It's unlikely, but yes. Or if we can't get him onto the plane or something. That's more of a possibility,' he added, 'but that's why I have Anne Chaffey with me, to prevent such mishaps.'

'Dying is scarcely a mishap, Adrian. Quite frankly, this scheme of yours terrifies me.'

'The event is to be launched tomorrow morning, at the press conference. Nothing's to be revealed before then.' Adrian wanted support. He didn't want to know about everyone else's worries; he had enough of his own. 'If I'm to take full responsibility for this, James, I have to be the one running the show. I've told you that already: I make the decisions.'

Before Balcombe had a chance to communicate any more of his concerns, Adrian said: 'I have to go. The immigration people are about to arrive.'

But the executive director of Africa Assist refused to be dismissed so easily. 'One more thing. I'll come and meet you at Heathrow.'

'Probably better if you don't. Everyone will be tired. Why not join us at the press conference tomorrow morning?'

As he put the phone down, Anne returned from the kitchen with a glass of milk. 'I suggest you offer this to him in a solemn manner, Adrian. It would be wrong just to put it down on the table in front of him.'

Adrian carried the glass across to where the young man was sitting. He didn't stir. Adrian said his name. He looked up. Although Adrian knew the young man couldn't understand him, he said: 'Here's some milk for you,' and held out the glass. It was a few seconds before the Ethiopian reached up and slowly, with both hands, took the glass off him. He bowed his head as if to thank Adrian, then gulped the milk noisily. Adrian was reminded of a small child, and half expected him to gasp and wipe his mouth with the back of his hand when he'd finished. He did neither. He simply let his hands fall back onto his lap, still holding the glass.

'Oh dear, that was far too fast.' Anne came up and stood next to the two men. 'I think we may be seeing that milk again somehow.'

'You mean…?'

'Yes.' She gently prised the glass from the young man's hands.

'Oh.' Adrian took an involuntary step backwards, and the two of them stood looking down at the skeletal figure, once again slumped apathetically before them.

'I was thinking, it doesn't matter if he's ill, just so long as he's not about to die.' Aware of how callous that might sound, he added: 'I'd be happier if he wasn't ill, of course; I certainly don't want him to suffer.'

'I'm pleased to hear that. Anyway, you won't get him into the UK if he has anything too serious. As for the ethics of doing such a thing…'

He stared at her for a moment, silent, as if he were ignorant of that particular word and needed time to work out what it could possibly mean. He was exasperated by what he perceived as her lack of co-operation.

He went back to the desk and started to type on the old typewriter. 'To whom it may concern. This is to say that I am leaving Ethiopia of my own free will, in the company of Adrian Burles, Chief Project Manager of Africa Assist and Partner of Talcott & Burles. I have agreed to fly to London in order to let the people of the United Kingdom learn of the desperate famine conditions in my country, and to help raise money for my compatriots. I absolve Africa Assist of any responsibility for what may or may not happen to me.'

He handed the sheet of paper to Anne. 'Would you translate this for Mujtabaa and ask him to sign it?'

'I'm certain he won't be able to write.'

'Make him put a cross then. Some kind of mark.'

She read the letter without comment. When she spoke to the young man, he neither moved, nor reacted. She struggled to place a pen between his fingers and thumb and hold it there, before attempting to guide his hand to draw an 'M' at the bottom of the page.

As Adrian took back the sheet of paper, he said, 'I'm sure we won't need it.' He didn't sound convinced, but he was more preoccupied at that moment with whether or not they'd be able to persuade Mujtabaa to get on the flight to London that afternoon without causing some kind of scene.

The terminal lay stretched out beside the empty landing strips, paralysed by the heat. Planes squatted immobile near the hangars, people slouched on seats inside the terminal, and the small number of taxi drivers at the front of the building hung listlessly out of open doors waiting for fares that seemed unlikely ever to materialize. The Arrivals and Departures boards clattered city names and flight times rarely and with complete uninterest, as if sensing no one had either the energy or the desire to read them.

A little before two o'clock, after receiving a laconic 'goodbye and good luck' from Rory, Adrian, Anne and Mujtabaa left what was rather ambitiously described as a Departure Lounge, and walked out of the terminal towards a jet parked on the apron.

Accompanied across the tarmac by many other passengers, each enveloped in their own damp, heavy, clinging mantle of heat, Adrian worried that Mujtabaa would create a scene and refuse to climb the stairs onto the plane. What could they do? What if an official ran forward and started asking awkward questions and the Ethiopian shouted that he was being taken out of the country against his will? He took reassurance by reminding himself of the stories he'd heard about the steady stream of Westerners leaving the country with local children in tow. Their hastily cobbled-together visa documents declared them to be adopted, but, if you had money – and not even a great deal of it – you could get your hands on documentation saying anything you damn well wanted it to say. He told himself there was no reason for him to worry; not only was their paperwork all in order, but Anne had reassured him the young man was accompanying them of his own free will.

It may have been because the plane was bigger than the one they'd been in earlier that day and he was simply unable to comprehend it, or it may have been that he found the presence of so many of his fellow Ethiopians reassuring, but Mujtabaa boarded the plane without a murmur. He climbed the stairs slowly, Anne supporting his elbow, almost with the air of a departing dignitary.

Adrian found his place in the Business Class section of the plane and Anne and Mujtabaa continued through to the rear. He settled into his seat and a minute later a steward brought him a glass of orange juice and a cool towel. He was relieved to find there was no one sitting next to him. He stared out of the window.

You're going to make it, Mujtabaa, he said to himself. You're going to be OK. So long as you don't go and die on me, I'll make you famous. This is going to be a huge coup for Africa Assist.

He was smiling as the plane taxied to the end of the runway. A few minutes later, after lumbering ponderously through the heavy heat haze rising off the tarmac, they were airborne. Stage one has gone without a hitch, Adrian told himself, and he ordered the first of a few celebratory glasses of champagne.

Some time later, after lunch, as he was flicking through the airline's in-flight magazine, he saw a map of the world that showed the countries the airline flew to, the routes exploding across the page like fireworks over the major cities of Africa, Europe and Asia. He studied the map closely, then, keen to share his thoughts, he stood up and, still clutching the magazine, made his way past the curtain that separated Business Class from Economy. He was pleased to find that Anne had put Mujtabaa in the aisle seat, as far from the window as possible. She was sitting in the middle seat, and a young European girl was by the window.

He held out the magazine to Anne, over the head of the young man. 'Show him Ethiopia and England, Anne, then he'll get an idea of how far he's flying.'

She stared at him, incredulous. 'He won't understand. Not a map.'

'Try,' he insisted, as eager as a young boy. 'Please.'

'He won't be able to grasp how you can put a whole country on a piece of paper. It won't make any sense to him.'

Adrian continued to hold the map before her face, obstinately thrusting it forward like an unwanted gift. Shaking her head in disbelief, as if dealing with a particularly stubborn child, she took the magazine and held it in front of Mujtabaa. She said a few words, pointing at the map. He lowered his eyes for a second, then returned to staring at the top of the seat in front of him. Anne handed the magazine back to Adrian. 'He's not interested.'

'You'd think he'd be keen to know where he's going.'

'When we get to London, Adrian,' she said with an uncharacteristic hint of exasperation, 'may I suggest you draw a map in the earth with a stick? It will probably make more sense to him.'

He noticed how, when she spoke to him, she would slightly lower her head – it was almost a bow, almost as if she felt herself unworthy to speak to him – and it occurred to him, just fleetingly, that maybe she was unused to speaking to her own people after having lived in Ethiopia for so long.

He stood in the aisle as if stranded in no-man's-land, at a loss where to go. 'How's it going then? Did you give him anything for lunch?'

'Very little.'

'That's good.' He stared at the top of Mujtabaa's head, without seeing it, and, unusually for him, without knowing what to say.

'A stewardess kindly mixed some dried food in the galley – faffa porridge.' Said as if Adrian should, in some way, have planned for this eventuality.

'It was bright yellow,' said the young girl by the window.

'Is that right?' Adrian smiled.

'And she' – the girl added, pointing at Anne – 'had to feed him with a spoon, like a baby. That's because he lives in a tent in the desert.'

'No, it's because...?' The old nurse raised her eyebrows.

'Because he's not well.'

'That's correct.'

'I'd better be getting back,' said Adrian, beginning to feel somewhat superfluous to the conversation, almost as if he were being deliberately excluded.

He was dozing, sitting bolt upright in his seat, his chin resting on his chest, a work file on his lap, when the plane ducked and draked along the wet runway at Leonardo da Vinci International Airport. There was an hour's wait before the flight continued to London. Anne and Mujtabaa stayed on board, while Adrian left the plane. In the terminal he bought some perfume for Judith and a leather writing-case for Emma. He toyed with the idea of buying Mujtabaa a photograph of the Pope, or one of the little plastic replicas of a Michelangelo statue, Moses or David, almost as a bit of a joke, but at the last minute decided against it. He considered buying him a leather jacket, but thought even that might not be appreciated.

Soon after seven, on a sublime, still, summer's evening, they soared smoothly into the sky and headed for London. The rain clouds had scattered to the horizon, and a brilliant orange sky now stretched like a theatre backdrop behind the seven hills. The Eternal City was bathed in an appropriately ethereal glow. Flying up the coast to France, it struck Adrian very forcefully, and for the first time, that his dream was about to be realized. He was almost home.

Two hours later they were flying low above the wide, translucent ribbon of the Thames. The sky was becoming dark. Adrian looked out of the window at the sights of London unravelling beneath them. He doubted Mujtabaa would be interested in seeing them, and was probably, as always, staring impassively to the front, seemingly oblivious of everything that was happening around him. Adrian was concerned by his lack of movement, but also by his separateness. And he was frustrated by the fact that he was only able to speak to the Ethiopian through Anne.

Right on schedule, they were taxiing towards Terminal 3.

Being one of the first to disembark, Adrian waited for Anne and Mujtabaa at the end of the airbridge. The nurse had asked for a wheelchair for Mujtabaa, so she was the last off the plane.

It was being pushed by a flight attendant. His perspiring face was directly above his seated compatriot, but they weren't talking. Mujtabaa sat, looking at no one, as silent and unresponsive as a piece of baggage.

'I thought it better to avoid the crush,' Anne said by way of explanation.

The flight attendant took them to Immigration and Passport Control, chatting all the time, as if that was what was expected of him. He left them in the queue, solemnly turning round and waving as he walked back the way they'd come. The immigration officer barely looked at Anne or Adrian's passports, and stamped Mujtabaa's visa after only the quickest of glances in his direction. Before handing it back to Adrian, he said, 'What's wrong with him?' He scarcely sounded interested in a reply.

'You mean, why is he in a wheelchair?' The officer nodded. 'He's from an area of famine, and has lost a lot of weight.' They were waved through with a world-weary flick of the hand.

They collected their luggage from the carousel along with Mujtabaa's *jile*, which had travelled as a 'special package' in the hold of the plane, from a desk nearby. At Customs, they walked through the Nothing to Declare gate. They were stopped.

'Has this young man any baggage?' The customs officer was looking at Mujtabaa.

'No,' said Adrian.

'No hand luggage, sir?'

'No.'

'A toothbrush, maybe?' he asked frowning.

'Not even a toothbrush. Never used one, doesn't own one, probably never seen one.'

The customs officer stared at them. 'What would Colgate Palmolive have to say about that?' He half smiled, revealing his own rather forlorn set of nicotine-stained teeth, then indicated they should wait. He walked away to consult a colleague.

'What's the problem now, for heaven's sake?'

'I'm sure everything's fine, Adrian. It's probably because they've never come across anyone without any luggage before.' She lay a protective hand on Mujtabaa's arm.

The two customs officers were staring at them from an inspection table further up the hall. A minute later they walked over. The new officer, an overweight, stern-faced woman and, from her demeanour, the more senior of the two, asked: 'What did you say was wrong with your friend?'

'I didn't. I told one of your colleagues at Passport Control that there's nothing wrong with him, apart from the fact he's hungry. He's been in an area of famine, but he's not ill.'

'Ethiopia, is that where he's from?'

'Yes. I work for the charity Africa Assist, and this man is helping us raise money for his people, for famine relief.'

The two officers, expressionless and silent, regarded Mujtabaa as if he were a dead fish washed up on a beach and they were uncertain whether to throw him back in the water or simply walk away.

'Is there a problem?' Adrian asked.

The woman looked at him, almost with reluctance. 'Is there? You tell me, sir.'

'I don't believe there is.'

'Can he stand?' the woman's colleague asked.

Adrian's heart sank. 'Yes, of course.'

'Will you ask him to stand for me, please.'

Anne spoke to Mujtabaa, but he didn't stir. She took both of his hands and gently attempted to pull him to his feet. She whispered to him, but his head remained sunk on his chest. The customs officers watched dispassionately, as if they had little interest in the outcome of their request. Adrian stepped forward. 'Mujtabaa, let's just give you a bit of a hand up.' He grasped the young man under one of his arms, and with the nurse on his other side, they lifted him gently out of the wheelchair. He stood between them like a rag doll. Adrian felt he and Anne could have been army privates supporting a friend at an officer's morning inspection, trying to hide the fact that he was drunk and incapable from the night before.

They stood there for what seemed an interminable time. Finally, the female customs officer said, 'He can sit down again.'

Thank God, Adrian thought. But no sooner had they lowered

Mujtabaa into the wheelchair than the woman said: 'If you'd follow me, please.' She led them to a small room at the side of the Customs Hall.

'Can you tell me what's happening?'

'Yes, sir. Because of where he's come from, I'd like one of our medical officers to look at your friend.' She picked up the phone and dialled a number. While she waited for someone to answer, she addressed Adrian: 'There's a Medical Centre here at Heathrow, or we can take him to Hillingdon Hospital.'

'I really don't think that's necessary.'

'He doesn't look well to me, sir. I'll ask someone from the Medical Centre to pop over.'

'He's fine–' His protests were cut short by the woman explaining the situation to someone on the other end of the line. When she put the receiver down, she addressed Anne rather than Adrian: 'It's regulations, you understand. We have to be careful. There's been a lot of publicity about the famines in Africa.'

They sat on chairs by the door. The customs officer sat behind a desk and stared at the Ethiopian. No one spoke. Adrian appreciated that, even though he'd anticipated the possibility of such a ruinous turn of events, he was confounded by it now that it had happened. Although it was too late to argue with the customs officer, he'd have to make sure he pushed his case at the Medical Centre. He was so close to realizing his idea; he couldn't let it slip through his fingers at this late stage, after they'd come so far. He glanced at Mujtabaa. It was possibly a stroke of luck that no one was able to talk to him. But could he rely on Anne to say the right thing? That was his main concern.

A few minutes later there was a knock at the door and a young nurse appeared. 'I've come to collect someone for the Medical Centre.' She appeared relaxed and confident, her shapely, muscular frame sheathed tightly in a clean, starched uniform, a friendly, open smile on her face.

The nurse pushed the wheelchair, while Adrian and Anne followed behind. 'The Medical Centre is in Terminal 2. It's not far.' The young woman smiled over her shoulder at them. The moment they walked out into the crowded, noisy Arrivals Hall,

Dave Parker appeared suddenly at their side. There wasn't much flesh on the man, and so little on his face there was scarcely enough to even feed a smile. Maybe it was because of his height – an inch or two over six feet – but he always seemed to be looking down on those around him. A look that was complemented, quite successfully, by his air of smug satisfaction. He'd been with Africa Assist for the best part of 15 years, so he knew the ropes sufficiently well to follow Adrian without asking questions. As they walked, Adrian introduced him to Anne Chaffey. 'This is James Balcombe's right-hand man.' It was his way of disowning the fellow.

Even at this late hour, there were people hurrying in every direction, or standing about aimlessly, looking lost. The small group headed for the underground walkway. A long pedestrian mover carried them between green, hospital-like walls, illuminated every few yards by an electric light. There was no one to be seen; everyone had suddenly disappeared. For one insane moment Adrian considered elbowing the young nurse to one side, grabbing the wheelchair and, with Anne and Dave in tow, making a run for it. He was sorely tempted.

When they reached the entrance to Terminal 2, they turned right and walked the dozen yards to the Queens Building: the Medical Centre was on the ground floor. The nurse ushered them into a small room, then disappeared through a door at the far end, saying, 'Dr Kadwell won't be a minute.'

Dave peered down at Mujtabaa. 'So this is the unfortunate soul who has to walk to Trafalgar Square?'

'There are a few – as you put it – unfortunate souls walking to Trafalgar Square,' said Adrian curtly.

Dave turned to him. 'Which is extremely noble-minded.' He smiled. 'But then I'm driving, so I would say that.'

Anne was watching Dave closely, as if uncertain how to take him. 'He doesn't look what I'd call conspicuously thin,' he said to Adrian. 'Do you think he's going to stand out sufficiently for our purpose?'

Adrian wondered if he was going to have to put up with this kind of negativity for a whole week. 'He'll certainly stand out in this country. In his own country he doesn't, but that's because everyone there is thin.' He didn't bother to keep the supercilious tone out of his voice. 'Also, you're only seeing his face at the moment.'

Dave was looking at him critically, perhaps reflecting on the fact that the public-relations consultant was an endomorph, while he himself was an ectomorph. Adrian was annoyed with himself for having given James Balcombe's man the opportunity to comment, but equally annoyed with himself for his barrel-shaped abdomen.

'Do we know how much he understands what's going on?'

'We believe quite a bit, although he doesn't say very much, so it can be hard to tell.' Anne spoke as if she were still addressing the child who'd sat next to her on the plane.

Dave took a step forward and lifted one of Mujtabaa's hands off his lap, clasping it briefly. 'Pleased to meet you. I'm Dave.' Mujtabaa didn't move. Dave placed his hand back on his lap. The three of them stared at the Ethiopian in silence, then Dave said, 'As you requested, Adrian, I've arranged a private lounge for us, when we leave here.'

Dr Kadwell appeared a few minutes later. He looked as if he were barely out of medical school, having the tired, haunted appearance of a student who works all day and night, and is permanently worried about making a wrong diagnosis. He strode into the room, walked straight across to the wheelchair, and bent down to examine Mujtabaa's face. He was so objective, so separate, he could have been a lepidopterist studying a particularly interesting specimen in a display case. He straightened up and announced to the room, even though he was still staring with great concentration at the young man, 'If everything goes well, this should take less than an hour.' Only then did he turn and ask, 'Do you wish to stay here or go and have a coffee?'

'We'll stay here, and I'd like Anne Chaffey to accompany you. She's his nurse.'

'There's no need for that.'

Adrian was insistent. 'This young man knows Anne, it will help him to relax. She's also the only one able to communicate with him.'

Kadwell said nothing, but left the room with Mujtabaa and Anne.

'I don't trust that fellow.'

'Is there anything he can do?'

Adrian imagined the worst scenario. 'He could attempt to get him admitted to hospital.'

'Would Mujtabaa pass a medical, do you think?'

'Anne says he isn't fit compared to a Westerner, but then it depends on the criteria you judge him by.'

'He doesn't look well to me.'

Adrian found his assistant's lack of enthusiasm disheartening. He should surely have to defend himself from the doctor, not from his own assistant. 'You have to take into account his background, his circumstances and the fact he's severely malnourished. Obviously, he's weak but, as far as Anne can tell, he's not ill in the sense that he's carrying any contagious or dangerous diseases.'

'How about AIDS? Did you ask her about that?'

'She said it's difficult to tell, but she doesn't believe so.'

'That's the big worry nowadays.'

'People are just paranoid. Fixated. That's all that is.' He was becoming impatient. He began pacing up and down the small room.

'I spoke to one of the Press guys before you got here, Adrian – part of the permanent media presence at the airport.'

He abruptly stopped pacing. 'I told you not to speak to anyone until we arrived. What did you go and do that for?'

'It was James's idea.'

Adrian swore under his breath.

'I played it down, just kind of mentioned it.'

'How on earth can you *just kind of mention* something like this?'

'I knew you were in the air, so I didn't think much could go wrong.' His smile looked vaguely victorious.

'For Christ's sake, Dave, just stick to what I tell you in future.' He resumed pacing. He felt unnaturally tense; he needed to relax.

'It's not a good idea to speak to anyone until the press conference tomorrow morning, OK? We can build it up quickly from there.' He shook his head. 'What came over you?'

Dave's smirk had disappeared; now he was sulking. 'I told James what I was doing.'

'You don't answer to him over the next week – just me. Is that clear?'

'Sure.' This was said with seeming indifference, as if he had no intention of obeying such an instruction.

Adrian started to think about all the things that had to be organized, but he also knew there was nothing to be done until they could be sure they had Mujtabaa back in their care. He hated being dependent on someone else's decision.

Eventually, Dr Kadwell came back into the room. His head was buried in a file, and he exuded an air of busy self-importance. He was alone.

'Mr Burles, can you tell me why Mujtabaa is in this country?'

'He's helping Africa Assist raise money for famine relief.'

'And how's he doing that?'

Adrian briefly described what was planned, but avoided the details, trying to keep everything as vague as possible.

Dr Kadwell briefly consulted his file. Adrian stared at him, tense. Dave remained silent. Finally, the doctor closed his folder with a deliberate emphasis. 'You appreciate Mujtabaa isn't a well man?'

'We scarcely needed a medical examination to tell us that, Dr Kadwell.'

'It was a precautionary measure, you understand. To come straight to the point, I believe that what you're suggesting for this man, this *young man*, would place him in real danger.' He hesitated, before adding: 'I don't believe I'm exaggerating when I say it could even amount to a death sentence.' Outside the room, very much in the distance, they could hear flight information being announced over the public-address system. A taxi went past the window.

'I disagree, Doctor.' Adrian's features twitched with the effort to remain calm.

'It's possible you're playing with a man's life here, Mr Burles.'

'If we were – and I don't believe that is the case – then we're risking one man's life in order to save the lives of many others.'

'You're surely not saying the end justifies the means?'

Adrian held up his hands as if startled by such a suggestion. 'Not at all. I'm not that callous.'

'What if he should die? What if he can't do all that you want him to do?'

'I'm quite confident he can do what's required of him.'

'To the best of my knowledge, you're not a medical man, Mr Burles, so how can you be so sure?'

'We know that over the past few days, before he reached Anne Chaffey's clinic, this young man had walked over a hundred miles. He walked over a hundred miles to find food. We're not asking him to do anything nearly as exhausting as that. We're also giving him food and taking care of him while he's with us.'

'He walked that distance in order to survive. Now he's not obliged to do anything in order to survive.'

'But he is. He needs to raise money for himself, his family and his tribe so that they can *all* survive. He chose to come here of his own free will in order to help them. Leaving your own family, that's a hard choice for anyone to have to make.'

'He doesn't need to do anything to raise that money.'

'You're wrong, Dr Kadwell. Africa Assist has been in this business long enough to know that the general public doesn't give a damn about the hundreds of thousands of Africans dying of starvation, but they do give a damn about an individual. That's the way it's always been. It'll never change.'

He spoke passionately, earnestly, waving his arms around, keen for his audience to understand his point of view. 'And when people see this one skeletal figure, when he's standing there right in front of them, people will care. The ordinary man in the street can't *imagine* someone like him – he's beyond their comprehension – but if they can see him, then they'll understand. That's why I've brought him to London, so that people will comprehend the scale of the Ethiopian disaster.'

There was a long silence at the end of this speech. The two

men looked at Dr Kadwell, waiting for his response. Finally, he spoke: 'That's very altruistic, very noble – I mean that sincerely. But it doesn't get away from the fact your organization is placing this man's life in danger, and I can't condone that. Live Aid raised a great deal of money without bringing starving Ethiopians into the country.'

'And that's what was missing from their campaign – the human touch. They had to rely on film.'

'They were very successful, despite – as you put it – relying on film.'

'Geldof did well, I'm not denying it, but I'm building on what he achieved. I'm making famine personal, that's the difference.'

The doctor seemed to waver. The two men stared at each other in silence. Dave still sat in a chair in the corner of the room, watching, almost looking as if he didn't care who won the argument. This time it was Adrian who eventually spoke. 'Is he ill, Doctor? Is that what you're saying?'

'It depends on what you mean by ill. So far as I can tell, he doesn't have any of the diseases one might expect him to have: TB, leprosy, typhus, typhoid or trachoma. And he isn't HIV positive.'

'There you are.' Adrian held his hands out wide, as if to say, well then, that's the end of our discussion, everything's fine. 'Wonderful!' He attempted to hide from the doctor just how relieved he was to hear this news.

'But the danger to Mujtabaa isn't what he can give us, it's what we can give him. He's so weak, a dose of common-or-garden flu could be fatal to him. That's my concern.'

'We'll be careful. But the point is, he's well – or, at least, he isn't ill.'

'That's a little simplistic.'

There was a brief silence before Adrian said: 'Thanks for checking him over, but I think we should get out of your hair now.'

Considering the doctor, despite his age, had only a fringe of fine hair around the base of his shiny cranium, this probably wasn't the most appropriate expression to use. Apart from moving the files he was holding at his side to an almost protective position in front of his navel, one hand over the other, the doctor stood motionless. His veins were prominent on the back of his polished hands. 'I'm suggesting most forcefully, Mr Burles, that this young man does not do anything apart from rest. What you're suggesting is not only dangerous, it's immoral.'

'The morality or otherwise of our plans shouldn't be part of this discussion.'

'It's hard to ignore.'

'I say this with the greatest respect, Doctor. Your business is Mujtabaa's health, that's all. If he doesn't have any health issues, then you have no grounds to detain him.'

It was a gamble to spell it out as clearly as that, but Adrian felt he was now getting the better of his young adversary. When the doctor didn't reply, he added: 'My feeling is, Mujtabaa's no worse off here than he would be back in the desert. In fact, I'd say he's probably better off with us because he'll have medical support with him at all times.'

Dr Kadwell's smile looked as if it was being squeezed out through a cake-decorating bag. 'No offence intended, but if you're referring to Ms Chaffey, she's only a nurse.'

'A highly qualified one. She's been working with people like Mujtabaa for about 40 years. She runs a health clinic in his country, and deals with hundreds of refugees every day. She has cared for thousands of people in her time. There's little she doesn't know about the treatment of the malnourished.'

Then he added, very much as an afterthought: 'I've also arranged for our family doctor to keep an eye on him – on a regular basis.'

'That reassures me a little.'

'It will be additional insurance.'

There was a long silence. It was eventually broken by the young nurse wheeling Mujtabaa back into the room, the wheels making a slight sticking sound on the linoleum. She was followed by Anne Chaffey.

Adrian looked at them, then turned back to the doctor. 'We must be on our way.'

'You're surely not planning to commence anything this evening?'

'Tomorrow morning.'

'Then might I suggest the young man spends the night in our Medical Centre? At least he'll have a qualified doctor with him on his first night in the country. We can keep him under observation.'

'Thank you, but I think we'll take him with us.'

'Where are you planning to stay?'

'We've booked a hotel.'

The doctor nodded. 'If he stayed with us, Mr Burles, he'd be in good hands – in the event of an emergency, you understand. We'd be able to take care of him.'

'We're not expecting there to be any emergency. Anyway, we'll only be two minutes away.'

'You're placing his life at risk, and quite needlessly in my opinion. If he dies tonight, you'll have that on your conscience.'

'I'll have to learn to live with that' – said with the faintest of smiles. 'But, as I said, our family GP is making himself available.' He held out his hand, but the doctor's hands remained clasped on top of his files.

'I've taken the Hippocratic Oath – as I'm sure you must know – to save lives at all costs. I'd be breaking that oath if I didn't speak out.'

Adrian wondered what the doctor was getting at, but decided not to ask him. He made to walk off, then stopped. 'Mujtabaa is here of his own free will, you know, Doctor. He understands that, by helping us, he'll help his family and tribe.'

The doctor said nothing to this; he simply left the room. The young nurse gave them a little smile as she followed him out.

On their way back to Terminal 3, Dave, who was pushing the wheelchair, said: 'I thought it was a good idea to leave Mujtabaa there for the night.'

'Did you?'

The assistant hesitated, perhaps reluctant to risk overstepping some imagined mark. 'It struck me as a sensible option. You know, a safe one.'

'It's too great a risk. You know what they say; possession is nine-tenths of the law.'

They took a few steps in silence before Anne murmured: 'I didn't appreciate that rule applied to people.'

Adrian couldn't tell if this was a straightforward claim to ignorance or if the nurse was being ironic.

'I'm pleased to hear you'll be contacting your GP as an added safeguard.'

'If it makes you happy, Anne,' he said magnanimously, 'I shall do just that.' He hadn't intended to.

When they reached the reserved lounge, Anne read a book, Mujtabaa fell asleep in the wheelchair, wrapped in a large grey blanket, while the two men discussed the printing and distribution of flyers, the placing of advertisements in newspapers, the organizing of an army of volunteers, and the arrangements with respect to the mobile home. Adrian also told Dave to confirm, first thing in the morning, Mujtabaa's attendance at the Sunday rally. This was a long-standing booking organized by the Disasters Emergency Committee, the umbrella group for British charities raising funds for emergency relief.

Dave stared at the young Ethiopian in his wheelchair, his head lying awkwardly on his shoulder. 'We're giving him food, aren't we?'

'Enough to keep him going. Over the next few days, until the weekend, we just want to keep him alive.'

Dave grimaced. 'That sounds fun.'

'He has to stay hungry, otherwise this won't work. Come Sunday, we can feed him up, but not until then.' Adrian shook his head. 'We don't have an option. The hungrier he looks, the better this will work for us.'

'I suppose so.' His assistant didn't look convinced.

'Don't worry, we'll take good care of him.'

'Oh, I'm not worried.'

But Adrian added, because he knew it would be faithfully relayed back to Dave's boss, 'He'll be in good hands at all times.'

Dave changed the subject: 'It reminds me of that joke you hear every time there's a famine in Africa.'

'Yes?' Adrian did his best to appear interested.

'A fat man runs into a thin man and says: "You should be ashamed of yourself. If a visitor to this country saw you before anyone else, he'd think there was a famine here." And the thin man replies, "And if he saw you straight after me, he'd know the reason for it."'

With a somewhat preoccupied air, Adrian nodded.

Soon after Dave left for home, Dr Somerville arrived, stooping, as if dragged forwards both by his age and the weight of his faded black medicine bag. He'd been the Burles family's GP for many years, back to the days when Adrian was a child. Adrian had always regarded him as part of that rare breed of doctors that takes the time to talk to each of their patients, to find out how their lives are going even if they only claim to be suffering from a headache. This meant he was always behind schedule, and his waiting room always crowded.

He examined Mujtabaa carefully, breathing heavily as he did so. Adrian looked on, deciding the doctor sounded far less healthy than the patient. Finally, the medical man straightened up. 'Malnourished definitely, but fit as a fiddle I'd say. If I were you, I'd dose him up on vitamins, and plenty of supplements.' He turned to Anne: 'Imagine you're doing that already, Nurse?'

She smiled back at him. 'I am, Dr Somerville.'

'Good woman. Obviously can't teach you anything.' And a few minutes later he left.

Adrian told Anne that he wanted the three of them to spend the night in the lounge. 'It's more authentic if it looks like Mujtabaa has just stepped off a plane when he starts his walk. It's not the same if he spends the night in a hotel, then returns to the airport the next morning.'

'That doesn't mean you have to stay here, Adrian. He'll be fine with me – just so long as you're nearby.'

He quickly agreed, grateful not to have to spend the night on a sofa. They said goodnight. He left Anne and the still-sleeping Mujtabaa and caught the lift down to the ground floor. He booked into the first airport hotel he stumbled across and, before going up to his room, called Anne to give her his room and phone numbers. 'Call me if you have any worries, any worries at all.' Then he ordered a double scotch at the bar. He was the only customer. He stared down into the amber liquid in front of him, swilling the ice around in the glass. He felt tired and lethargic, and briefly wondered why. This was no time to take his foot off the accelerator; this was his moment. This project could be the biggest thing he'd ever done.

Monday

*I*n the early hours of the morning, Anne woke to find Mujtabaa standing on one leg, his other foot placed against it at right angles just above the knee. He was staring blankly across the room, motionless, frozen in the centre of an alien place.

She asked if he needed anything, but it was as if he didn't hear her. Not wishing to disturb him, she lay back down on the sofa. Her heart went out to him. This is no place for an Afar warrior, she thought, and momentarily she wished they were both back in Ethiopia.

She remembered what he'd said to her earlier, on the plane. It had been garbled, at times almost incoherent, and her poor knowledge of the Afar language had scarcely helped. He had told her a story – and for a while she wondered if it had been just that, a story – about a creature that had attempted to kill him on his long trek across the Danakil.

Shivering with cold – or fright, she wasn't clear which – he'd become aware at some point in the journey of a creature with red eyes looming over him in the darkness. This creature was so close to him, he'd been able to smell its breath. Other creatures were there too, equally malignant, but always lurking in the background, their shadowy shapes scarcely visible in the darkness. Mujtabaa told Anne they'd been following him for days, but only appearing after the sun went down, and that the whining, shuffling and predatory postures of the creatures – especially of the leader, the one he called Red Eyes – meant they were about to attack him. He had wanted to tell them not to waste their time: he was no more than skin and bone and as hungry and thin as they were.

Yet there was a part of him that wanted these creatures to

attack, for his ordeal to be over. It was like he had neither the strength nor the will to keep them at bay any longer. He either wanted to be taken by He Who Is Always Hungry, or to be left alone to continue his walk in peace. Which of these it was to be, he did not care.

But on this particular night, he could tell Red Eyes was about to attack. The creature was closer than ever before, so close that Mujtabaa felt he could reach out and touch him. He swung his *jile* wildly through the darkness, and struck the creature just to the left of its eyes, perhaps on its head, perhaps on its shoulder. The bone-splintering blow caused it to retreat with a snarl of pain and anger. Without hesitation, the other creatures then turned on their stricken companion and tore him to pieces just out of sight of Mujtabaa.

The recounting of this story was disjointed, and Anne found herself forever trying to fill in the gaps or join the dots. So she wasn't surprised when suddenly, without any logic – or none that Anne could understand – he told her how he'd fallen over. (She guessed this was at a different time and in a different place from the Red Eyes attack.) It happened because he was weak – 'like a woman' was the phrase the nurse picked up on. He'd wanted to stay on the ground and sleep, but had been unable to stop his thoughts turning to Safia. He said she was walking with him, comforting him, encouraging him to keep going. He'd left her many days earlier in the *ari*, lying on the skins with their son, and yet it was like she was still with him, at his side. She even lay with him on the sand, her arms around him, so that he could feel her softness and warmth, the dampness of her skin against his. He told the nurse – or perhaps just himself – that he had never before experienced such peace. And, as he drifted in and out of sleep, he accepted that He Who Is Always Hungry was about to claim him.

Instead, it had been the white ghosts who had come for him, and he found himself flying through the sky. The desert was falling down into the sky and he was being lifted up, higher and higher, towards the sun. He peered through the small glasses that lined the side of the machine he found himself in, and saw only clouds. Even more astonishing – and quite beyond his understanding – the clouds were below him, not above him where they should have been. How was it possible to be on top of the clouds?

They were now so high, he knew he must be dead. Even though the white ghosts were still with him, he must now be a spirit. But how could that be? Everyone knew white people didn't have spirits, so it was impossible they were to spend time with him in the land of the spirits. He wasn't so wicked that he deserved that.

Adrian looked like he'd been tossed onto the mattress by a giant wave, and discarded there, like an overly large piece of jetsam, half unconscious, face down in retreating white-sheeted foam.

In the street below, a car went past scattering rock music through open windows, then was swallowed by the night. Someone walked along the corridor outside his room. From the sound of soft, intermittent thuds, he supposed they were delivering the morning newspapers. He pulled the covers up higher over his shoulders, against the coolness of the air conditioning, and tried to go back to sleep. It was impossible. His mind, like a dog set loose in a forest of lampposts, ran from one thought to another.

What a coup! What will the other charities say when they realize what I've pulled off? It's the perfect follow-up to Live Aid: a completely different, but just as original, idea – no, a more original idea! No one's ever done anything like this before, ever. It's going to reignite the public's interest in the problems of the Horn of Africa. The other charities will be crazy with envy. And it's not the kind of exercise you can repeat, so they'll just have to suffer in silence. I've changed fundraising for ever; Adrian Burles is a true pioneer! As for the young Ethiopian, he'll be all right. We'll take care of him, wrap him in cotton wool as much as possible. We're not making him do too much, and we'll be giving him more food than he usually gets. We'll have to prove that doctor wrong, and make sure the Ethiopian survives, that he makes it all the way to the Trafalgar Square rally. So many people are depending on that. We also have to make sure he gets back to his own country and takes a ton of cash with him. He'll be fine; Anne will take care of him. Not sure how to take that one. She's good, no doubt about it. Very dedicated, efficient, but she's a bit too closed in for my liking, a bit too private. Seems to lead a hospital-bed-corner kind of life: everything very neat, tucked in and orderly. It's certainly impossible to know what she's thinking. She says she's behind the project, and I tend to believe her, but I'm also sensing that she has some reservations. I'll have to keep an eye on her. She can't be allowed to sabotage my plan. If she starts causing any problems, I'll get rid of her, find a replacement. That shouldn't be too difficult in London, but it's not ideal. I'll certainly be hard pushed to find anyone else with her depth of experience of malnutrition at such short notice. And introducing a stranger into the proceedings at this late stage could be inviting disaster. Best not to worry about it, everything's going to be fine. A lot of good will come out of this walk. God, it makes me excited just to think about it. No wonder I can't sleep.

He stared up at the ceiling, going over every aspect of the plan again and again, persuading himself it was going to be a success, trying to block from his mind the ever-intrusive possibility of failure, while the hotel hummed around him, like a huge engine in the night.

He breakfasted alone in the dining room. While enjoying his bowl of muesli and fruit, followed by bacon, eggs, mushrooms and tomatoes, then marmalade and toast, with several cups of coffee, he flicked through the morning newspapers – five of them.

He sat in the hotel's reception and waited for Dave. A fountain was playing in the centre of the high, predominantly glass area. Palm trees clustered for comfort near the main doors, as if pondering a quick escape from this foreign environment. A forlorn group of Japanese tourists stood awaiting orders from their guide, looks of expectation on their faces, possibly nursing hopes of having now 'done' England and trusting that they were about to be given permission to leave this strange country and return home with their holiday snaps. He pondered how they soon wouldn't have to bother to make such journeys, wouldn't have to suffer the rudeness, stress and inconveniences of international travel, because they'd be able to visit the Tobu World Square theme park and get their overseas experience without ever leaving home.

Dave was suddenly standing beside him. Adrian wondered if he always made his entrances like this, sly and ghostlike. He shook Adrian's hand, but in a distancing way, as if to keep him at arm's length. He looks devious, Adrian thought; even his admiring glances round the hotel foyer lacked sincerity. Fifteen minutes later they were back in the airport lounge with Anne and Mujtabaa.

'He didn't sleep well,' said the nurse. 'I think he found it very noisy with all the aircraft.'

The young man was sitting in his wheelchair, looking like he hadn't moved all night. He didn't acknowledge the two men when they entered. It went through Adrian's mind that he looked as out of place in the room as those palm trees in the hotel foyer – a monochrome apparition in a full-colour setting.

'Did he sleep on the sofa?'

'He lay on the floor with a blanket over him.'

'How about food?'

'I gave him a little porridge.'

'He managed to eat it all right?'

She nodded. Adrian walked across to where Mujtabaa was sitting and reached out to touch his hand. 'Good morning.' The Ethiopian didn't stir. He looked vulnerable, and Adrian wondered briefly if he'd ever be able to bridge the gulf that lay between them.

He frowned, and turned away. 'We should get over to the conference centre.' He spoke to the nurse: 'I think it's a good idea if you wear your white coat over your dress, Anne. It tells people who you are, and also that you're medical.'

It was a fairly modest turnout by the press, although there was a representative from most of the major newspapers, as well as the BBC. The commercial stations had obviously decided that 'an important message from Africa Assist regarding a revolutionary fundraising scheme' was not of sufficient interest to them.

Most, if not all, of the reporters were permanently situated at the airport, just to cover departing and arriving celebrities or politicians.

Anne and Mujtabaa sat in chairs in the front of the room, along with James Balcombe, who arrived at the last minute and faffed around uselessly, getting in everyone's way and causing unnecessary stress. Adrian addressed the journalists.

'The young man you see here is Mujtabaa. He's flown here from his home in the Danakil Desert, in Africa, and he's about to set off on a walk from Heathrow to Trafalgar Square. The aim of this walk is to bring the world's attention once again to the plight of Mujtabaa's fellow Ethiopians. He wants to raise money to feed them. As you know, many parts of Africa are still suffering from – in Michael Buerk's famous phrase back in October 1984 – "a famine of biblical proportions", and Mujtabaa is the face of that tragedy. Anne Chaffey, a nurse who has worked in Ethiopia for over 40 years, will accompany him on his walk. The walk will end in Trafalgar Square at a rally against world hunger on Sunday.'

This brief statement was followed by questions.

'How far are you hoping to cover every day?'

'Trafalgar Square is about 25 to 30 miles from here, depending on the route. We intend to start on the A4, then take the A3006 – the old Roman road – through Hounslow and Brentford.' He indicated the map on the wall behind him. 'We'll cross the Thames into Richmond, possibly Barnes, then walk through Chiswick, Hammersmith, Fulham, Chelsea and, finally, Westminster.'

'So you're not intending to walk far every day?'

'Mujtabaa's welfare is our primary concern, so we intend to make absolutely sure that he doesn't over-exert himself. We have to be in Trafalgar Square on Sunday, so that gives us six days, which should work out at an average of five miles a day. But that is flexible, to a degree – like the route. We'll take each day as it comes, rather than stick rigidly to a schedule. Some days we may do more, some days less. We may spend hours in a shopping centre, for instance, or Mujtabaa may need to spend a day resting, we just don't know. But that's the beauty of living out of a mobile home: we can stop wherever and whenever we please.'

'Didn't Band Aid and Live Aid do everything that could be done to raise money for Ethiopia?'

'They did an excellent job, no doubt about it. But in my opinion – and in the opinion of many people – those two events created an almost insurmountable distance between the donors and the recipients. Our intention with this walk is to bring those two groups together. Quite literally, the distance between this young man and those who will help him will be no different from the distance between you and me in this room. We believe that will have a major impact on our fundraising.'

Another reporter asked: 'Do you think a public-relations exercise – because that's basically what you're proposing – is the answer to malnutrition in Africa?'

'Good question. I'd say people in the West won't donate unless they know there's a problem in the first place. And I'd remind you that it was the media that first drew the world's attention to the Ethiopian famines, and it was the media that basically brought about the solution. And the media is no more and no less than public relations.'

After the press conference finally wound up, and James Balcombe had departed with vague promises to visit them again soon, they put a blanket over Mujtabaa's knees, and pushed the wheelchair back to the Arrivals Hall.

'What about the cops?' Dave asked Adrian. 'Do they know the exact route we'll be taking?'

'They seemed surprisingly relaxed when I discussed the walk with an Inspector Davidson just before leaving for Ethiopia. That doesn't mean they won't try and pin us down to a route if this becomes big. I suspect they don't have any idea what this could turn into – maybe none of us does. But I played it down anyway, just to get them onside.' He grinned, satisfied with his tactics.

Anne asked: 'Do we know what the weather forecast is?'

'They say the next few days will be fine and hot,' Dave said. 'Around 70 degrees.'

'Thank you, God.' Adrian grinned, raising his eyes to the

ceiling. 'Perfect August weather. Someone up there's on our side. Mujtabaa should feel comfortable enough in that temperature, don't you think, Anne?'

'It's a good deal cooler than he's used to, but it will help.'

Dave looked stunned. 'Me, I'm down to my swimming costume when it gets that hot – oops, sorry, Anne.'

She smiled. 'Not at all, Dave. It's a charming picture.'

'Only if you haven't seen it.' He rolled his eyes in a self-mocking way.

They stopped in the approximate centre of the Terminal 3 Arrivals Hall, and stood around Mujtabaa's wheelchair. He was watching them, unblinking and without expression. He appeared oblivious of the stares of passers-by. Adrian turned to Anne. 'We need to tell him it's time to start our walk.'

'There should be an official starting place,' Dave said, 'something that says, right, let's start here.' They looked round the glass, steel and concrete hall, at the people, either rushing purposefully by or standing with bemused expressions as they waited for their flight announcement, but there was nowhere that stood out.

'Where are those collectors, Dave?'

'Waiting for us by the main doors.'

'Why aren't they inside the terminal? This is a good money-collecting opportunity.'

'It's against the local bylaws.'

Adrian swore under his breath. 'In that case, they'll have to begin collecting as soon as we set off.'

Anne bent down to talk to Mujtabaa. She removed the blanket, and took one of his hands to help him out of the wheelchair. He stood before them, fragile, a little shaky, like an old man. She took his goatskin waterbag off him and placed it on the wheelchair. 'I'll carry that for him.'

'Anne, you'll have to remove his *shämma*.'

Still firmly holding the young man's arm, she turned to Adrian, 'But he only has his *sanafil* on...'

'I've already told you, that's all I want him to wear. That's how he usually goes around, isn't it – back home?'

'Often, yes...' She appeared at a loss. 'But we're in London now, in an airport building.'

'That's what I want him to wear, just that skirt thing. We'll carry his *shämma*.'

'But what about his dignity?'

'I'm not interested in his dignity, Anne. Anyway, starvation is scarcely dignified, you know that. I want to shock people, and they won't be shocked if he's covered from head to foot.'

The nurse hesitated. She looked from Adrian to Mujtabaa, and back again, indecisive, suddenly looking her age. 'I don't think that's right,' she said, her voice barely audible against the sounds of the terminal.

'Well, I do. Not just right, but necessary. I'm sorry, it's not up for discussion.'

The nurse was blinking, her head moving this way then that, one hand grasping the other and then, as if hoping to provide each with a little comfort, the other way around. No one spoke. The announcements of flight arrivals continued above their heads, almost without a break. A passing couple stared, momentarily hesitating, like they were in the audience of a theatre in the round. The Africa Assist group of four was already a spectacle.

Adrian was insistent, leaning forward to emphasize his words. 'People have to see him. It's the only way. They have to see how thin he is.' He looked like a man who was used to giving orders, possibly even shouting them, and was now making an enormous, as well as unusual, effort to be more reasonable and democratic. 'I hear your concerns, Anne, but I won't entertain any alternative.'

Dave was watching them both, making his non-engagement very obvious, as if he hadn't yet decided whose side he was on.

'But what if he gets cold?'

'We'll make sure he doesn't,' Adrian said. 'He'll have to put up with a little discomfort for a few days, Anne, but nothing he won't be used to. It's cold in the desert at night, everyone knows that.'

She blinked nervously. She looked like she was about to cry. She turned to the young man and said something. He didn't move.

'I don't think he understands.' She half glanced at Adrian, her hands now clasped together as if in supplication to a higher being, peering up at him from beneath the rim of her straw hat like some small, shy desert creature surveying the lie of the land from its hole in the sand.

He wasn't in the mood to back down. 'You take it off him then.'

She still hesitated. Adrian stepped forward. 'Maybe I should–'

'Thank you. I will do it if it must be done.' She began to remove Mujtabaa's belt and *jile*. She didn't hurry. Then, standing on tiptoe, she reached up and undid his *shämma*. Gently she unwrapped it from around him. There was a tenderness in her movements, as if she were undressing an overgrown grandchild for bed. She stood back, her face averted. The young man was naked apart from his *sanafil* and the sandals on his feet. An old woman passing by with her husband gasped. Adrian heard her say, 'Oh dear, that's terrible. The poor chap.' Her husband put an arm round her shoulders, urging her to keep moving, not to upset herself by looking.

Mujtabaa put his belt back on, slowly, like a man who was drugged. He was a living skeleton, a collection of bones, a walking corpse. Every rib could be counted. His collarbones stood out, impossibly stretching the covering of flesh. His arms hung by his side, his elbows, like his knees, painfully knobbly. The circumference of his thighs was little wider than that of his thigh bone, and beneath the proscenium of his rib cage, his *jile* jutted sideways, obscenely large in its sunken, scrawny setting.

In an attempt to snap everyone out of their musings and doubts, Adrian spoke. 'We'll make a start then. You have to stay with him at all times, Anne. Don't ever leave his side. I'll walk ahead. Dave, you have to follow behind until we're outside, but keep close. We can't allow anyone to jostle Mujtabaa, especially here in the terminal. We must protect him. We're all responsible for his welfare.'

Dave suggested that Adrian say something to the handful of inquisitive people who were standing nearby watching. 'Tell them what's happening. Announce the start of the walk. It's good publicity. We shouldn't pass up the opportunity.'

Adrian thought for a moment, cleared his throat self-consciously and said: 'I'd just like to say a few words.' One or two people passing by stopped, uncertain, unsure that they were being addressed. He continued, more confident now that he had an audience. He explained what Africa Assist was planning, even mentioning Live Aid in order to put the walk into context.

He stared at his audience. Many appeared to have just returned from a holiday on the Continent, others to have come to the airport to greet returning family and friends. He regarded their unwavering gazes. Like cows, he thought, just staring at me, not comprehending. There was likely to be much more of this over the following days; he had to try to be patient. This was his market.

He ended up: 'I'm sure you'll all join me in wishing Mujtabaa well.' And, in the face of his silent audience, Adrian also fell silent.

Awkward, almost painful seconds ticked by. As he turned away from the gawping strangers, one person started to clap half-heartedly, but stopped almost immediately. Two police officers were approaching, screened off and threatening behind their dark glasses.

One of the officers addressed Mujtabaa. 'Excuse me, sir, you can't carry a knife like that around the terminal.' He was seemingly unfazed by the sight of the young man's body.

Adrian stepped in. 'He doesn't speak English, Officer. Can I help?'

The policeman pointed at the knife. 'Carrying weapons in a public place is an offence, sir.'

'But it's ornamental.'

'Makes no difference, sir.'

'We're just leaving.'

A disembodied voice announced a flight arrival from Johannesburg. Mujtabaa, bewilderment on his face, stood before them, almost naked, looking starkly out of place against the chrome, glass and polished-vinyl floors of the airport. The officers stared at this sliver of humanity, about half their own width, and obviously had no idea what to do. They still addressed Mujtabaa. 'You'll have to leave the airport, sir. We'll escort you to the exit.'

'Thank you,' Adrian replied on his behalf.

Anne took Mujtabaa's hand, leading him gently forward. Some tourists were about to take photographs, yet suddenly seemed reluctant to do so, as if they'd all reached the same conclusion at the same time, that they had no right to photograph such a figure. No one spoke. The crowd parted in front of Adrian, as softly and slowly as a stage curtain, with Anne and the young man following close behind. The two officers, suspicious and distrustful, brought up the rear. Adrian looked at his watch; it was a little after ten. He made a mental note of the time. He intended to keep a diary of the week's events; it could be an important historical record.

'I should find a public phone and call Inspector Davidson. Get clearance for that knife before we have any more problems.'

'I've got one of those mobile phones in the Winnebago,' Dave said. 'Why not call him on that later? It'll be easier after we've left the airport.'

They continued through the terminal. People stopped and stared, some now taking photographs, others shouting questions. They followed the small Africa Assist group, jostling for position, straining to get a better view of the young man. Passengers walked over from the other side of the terminal, curious to see what was happening. And, for the first time, Adrian thought: This is going to work. People are interested. They really want to know, to see the face of hunger for themselves.

He headed for the escalators. Anne called after him, incredulous: 'You can't take him down there, Adrian.'

He nodded, annoyed he hadn't thought of that. He veered away and headed for the stairs. They descended the stairs, slowly, followed by a sizeable crowd. One man – he appeared to be an American – was walking backwards down the steps ahead of them, taking photographs as he went. Something to show the folks back in Omaha, went through Adrian's head.

70

As they passed through the automatic doors to the outside of the terminal, they were joined by six collectors wearing the eye-catching scarlet vests of Africa Assist and carrying collection tins. After a brief discussion, watched by the police from just inside the terminal doors, they set off. They were walking past the queue at the taxi rank when someone turned and said: 'Jesus, look at him, will you?' Everyone was looking at him anyway, so the comment scarcely seemed necessary. 'That's obscene. It shouldn't be allowed.'

'Yes, then why don't you do something to stop it,' Adrian snapped, angry at such ignorance. He pointed to the Africa Assist collectors: 'They'll be happy to receive your donation. That's how you can help end this obscenity.' He suddenly felt the urge to hurry, to get away from the airport as fast as possible. For some inexplicable reason he felt they couldn't begin their journey until they left the airport, even though the airport actually was the beginning.

He walked across a pedestrian crossing. Cars stopped. Drivers and passengers stared through the windows, transfixed by the skeletal figure. Was he ill? Was he anorexic? Was this some kind of stunt? Maybe it was a film?

Adrian turned round. Anne was following him and, immediately behind her, at her heels, trailed Mujtabaa. His head was held high, making him look aloof from the proceedings, separate, almost disdainful. A few yards behind him came Dave.

Adrian skirted one side of a multi-storey car park. He wondered what the Ethiopian must be making of all this. Dave caught up with him. He was short of breath. 'It's not easy to walk out of the airport with all these one-way streets and roundabouts and car parks. It's been designed around cars. Tomorrow will be more straightforward.'

'What are you saying, Dave? Which way do we go?'

'You have to walk through that tunnel.'

'It says No Pedestrian Access, for Christ's sake.'

'Ignore it. It's the only way out of here that I could find. Believe me, it's all right. I've done it.'

'Not with a crowd like this, you haven't.'

'They won't follow you. Anyway, it's the only option. I'll be off to pick up the cases and collect the Winnebago from the car park. I'll wait for you at the agreed spot.' As he walked off, Adrian shouted after him: 'Where are the collectors?'

'Still back at the front of the terminal. People won't let them get away.'

At least there was some good news. He felt dissatisfied with the way things were going, but wasn't sure why. Rather, it was something he sensed, an unpleasant, gnawing feeling of unease, almost dread of some impending disaster.

The three of them entered the 15-foot-high tunnel; Adrian followed by Mujtabaa, followed by Anne. No one followed them, just as Dave had predicted. There was a narrow footpath on the left-hand side of the tunnel, separated from the single-lane road by railings. Between the railings and the road was a narrow cycle path, picked out in red. Large ventilation fans and surveillance cameras were spaced every 50 yards or so above the footpath. Adrian wondered if they were being watched. What would the security person think of this bizarre procession heading through his tunnel? On the far side of the roadway, against the wall, were strip lights encased in protective cages.

There were no other pedestrians and only a few cars. Those that passed them were travelling fast and paid no attention to the small group walking along the footpath. Adrian wondered how Mujtabaa would see this, a 200-yard tunnel beneath the ground. He certainly wouldn't realize that huge jets were landing above his head, right on top of him. Suddenly Anne was calling to him to stop. He turned round to see Mujtabaa on his knees, clutching the railings. He rushed back.

'What happened?' Anne was bent over the young man, her hand on his brow.

'I don't know. He just reached out for the railing, then fell to his knees.' A car went past, inches from them, sounding its horn. 'We have to get him out of here.' Between them, they managed to get Mujtabaa to his feet. They stood next to him, hands out, ready to catch him if he fell again. Anne took his pulse. She was frowning, whether from concentration or worry Adrian couldn't work out. They continued slowly along the footpath, Mujtabaa holding on to the nurse's arm.

It took ten minutes to reach the far end of the tunnel. They blinked when they emerged into the light. Directly in front of them was a large roundabout covered in flowers and grass. They walked to the left. They had to cross three busy roads that fed traffic onto the roundabout before they were able to turn left up a hill, past the Heathrow police station. Mujtabaa seemed to have recovered and, although he no longer held on to Anne, he continued to walk painfully slowly. In Adrian's eyes, this was perfect.

Two police officers sitting in their car outside the station eyed them with only passing interest. They either didn't notice, or weren't bothered by the *jile*. Adrian thought their view of the world must be so jaundiced that he wondered what it would take to get them out of their car. A few yards further on, they turned right onto the A4, signposted for 'Central London, Harrow and Hounslow.'

Adrian halted. 'Thank God we're out of there. That has to be a pedestrian's worst nightmare. How is he?'

At that moment a horn sounded from across the dual carriageway. It was Dave, parked outside a service station. Adrian told Anne to wait with Mujtabaa, and crossed the road. The volunteers were piling out of the side of the mobile home. It was covered in posters advertising the walk. Adrian instructed three volunteers to collect money along the left-hand side of the road, and the other three to follow the Ethiopian on the far side.

It wasn't the ideal place to start the walk: it was a dual-carriageway arterial road with a barrier down the middle. Most cars were travelling too fast to stop. The pavements were wide, empty and dirty, but Adrian knew this road was still better than the only alternative – the M4 motorway.

The noise from traffic and aircraft was both incessant and mind-numbing. Hotels lined the route: large, impersonal structures with drawn, shut-out-the-world lace curtains in every room. On the right-hand side of the road, between the hotels, planes could be glimpsed on the tarmac. Every now and again there was a roar as one took off, and each time this happened, Mujtabaa jumped and put a hand to his *jile*. At Harlington Corner, there was a road off to the right to Terminal 4, and an historic milestone indicated that the centre of London was 13 miles away.

It was midday before they reached the first houses since leaving the airport. It was a rundown area which had been completely subjugated by the car. The world either drove straight through it, or bypassed it. The collectors went into the White Hart pub, a mock Tudor building adjoining an Esso service station. One or two drinkers came to the door to have a look at what was going on and to see whom they were giving money to.

The Africa Assist group stopped for a break at a community centre, and Adrian took the opportunity to use the public phone. First he called Inspector Davidson, the man he'd been dealing with over the various aspects of the walk, and received clearance for Mujtabaa's knife. It was given somewhat reluctantly, and only because Adrian placed great emphasis on its ornamental nature, lied about how blunt it was, and promised that it would never leave the scabbard. He was very persuasive.

Next he called home. 'Let's go out this evening; you, me and Emma. There's a reasonable-looking restaurant next to the Grand Union Canal – where it crosses the A315. I went past it a couple of weeks ago when I reconnoitred the area. I don't remember the name, but you can't miss it.'

'Will you have got that far by then?'

'We'll probably stop somewhere in Hounslow this evening, but I'll catch a cab there. See you both at 7.30. We shouldn't have to book, not on a Monday night.'

He wasn't happy with the way the walk was progressing. Cars were slowing down for a look as they passed, but few stopped. Pedestrians were generous, but there were not many of them. There was also the tedium of the walk itself: alongside a noisy dual carriageway, past hotels and acres of derelict ground, across endless roundabouts, down streets full of nondescript 1950s housing and uninviting shops and takeaways. He briefly considered taking a side road, but knew there'd then be even fewer people, and so they'd receive even less publicity. Publicity was the lifeblood of his venture, and he briefly lamented the absence of the media.

Immediately after the Waggoners roundabout, they passed a large McDonald's. Adrian briefly wondered if the restaurant would ever have a franchise in Ethiopia. He remembered reading that there wasn't yet one in South Africa, but that was because of apartheid.

They turned onto the A3006, a single-lane road, with a narrower road running parallel and adjacent to it behind a high hedgerow. They walked along this smaller road, in front of a row of houses. They were almost directly under the flight path now and, as every jet screamed low overhead on its final approach, they could turn their heads towards the northeast and see the next jet already lining up in the distance. Mujtabaa looked up as every plane passed above them on its landing run. The first time it happened, he crouched down close to the ground and, drawing his *jile* from its scabbard, raised it in the air and shouted ferociously, staring transfixed at the enormous fuselage with its blinking lights and undercarriage already down. Adrian blinked nervously at the fearsome, razor-sharp blade and was grateful Inspector Davidson wasn't around to see it. Anne tried to reassure the Ethiopian, shouting to make herself heard over the roar of the engines. Although he started to leave his *jile* in its scabbard as other jets bellied earthwards, he continued to clutch it, looking as if he were still ready to do battle.

They reached their first Underground station, Hounslow West, and stood outside for almost an hour collecting money from commuters already beginning to return from work. Most of the people had that stressed, eyes-down, I-must-hurry-home look which precluded any real connection with the event, no matter how extraordinary, unfolding before them.

They found Dave parked outside the Windsor Castle pub on the corner of Wellington Road North. 'Don't worry, I've not been inside,' he shouted to Adrian from the cabin of the mobile home. 'Can't say I didn't think about it, though.'

The two women were a study in contrasting body language:

one tight, the other loose. The mother sat very still and upright at the table, as if not wanting to draw attention to herself. She had a slightly wary, almost beaten, look about her, yet there was a stubbornness still lingering around the corners of the eyes and mouth that hinted at the possibility she may not have been entirely subjugated – despite her forty-something years. The other, the 14-year-old, lay rather than sat on her chair, arms hanging by her side, eyes down, listening to her Walkman. She looked as if she were attempting to impersonate a tormented, romantic soul in a state of drug-induced inertia (and was doing a very good job of it).

There was a commotion by the front door of the restaurant, just enough to register through Michael Jackson's high voice. She looked up to see the waiter leap forward, only to be brushed aside – like he was something of a minor nuisance – as her father weaved his way through the empty tables towards them. Her mother, before taking a quick mouthful from her glass of wine, said, unnecessarily, 'Here's your father.'

Adrian frowned at his wife across the table, at her newly spiked, highlighted hair. 'Like it?' she asked.

'It's certainly different.' He moved round the table, bent down and pecked her on the cheek. 'Not sure it suits you, Jude, but maybe I just need more time to get used to it.'

Without waiting for a reply, he moved round to his daughter and enveloped her slouched body in a bear hug. He turned his head to look her directly in the eyes and silently mouthed some words. She wriggled from his grasp, saying – as she took the headphones from her ears and rolled her eyes – 'Very funny, Dad.'

He tousled her hair. She ducked away from his hand, protesting.

'I can't make it any messier than it is already, can I?' He sat down, hands clasped on the tablecloth, and looked at each woman in turn. Judith sighed. 'And it's good to see you, too, Adrian.'

He put on an innocent air. 'What?'

Her eyes closed, and she shook her head briefly as if denying there was anything the matter. 'I ordered a bottle of Cabernet

Sauvignon.'

'As well as whatever it is you have there?' – indicating her glass of white.

'I needed something while we were waiting.'

Emma was annoyed that her mother felt it necessary to make an excuse.

'How did you know that's what I wanted to drink this evening?'

'You always drink Cabernet Sauvignon, Adrian – always. And if tonight is the exception, then I will drink it. How about that?'

'You probably would, too.'

'Meaning?'

'If you two are going to fight, I'm going to listen to my Walkman.'

'We're not fighting, darling, just discussing the wine.' He patted her on the arm. 'Now, does everyone know what they want to eat?'

There was a brief lull as they studied the menu. A minute later the waiter approached.

'Seeing that my wife has ordered a bottle of your Cabernet Sauvignon, I'll have the rump steak with béarnaise sauce – medium rare, please.' He didn't bother to look up from the menu.

Emma ordered the fish of the day – 'with vegetables, please, not fries.'

'Have some fries, darling, they'll fill you up.'

'I'm putting on too much weight.'

'Rubbish. That's just puppy fat.'

'Thanks, Dad.'

He looked surprised. 'But it's true, darling. It's quite normal. You're lovely.'

Judith also ordered the fish of the day.

'You're not drinking the Cabernet Sauvignon with fish, surely?'

'I don't mind.'

'Why not order another glass of white?' She shrugged. 'Or a glass of the Traminer Riesling? You like Traminer.'

'Do I?'

'You do.'

'If you say so.'

He turned to the waiter. 'A glass of Traminer.'

Emma ordered a Coke.

'If you're really worried about your weight, darling, you shouldn't drink that stuff. You know how much sugar it has in it.'

While the waiter was collecting the menus and rearranging the cutlery, Judith asked, 'And what's your Ethiopian eating this evening?'

'He eats cereal most of the time.'

She said nothing, but after years of practice her silence successfully conveyed her thoughts as eloquently as any words.

'There's no point both of us starving, if that's what you're thinking, Judith. That wouldn't help anyone.'

The waiter departed.

'I'm sure.'

Emma watched her father straighten his cutlery, moving the knives a fraction one way, the forks a fraction the other, then push the dessert spoon and fork slightly forward. He did it every time he sat down to eat, like a dog will always turn round and round in circles before it lies down. She also saw the flash of irritation that crossed her mother's face. And it struck Emma for the first time that maybe he moved his cutlery around simply to annoy her.

'So, is it going well?' Her mother sounded determinedly neutral, perhaps still undecided whether to take a positive or negative approach towards her husband's latest venture.

'Really well.'

'It's exciting, Dad. Can I walk with you?'

'Of course you can; I told you that. I want you to. You'll learn a lot.' He turned to his wife: 'Are you going to join us on one day?'

'You know how I loathe things like that – the crowds,' she added with obvious distaste.

Emma noticed that her father didn't seem upset by this decision. She asked: 'Am I coming back with you after dinner?'

'Did you bring some clothes? You can't walk with us in the

torn jeans and ripped T-shirts you normally wear, you know. You may be on television, on the News, so you have to dress appropriately.'

She sometimes suspected she wasn't beautiful enough for her father. He never said anything outright, but she did sometimes wonder if he would have loved her more if she'd had long blond hair, a sweet face and a perfect schoolgirl figure. She didn't think he was exactly ashamed of her, just possibly not proud. Like he somehow managed to make her aware of her mousy brown hair, her braces, spectacles and old clothes. 'Not all of my jeans are torn, you know, Dad,' she said. 'Anyway, I brought plenty of stuff in my backpack.'

He turned to his wife. 'It's going well. It's not great yet, but I'm certain things will pick up. We only started this morning, and it may take a day or two. By the time we get to Trafalgar Square, there should be a lot of interest.'

He popped a piece of grissini in his mouth, and lent across the table. 'This could raise so much money, Judith, so much.'

The smile she gave him lacked sincerity. Her expression was that of someone long wary of sudden intimacies.

There was a glow of satisfaction on his face. He was still chewing. He leant back in his chair as if he'd divulged a great secret and was now expecting to see his listener's breath being taken away.

'That must be very pleasing for you.' She also took a grissini from the glass holder, possibly because she was unable to think of anything to say. She snapped it in half, in a gesture that was faintly punitive.

'I wouldn't be surprised if some of the other charities try to jump on our bandwagon, but I'm not going to let them. Why should I do all the hard work, take all the risks, and then let them steal our thunder?'

'Surely if other charities can benefit from the walk, that's a good thing?'

'Right now I don't give a damn about them. I don't wish to sound harsh, but this is a business I'm running – a competitive business. I keep telling James Balcombe that. We're all fighting for the consumer's money, that's how it is. I have to make Africa Assist famous – a brand. That's how they'll raise more money in the future.'

'I suppose so.' She didn't sound convinced.

'The days of the do-good, liberal amateur – the stall at the local market on Saturday mornings, the Christmas dinner and the ball at the Connaught – those days are gone forever, Jude. Charity is now fundraising with a capital F.'

The waiter appeared with one glass of white wine, then poured Adrian another glass of red. He departed.

'I wouldn't be surprised if we raise a record amount.'

'And how much would that be?'

'I don't know exactly. But I'm talking millions of pounds.'

'That is a lot.'

'We need it. Live Aid isn't pulling in the money now. The public are already forgetting about the problems of the Third World. They lose interest in anything unless it's right there, continuously, in front of their eyes. Compassion is shallow, fickle. And the situation isn't helped by Thatcher, who keeps on cutting overseas aid. Now she's won a third term, it doesn't bode well for government support.'

'You're surely not criticizing your beloved Conservatives?'

He didn't rise to that, so Judith took the opportunity to change the subject. 'What's the nurse like, the one you brought from Africa?'

'I think she'll be OK. She's the only way we can communicate with Mujtabaa, so she's kind of essential.'

'How old is she?'

'Sixties, I'd say.'

His wife smirked, possibly thinking that even her husband wouldn't be tempted by such longevity. She turned away and looked round the restaurant, perhaps deciding not to risk Adrian looking into her eyes and seeing the satisfaction there. There was a couple near the far wall – the only other people in the restaurant – a furtive, nervous man in his forties and a woman who must have been 20 years younger: blonde and dumb-looking. Emma caught the flash of contempt in her mother's eyes as she turned back to their table, but wondered if it might have more to do with her father.

Later, when Judith was already on her second glass of wine – which her husband generally took as a warning signal – she said: 'You realize, of course, the example you're setting your daughter?'

'I'm sorry?'

'I'm talking about that Ethiopian fellow. What do you think it's showing Emma?'

'I don't know. What is it showing you, Emma? That you can help people and make a difference in the world?'

Their daughter continued eating, refusing to lift her head.

'I'd suggest that it's showing her how you can use other people to attain your own ends. How you can manipulate people without any thought for their own welfare.'

'That's rubbish, Judith, as you well know. We'll make millions of pounds for Africa, money that will save millions of lives.'

'I understand there are now many people who think charities are destroying Africa rather than saving it.'

'That's ridiculous.'

At that moment the waiter brought the main courses. The three at the table fell into an uneasy silence. The vegetables were served, the pepper grinder was offered to each in turn, Adrian's glass was refilled, then they were left alone. Judith, eyebrows raised with an air of forced carelessness, said: 'Emma tells me your native's in a bad way.'

'I said he was hungry, Mum, that's all.'

Her father tried to support her. 'That's true enough. He is hungry, of course he is.'

'What you actually said, darling, was...' Judith paused meaningfully, leaning slightly towards Emma, attempting to enlist her support through physical proximity: 'What you said was, you're worried the walk is going to kill him. And, if I'm honest with myself, that worries me, too.'

Adrian put down his knife and fork. He shook his head, as if it were all too much for him. He picked up his glass and gulped a mouthful of wine. 'I'm sure that's an exaggeration,' he said, putting the glass down exactly where it had rested before.

'I didn't say it like that, Dad. I'm worried about him. You know...'

He patted her hand as if to reassure her, and leant back in his chair. 'Look, I'm not overly happy about asking Mujtabaa to complete this walk, but if it's the only way to make people aware of the problems in Africa, then I'll do it. And another point to take into consideration: he has *agreed* to do the walk.'

'Did you blackmail him?'

'For heaven's sake, how could I blackmail him?'

'I don't know. Perhaps you told him that if he didn't do the walk, you wouldn't help his people. That would be blackmail.'

'Not true. I don't know how you come up with these ridiculous ideas. We help his people anyway. You're forgetting that.'

'Does he know that?'

'He may be aware of the work Africa Assist does for his people, although, from what I understand, the Mengistu government tries to keep the reality of Western aid a secret from their people. And I wish you'd stop calling him *my* native. He isn't. He isn't anyone's native.'

Their eyes met, and although there might once have been love there, it was no longer present now. For her, it had been replaced, possibly by indifference, but more likely by scorn. Scorn for the male's bewilderment at having absolutely no idea how things could have got to such a pass when he was so completely unaware of there ever having been a problem. She turned away.

A minute later she said: 'I've told you before, I think you're incapable of telling the difference between right and wrong, Adrian.' She picked up her knife and fork as if declaring she could no longer be held responsible for his moral welfare, but that didn't mean she was about to abstain from nourishing her own. 'I suppose I should be pleased you're doing something with your life at last,' she added after her first mouthful.

Emma wondered how her mother could say such a thing about her father – he was so successful in everything he did.

'What are you making out of this walk?'

He stared at his wife with disbelief. 'Me, personally? You're surely not suggesting…? Unbelievable! Nothing, not a penny.'

'You're doing this out of the sheer goodness of your heart?'

'Of course.'

'That's a change.'

'Meaning?'

'I thought you might be doing this to make a name for yourself as some kind of PR wizard. A legend in your own lunchtime, isn't that what you always say?'

'It's my job to help people, Judith. That's how I earn my money. I help companies prosper, they employ more people, everyone benefits.'

'Oh, I'm sorry, I've always been under the impression you were only interested in making money for yourself.'

'Mum, drop it. I think what Dad's doing is great.' Emma rarely took sides, but she wanted her father to know, even though she found it hard to say, how much she admired him for what he was doing. He was trying to change things, trying to make the world a better place, and that was good. For once he wasn't simply trying to persuade the public of the merits of the dubious activities of some global conglomerate.

'Why should I drop it? I can tell you, young lady, your father doesn't care about anyone but himself. Not unless a leopard can change its spots.'

'You're crazy! He's caring for millions of people.'

'It's not the same thing, darling. Those Africans aren't human beings; they're statistics.'

The waiter approached their table and they both withdrew behind their front of marital harmony as he asked if they were happy with the food. When he walked away, Emma put her headphones back over her ears. Judith said, 'Emma, I don't think–' but Adrian interrupted: 'You can't blame her. Leave her alone.' She didn't bother to argue.

Later, when their table was being cleared, Judith said to her daughter, 'I remember when you were very young, I once told you to finish the food on your plate, and you asked me why you should. I said, because there are thousands of children in Africa who don't have enough to eat. And quick as a flash you replied,

"Name one."' She laughed. 'And of course, I couldn't.'

'Cheeky little monkey.' Adrian leant over to hug his daughter, then added, 'And you still are.'

She returned his hug, almost dismissively, and said, 'Dad, know what I found out at school the other day?' Her father shook his head. 'That there are about a billion hungry people in the world, and about a billion people who eat too much.'

Seemingly by rote, he replied: 'So if all the starving people got together with all of the people who are overfed, they could swap weights.'

Emma looked surprised. 'How did you know that?'

'It's an idea that's been around for a while. To be honest, it's a little impractical – sadly.'

Later that evening, after a drive spent in a strained silence, Judith dropped Adrian and Emma at the mobile home outside the Italian Romanesque Catholic church of St Michael and St Martin on Bath Road in Hounslow. Mujtabaa and Anne had already gone to their bunks, and Dave was watching TV, with the sound turned down. He switched it off when they entered. The Ethiopian's feet were sticking out of the end of his bed and halfway across the doorway. Emma giggled as they squeezed past.

There was a double bed over the driver's cabin, and Adrian explained to his daughter that she'd be sharing this with Anne.

Lowering her voice, in a panicked whisper: 'Dad, I can't do that. I don't even know her.'

'I've checked it with Anne. She's fine with it. Just lie on the bunk in your clothes if that makes you feel more comfortable. And you have your own sleeping sheet. We're all going to have to rough it over the next few days.'

The main table and bench seats on the driver's side also converted into a double bed, with a single bed above it. The double bed Adrian had taken for himself, while the single one was for Dave. On the opposite side of the vehicle, directly opposite Adrian and Dave, a smaller table and bench seat converted into another single bed. This was for Mujtabaa. At the rear of the vehicle, on one side there was a toilet, washbasin and shower; on the other a stove, microwave and workbench; while in the centre there was a sink. Beneath that, there was a refrigerator. High up, to the right of the entrance, was a small television set.

For a short while, Adrian and Emma talked quietly with Dave, then everyone went to bed. Before climbing into her bunk, Emma leant forward to see if the Ethiopian was still awake. Although the mobile home was poorly lit, she could see that his eyes were open. Startled, she said hello, but he didn't reply. She stepped hastily backwards, hitting her arm against the side of a cupboard. 'I thought he was asleep,' she whispered to Dave.

She tried to lie on the edge of the bunk. The nurse didn't move. She was lying on her back, hands folded across her stomach, breathing slowly and rhythmically. She resembled one of those brass figures in the crypt of a church.

Tuesday

*F*oetal, enveloped in a cocoon of blankets, sheets and clothes, she lay heavy and still, while voices rose and fell in her head like a poorly tuned-in radio station. Slowly she drifted back up to the surface of the day. Keeping her eyes closed, she tried snuggling even deeper into her lair, wishing, despite being barely conscious, that she could return to her world of dreams. Then, suddenly remembering, startled, she raised her head and turned to look behind her: the brass figure in the crypt had gone. Relieved, she let her head fall back onto the pillow, pulled the bedding closer around her and burrowed gratefully back into her seclusion.

She manoeuvred her head a tiny degree to clear the ear she wasn't lying on of blankets. Dave, his voice deep and London, and seemingly oblivious of anyone who might still be asleep, was talking to a woman – most likely the brass figure. She was making little sounds of sympathy and saying a few words of encouragement every now and again. She spoke softly, with a faint burr.

There were the reassuring, comforting sounds of domesticity, of crockery and cutlery, water being poured into a kettle and the fridge being opened and closed. Emma lay curled up behind the curtain of her bunk, listening, with little interest, to the two strangers.

She wondered where her father was. He certainly wasn't in the mobile home; he would have made his presence known. It came to her that Dave and the nurse – what was her name? – were working for her father, that he was the boss, and for some reason this made her proud. All of this was happening because of him. He always made things happen, and she admired him for that.

The way he pushed his way through life, full of enthusiasms, and she, with her mother, followed in his wake. And she was comforted by the thought that he was always there for her, protective and caring. She felt safe when he was around. He could be bossy – and this would sometimes irritate her, but then he'd grab her in a bear hug and all would be forgiven. And she thought how he hugged her more than he hugged her mum, and she was sad about this. She wished her parents got on better. When she'd been younger they'd seemed much happier together, but then maybe that was just her imagination.

Suddenly her father threw open the door of the mobile home. 'This will put the cat among the proverbials,' he said. 'Kadwell's written to *The Times*.'

Emma heard either Dave or the nurse put down their coffee cup – like a slightly delayed exclamation mark to her father's statement.

'What did he say?'

'Much as you'd expect.' There was the sound of a newspaper being opened. 'Listen to this. "Sir, On Sunday evening, as resident doctor at the Heathrow Medical Centre, I examined a man who had just arrived in this country from war-ravaged Ethiopia. He was in a state of advanced malnutrition, exhibiting symptoms of extreme weight loss, lack of body fat, wasted muscles, as well as mineral and vitamin deficiencies. He was in the care of the charity, Africa Assist. I was informed by one of its management team, Adrian Burles, that the Ethiopian was to undertake a walk from Heathrow into the centre of London..."'

His voice took her back to when he used to sit on the edge of her bed and read to her last thing at night, before she fell asleep. It may have been the confined space of the mobile home that conjured up this memory of her small attic bedroom, or it may simply have been the fact he was reading out loud, but she could recall her father's reassuring closeness, and the sound of his voice as it lulled her into the deep, deep sleep of childhood.

When he finished reading the letter, there was silence. Then the nurse said, 'Oh dear.'

'It's not "oh dear" at all, Anne. Quite the contrary, we must thank the doctor for having done us a huge favour. He says the walk is taking place against his advice and displays a "shocking disregard for the welfare of the young man". As we know, that's rubbish. So we'll continue with our plan, and people will be able to make up their own minds. It's great publicity!' Her father folded the newspaper carelessly and threw it down onto the table. 'Now, where's my daughter?'

'I'm awake,' she answered, pulling back the curtain around her bunk.

'You should be thinking about getting up, young lady.'

From her bunk, she watched Dave pick up and open the newspaper. His head moved from side to side in an exaggerated fashion as he read each line of the letter. 'It says, "This obscenity should not be allowed to proceed on moral grounds, and should certainly not be allowed to proceed on medical grounds. I remain, sir..."' He looked up, frowning, as if struggling to understand the PR benefits Adrian had discovered amongst the narrow pillars of grey, compressed type. 'Well, that's a turn-up for the books. And you think this is good, Adrian?'

'Believe me, a storm of moral outrage will do us the world of good. Always works without fail.'

Dave looked thoughtful, perhaps attempting to grasp what was to him an unusual interpretation of the letter. The nurse was feeding the young Ethiopian, but she looked up briefly and smiled at Emma. 'Hello, you must be Emma. I'm Anne, and this is Mujtabaa.'

'Hi.'

Emma watched, fascinated. Each time Anne held the spoon to the young man's lips, he opened his mouth and she put the spoon in, then he closed his mouth and she took the spoon out. And each time the food disappeared. Apart from blinking now and again, and swallowing as soon as the spoon was taken from his mouth, he did not move. He was like an automaton or, perhaps, an over-sized baby.

Emma climbed down the ladder from her bunk.

'Did you hear that, darling? We're in the papers.'

'Yes, Dad.' Bleary-eyed and tousle-haired, and with the

briefest of nods to everyone, she disappeared into the toilet. 'It's only a letter in the newspaper,' she shouted as she closed the door behind her.

'There are a couple of other articles too. Nothing major, I grant you, but it is early days. Now hurry up, we're about to have breakfast.'

Dave, seemingly still struggling to understand the merits of the letter, folded the newspaper with a dismissive grunt and stood up. 'I was waiting for you to get back, Adrian. I'll get on with the cooking.'

In the bathroom, through the flimsy door, Emma could hear the conversation clearly.

'I'm sorry, Adrian, but I don't think that's a good idea.' The nurse didn't raise her voice, but Emma could still hear the strength and firmness in those few words.

There was a clatter of dishes at that moment, probably caused by Dave, so she failed to hear what her father said in reply.

'I didn't understand you were intending to cook bacon and eggs.'

'What did you imagine we were going to eat, Anne?'

'A bowl of cereal or a piece of toast maybe.'

'That's hardly going to get me through the morning. I always need my breakfast.'

Emma held her breath. It had suddenly gone quiet on the other side of the door. Even Dave seemed to have stopped his preparations in the kitchen.

'I take it this is about Mujtabaa?'

'It is.'

'There's no reason we should all go hungry just because he is.'

'Well, I'm sorry, Adrian, but I happen to think there is. And also, Mujtabaa isn't hungry, he's starving. There is a difference, you know.'

Wow! Emma thought the nurse was brave to talk to her father like that. He wasn't used to being spoken to in that tone of voice. She wanted to stay where she was, out of sight, but told herself she was too old to hide away like that.

Her father didn't look at her when she emerged from the

bathroom. He was standing over the nurse, hands on his hips, scowling at her. 'Anne, you eat in Korem, don't you?'

The nurse sat, eyes lowered, hands folded on the table in front of her, looking like she might have been praying. To Emma it appeared that her father was somewhat unnerved by this possibility, even more so when Anne raised her eyes and smiled at him. 'Of course I do, Adrian. I have to stay alive if I am to help my people.'

He won't be able to cope with her politeness, his daughter thought. She's far too calm, he won't like that. He likes people to shout back at him, then he can do the same.

'You must explain the difference to me. I have to admit to finding your logic a little hard to follow. I would have thought that I also have to stay alive in order to help Mujtabaa. And to stay alive, I also have to eat.' Emma never felt comfortable when her father was sarcastic. 'Is that not the case?' he asked, not bothering to hide the aggression in his voice. 'Or am I missing something here?'

'Of course you have to eat. But bacon and eggs is very different from a piece of toast. The smell, Adrian, that alone...'

'Jesus! I don't believe I'm hearing this.'

'Please don't blaspheme.'

Her father was dumbstruck by this, as if it were an argument he'd never come across before, but it silenced him only momentarily. He shook his head in disbelief. 'Well, I'm eating a decent breakfast, Anne, and I suspect Dave and Emma will too. So if you and Mujtabaa have a problem with the smell, I suggest you both sit outside.'

The nurse regarded Adrian dispassionately for a moment or two, then stood up. 'That's the most thoughtless, selfish thing I've ever heard a person in your position say, Mr Burles.'

'I can say much worse than that, believe me.'

'Well, I'm pleased this young man doesn't understand you.' And, as if she had all the time in the world, she took Mujtabaa by the arm and guided him down the steps of the Winnebago.

Adrian punched his fist into the palm of his other hand with such force it made Emma jump. She sat down heavily on the bench where Anne had been. She wanted to speak, but couldn't. Her father's temper frightened her.

Dave made a valiant effort to fill the silence. 'I'll see what I can rustle up.' And he again began to busy himself in the kitchen area, but not before saying, half to himself, 'Knew that one wasn't to be trusted.'

Her father grabbed a newspaper and, without a word, started to flick through the pages. Emma picked up her Walkman. Soon, the smell of bacon and eggs filled the mobile home. Dave put cutlery on the table then, a few minutes later, plates of bacon and eggs.

'No thank you, Dave. I'm not hungry.'

Her father turned to her. 'Nonsense, Emma. You have to keep your strength up. We've got a long day ahead of us.'

'I only want tea or coffee.'

'Dave has gone to the trouble of cooking this for you.' He was staring at her, his face a mask of exasperation and frustration. Dave stood beside her, poised over her plate of bacon and eggs, smirking as if he'd been revitalized by the family discord.

'Eat something this morning. You don't have to have a cooked breakfast every morning if you don't want to.'

She knew he was asking for her support. 'I can't.' She looked out of the window, possibly in the hope of seeing Mujtabaa. 'I'm sorry, Dad, but I can't eat – not while he's with us.'

'It's really not going to do him any good if you starve yourself – as I just tried to explain to Anne.'

'Not eating breakfast is scarcely starving yourself.'

Adrian looked meaningfully at Dave as if saying, what can one do? He took the plate off him and split the food between the two of them. Emma sipped her tea and watched the men eat. She was hungry, but she was angry with her father and Dave, and agreed with Anne wholeheartedly: how could they?

No one spoke. She looked out of the window. Despite the fact he was outdoors, the Ethiopian's presence still filled the mobile home. He was sitting on a wooden seat, like a waxwork, neither moving nor speaking, seemingly oblivious of having been the cause of any discord.

Her eyes wandered to Dave, sitting across the table from her. He was eating with quick, jerky chewing motions, his mouth open, toast and egg being masticated in full view of everyone. Small, wet smacking sounds accompanied this sight, and every now and again, before his mouth was empty, he'd take a mouthful of tea. To distract herself, she busily stirred sugar into her cup.

She stood up. 'I'm going to sit outside with Anne.' The men said nothing. She carried her cup of tea down the steps of the Winnebago and sat on the bench next to the nurse. Neither woman spoke. The young girl leant forward so that she could see the young man sitting on the other side of Anne. 'Doesn't he ever wash?'

'Not because he doesn't want to. Your father has forbidden him to go anywhere near water for the rest of the week.'

'Why's that?'

'He wants Mujtabaa to look as if he has just walked out of the desert.'

'Is it so important that he looks like that – dirty?'

'It's probably how he normally looks. That's why your father doesn't want him to wash.'

'But he...' And the young girl screwed up her nose in a gesture of dismay.

'It's not his fault, you know.'

Which made Emma regret that she'd said anything. She didn't like herself for that.

After breakfast, the volunteer collectors arrived in an Africa Assist van, and Adrian and Dave gathered them together for a briefing outside the Winnebago. They were all ages; the younger ones appeared to be predominantly students, the older ones retirees. The latter were almost exclusively women, although there were some couples. Emma went back inside the mobile home, where the nurse was saying something to Mujtabaa.

'What are you telling him, Anne?'

'I'm trying to explain that we'll be leaving soon.' She spoke some more, but he didn't respond. 'I'm also asking him how he's feeling.'

'Doesn't he understand?' the young girl asked, sitting down.

The nurse sighed. 'I'm not sure that he does. My Afar isn't as good as it might be, but I thought I could make myself understood. To be honest, it worries me that he rarely says anything.'

'But you speak his language?'

'To a degree. But there are more than 80 languages in Ethiopia, Emma, and I'm afraid I speak Amharic – the main language – better than Afar.'

Half an hour later Adrian put his head through the door. 'Are we ready to go?'

'He won't speak to me.'

Dave started the engine.

'Tell him we're waiting, Anne.'

'He's not responding to anything I say.'

Adrian heaved himself up into the mobile home. 'Come on, Mujtabaa, we have to leave now.' But the young man continued to sit motionless, his hands on his lap, eyes staring straight ahead, like a statue – and just as silent.

'He doesn't understand you, Dad.'

'This is all we need,' her father said, banging the heel of his hand against his forehead. 'What's up with him?'

'I don't know. He's scarcely moved or spoken since he woke up.'

'Ask him what's wrong. Tell him we're concerned about him.'

She spoke to the young Ethiopian again. He blinked, but that was all. He could have been in a different place.

'Try asking him if there's anything we can do for him, anything he wants.'

Again the nurse spoke to Mujtabaa. Then she turned to Adrian: 'I feel confident he understands what I'm saying.'

'There has to be a reason for this.' Adrian closed his eyes, placing his fingertips against his forehead, trying to puzzle out the answer. He stayed like that for almost a minute before dropping his hands and taking a deep breath.

'Somehow you have to explain to Mujtabaa that he has to walk. It's not a case of whether he wants to or not. We haven't brought him all the way from Africa so that he can sit on his backside.'

'He's not saying he won't walk. I don't believe that's the issue.'

'If he's saying nothing at all, in my book that means he won't walk.'

The nurse's lips tightened, almost imperceptibly, a tic that indicated the expectation of a possible verbal attack by Adrian. She spoke to Mujtabaa again.

'Why does he have to walk, anyway, Dad, if he doesn't want to?'

'He has to walk because we've brought him to London to walk.' He was frustrated, causing his voice to rise. 'He's obliged to walk.'

'You can't always make everyone do what you want, you know.' Emma raised her eyes to the ceiling and threw herself down on one of the seats across the aisle from Mujtabaa.

'You're not being helpful,' he said.

Dave switched off the engine. They heard him get out of the cabin and close the door. A second later he climbed into the back of the mobile home. 'What's up, people?'

'Seems our friend here doesn't want to walk.'

'One day enough for him, eh? Can't say I blame him.'

'Maybe he's ill, Dad. Maybe he doesn't feel well.'

'Then why doesn't he tell us that?'

Everyone stared at Mujtabaa, but it struck Emma that he was unaware of their presence.

'We're trying to help him and his family. Tell him that, please, Anne. We want to help his friends. If he won't walk, we won't be able to help anyone.'

The nurse again attempted to translate, but the young man might have been deaf for all the reaction she got.

Adrian sat down heavily at the large table next to Dave. Emma had never seen her father like this before – in a situation where he wasn't in control of what was happening. He always had an answer, always had the solution to any problem. He looked up at Anne. There was an uncharacteristic weariness in his voice: 'Be honest, Anne, is what I'm trying to do so terrible? Am I being cruel? Am I being unreasonable? Is there a better way of doing this?'

No one moved while they waited for the nurse to answer. Emma could see her struggling for the right words. Finally, she spoke. 'I have no doubt you're acting with the best of intentions, and that your motives are well-meaning, but...' She paused, and it was obvious she was seeking even more earnestly the words that would satisfy both herself and her benefactor. 'I do wish there was another way we could raise money.'

'It would have been better if you'd expressed your doubts earlier than this, Anne. I thought you were in agreement about the walk? It was thanks to you that I came up with the idea in the first place.'

The nurse was flustered. 'I do agree with it – in principle. But that doesn't stop me at the same time worrying about whether it's the right thing to do.'

Adrian groaned.

'I also think you have to try and see things from his viewpoint.' She placed a hand protectively on the young man's arm. 'He's done so well, and under very trying circumstances. Maybe you need to understand that. He's been plucked straight out of his own country and put down in an alien environment, a world he can scarcely comprehend. It's not surprising he's upset. He wouldn't be human if he wasn't.' She could barely contain her disapproval.

'But what can I do now, at this late stage? Tell the volunteers to go home, tell journalists the walk is over? Tell everyone that our friend here has suddenly taken it into his head to down tools – after we've brought him all this way? It's the start of day two, and it appears he's already given up. Maybe *he* should try and understand things from *my* point of view. We've invested a lot of money to bring him here. Maybe you're also forgetting that.'

He stared at Mujtabaa belligerently, as if he might be considering wrestling him to his feet.

'Maybe he's just hungry.'

'That, Dave, is stating the bloody obvious.'

'Only trying to help.'

'Well don't, not unless you've got something constructive to say.'

'Stress less, Dad.'

'I wish you wouldn't use that expression, Emma. You know it upsets me.' He closed his eyes, sinking into a reverie. A minute later, leaning forward, hands clasped earnestly together, he addressed the nurse. 'Anne, I have Mujtabaa's welfare at heart, but I can't help him if he won't help himself.' He stared meaningfully at her, demanding she see his point of view. 'If only we could make him realize that we have his interests at heart.'

'I've tried, Adrian. Believe it or not, I've tried.'

He half smiled. 'I know, and I appreciate that.' He suddenly changed tack. 'Is there some delicacy we can tempt him with, something he would really like?'

'All I have is porridge. I certainly can't feed him bacon and eggs, not in his condition.' Emma flinched.

'This is surely not about the bacon and eggs?'

'That is not what I'm saying.'

Adrian stood up. Everyone stared at the Ethiopian. Emma put her headphones over her ears, switched on her Walkman and closed her eyes. Her father said, 'For once in my life, I don't know what to suggest.'

For the next hour, they remained inside the mobile home, making cups of tea and coffee for themselves and the volunteer collectors outside. Apart from the priest from St Michael and St Martin's who fleetingly put his head through the door to say good morning, no one came near them. Conversation was spasmodic. Every now and again Adrian would mutter: 'This is so frustrating. I really don't know what to do. We could be achieving so much, instead of sitting here wasting time.' Sometimes he threw in a few expletives, often blasphemous, at which point Emma would say, even though she was listening to her Walkman, 'Dad!' and he'd then turn to the nurse and apologize.

Anne went off by herself to look for some shops where she might find something to tempt her ward. Adrian and Dave went outside and sat on the grass, one minute whispering intently to each other, the next talking to the collectors. Emma remained at the big table, feet up on the bench seat, listening to her music.

She watched the young Ethiopian out of the corner of her eye. He was staring at the table directly in front of him, his forehead deeply furrowed. She thought how sad he looked, like a child in kindergarten, alone in the corner of the room because the other children wouldn't play with him. He was probably missing his family. She wondered if he had a family, a mother and a father, maybe brothers and sisters. She realized then that none of them knew what kind of person he was, or what kind of life he led; none of them had any idea about whom he loved or who loved him. He was a complete stranger, living amongst them, yet existing in his own separate, unknown world.

She swung her feet off the seat and turned to face him. She lifted the headphones off her head. Outside, just faintly, she could hear her father talking. In the distance there was the never-ending hum of London traffic. She cleared her throat. Her mouth was dry. She told herself not to be stupid. She felt so hot – God, she was blushing! The edges of her spectacle lenses were misting up. She forced herself to stand up, move across the aisle and sit down next to the young man. He didn't look up. For several minutes she sat there, and he didn't even seem to be aware of her.

She said, 'Hey, have a listen to this.' She held the headphones up to one of his ears. He jerked his head away, startled. 'Don't worry. It's Madonna.' He was staring at the headphones, his face half turned away, suspicious. 'It's pretty cool, actually – for her. But maybe you're more of a Paul Simon man. I've got the *Graceland* cassette here.' She leapt up and scrabbled in her backpack, amongst her other cassettes. 'My Mum likes this.' She changed the cassette while she was talking. 'Reckon you might like it too. It's kind of African. Here, listen.' She held out the headphones, but he leant away from them. She put them back over her own ears. 'See, that's all you do. You put them over your ears and listen. It's okay, they won't hurt you.' She took her headphones off and laid them on the table. 'Maybe I'll show you another time. You must be into music.'

They sat together, side by side, in silence: the young African man, ebony black and so thin he could have been a wire coat hanger bent into the shape of a human being, and the white girl, heavily built, almost ungainly, with her slightly rounded shoulders and her mousy hair, lank and uncared for. She wished she could speak to him. Finally, biting her bottom lip and screwing her eyes shut, she reached out, slowly, tentatively, as if about to stroke a wild animal, and laid one of her hands on his. He didn't move. This surprised her. She opened her eyes. His hands were hard and dry. There was no flesh on them. She was aware of the softness and plumpness of her own hands, and was suddenly ashamed. They were too pampered.

'I'd really like to be your friend.'

The young man smelled strongly; a sharp, almost rancid odour that was far from pleasant. She tried to breathe as shallowly as possible, but hated herself for it, and immediately forced herself to breathe normally again. He turned slowly and looked down at her, across his left shoulder. It felt to her as if it was the first time he'd moved all morning. His soft, limpid eyes were black and huge beneath his arched eyebrows. His nose was strong and straight, his cheekbones so prominent they were almost angular. His features were covered by a fine, whitish dust, and on his forehead, rimed with salt, there were tiny irregular cracks, like the bed of a dried-out salt lake. His lips were full and perfectly formed, turning down just a little at the corners of his mouth.

He didn't say anything, he simply looked at her – almost through her. It was as if she wasn't there or, if she was present, only in the very distance. Despite their being about the same age, there was a gulf between them, and his look made her aware of this. She turned away, unable to bear his gaze, embarrassed by how small he made her feel. But she forced herself to leave her hand resting on his.

Looking down at the table, she said, 'I think it's great what you're doing.' She spoke almost in a whisper. 'You'll really make a difference. That's what my Dad's trying to do, too. He wants to help you, you know. He can be a bit up himself at times, but he's kind of cool most of the time – nice. You know what I mean? Together, you can do so much for so many people. You can change the world. You should be proud of yourself, Mujtabaa. I just wanted to tell you that.'

She was aware of how hot she'd become. Her face must be like a tomato. That thought made her blush even more. He must think she looked ridiculous, what with her red face, her spectacles and train tracks. She plunged in again because it seemed like a better idea than remaining silent. 'At school now, we're studying history, and there's this man, William Wilberforce, who's trying to end slavery. He told everyone how awful it was, that it wasn't right, and that it had to be stopped. I know you're not ending slavery or anything, but you're changing the world just like he did, and that's brilliant.'

A few minutes later she turned and grinned at him. 'Can I call you Moosh? It's kind of easier than Mujtabaa.' She pointed at him: 'Moosh.' She said it slowly, several times, pointing at him each time she said it, and each time he frowned. But finally he gave the faintest of smiles and said, 'Moosh.' His voice was soft, surprisingly soft; she had expected something stronger, deeper. She was a little disappointed.

She clapped her hands. 'Hey, you understand. That's great.'

There was a long silence. She saw the digital clock on the oven door change from 11.21 to 11.22. She would always remember that. It was one of those moments, she told herself.

'I wish I could do something like that, something that would benefit other people and make a difference to their lives. I think that's the only reason we're in this world, to help other people. That's what I think. And that's what my Dad's trying to do, and that's what you're doing. It's really cool.' It came out in a bit of a rush, but it was pretty close to what she wanted to say, so she didn't feel too bad about that.

She looked at him again. Her eyebrows shot up. 'You haven't got a clue what I'm saying, have you? No idea at all.' She grinned. He turned his head slowly and stared back at her solemnly. 'You poor guy, you must be so hungry. And I bet you think I'm really fat. I'm trying to lose weight, actually. And you probably think that's obscene, really obscene – me trying to lose weight, that is. I hope you understand, but I don't suppose you do.'

She could hear Anne talking outside, and a few seconds later the nurse climbed the steps into the mobile home. She looked at

Emma quizzically as she passed to the back where the stove was situated. 'You two having a chat?'

Emma stood up. 'It's difficult when he doesn't speak English, but I've told him that I'm going to call him Moosh, and I think he understands that. Did you manage to find something for him to eat, Anne?'

'I got him a little lamb, which I'll cook up. I think your father's terrified it's going to make Mujtabaa fat.' They laughed together, complicit in the idea of the absurdity of the male sex. 'His stomach should be able to cope with a very small amount, if I cut it fine enough, almost mince it. I hope he'll find it a bit of a treat.' She was rummaging in a plastic shopping bag.

'Does he eat meat, do you think?'

'It's unlikely to be very often. Animals are too precious as a source of milk to be killed for their meat. An Afar's main food is milk and a kind of bread they call *ga'ambo*.'

'What else would he eat at home?'

'A real luxury would be durra, which is a sweet cereal grass. They obtain that by barter – or they did once upon a time. Another favourite delicacy is a mixture of ghee and red pepper mixed with curdled milk.'

'Yuk, that sounds gross.'

The nurse smiled. 'It may not be to our taste, but...' She stopped in mid-sentence and stared over Emma's shoulder. Mujtabaa had stood up. He said something.

'What's he saying?'

'He's saying he'll go now.' Anne hastily put the meat in the fridge as she spoke quickly to the young man. As they were leaving the mobile home, she patted Emma on the arm. 'I don't know what you said to him, but whatever it was, it seems to have meant something to him.'

The schoolgirl grinned. 'I didn't say anything, at least nothing he'd have understood.'

'You can never be sure. There's intuition, you know.'

Emma proudly helped Mujtabaa down the steps of the Winnebago, followed by Anne clutching her small medical bag. As they emerged into the sunlight, everyone leapt to their feet.

'Mujtabaa says he'll walk,' Anne said.

Adrian didn't question her. As Dave walked round to climb into the driver's seat of the mobile home, and the volunteers rushed to get their tins, Adrian said, 'You'll have to take his *shämma* off him again, Anne.'

'Do you think it's wise when he's like this?'

'I'm sorry, but it has to come off.'

When Emma saw Mujtabaa standing before her with just a cloth around his waist, she couldn't hide her dismay. 'Oh, Dad, that's terrible!' She could see that his skin, like papier-mâché, was shrunk across his torso. He looked wraith-like, like he could have been blown away by the smallest puff of wind. She had a hand to her mouth, and she was blinking furiously to stop the tears falling.

The young man glanced in her direction, and she was ashamed of her outburst. She prayed she hadn't upset him, that he didn't understand what she was saying.

Adrian saw the tears in his daughter's eyes, and put an arm round her to give her a squeeze. He didn't say anything. It was possible he didn't know what to say, so he just gave her a cuddle.

'Does he have to walk like that?' she murmured.

'Yes, people have to see him as he is.'

'But it's so...'

'Demeaning, yes. But starvation is demeaning, that's the reality of it. If this is to work, people have to see what malnutrition does to a person. We have to thrust it under their noses. It's the only way, darling. That's why we've brought Mujtabaa 4,000 miles to England.' He sighed, throwing his hands outwards in a gesture of hopelessness. 'I don't think he minds too much.' But it was obvious to his daughter that he wasn't truly convinced by what he was saying.

Anne guided the young man to the Bath Road, and he started walking back towards Heathrow. She reached out and placed a hand on his arm. 'No, the other way, Mujtabaa.' He stared at her, puzzled. She pulled him gently round until he was facing towards central London, and, like an automaton, he set off along the Roman road in silence, followed by Adrian and Emma.

Hounslow's main shopping mall, an outpost of commercialism surrounded by poverty and deprivation, conjured up the one-store, one-hotel, one-brothel shanty towns that once dotted their way along the wagon trails during the opening up of the American west. It was a convenience doing its best to become an essential. In a district that comprised endless, uniform rows of dull terraced houses on narrow, car-lined streets – in which the prevalent smell was curry – and a continuous stream of thundering semi-trailers on dirty, dusty arterial roads – on which the prevalent smell was carbon monoxide – this almost clean, almost spacious pedestrian walkway was a shopping oasis lined with trees and dotted with fountains – where the prevalent smell was commerce. The big stores all had a presence here: Woolworths, HMV, Littlewoods, WH Smith and Superdrug, as well as many smaller ones. For the people of the surrounding district, this was where they chose to spend the little money they had to spare.

When the Africa Assist group arrived at the mall, it was busy with midday shoppers and those enjoying an early lunch. They meandered aimlessly beneath the summer sun with their pushchairs and shopping trolleys, clasping sandwiches and soft drinks to their bulging stomachs, or stood in groups chatting – sometimes smoking – or sat on benches watching others stroll by. Children ran amongst them, in all directions, laughing, shouting and getting in everyone's way.

Scarcely anyone paid any attention when the Africa Assist group crossed from the High Street into the mall, but as the collectors fanned out among the pedestrians, pointing the Ethiopian out to them and explaining what he was doing, they began to take an interest, and the more who took an interest, the more others were dragged in. They stopped and stared; they pressed closer, and they started to question Adrian, Anne and Emma about this stranger from a distant desert. Who is he? What country is he from? Where's he going? Why is he doing this? Mujtabaa could have been an exhibit in a museum. The questions, which began as a trickle, soon flowed with increasing speed. Adrian answered patiently. It wasn't in his nature to be patient, but he made an effort to be so now. He knew how important it was to get people on side.

Young and old seemed genuinely concerned for Mujtabaa. Even though they themselves were poor, it was obvious they had never witnessed poverty such as this. They were fortunate enough to live in a land of plenty, and here, amongst them now, was a human being who possessed nothing but a simple cloth around his waist, sandals, a walking staff and a dagger. They were moved to see a man reduced to such circumstances, and responded in the only way they knew how, by giving money. Emma saw several people actively search for an Africa Assist volunteer and thrust coins as well as notes into their tin. They did this with a grim determination, as if by doing so they might fend off the horrors conjured up by the black apparition that walked amongst them. She saw one man, an office worker halfway through his lunch, who, when the Ethiopian approached, hastily put his sandwich back in its paper bag and placed it beside him on the bench like he desired nothing more than to disown it completely.

The group, halting every few feet, progressed slowly through the mall, many people stepping forward to speak to Mujtabaa and wish him good luck. When Anne explained that he didn't speak English, they weren't in the least put out, many continuing to chat away as if the young man understood their every word. A middle-aged Indian immediately changed from English to Hindi, possibly believing this might prove more successful, and one old woman simply said, 'It's no matter, love,' and smiled as she went on her way.

Emma could see how pleased her father was. He was in his element being in charge, instructing his small band of assistants in what to do. She thought he looked a little incongruous in his shirt and tie and neatly pressed trousers amongst so many casually dressed people, but appreciated that it was a part of 'the sell'. He'd told her before often enough that people don't buy from the poorly dressed.

Because she was following immediately behind Mujtabaa, Emma was the first to notice that anything was wrong. She almost bumped into him when he stopped. He raised his left arm and he was turning back towards her. She wondered what he wanted. She held out his waterbag to him, but he ignored it. He gripped her forearm with his free hand, not looking at her, but past the people crowding around them and down the mall, into the distance, towards the bus station at the far end. His legs buckled, as quickly as if someone had kicked them away from beneath him. She cried out, 'Dad, Dad!' and he and Anne stopped. They rushed back to where Mujtabaa was now kneeling on the footpath, still holding on to Emma's arm. She was bent forward over him, her free hand pushing the hair back from her face. Adrian crouched beside them. 'What is it? What happened?'

'I don't know. He just fell.' Her frightened face turned back and forth between Mujtabaa and her father, desperate for one of them to say that everything was all right.

The crowd pressed forward on every side. Anne moved behind the Ethiopian, placing her hands under his armpits, practical, matter of fact. 'Let him lie down.' Together they lowered Mujtabaa to the ground. He lay on his back, his eyes closed. He was breathing fast, almost panting.

'Keep back. Keep back, please.' Adrian waved his arms in the air. 'Give him space, let him breathe.'

Anne, looking very much the part in her spotless medical coat, was kneeling beside the young man, taking his pulse, when there was suddenly a commotion in the crowd. A man in a greasy, torn overcoat, tied at the waist with string, incongruous in the summer heat, pushed his way past everyone until he stood at Mujtabaa's feet. He had flaming red hair and a beard, both in disarray. He looked down at the fallen black man lying on the patterned bricks, and let out a whoop of glee, giving a small kick to the bottom of one of the young man's feet as he did so. His mouth spread wide in the rictus of a crazy grin, and he yelled again, like a shout of victory. Emma stared at him in dismay.

Her father ignored the man and concentrated on helping Anne. This became almost impossible, however, when the tramp started to dance around the Africa Assist group, whirling and cavorting, his filthy coat flying in the air while his sandalled feet, with toes protruding from blackened socks, performed to some tuneless jig in his head. The onlookers fell back on all sides.

It could have been an artistic parody: the tableau vivant of Christ taken down from the Cross – by Velasquez possibly – then thrown together, without due care or consideration, with some character straight out of Edvard Munch.

'Will someone get this idiot out of here?' Adrian shouted at the people around him, but no one heard him or, if they did, they chose to ignore him, obviously considering it both unwise and foolhardy to tangle with such a bizarre character.

'Please do something,' Emma pleaded with the crowd, trying to keep her eyes away from the leering, jeering face so close above her. '*Please!*' People shuffled uneasily before her pleading eyes, then turned away.

Anne attempted to pour water into Mujtabaa's mouth, but it only dribbled over his chin and down onto his chest, forming rivulets between his ribs. 'Adrian, you have to get this man away from us.' She could imagine how this figure must appear to the Ethiopian, as some kind of devil dancing over him, a contorted, leering mouth screaming above his prostrate figure, an evil spirit come to take his soul away. She held him closer, trying to shield him from the stranger. 'Don't you worry, Mujtabaa, no harm will come to you,' she whispered. 'I'll make sure of that.'

Adrian raised himself to his feet and tried to half push, half shepherd the man further down the mall. 'Move away. This young man needs help, and he's not going to get it with you leaping around the place like this.'

The man threw Adrian's hands off, shrieking obscenities and spitting hatred in his face. 'What about the poor people in this country, you fucker!? Why don't you collect money for them? They're the ones who need help. Not him, not some fucking African. Send him back to his own country. He don't deserve help.' And his language became increasingly foul, so much so, Emma became concerned Anne wouldn't be able to cope with it. The tramp was shouting at the top of his voice, and at one stage leant past Adrian to spit at Mujtabaa lying comatose in the nurse's arms. The elderly woman, calm and composed, wiped the phlegm from where it had landed on Mujtabaa's stomach with a tissue handed to her by a woman in the crowd.

Adrian again tried to push the man away, but without success. The tramp's face, all hair and dirt, with patchy, purplish skin and broken blood vessels, was as close to his own as it was possible to be without touching. Adrian jerked his head back, trying not to inhale the man's foul breath.

'I hope he fucking dies, the black bastard,' the tramp screamed, filthy fingers sticking out from grey mitts like unsheathed cat's claws, scrabbling at Adrian's shirt-front. 'There are plenty of us in this country more deserving than him. Why don't you get money for us, you fucking nigger lover?' The man broke away and started dancing again, more peacefully now, as if he'd said his piece and needed time to catch his breath. 'Charity fucking begins at home,' he repeated, still breathing hard, in a sing-song voice. 'Charity fucking begins at home.'

Suddenly Dave appeared out of the crowd. He grabbed the shambling figure from behind, twisting an arm behind his back and putting him in a headlock. 'Good grief, you smell terrible,' and the onlookers standing nearby laughed, pleased that someone else had taken things in hand. 'This way, my friend. Let's be having you,' he said, like some off-duty bouncer. And he marched the swearing, struggling tramp away across the pedestrian mall. Adrian saw him give the man a mighty boot up the backside, and was surprised at how little he knew of his assistant. Despite his wiry frame, he appeared to be unexpectedly strong. The tramp continued to shout obscenities back at them as he stumbled away, but made no further attempt to approach.

Anne said, 'Help me move him to that bench.' Mujtabaa's eyes were now open. Emma, crouching next to him, stared intently down at him, looking helpless. 'Moosh, are you all right?' she kept asking. She looked at her father for guidance. As he stooped to pick the Ethiopian up, a shopper stepped forward, 'Here, let me help.'

The stranger helped Adrian lift Mujtabaa to his feet and they half walked him, half carried him over to a bench. Emma sat down next to him and held his hand.

'Should I ask one of the shops to call an ambulance?' the stranger asked.

'Thank you,' said Adrian, 'but that won't be necessary. We have a trained nurse here to care for him.'

Anne said, 'He needs to rest, Adrian.' She lowered her voice: 'I'm going to give him some food. He's too weak to continue like this.'

'Is that wise…?'

She picked up her medical bag and, without waiting for his consent, marched across to the Superdrug store on the other side of the mall. She emerged a few minutes later with a plate of baby cereal, which she fed to Mujtabaa under the gaze of a fascinated crowd. Many people took photographs. The Africa Assist collectors again fanned out amongst the pedestrians, and children once again started to run around the mall. There was almost a festive air about the place then. Even Mujtabaa, after eating, seemed more aware of what was going on around him. He was looking at everyone and once, obviously fascinated, held out his hand to put it on the head of a small blonde girl. She giggled and ran to her mother, where she was told not to be stupid and to be nice to 'the poor black man'.

For half an hour they stayed by the bench. People came and went, many stopping to chat. Everyone Adrian spoke to was asked to tell their family and friends about the walk. Almost all of them were well disposed towards the Ethiopian and his undertaking. They possibly saw him as one of themselves, someone who was down on his luck, but battling to get up and have another go. Or that's how Emma chose to see it. Certainly there were many faces amongst the passers-by that were pinched and drawn, showing a lifetime of struggle and deprivation; something which, as she was becoming increasingly aware, she knew nothing about. Maybe, she told herself, in their own way they have to battle against the odds as much as Moosh, and so they see themselves as being the same as him. She felt a little proud of her deduction.

An old woman approached and thrust a one-pound coin into Mujtabaa's hand. She went away muttering to herself, no one able to understand what she was saying. Adrian, smiling and earnest, took the money out of the Ethiopian's hand and held it up before his face. 'This small coin will help to buy your village a well. Can you translate that for me, Anne?'

'I'll try.' But as she spoke, the young man simply stared at the money, frowning and intent, possibly expecting Adrian to perform some magic trick with it. Adrian patted him on the shoulder: 'You'll understand what it's all about soon enough, Mujtabaa. Wait till you see what we're going to collect for your people.'

The owner of a café brought them coffees. He went back to get a glass of milk for the Ethiopian. Adrian tried to pay, but was told they were on the house. A small boy offered Mujtabaa a cream bun which he'd already taken a bite out of, and Anne had to explain that it wouldn't be good for him because 'his stomach isn't strong enough.' So the boy stood before the Ethiopian and ate the rest of the bun himself, slowly and thoughtfully, looking at Mujtabaa with an objective eye as he did so.

'How is he?' Adrian asked.

'I think he has recovered,' Anne said, then added, 'I don't think you appreciate how tough he is, Adrian.'

'I do.'

'I don't think so. In my opinion, most people in his condition would be dead by now, or at least in hospital. I don't think you understand that.'

'I fully appreciate what he's doing, honestly I do.' But his protest sounded weak, and it was clear the nurse was sceptical.

'Then I think you should make the effort to acknowledge it more.' It was the slightest of reprimands, but it still stung him – or so it appeared to Emma.

They left the shopping mall soon after two o'clock. Several of the people who had spent time with them waved and cheered them on their way, like they were witnessing the departure of some exploration party into the wilderness. They continued down the mall, past the Hounslow bus station, along London Road, past the bingo hall and the Coach & Horses pub, then on to Thornbury Road.

At the West Thames College, students were milling around the grounds and outside the high wire fence as the Africa Assist group approached. They wandered over, casual and relaxed, when they saw Mujtabaa. They wished him luck and even patted him on the back, until Anne was forced to plead with them not to touch him. There were a few Africans in the crowd, more reserved than the others, holding back, watching uneasily, as if they were being shown up by one of their own. Two of them approached Adrian, scowling, managing to look both disdainful and angry at the same time. 'You are making a mockery of Muhammad,' one of them said in a low, threatening voice.

Adrian grasped one of the men by the upper arm, but was thrown off. 'I can assure you, I have not the slightest intention of offending the Prophet. Quite the opposite, I am trying to help his people.'

The second man said, 'It is God's will that some are without food. You have no right to interfere with His universal plan.' Then, nodding quickly in the direction of Mujtabaa – 'You must send him home. It is not right that he is here.' With that the two men turned and strode away.

They stopped for the night near Syon House, the Georgian masterpiece by Robert Adams and Capability Brown. In the distance was the great glass dome of the Syon House conservatory. Across the Thames, immediately below them, were the Royal Botanic Gardens, and nearby, on the same side of the River, the London Butterfly House. Even though they were near the centre of London, they had 200 acres of greenery spread out before them.

They hadn't been in the grounds of Syon House long before a reporter from *The Times* appeared at the door of the mobile home wanting to do an interview. His interest had been sparked by Kadwell's letter. He told them he'd been touring the area, questioning shopkeepers about whether they'd seen a 'starving African walking towards the City.' He claimed it had been an easy trail to follow.

'We've had a few letters from readers about what you're doing, Mr Burles.'

'Supportive, or otherwise?'

'It's about 50-50 at the moment, I'd say. But we'd like to do a story, tell our readers what you're hoping to achieve.'

'Will it make tomorrow's paper?'

'That depends on a couple of factors: how interesting my editor finds the story and what other stories are breaking.'

'In that case, we'll have to make it as interesting as possible.' And over the next hour he told the reporter everything about the walk, the justifications for it, about the conditions in Ethiopia, and what Africa Assist was doing to alleviate the famine. He also gave him prints of several photographs Dave had taken of Mujtabaa walking the previous day.

While Adrian spoke to the reporter, Dave went down the road to look for a pub. Mujtabaa lay on his bunk with his eyes closed, and Anne sat nearby, reading. At first, she thought he was asleep, but soon he started to speak – not so much to her, but to himself. She understood his need to talk, to break out of his isolation, to try to communicate with those with whom he now found himself, so she put her book down and listened carefully. She refrained from speaking herself, and concentrated solely on understanding what he was saying.

He said he was doing the walk for Safia, to get help for her and the child. When he left them, she'd been lying in the shadows of the *ari*, covered in grey sackcloth, the baby asleep on her chest.

He had picked up a water bottle, then gone to stand next to his wife. When she looked at him, he could see the fear in her eyes. He was also frightened, but he didn't want her to know that, otherwise she'd think he was like a woman. 'I was ashamed,' Mujtabaa said to Anne. 'She has not been my wife for many seasons, and already I am unable to provide for her. I only have one wife, and still I cannot take care of her.' He said that if his child were taken by He Who Is Always Hungry, it wasn't so important. They could make more babies when times were better, but he couldn't make another Safia.

All he had said to Safia was, 'I'm going to the town.' She hadn't questioned him; it wasn't her place to do so. She simply raised her free hand, the one that wasn't supporting the baby, and grasped his. He knew they were unlikely to hold hands again, that she and the baby would die, but he also knew he had to try to save them.

Later, he told Anne, without making it clear if it had any connection to his stories about leaving Safia or the creature with red eyes, he heard a noise. It was a far-away, deep and incessant sound, and it continued to become louder, to gnaw and worry at the peace and quiet within his head. It sounded like a jackal at the carcass of an animal, he said. Slowly, he came to understand that it was not one sound, but many. It was the sound of his friends bringing the goats back into camp. They were excited, laughing and calling out to each other. The goats were bleating and there was the growl of a camel. Everyone was happy to return home.

Mujtabaa was smiling, desperate to jump up and join them, but he didn't have the strength to stir, not even the strength to call out. He listened for familiar voices. His friend Tsegai must surely be amongst them? And what about Safia? She must also have gone to bring in the animals from the dangers of the night. He was listening to all their voices, trying to distinguish one from the other, but then slowly realizing that they were speaking in a tongue he didn't understand. For a while he was unable to work out what this meant, until it finally came back to him where he was. The voices he could hear were those of the woman in the straw hat, the headman, and the girl with glass over her eyes. There were others, too, strangers, all forcing themselves into his head. It made him sad. He wanted to be left alone. He didn't want to listen to those voices.

Then Mujtabaa was saying – and because his words lacked a certain logic, Anne couldn't be sure she was remembering it all in the correct order – that he opened his eyes and there was an evil spirit dancing over him. It also had red eyes! Only this creature had red hair, too. He had closed his eyes against the apparition, but when he opened them again, the evil spirit was still there, still dancing. It was the creature in the desert (which Anne guessed had been a hyena) who'd come back to claim him. He had no doubt about this. But no sooner had he convinced himself of this than he saw flailing arms and legs and flying robes, and a contorted, leering face screaming and laughing above him. Then he understood that this wasn't the four-legged creature from the desert. It could only be the evil one himself who'd come to claim his soul.

When the apparition stooped over him, red eyes flashing hatred, he shrank back as far as he was able. But the evil one spat at him, and Mujtabaa was terrified of being taken from the land of the white tribes instead of from his own place. From what Anne understood, it was important he be amongst his own people when the spirits came for him.

As quickly as he appeared, the evil one disappeared. Mujtabaa lowered his hands from his face, and the figure was gone. What kind of magic was this! But from that moment on he was convinced he was condemned to stay in the land of the white ghosts forever. He would never return to his own home. The evil one would never let him go.

Anne did her best to reassure him, to make him understand that he would return home very soon, but he did not look like he had faith in what she said.

Emma lay outside on the grass, a short distance away, listening to her Walkman. She lay on her back with her hands behind her head and stared up at the wisps of cloud drifting high overhead. She wished her mum was with her. She wanted to talk to her about the walk. Her mother had the ability to make things seem straightforward and simple, even when they were complicated. She always had an answer, and whatever it might be, it usually made sense to her daughter. Emma didn't think her dad always had the answers – even though he thought he did – and, anyway, if he did have them, she wasn't sure they were always the right ones. She sensed, at times, that his enthusiasm overrode his common sense, and that he didn't see what he didn't want to see. Although she found this quality appealing, it also meant her father could sometimes seem, even to her, a little immature. No, she needed her mum; she was the more trustworthy one.

The doubts in her head nagged away at her. On the one hand she thought it was wonderful that Moosh was doing this walk and making lots of money for his people back in Ethiopia, money that would buy them food, farming equipment, wells and an education. She understood that. She also understood how much the West could do for Africa, and was obliged to do. She'd been taught that at school. She believed utterly that the haves of this world must look after the have nots; it was a moral duty. The walk was a way of achieving this, of helping those who were unable to help themselves. She agreed with all of that. But she also felt there was something… well, something not quite right about what they were doing, something that didn't feel good. She felt Moosh was being used, that other people were benefiting more than him, that he was being tainted in some vague, indefinable way by the materialism and vulgarity of the very world in which she herself lived. Why couldn't the walk be a spiritual event, something pure and untarnished, like the country it was intended to help? That was the way she saw, or imagined, the land Mujtabaa came from: a pure, idealized landscape, populated by a noble tribe, uncorrupted by the 20th century – possibly even by the 18th or 19th centuries. She asked herself if perhaps hunger was something wreaked by Nature and therefore, in its way, as honest, straightforward and natural as the people who suffered it.

The walk aroused in her the same emotions that photographs of modern-day wars and atrocities aroused in her, feelings of both revulsion and fascination. She could look at a war photograph, like from the Iran-Iraq conflict, and think, this scene I'm looking at is so wrong and so horrible it should never have been allowed to happen, and it should certainly never have been photographed. But at the same time there were feelings of fascination, almost titillation, caused by this covert viewing of someone else's suffering. The photographer may have had the right intent – to make people aware of the horrors of war – just as her father had the right intent in organizing this walk – to make people aware of the horrors of famine – but she worried that Moosh's suffering was too private to parade publicly through the streets of London. She thought there was a danger of him becoming some kind of freak show. At school she'd read how London high society in the 18th century had flocked to Bethlem Hospital, Bedlam, to be entertained by its lunatic inhabitants. It was regarded as an amusing excursion to help pass the time of day. Was this walk any different? It was almost as if their emotions – the feelings of herself, her father, Dave, possibly even Anne – were suspect, unreal and insincere, and so the viewer, the person in the street, should therefore not be allowed to experience them. Isn't that how it was? She didn't know. She was unable to work it out.

Her mind was in turmoil. Her dreams were vague and indefinable, and her hopes changed, if not day by day, then certainly week by week. She knew more about what she did not want, than what she wanted. That she needed to break away from the stifling conformity of her parents' lives, and the materialism and emptiness of their existence, went without saying. In her eyes, she was living in a society that had an excess of everything – not only cars, refrigerators, TV sets and dishwashers, but toothpastes, chocolate bars, cans of beans, biros, clothes, even such commonplace items as buttons and paperclips. And her father was adding to the problem. His work was all about companies making more money, selling more goods, growing bigger and bigger, and usually at the expense of ordinary people and the environment. There were no longer basic needs in the Western world. The luxuries of yesterday had become the necessities of today. There was no hardship any more, no spirituality. She yearned for purity, but felt the only place it was to be found was inside her head. The world itself lacked purity. It was full of greedy people grabbing as much as they could for themselves, grasping onto material things. And for what gain? On the surface, it was so that everyone could live a better life, live *more*, but if this was the case, then it obviously wasn't working. People's lives today, so far as she could see, were more impoverished than ever before; they certainly weren't fulfilled. And although their needs were now satisfied, their wants never seemed to have an end. She had no desire to live like the parents of those she went to school with, or the people who lived in the same suburb as her. But then that begged the question: how did she want to live? That was the question she had no answer to. In fact, the truth of the matter was, it was the question she didn't even know she was asking.

Grey, almost black clouds were starting to amass to the north, piling up on each other, billowy heads peering over billowy shoulders, appearing to be held in check by those at the front, or maybe just tentative about stepping into the ring of blue that lay unsullied before them. The clouds were streaked with orange and purple from the rays of the setting sun, as if a fire was burning out of sight, somewhere over the horizon. The colours on the lower clouds were fast disappearing, retreating before the creeping darkness, contracting until only the smallest of splashes could be seen on just a few of the bases. Some were highlighted, others not, and then the plug was pulled, quite suddenly, and all of the colour disappeared from the sky. Rain was on its way; she could smell the dampness in the warm air.

Her father came and stood above her in the dusk, looking down at her lying on the grass. She opened her eyes briefly and smiled up at him. The thump of music through her head had the effect of separating him from her, making them like strangers. He was distant, watching her, and she knew he had no idea what she was thinking. That will annoy him, she thought, and smiled, happy that there was an area of her life he could not control. She also knew, for certain, that he'd think she was smiling at him, and that this would make him worry that she found him amusing.

He said something. She took the headphones off her head and sat up. 'What?'

'I said there was a battle here.'

'Yes?'

'In 1642. Between the armies of Charles and Cromwell.'

She wondered why he always felt he had to try to teach her something, but also why she always felt she had to respond. 'Do you have those soldiers in your collection?'

'I only collect toy soldiers from the period of the British Empire. You should know that by now.'

And the first splashes of rain fell from the sky.

———————

Wednesday

*T*he word 'charity' had always been alien to her. Being a naturally generous person, she had never considered what some would call the business or political side of giving. There was no quid pro quo to her benevolence, never any calculations as to what might be in it for her. More importantly, she never had any feelings of obligation; the sense that one *should* do something to help another less fortunate than herself was something she never experienced. Her motives were pure – so much so that she couldn't have been said to have any motives at all. She was, as some would put it, a naturally kind woman; what others might call a saint.

She'd always been that way. Until the age of 17, she had lived with her parents and a younger sister in the suburb of Croydon, and when very young – about four or five – when her parents had either not been around or too busy doing whatever parents did, she would invite tramps into the kitchen and feed them. Sometimes this consisted of sandwiches or toast and jam, sometimes a bowl of cereal. As word spread through what in those days was a relatively small homeless community, such drop-ins became increasingly regular. Finally, her mother, with a smile and a shake of the head that was simultaneously approving and despairing, told her that such visits had to stop. Anne had no recollection of any of this, but was told about it by her mother when she was older.

What she could remember, however, from when she was quite young, was that she had always wanted to travel. Her parents were subscribers to *National Geographic*, and she spent hours poring over the pictures of foreign countries, exotic people, and strange or bizarre customs. She found herself falling in love with names on the map. There was Coonabarabran in Australia, Timbuctoo in Africa (less unexpectedly), and San Miguel de Tucuman in South America. The jumble of so many letters on the page, small print against a brown, orange or green elevation key, and the fact that the roads leading to such places were usually minimal, invariably made her heart race and her eyes mist over, and she would immediately be transported thousands of miles from her home. And when she first saw photographs of the 12th-century rock churches at Lalibela, she knew immediately that she had to visit them.

Africa had always been the continent she most wanted to see. To her it seemed insanely magical, especially when compared to the austere, grey, conventional life of post-War England. When she moved into her own flat, after studying nursing at King's during the War, she spent many evenings putting together an itinerary. It included Tanganyika, Uganda, Kenya and Ethiopia. To the surprise of most of her friends, she travelled alone, and with only a rucksack on her back. She was ahead of her time.

The highlight – or turning point – of her whole trip was in Weldiya, on Ethiopia's main north-south road, on her way back from visiting Lalibela and en route to Addis Ababa. This was where she met Miss McKenzie. She could still picture, quite clearly, their first meeting. Anne had just climbed down from an ancient, rusting, overloaded bus and was trying to explain to the grinning, but exceptionally unhelpful owner of the store in the service station that she was looking for somewhere to stay. Their mutual incomprehension came to an end when a small, middle-aged woman strode towards them. She was like a whirlwind, and she had the loudest voice Anne had ever heard from a woman.

'Need any help?' she shouted, as if facing into a Force 10 gale. Anne had already spotted the owner of the store running around helping this woman, speaking to her as if she were someone important, in complete contrast to the way he spoke to Anne. The two women started talking, and it turned out that Miss McKenzie – who was never addressed in any other manner anywhere on the planet, as far as anyone knew – was from 'a good family' (as she put it) in Kenya and had moved to Ethiopia 'a long, long time ago, dear. Oh, I don't like to think…' She'd wanted to help out, and had simply stayed on. 'Served here with the RAMC during the War. Never bothered to leave afterwards. Too much bother, you know.' All of this was shouted as if the young traveller had been standing a hundred yards away. Miss McKenzie ran the small hospital ('more of a health clinic, if the truth be told') on the edge of town, with her patients coming from as far as a hundred miles away.

When Anne told her she was a nurse, Miss McKenzie invited her to visit the clinic and stay the night. So she went. She'd never seen anywhere like it before; just a large room with six or eight beds, and every inch of floor space covered by mattresses. 'Most of the cases are TB,' Miss McKenzie shouted at her as they surveyed the scene from the doorway. One or two of the patients lifted their hands to greet the two women, and one cried out. An old man appeared at their side, both birdlike and sheepish. 'This is Nyoto,' Miss McKenzie said, 'my head nurse.' He was barefoot, wearing a filthy pair of trousers secured at the waist with a length of string, and – obviously his badge of office – a white jacket, torn and badly stained, with nothing between it and his scrawny chest. Anne thought him noticeably different from the starched, large-bosomed matron with polished pink skin that she was used to dealing with in London. 'I'm pleased to meet you, Nyoto,' she said. He responded with a huge smile, one that was quite bereft of any teeth.

Anne asked if Miss McKenzie did all of the work by herself, and she answered yes. She received a little money from the government and some help from the Red Cross, but that was it. Anne gave her a hand in the ward, and ended up staying three nights. They talked for many hours that first evening, and the following two evenings also, and on her final morning, before continuing her travels, Anne told Miss McKenzie that she'd like to return from London and help her. She'd been thinking about it throughout her visit. The private nursing she did in England, with her rich patients – almost all of whom were hypochondriacs – suddenly seemed far from satisfying. Miss McKenzie agreed to her coming back, perhaps thinking she'd never hear from Anne again once she had returned to London.

The middle-aged woman stood in the dust at the edge of the narrow strip of bitumen, the flimsy thread of civilization that stretched between Addis Ababa and the north, and as Anne climbed into another rust-bucket bus, she shouted her farewells as if the young girl were already many miles away.

Anne resigned from her job as soon as she was back in London. She felt guilt-stricken about leaving. In their own way, she realized that her patients needed her, and she had to remind herself quite forcefully that there were people in Africa who needed her more. She rented out her flat – just in case she ever returned – and joined Miss McKenzie two months later. With two nurses – and not forgetting the invaluable assistance of Nyoto – the hospital, or clinic, or whatever one wished to call it, was soon able to expand. They added a whole new ward (or 'room' as Anne described it in a letter to her sister back home), raised more money and cared for more patients. But the problems were Sisyphean, and Anne frequently thought – always late in the evening, the only time she ever had the chance to think – that their efforts were no more than a drop in the ocean. This was especially true during the 1958 Tigray famine when over 100,000 people died of starvation.

In 1962, ten years after moving to Weldiya, Anne travelled 25 miles up the road to set up a health clinic at Korem. The refugee camp that was eventually to appear on the outskirts of the town was still many years off. She hadn't wanted to leave Weldiya, but one of the women had to, and it seemed only fair that it should be Anne. The droughts were terrible, as was the fighting, and famine was again on their doorstep, only this time it was spreading to almost every corner of the country. Miss McKenzie was in her seventies by then and, as she herself said, couldn't do what she used to. 'I'm still healthy, dear,' she shouted down the phone at Anne, 'just slower. I'm getting slower. My batteries are running low. I get more tired than I used to.' But her vocal chords showed no signs of deterioration.

At her new location, Anne battled with government bureaucracy, inefficiency and downright dishonesty while trying to cope with the rising flood of refugees. With inadequate resources and little help, she attempted to stem the wave of human misery. At times, as during the Wollo famine in the early Seventies, she was overwhelmed. Even though she loved the work, the people and their country, and even though she didn't have a minute of the day to herself, she felt free. She didn't have to answer to anyone.

The crisis grew bigger by the day, and she was increasingly at the mercy and generosity of those passing by, those who were willing to put their hands in their pockets and help. Sometimes it was her adopted country's own government she was forced to rely on, the very people who'd caused most of the problems in the first place by starting a civil war in 1974. They now made little more than token gestures towards solving them. More often than not it was the people of the developed world that she turned to for support. Ethiopia had become a beggar on the streets of the West, head down, cap in hand, with a piece of old cardboard on which was scribbled the word '*Hungry*'. Anne had doubts about whether aid was the answer at all. She even had doubts – although they were less frequent – about whether the work she did was the right path to follow. Did this so-called charity simply perpetuate the problems it was intended to solve? Was it only given in the hope of salving the donors' conscience? Should her work even be listed as charity? She never seemed to arrive at a satisfactory answer to any of these questions. Sometimes she suspected there were no answers, and so she carried on with what she was doing, and stopped questioning her motives altogether. The one thing she did come to appreciate very quickly was that food, along with clean water and shelter, was the number-one priority, coming well before medical and health services and anything she was able to provide.

Africa Assist was one of the charities that supported her work. As a consequence, she had to put up with a steady procession of visitors from the UK. Visitors were part of the deal, the quid pro quo for any organization that received overseas aid; it was described as reciprocity. The charity, as well as the media, wanted photographs of starving people, preferably babies or those who had lost limbs in the fighting. Celebrities wanted to donate money to Anne in exchange for photographs of themselves looking, with pitying eyes, upon the starving. Equally disruptive, government officials would drop into the clinic unexpectedly to ask impertinent questions and try to ascertain whether she was giving succour to the rebels. Included in this category, unfortunately, was any attempt to heal their wounded.

Once, she had looked forward to visitors; it confirmed people had heard of the work she was doing and wanted to help. But then she'd grown to suffer them; they got in her way, messed up her schedule and wasted her time. Almost all of them fell into one of two camps: they were either young, naïve and of the generation that approaches a task with enormous enthusiasm, then quickly loses interest; or they were middle-aged and jaundiced, and only visited her hospital because they were expected to do so. That crowd couldn't wait to get back to their five-star hotel in the city, lie by the pool, drink cocktails and even, from what Anne was told on occasion, order up a local girl to visit them in their room. It was not in Anne's nature to despise these people – to despise anyone – and yet it struck her, as one such group toured her hospital, that they resembled a fastidious person being asked to stoop down and pick up a particularly soiled and smelly rag from the gutter. They weren't always able to hide their distaste; some didn't even attempt to try.

When Adrian Burles visited her at Korem, she wasn't sure which group he belonged to. He was naïve, certainly – how could he not be when he didn't even work for a charity? When she learnt of his history, that he handled public relations for Africa Assist, she hadn't been particularly interested, although she did wonder, briefly, how a public-relations executive could possibly understand or empathize with the suffering of the Ethiopian people. Yet it seemed she'd misjudged him. When she had seen the tears as he stood amongst the refugees outside the clinic, it had caught her totally by surprise.

She was critical of herself for making such a misjudgement, before having given him the opportunity to prove himself, and admonished herself for being so uncharitable. Reassuringly, he regarded her patients with neither disgust, disdain nor mawkishness. Rather, he was practical, businesslike, almost aloof, neither showing exaggerated interest nor lack of interest in what she was trying to achieve. He was both charming and persuasive (his public-relations background, she supposed), explaining to her that Africa Assist was willing to finance an extension to her clinic, supply much-needed medical equipment and, if required, pay for more staff. (She never once suspected that he made these promises without any authority to do so, simply on the basis that he knew he'd be able to persuade James of the benefits of such an investment.) They placed great value on her work, he said, and wanted to give her all the financial assistance she needed to guarantee the future of the clinic. But then his mind – especially on that second, unexpected visit – had obviously been on other things, on what he called his special project. That was all he could talk about. But if those proffered funds were in any way contingent on her flying with him to London and accompanying a malnourished man on a walk through the city, the link, so far as she could remember, had never been made. Rather, what she remembered was Adrian discovering that she had a sister in Yorkshire whom she hadn't seen for more than 20 years, and emphasizing, with great enthusiasm, the merits of a reunion. 'What a wonderful opportunity for you both to get together.'

When Adrian and Dave had finished their cooked breakfast (in Anne's opinion, eaten by Adrian in order to make a point, rather than for enjoyment), she and Mujtabaa returned to sit inside the Winnebago. Emma remained outside in the sunshine, with a book. She sat on a bench, the grass still being wet from the overnight rain. Dave was meeting with the volunteers to organize them for the day ahead.

The nurse was reading one of the morning newspapers while she had coffee, her white hair just peeking above the opened broadsheet. She hadn't spoken for at least ten minutes, not because she hadn't wanted to, but because she'd never been inclined to speak up, to push her own views on people. But finally, she put down the newspaper and, overcoming her natural reticence, said, 'Adrian, may I ask how you know all of this about Mujtabaa's family?'

He didn't seem surprised by her question. 'I don't.'

'You made it up about his parents, brothers and sisters all dying of starvation?'

'Yes.'

She was shocked. 'But it's not true.'

He was smiling. 'Isn't it? How do you know?' She could see he was in a good mood. 'Probably even Mujtabaa doesn't know what's happened to his family, but it's a pretty safe bet that they're dead. And it certainly makes a better story.'

'You're saying a better story is more important than the truth?'

'It's called spin, Anne. That's what we do in PR. We interpret an event to make the public feel favourably towards us. It's a quite acceptable practice. Look at all the free column inches we've been given, and all the photographs. That kind of publicity can't be bought.'

'From what you're saying, it sounds to me like it can.' She didn't bother to hide her look of disapproval. She shook her head, folded the newspaper and pushed it away from her across the table as if it might be contaminated. 'I don't feel that's right, Adrian. If you don't mind my saying so, what you've done is scarcely honest.'

'I'm sorry you feel that way, Anne, but please don't worry about it. First, what I told them about Mujtabaa's family is more than likely the truth, and if it isn't true then it will be on my conscience. Second, I don't actually think it's that important.'

At that moment there was a commotion outside. Emma put her head round the door. 'Dad, there are TV crews here, and reporters. They want to talk to you.'

Adrian went outside. Anne followed him to the door of the Winnebago. There were five or six reporters, as well as two commercial TV stations, and the BBC. A press man was holding up the morning edition of *The Sun* with its black banner headline, 'MUST WE STOMACH THIS?' over a photograph of Mujtabaa lying on the road. Adrian had already read the article. In short simple phrases, mainly in words of one or two syllables, it questioned both the validity and the morality of the walk, saying that it was no more than a barbaric publicity stunt. It claimed the British were amongst the most generous of nations when it came to donating to charities, and insisted that 'every man, woman and child in the country would be happy to dig deep to help Mujtabaa and his fellow Ethiopians without the necessity of this cruel charade.' It pilloried Adrian and Africa Assist, saying that, however noble the original intention, the event – or 'the walk' as it was now called – was in danger of degenerating into a media circus. Demonstrating the remarkable blindness and hypocrisy of the tabloid press, this particular newspaper didn't see itself, however, as part of that circus, but rather as the voice of reason, concern and objectivity.

'What do you say to these claims, Mr Burles?'

'*Your* claims, Jack?'

The reporter shrugged, indifferent – if not proud – to be recognized as the author of the piece. Adrian had known him for many years. He was a hard-drinking, nicotine-stained, foul-mouthed and cynical individual, who despised the public whose opinions he herded like sheep, and loathed, with equal fervour, Rupert Murdoch, the proprietor who paid him.

'I say this to your claims. This walk is not, as you put it in your piece, barbaric. The conditions in which Mujtabaa and a large percentage of his people are still forced to live, those are barbaric. I say that the Mengistu dictatorship, which moves its people around the country like so many head of cattle, is barbaric. I say that existing on two litres of water a day is barbaric. That walking five miles to a well for that water is barbaric. That existing on one so-called meal of gruel a day is barbaric. I say that *existing* instead of *living* is barbaric. I'd further suggest that your newspaper, Jack, doesn't know the true meaning of the word barbaric, and if you'd like to borrow a dictionary so that you can discover its true meaning, then I'd be more than happy to lend you one.' Everyone – apart from Jack – laughed.

Anne, standing in the door of the Winnebago, didn't know how she felt about what Adrian had said. She thought it had been a spirited, even heartfelt rejoinder, yet she was still unable to overcome her doubts about what they were doing. She was living in a world she understood very little about, and it unsettled her. The borders between good and bad, between what was right and what was wrong, seemed to be becoming harder for people to recognize. These borders were nebulous now, ill-defined, amorphous, very different from when she was young.

She watched Adrian take a handkerchief out of his pocket and wipe his forehead. He was breathing heavily.

Another reporter pushed forward. 'Mr Burles, don't you think Africa Assist could raise money without putting Mujtabaa through this ordeal? Live Aid didn't make anyone walk through the streets of London, and they raised millions of pounds.'

'We can't just continue to repeat Live Aid every year to raise money – as much as we might like to. We need something new to grab the public's interest. I do appreciate that the people of Britain are extremely generous. Every year charities raise the equivalent of two pounds from every man, woman and child in the country – over £120 million in total – but they need to be given a reason for parting with their money. Famine in Ethiopia is unique in that it recurs with mind-numbing regularity – already they're talking about another famine next year – and I believe this calls for unique money-raising methods.'

Anne was watching Emma. She was standing to the left of the group of reporters, biting her fingernails and looking worried. In her own way, she looked as frail as Mujtabaa. The nurse wanted to hug her.

'Although we're not in a position to release figures yet, Africa Assist is already raising more than we could ever hope to raise through newspaper advertisements or a door-knocking appeal. We'll release the exact figures after the Trafalgar Square rally on Sunday.'

Another hand went up. 'Some people have described this walk as being a Hunger March for the Eighties. Do you see a similarity between what you're doing and the marches of the Twenties and Thirties?'

'Interesting question,' said Adrian, nodding his head. 'But I think it's a little misleading. Certainly, Mujtabaa is walking for food and for recognition of his plight, but he isn't walking for a job. So I'd say hunger is the only similarity. Employment simply doesn't enter into the equation in Mujtabaa's part of the world – or not how we think of employment. Also, on this walk I'm pleased to say there has been no violence – as there was in those hunger marches of the Twenties and Thirties – and there's no reason why there should be any, of course.'

Some half hour later the reporters and TV crew dispersed to their cars in order to go back to their offices to file their stories. Before leaving, some of them reassured Adrian that they'd catch up with the walk later in the day. After this unscheduled news conference, Emma went up to her father and hugged him. 'You were great, Dad.'

Later that morning they followed the loop of the Thames northeast to Kew Bridge, and there they headed south across the River. They were forced to stop in the middle of the bridge while Mujtabaa stood at the parapet and stared down into the grey water, watching wide-eyed as barges wallowed by, and a ferry tied up at Kew Pier, a little downstream. He could have been a four-year-old, his look was so intent. 'He'll never have seen so much water before in his life,' Anne explained. Emma watched the young man leaning against the structure and was saddened by his separateness, by her inability to share with him the excitement of his various discoveries. It was like viewing someone in a soundproof glass box, unable to hear or feel what they were experiencing, completely cut off from each other. Eventually, Mujtabaa had to be pulled away – 'otherwise we'll be here all day,' Adrian said.

They walked slowly through the faded suburbs of west London, where roads and railway lines vied for position with the Thames, and the houses had been forced to settle haphazardly into the spaces left in between. Grey brick, spiritless terraces, with windows framed in peeling white stone and unapproachable front doors, were planted either side of the furrowed streets. Here and there, battling for space amongst the rundown corner shops and factories, the deserted churches, the postboxes, traffic lights and parking meters, could be found small patches of grass. The grass struggled for air beside the railway lines and in backyard allotments, on derelict land, even in the parks. It wasn't a very green grass, more a kind of murky, dirty, dusty yellow – etiolated in its battle for survival. The trees, also, were covered in dust. The dingy, dull smell of London dust, reminiscent of a rarely visited attic in summer, pervaded everything.

Soon after crossing Kew Bridge, on Mortlake Road, Mujtabaa stopped and bent down to speak to Anne. She was trying not to smile as she turned to Adrian: 'If I understand him correctly, he's saying that he'd like to have a ride in a car. He calls them "small trucks".'

Unlike Anne, Adrian wasn't amused. 'Tell him, when he gets to Trafalgar Square, he can have all the rides he wants, but not until then.'

'You should see it as an encouraging sign, Adrian. Our young man is becoming more aware of his surroundings.' He grunted, non-committal. She spoke to Mujtabaa, and his mouth parted into an ellipse of brilliant white. He started walking again, and Emma could have sworn there was more of a spring in his step.

Kadwell's letter to *The Times*, the articles in that morning's newspapers, the segments on the evening news programmes, the fliers that had been distributed overnight along the route and in the surrounding area by volunteers, also word of mouth, had all stimulated interest in the walk. People were now turning out especially to see them. Many cars stopped in order to donate, often causing chaos while they did so. When traffic lights went red, the collectors ran from car to car before springing back to the safety of a pavement or island as soon as they turned green. Many pedestrians accompanied the walk for short distances, and a teenager in Richmond pedalled alongside them for most of the morning, grinning at Mujtabaa as he cycled, shouting over and over again, 'How you doing, man?' The young Ethiopian never smiled, but stared at the bicycle wide-eyed, which was more than enough to keep the teenager content.

Dave pulled up alongside the walkers and called out to Adrian. 'James just called on the car phone. He's on his way over.'

'What does he want?'

'Wouldn't say. "Too hush-hush", he said, "have to talk to Adrian."'

Adrian rolled his eyes. 'Unbelievable.'

On the next street corner, they ran into a group of musicians. There were two drums, a guitar and a woman, at the front, shaking some maracas. She was swaying in time to the one-drop rhythm of her singing. The men wore yellow, red and green crocheted hats, and the woman had a crocheted shawl over her dress. They shouted greetings when they saw Mujtabaa, and he stopped to watch them. The music had a haunting sound, and each drum its own individual voice. Soon his feet began to move, but only a little. They shuffled first one way, then another. He closed his eyes as his feet picked up the rhythm. The woman with the maracas moved to his side. She was laughing as she sang, and her eyes sparkled with joy. She moved her body in time to the music, and they could all see that Mujtabaa wanted to find the strength to move with her. However, he could do little more than sway; he looked exhausted. At that moment, Adrian stepped forward, alongside Mujtabaa, and he also started to dance. He lacked both rhythm and grace – very much the cliché of the stiff, unbending business executive – but he clapped his hands and grinned, and appeared to be in the best of spirits. Everyone understood why he was joining in, and the woman encouraged him with her eyes and Emma cheered.

When the music stopped, Mujtabaa held on to the woman's arm, as if for balance. She spoke to him, and he stared at her, like a child, unable to comprehend what she was saying. She put her arms round him then and held him. She was a large, maternal woman; her hair was braided and her eyes were closed. After what seemed like a long time, she gently squeezed his arm and released him. The Ethiopian looked like he wanted to stay with these people, as if he were unwilling to continue with the walk, and yet he did – with a little encouragement from Adrian.

As they walked off, the woman sang and laughed and waved them on their way. The other musicians clapped their hands, and started to play their instruments again, but now it was like they were playing for Mujtabaa, attempting to give him the strength to keep walking. They shouted their farewells to the Africa Assist group and, even though he was tired, Anne could swear that Mujtabaa was walking with a lighter step. Music must make him feel good inside, she thought.

James Balcombe appeared, breathless and full of self-importance, an hour later. Dave parked the mobile home at the side of the road, and they met inside, but not before James had time to peer, with blatant curiosity, at the Ethiopian resting on a seat at a bus stop, next to Anne.

'Coping all right, is he?'

Adrian reassured the chief executive. Balcombe wasted no time on preliminaries. He threw a letter onto the table in front of Adrian. It was from the Ethiopian embassy. Basically, it suggested the walk was propaganda, 'besmirching and sabotaging' the efforts by the Ethiopian government to contain the effects of a debilitating drought, and claimed it painted an unfair picture of their country's way of life. If the relationship between Ethiopia and the United Kingdom was to remain cordial, the walk should be stopped immediately.

'That's wonderful,' said Adrian.

'What do you mean, wonderful?' Balcombe sat down. 'How can you say that, Adrian?'

'It shows we're doing the right thing.'

'I don't think you understand.'

'I understand only too well. It's quite obvious Mengistu considers it an insult that a famine exists in his Marxist-Leninist paradise, so he denies it. What do you expect of the man? Release that letter to the press and we'll have the whole of Britain behind us, immediately. Even the handful of people who are objecting to the walk now will be won over. Everyone will see it for what it is: an attempt by a dictatorship to silence criticism of their relocation policy.' He made to move away.

'But what about diplomatic relations? What if the Foreign Office becomes involved?'

Adrian turned back to Balcombe. 'Why would they? Even if

they objected, which is extremely unlikely, it's no concern of ours. Everyone in this country knows what a disastrous mess Ethiopia is in. No one's going to have any sympathy for a government that created that mess in the first place, then compounded the mess by doing little or nothing to fix it. In fact they're making it worse with their civil war. Release that letter to the press, James, or ignore it. It's up to you. But whatever you do, I suggest you don't reply to it.'

The chief executive rose to leave. Outside the mobile home he stopped and eyed Mujtabaa uneasily. Although the young man didn't appear to see him, James nodded, as one passenger might nod to a fellow traveller when leaving a railway carriage on arrival at their destination. He smiled distractedly at Anne, then obviously decided that he should go up and say hello. After a few brief, perfunctory words, he turned and walked off. Dave accompanied him, seemingly deep in conversation. I don't trust that man one little bit, went through Adrian's head. He could have been referring to either man, although the sentiment was in fact aimed at Dave. He watched them go, shaking his head, puzzled. Even now, I don't believe James really understands what we're trying to do here.

Once again they set off. Anne walked with Mujtabaa. She was only happy when she was not too far from her ward. Adrian, always out in front, led the way. He appeared to walk with his chest stuck forward, or perhaps it was with his arms pulled slightly back, but whichever it was, the overall effect was of a man wading into the sea, breasting the waves, battling the odds with grim determination. To the others it must have appeared that he had little interest in his surroundings or in the suburbs they passed through, that he was concentrated solely on his destination. It was like Trafalgar Square was always in his mind, occupying his every thought, and in the background there was always a clock ticking. He had to get there before time ran out, before something went wrong. Probably, he worried that Mujtabaa might not have the strength to reach the Square, but other worries were equally pressing, if a little more nebulous: that an official, an all-powerful bureaucrat, would descend out of nowhere, confiscate the young African, and carry him off into the bowels of Whitehall, never to be seen again. Now and again Adrian would turn and look back over his shoulder to check that the Ethiopian was still there, and to make sure he himself hadn't advanced too far ahead of the others. If he had gained too much on them, he either stopped or turned round and walked backwards for a minute or two, all the time watching the young man, the nurse and his daughter walking towards him. At times he gave the impression he wanted to rush back and grab Mujtabaa by the hand and drag him forward, hurry him through the streets to their destination because there was no time to spare. The two women could feel his impatience.

Emma walked a little behind Mujtabaa – about three or four paces – and a little to one side. Already it was her recognized spot, her official place in the procession, and she never moved from it. As the newspapers began to publish more and more photographs of Mujtabaa, there in the background, almost unfailingly, was Emma, clutching his goatskin waterbag. She was his shadow, and that's what Anne called her: 'You're Moosh's shadow, dear.' Later, in the mobile home that evening, Anne attempted to explain this to Mujtabaa, and he'd been delighted. He briefly clapped his hands and laughed, his mouth wide, his teeth a startling white against the darkness of his face, and the young girl was reminded of those dancing, grinning skeletons in funfairs, the ones that leap out at you on ghost-train rides.

'You know what he calls you when he talks to me?' the nurse asked the young girl. '*The girl with glass over her eyes.* Do you like that?'

Emma smiled, pleased most of all to hear that he sometimes talked about her.

'Your father is *the headman.* And I am *the lady in the straw hat.* That's how he sees us.'

The young Ethiopian had become like a magnet, attracting more and more people as the walk progressed. They lined the sides of the road, many respectfully applauding, others – fewer in number – heckling, as if they might stop the walk by showing their disapproval.

The more people were drawn to the spectacle of the African walking through the streets of the city, the more stressed Anne became. 'They all want a part of him,' she'd say to no one in particular. Earlier that day, in a shopping mall, a woman had approached the Ethiopian. She'd been wearing a long blue dress, like a *shämma*, covered with many different-coloured flowers. Around her neck and waist were lengths of other materials, also in many bright colours, and bracelets of gold and silver on her wrists and ankles sparkled when she moved. Her uncombed hair was a brilliant red that reached down to her waist. Everyone stopped – they were compelled to stop – before this striking figure, and everything went still and quiet. The woman smiled, a gentle, sorrowful smile, but also a smile that was very knowing; like a woman who was fully conscious of what she was doing. She stood before the young man, burning with a strange fire. Her feet and arms were bare, and her mouth was a startling streak of red. But what was really noticeable, above everything else, was the white cloth she clutched tightly to her chest. It was all about that cloth. Everyone could see that, but at first no one understood why. They stared at this apparition before them. The woman spoke to Mujtabaa, and he listened. It was almost as if he appeared to comprehend what she was saying. Certainly, he showed no sign of alarm, perhaps because her voice was so soothing, little more than a whisper, and as restful as a breeze through grass. She held up the open white cloth before her as she spoke, raised so that it almost obscured her face, but also so that everyone around them could see it. Somehow it was obvious to the onlookers that she was fully aware of the photographers in the vicinity. Mujtabaa swayed slightly, uncertain as to what was expected of him. When she stepped forward, he put a hand on his *jile*; a movement that was more reassuring for him than threatening to her. The woman stood directly in front of him, placing a hand behind his neck as if to hold him, and then wiped his face with the white cloth. She wiped his face slowly, carefully, gently, all the while talking to him in a quiet, soothing voice. Flashbulbs exploded all around them, but neither the woman nor the young man appeared to be aware of them.

At that moment a police officer walked up and stood next to the woman. He placed a hand on her arm, but she shook it off as if he wasn't important to her and she didn't want to waste time with him. Adrian said something to the officer, who then stepped back. The woman with the long, red hair dropped to her knees in front of the Ethiopian and kissed his hand – the hand that was holding the walking staff. It was all very theatrical, very staged. She knelt, motionless for a while, her lips pressed to his hand, then slowly raised herself to her feet, still clutching the white cloth to her skinny chest. There were tears in her eyes as she crossed herself. Then she stepped away from him, as if to tell him that the performance was over, that he must now continue with his walk.

Anne said, with just a hint of impatience, even disapproval, 'People have to be kept away from him, Adrian. There's no place for this kind of behaviour here. It's verging on sacrilegious. And, anyway, Mujtabaa has to rest.'

Adrian wanted him to sit outside the mobile home, where people could see him, but Anne was adamant. 'He's exhausted. If you continue to push him like this, you'll make him ill.' So the two women barricaded themselves inside the mobile home with the young man, while Adrian gave interviews to the media outside, and to the listening crowd.

An hour later, after Mujtabaa had rested and been fed a small plate of porridge, Anne said he could continue the walk. She was obviously reluctant to step outside the mobile home, and Emma sensed this: 'Don't worry, Anne, I'll come with you.' There was surprise on the nurse's face, as if she hadn't expected support from such a young person, but she squeezed the proffered hand gratefully. Finally, steeling herself to open the door, she left the Winnebago. It was chaos outside; a large, milling, inquisitive crowd, with the Press and the police now out in force, people shouting and jostling, everyone vying for a glimpse of the young African. With people pressing in on all sides, the small party struggled to make any kind of progress. Anne and Emma, on either side of Mujtabaa, encircled him with their arms, both women desperate to keep him safe, while Adrian attempted to force a passage for them through the crush. He shouted at people to let them past, and yet many in the crowd were already shouting, 'Stand back! Give him air! Get back!' so his task was relatively simple. Some police also helped to open a passage through the throng.

They set off through North Sheen and Mortlake, followed by a small army of supporters and the inquisitive, past terraced house and stuccoed semi, stopping for several minutes beside the North Sheen cemetery. 'Does he understand what it is?' Emma asked Anne.

'I've just tried to explain it to him, but he already knew. It's not that different from how his people bury their dead.'

Mujtabaa stood regarding the hundreds of headstones, his face quite impassive.

Anne continued: 'His people wouldn't have this number in one place, because they bury the dead where they fall, but they put them in the ground and erect headstones just like us – although not as elaborate, of course.'

They crossed Chiswick Bridge and went northeast, along the busy A316 towards Hammersmith. They were in the heart of suburbia now, halfway between the innocence of the countryside and the go-getting, yuppie ways of the city. The smells of London began to surround them, invading their nostrils: the stagnant stink of rancid fat from fast-food places, the fustiness of long-term poverty, the dull smell of exhaust and the close sweat of countless bodies. Everywhere, the heat clung, making it difficult to breathe.

They stopped for the night in Chiswick, in the grounds of a school on the edge of Duke's Meadows. Inspector Davidson, the middle-aged, genial police officer who was in charge of the walk, dropped by to chat with Adrian. He wanted to discuss the progress so far – 'It's bigger than I thought it was going to be,' he confessed to Adrian – but also to go over the plans for the coming days. He said he was keen to help make the walk a success because he, personally, felt so badly about anyone in the modern world not having enough to eat. 'It's a terrible thing, this starvation business,' he said, glancing at Mujtabaa, and Adrian politely agreed with him.

Later that evening, after Adrian had departed for an interview at Thames Television (they had shot footage of Mujtabaa for the bulk of their programme earlier that day), and Dave had gone into the Africa Assist offices to organize a few things, Emma sat next to Mujtabaa, on a bench seat in the Winnebago, attempting to show him how the television remote control worked. He started to flick from channel to channel, pressing the buttons carefully, and with almost painful deliberation, as he raised his head quickly to try to catch the change from one programme to the next. His face was a picture of solemn concentration, although guttural sounds of surprise did issue periodically from his mouth when he was fortunate enough to spot the changeover.

'He's so cute,' Emma said.

Anne smiled. 'I'm not sure an African warrior, even one still in his teens, would appreciate being called cute.'

'What is his life normally like, Anne, do you know?'

The nurse put down her book. 'I can tell you more about what it was like before the famine came than what it's like today, although Mujtabaa has told me a little. Life is very different for his people now.'

She sat in silence for a few minutes collecting her thoughts, for so long in fact that Emma began to wonder if the nurse had forgotten the question. Her hands were clasped together on her lap and her head was bowed. She could have been praying. Then, without unclasping her hands, she raised her head to look at her young charge and started to speak.

'He comes from the middle of the middle of nowhere. It's hard for someone like you, Emma, living in one of the busiest cities in the world, to appreciate just how empty the desert is, and how barren. It stretches for 200 miles between the mountains that run down the centre of Ethiopia – the plateau, where I live – and the sea, and much of it is below sea level. The Danakil is an unforgiving land of sand and stone, salt lakes and lava streams. The black rock is cracked and barren, and the sand is seemingly without limit. You can see pillars of rock and salt in every direction. The only vegetation is thorn bushes, gorse and tufts of hard, dry grass, and they're forced to hug the ground in an attempt to hide from the rays of the sun. It's very desolate and harsh. On the few occasions I've been there, it always reminds me of how I imagine Mars must look. There are no roads and no trees. Hyenas and jackals roam the fringes of the desert, and the heat is hotter than anything you could imagine. The air is sulphurous. It actually sears your throat when you breathe.'

Emma sat in silence, her eyes wide. It was much more interesting than any geography or history lesson at school had ever been.

'It's in this environment that you find a race of fierce, warlike warriors – the Afar. The most important thing you have to understand about Mujtabaa is that – even though he's young – he's a warrior. His people have fought all their lives, as have the generations before them. They're amongst the most feared tribes in the whole of Africa. They're always at war, that's how they spend most of their days. They fight against Mother Nature of course, but also against other nomadic tribes, tribes that want to graze their animals on the scarce desert grasses and near the rare watering holes.'

Anne, for the first time, turned her eyes away from the young man and looked at Emma.

'It's a world in which might is right. The most prized manly virtue amongst the Afar is prowess in battle. The men are brought up on an ethic of extreme aggression.'

'How exciting,' the young girl said, hugging herself.

'They're strong, and they're brave. They hunt, they care for their cattle and camels, and – as I said – they fight other tribes. They say it's not worth living if they haven't killed another warrior. In fact, tribal custom doesn't allow them to marry unless they have.'

Emma gasped. 'You mean Moosh may have killed someone?' She looked across at the young man, a picture of innocence, pressing the buttons on the remote control. She could not believe such a thing.

'Well, from the little he tells me, yes, he is married.'

'So, if that's right, he's killed someone?' She was leaning forward in her seat, her eyes wide. 'But that's horrid!'

136

Anne smiled. It was a gentle smile, the understanding smile of an adult for a child. Although she was sympathetic to the conflicting feelings the young girl was experiencing, Anne's lifetime had been one of always following the truth, no matter what the cost, of never avoiding what others might simply regard as too narrow or too difficult a path.

'They live in a harsh, unforgiving landscape, Emma, and the people are a reflection of that environment. The gods they believe in can be vengeful, unlike our own God who is all-forgiving.'

She paused, possibly uncertain as to how she could best express what she wished to say. 'When one of their warriors kills a warrior from another tribe, he will keep a certain part of his enemy's anatomy hanging from his belt. As a trophy, you understand.' She stared meaningfully at Emma, as if defying her to discuss the matter any further. 'I don't wish to go into more detail.' The young girl looked both fascinated and appalled, her imagination working overtime. 'No! Really? Oh, but that's so cruel! How awful.'

'It's likely they would regard many of our own customs as cruel. For instance, they'd never lock people away in prisons for decades, as we do; they couldn't understand something like that. And on this walk through London Mujtabaa will have seen individuals suffering hardships and loneliness that would never be allowed in the desert. They're nomads with almost no possessions, and yet they share everything they do have without a second thought: what's yours is mine and what's mine is yours. So it's utterly wrong to think of them as cruel. If you ever go to the Danakil, Emma, I can guarantee you'll find the Afar have basically the same feelings as you do yourself, and identical dreams about what they want for themselves – not to mention their families and the future. I'm sure you've heard the expression, people are the same the world over?' Emma nodded. 'Well, it's true. The similarities between us are what makes us human, the differences are merely cultural.'

She paused for a moment, leaving Emma time to feel suitably corrected, if not gently chastised. As she waited for Anne to continue, Mujtabaa rose slowly to his feet and crossed towards the television set. He stood before it for a moment, then leant forward and looked upwards as if attempting to see behind it.

'What's he doing?' Emma whispered.

'He thinks the people on the screen are behind the television set.'

'Really?'

A few seconds later, Mujtabaa straightened up and, with a look of bewilderment on his face, went back to where he'd been sitting.

Emma turned back to Anne. She was already more absorbed in her friend's past than in the present. 'He has told you he's married, hasn't he?'

'He says her name is Safia–'

'That's such a beautiful name.'

'And he's also spoken of a friend, Tsegai…'

Anne then told Emma, as best as she was able, how Mujtabaa had spoken about life in his village – or *mela*. How, when he was still a boy, not yet a man, he would rest in the shade beneath a tree with the elders of his people while they spoke of animals and the prices at the markets, of the lack of rain and the shortage of food, of the soldiers that appeared out of nowhere and the tribespeople who disappeared, of what could and could not be done in such harsh times. Every day the talk was of the same things, and at the end of all the talk nothing was ever any clearer, nothing was ever decided.

While he was sitting listening to the elders, he used to watch the women go about their business nearby. They were taking the huts off the backs of the camels, collecting wood for the fire and grinding durra into flour. He wasn't really watching all of the women, just Safia. He was admiring the anklets on her legs, the bracelets on her arms and the coloured beads that fell from around her neck onto her breasts. Sometimes she would glance at the men in the shade – not often, because she was too modest – just sometimes. And when she did steal a look in their direction, it was always quick. Mujtabaa knew she was looking at him and not the older men, and each time her face turned towards him, his heart beat faster. But he also knew that she was waiting for him to prove himself a man. She saw that he was sitting with the men, but understood that it wasn't the same thing. They both understood that, and they both understood what he had to do.

She had last spoken to him before the time of the full moon. She had listened to what he had to say, but kept her eyes downcast all the time. They were together in the darkness, some distance from where the others sat, but they weren't allowed to touch. She whispered to him, 'Why do you come to me, a woman, when you are also a woman?' It was what she had to say, what she was taught to say. She was keeping herself for him, but she wasn't permitted to tell him that. How long would she wait for him? Not forever, that was certain. He must do what had to be done, and soon, before another man fixed his gaze on her. He had to find an enemy warrior to kill...

Anne explained to Emma that if she didn't fully understand what Mujtabaa told her, she preferred to guess rather than interrupt him. She was scared of him withdrawing back into silence. The only time she risked interrupting was if he was speaking too fast or, once or twice, too quietly. Generally, however, she was patient. She knew she was his only contact with the world he now found himself in, and that he was as dependent on her as a blind person with a guide dog.

He told Anne, who then recounted the same story to Emma, of the time when he owned five cows. Those were the names he'd been able to remember and call out when he'd been cut by Birru. Five names screamed by him into the blackness of the night, despite the tearing between his legs and the bloodied knife held in the old man's hand. He hadn't fallen though, despite his legs having no strength. He'd stayed on his feet and then walked away.

His father hadn't said anything to him, but that didn't matter because Mujtabaa saw the pride in his eyes and knew he'd done well. His father was a brave man who'd killed many enemies, and at the ceremony he'd watched his son become a man, and nodded his approval.

With five cows, his life had looked good. He would spend his days watching his animals graze and dreaming of all the other animals that would one day would be his. He dreamt of other things, too. He dreamt of the girls in his tribe and in the neighbouring tribes he wanted to marry. He pondered the question of how many wives he'd have, and how many children they'd give him. He wanted lots of children because he knew it meant a secure and prosperous old age.

But now his dreams lay about him, shattered and sterile, like the rocks in the desert, cracked into many pieces by the heat of the sun. Now he didn't own one cow, not one. Now his only dream was to stay alive, and try to help his wife, his only wife. There was nothing else to hope for.

'That's what Moosh said to you?'

Anne nodded. 'He said it was a very different time from when he went with his father to the market to trade with the people of the highlands. In those days they traded cattle, goats, sheep, salt, milk, hides and ghee for grains, vegetables, eggs, spices, jewellery and clothing. In those days everything was different.'

The two European women sat with the Ethiopian in the gathering gloom of the mobile home. The high-pitched, distant cry of a fox punctuated the soft, steady hum of the television set.

Eventually, Emma said, 'Imagine being a husband at his age. It seems so young.'

'He's also a father.'

And the younger of the two women suddenly became acutely aware of the presence of a third, an unknown woman she could only imagine. And it was maybe at that moment, when she understood Mujtabaa was doing this walk for his wife and child, that the 14-year-old first fell a little in love with him herself.

Anne had resumed her own account of the Afar people. 'Although I don't know a great deal about their lives, Emma, I do know their lives can be harsh. But there are good times, too. They aren't always fighting, you see. After the rains, the earth comes to life – even in the desert. Everything begins to grow. There are flowers amongst the sand dunes. It's very beautiful, although I've only been fortunate enough to see it once or twice.'

'Flowers in the desert?'

'It's hard to imagine, but yes. And after the rains, the pasture

140

becomes more abundant, and there's also milk and meat. So the tribe gets together and feasts. When times are hard, their camp – called a *burra* – may consist of just two or three dome-shaped huts, but when it rains, you can find groups of up to a hundred people together.

'Those are the days when marriages are negotiated, and weddings celebrated. It's probably when Mujtabaa and Safia got together. After months of hard work, the men relax. They live in friendship and joy. They hunt during the day, and at night they squat, singing with their friends and family. They dance with the young girls. They know all of them because they've played together since childhood. Everyone knows each other. Everyone is happy.'

'So they're not always fighting?'

'Certainly not. Although the faces of the Afar can sometimes appear unfriendly, almost cold and scornful, they have warm and honest smiles. They're a very sociable people, always singing and laughing, and they just love to talk. They like nothing more than to sit down together and chat, often for hours on end.'

'Moosh certainly isn't like that. He never says a word,' then she added, almost resentfully, 'except to you.'

'You're forgetting the language barrier. Also, he's not with his friends now.'

They both looked at the young man, alone on his seat, still with the remote control, flicking from one channel to the next. 'I'm his friend,' Emma said quietly, and Anne nodded. 'You are, dear. That's true.'

At that moment Adrian burst into the mobile home.

'How did it go, Dad?'

He sat down heavily. 'Look, it went all right. Or it did until the interviewer practically accused us of being like some of those other, less reputable charities we all know about.'

'What do you mean, Adrian?'

'He brought up those tired old stories about senior managers lying like beached whales beside the swimming pools of Addis's international hotels. You know, sipping ice-cooled drinks and nibbling gourmet finger food while their fellow human beings, just down the road, are also pot-bellied and comatose, but in their case through lack of food.'

'But Africa Assist isn't like that!' Anne was most indignant.

'That's awful, Dad. How can they say that?'

'Because they're the media, darling, that's why. They can make everything up if they want to. It'll be on the breakfast show tomorrow morning, so there's a chance they'll cut that bit out. I think they might, because I gave them a pretty spirited rejoinder.'

Emma hugged him, 'I bet you were brilliant. I'm so proud of you.'

Anne smiled, although she still looked concerned. 'I'm sure they won't say anything that's not true, Adrian.'

He glanced at her as if marvelling that someone could be so naïve, then went on to tell Emma about what had happened at the television studio, and about the number of people who'd phoned the station during the programme. 'Their switchboard was jammed. They told me later that it was the biggest response they'd ever had to a live show. And the people who called in were pledging a lot of money – and I mean a lot.'

Anne picked up her book and tried to read, but was unable to concentrate. She regarded her companions over the top of her paperback. He must be in his mid-forties, she guessed. He was a little overweight – not especially so, but rounded and soft, almost the opposite of the men she saw in Ethiopia. He'd probably been handsome a few years ago, but now there was a layer of fat over his cheeks and jaw, and a faint hint of lines beneath his eyes and across his forehead. He held himself well still, although he was perceptibly round-shouldered. What she liked was the way his features became attractively animated when he spoke. There's a charm there, she thought, mixed in with a young person's enthusiasm, although it wasn't always immediately apparent. She also appreciated that, beneath the public-relations bluster, there was a sensitive man. She still recalled how surprised she'd been when he had cried on his first visit to her clinic.

Emma was laughing at something her father had said, her spectacles flashing beneath the lights of the mobile home, and Anne thought how innocent she looked, how full of life and optimism one moment, then moody and withdrawn the next – a typical teenager, she supposed. Physically, she was very much her father's daughter: a little overweight also, but with a kind, open face, and a readiness to smile. She was still a child really, still filled with hope and happiness, still a stranger to disillusionment. And, momentarily, Anne felt sad for Emma's future, for a young girl – so far as she could tell – without the bedrock of a belief in God.

Thursday

*T*he next morning there were piles of black bin liners full of old clothing outside the Winnebago. As Dave put them inside the mobile home to take round later to the local church, he remarked, 'It would have been better if they'd left money.'

'That's a little ungracious of you, Dave.'

He eyed Anne thoughtfully for a moment or two, then shrugged. 'Maybe. But this walk's supposed to be raising money, isn't it, not collecting old clothing? Money buys Africans food, wells, medicine – lots of stuff – but clothing's not going to help anyone.'

'It will mean a lot to a homeless person.'

'My point exactly: only to someone in this country.' And he abruptly turned away as if intent on cutting the conversation short.

Despite Adrian also being exasperated with people leaving their old rags outside the Winnebago, he was reluctant to take sides with Dave. He felt his assistant never missed an opportunity to subtly undermine the aims of the walk, probably under the misapprehension that James would want him to do that. Also, it was unfair taking his frustration out on the nurse.

Although he himself felt impatient with Anne at times, with her slowness and what he perceived as her old-fashioned ways, he could see her many merits also. He admired the unobtrusive way she went about her business, without any fuss, without seeking anyone's attention. It wasn't how he worked, but he understood there was a place for such an approach. Personally, he'd never had any patience with the sorry-thank-you-excuse-me meekness of the British, their let's-muddle-through incompetence and the complacency with which they accepted mediocrity and the status quo. Although he wasn't inclined to pick up the dumped clothes, mutter a polite thank you and pass them on to the local church, nor did he lean towards the complaining negativity of Dave. He preferred to bang heads together, shout at people until they woke up, not just to make things happen, but to make them happen now. He was impatient in his desire for achievement and for progress.

That morning, after Mujtabaa had eaten his bowl of porridge and taken his vitamins and minerals, Adrian, Anne, Emma and Dave all sat down together for breakfast. They had toast and tea. That morning no mention was made of bacon and eggs, so Anne allowed Mujtabaa to stay inside the mobile home. The morning newspapers were spread across the table and they read them while they ate, as well as watched the various TV stations. Every newspaper, both tabloids and broadsheets, carried the story of the woman with the white cloth wiping Mujtabaa's face. It had knocked Thatcher and Mitterrand's go-ahead for the building of the Channel Tunnel off most of the front pages. Although none of the TV stations had been in the shopping mall at the time, they all mentioned the incident on their news programmes. The photographs on the front page of the *Sun* and the *Daily Mail* were headlined, 'HANKY PANKY IN KEW' and 'MODERN ST VERONICA'.

'This is it!' shouted an elated Adrian, thumping the table and even making Mujtabaa look up. 'We have lift-off. This is where the story gets big. And I mean *big*.'

The self-styled head of public relations at Africa Assist knew enough about the charity business to appreciate that it was all about reaching people – touching them. And that's exactly what they'd now achieved. Mujtabaa had reached out and touched the people of London; they had taken him to their hearts. And, as Adrian never tired of pointing out to anyone who would listen, the reason they'd done that was because the young man was there, in London, amongst the very people who could help him. It was like seeing a picture of a starving child in a magazine, then multiplying that effect a hundredfold, even a thousand or a millionfold, by actually depositing that same child in everyone's front room. For the first time (without confessing as much to the others), Adrian felt truly confident.

Emma giggled. 'Did you see what she said to him?'

'What was that, darling?' Adrian asked, still scanning the inside pages of one of the papers.

'"God bless you, son, for showing us the way." That's kind of weird, isn't it?'

'She's a religious nut, so it's not really weird,' he said, throwing one newspaper aside and picking up another. 'Although it's possible the paper just made it up.'

Anne said, 'I'm sure the lady meant well.' It was said very quietly.

Adrian ignored her comment, saying to Emma: 'We knew they'd appear some time. It was to be expected.'

Emma didn't reply. She was waiting for her father to say something to Anne, to acknowledge what she'd just said. He could sometimes cut people dead in that way, as if they didn't exist, and she hated it when he did it. But instead, Dave spoke: 'Who's that, Adrian? Who would appear?'

'The freaks.' Her father stirred some sugar into his second cup of tea. 'I'm saying we knew the freaks would appear eventually. They always do. But it won't harm the cause; it's more likely to help us.'

'Why's this woman a freak, Dad? That's not very nice.'

'What else is she? She's certainly an attention seeker, probably desperate for her 15 minutes of fame.'

'Maybe she was just being kind. Isn't that possible – that she was just being kind to Moosh? You're so cynical at times, Dad.'

Turning to his daughter, 'You're quite right, darling. I'm sure that woman's heart was in the right place. I apologize.'

'You can't see any good in people, ever.' Her face was flushed and she was blinking indignantly.

'I'm sure her heart's in the right place. It was uncharitable of me. And, anyway, I don't know why I'm complaining. As I always say, all publicity's good publicity.'

Mujtabaa was sitting by himself across the aisle. Unnoticed by the others, he had picked up the TV remote control and, as if worried someone would stop him, was surreptitiously flicking from channel to channel. His forehead was creased with concentration.

Emma whispered, 'Look, Dad. I showed him how to do that yesterday.'

Despite the fact that everyone was now watching him, the Ethiopian remained unaware of the attention. Emma leant towards him and pointed out one of the many photographs of him in the papers. He glanced at it without interest.

'I don't think he recognizes himself. Is that possible, Anne?'

'I'm not sure that nomads have mirrors. I've heard stories of them being shown photographs of people who are standing right next to them and they don't recognize the likeness. It's as if they're unable to make the connection.'

'So he may never have seen his face before.' She held the photograph up before Mujtabaa again. 'Moosh,' she said, pointing. 'There's Moosh.' But he turned away from her and went back to pushing the buttons on the remote control.

Adrian reached across the table and showed *The Guardian* to his daughter. 'Talking of photographs, here's a good one of you. One for the album, I think.'

She peered across the table. 'Yuk! Dad, put it away, I look awful.'

Anne smiled.

After crossing Hammersmith Bridge, the area became noticeably more affluent. The houses opposite the grounds of St Paul's private school were detached and double-fronted, with mature trees in the front gardens and large driveways. Expensive cars were parked on the gravel. Adrian told the volunteers to knock on every door. 'There's money in this street,' he said, 'and I want all of it.'

But the people in this neighbourhood turned out to be less willing to part with their money than the people in some of the poorer districts they'd passed through. The women who opened the front doors would say, 'Stay here a moment,' before disappearing into the back of the house. They'd return after a sometimes lengthy period with a one-pound coin, hand it to the collector as if satisfied with their generosity, and close the door with an air of finality. Others closed their doors as soon as they realized it was someone asking for a donation. 'No thank you, we have our own charities.' In the whole street, only two people bothered to step outside their front gates in order to see Mujtabaa.

'We should have kept to the working-class suburbs, Dave.'

'It'll get better. They can't all be as tight-arsed as this lot.'

'At least it gives the TV crews a bit more space.'

There were now media people with them for all of the day, posing shots and shouting instructions to Mujtabaa to do this or do that. He paid no attention to them, and probably had no idea who they were or what they wanted of him. This made Emma giggle. She whispered to him: 'Good for you, Moosh. That's it, ignore them all.' And he'd grin at her, even though he didn't understand what she was saying either.

As she walked along, closely shadowing the young Ethiopian, she went over in her mind what he'd said to Anne about the people of London.

'He finds us odd,' said the nurse. 'He thinks we're like strangers who never talk to each other. He says that when we do talk, we're like camels: we bark. And we rarely look at each other because we're so busy rushing through this world that we're not interested in what we see around us. He watches us in the street, very close together, and he thinks we're far apart, as if we're all living in our own little world, and always in a hurry to go somewhere else. We keep space around us, and guard it carefully. We don't touch one another when we talk, or even hold hands. All in all, I think he finds us rather strange – and not very happy. He says we look like we're all busy arranging our own funerals.'

She went on to tell Emma that, according to Mujtabaa, there was always laughter and chatter in the marketplace at home, even when people were hungry. He told her that standing in the sunshine, drinking cold water from the well, and talking to friends and family were the best things in the world. 'What's the point in being sad?' he asked her. 'Being sad makes you unhappy, but being happy makes you happy.'

'It's not good that he sees us like that. Do you think he's right, Anne?'

She didn't answer. 'He says the remedy is for all of us to go with him to his well.'

'I'd love that! But why, what would we do there?'

'Nothing, nothing at all. But after a while of doing nothing, he says we'd start to talk – about friends, or the price of camels or ghee, anything at all – and after another little while we'd start to laugh.'

'I'm sure he's absolutely right.'

'"White ghosts don't laugh enough," he told me, and he thinks that's because we're unhappy, but he doesn't understand why. He says we all look well fed, so it can't be food we need. And he's seen the huts we live in, so we obviously don't have to walk long distances to find shelter. He thinks we have everything we need, so why aren't we happy?'

Anne said that Mujtabaa had been shocked by one particular incident. He saw two small children laughing as they ran in and out amongst the legs of adults, and their mother had caught them both and hit them over the head, shouting at them as if they were doing something wrong. No one else seemed to notice this, he said, and those who did behaved as if it were perfectly natural.

'Do you think he's unhappy, Anne? It would be horrible if he's not happy.'

'It would be asking too much of anyone in his situation to be happy. He's obviously overwhelmed by all that's going on around him. He described his head as always being fuzzy, that's how he put it to me, like he's spent the night chewing *qat*.'

'What's *qat*?'

'It's a shrub. They use it as a stimulant, like a drug. I think he feels that way because he's weighed down by the vastness of the city. It's like the vastness of the desert, but it isn't uplifting like the desert. It's the walls that make a difference – even I notice those. It's like there's no room for emptiness in London.'

Halfway along Castelnau Road, Mujtabaa reached out and took Emma's hand. She blushed scarlet, and the fact there was a

149

camera crew filming them at the time made the whole thing even more embarrassing.

Anne smiled. 'It's their way, Emma,' she said. 'It's quite normal for men and women to go round hand in hand, even for two men or two women to hold hands. It's a sign of friendship. You should be flattered.'

'It's cool,' she said, and tried to look as if she was relaxed about it, but they were an incongruous pair. Walking side by side and holding hands only emphasized their differences: one six foot three, the other a little over five feet; one stick thin, the other almost chubby; one black as ebony, the other as white as a pink rose. It was a convergence of opposites, of two very different worlds.

A little further on, just before Barnes Common, the walkers were confronted by a group of demonstrators. There were about 20 people on either side of the street. Adrian spoke to Anne: 'I'm guessing the lot on the right are the dolphin- and tree-loving mob. Must be taking time out from their anti-fox-hunting demonstrations, or anti-G7 demonstrations, or however it is they spend their days.'

'You're being uncharitable, Adrian.'

He saw this small congregation of middle-class righteousness as posing little threat, as quite harmless in fact, like the placards they were waving: ANGER NOT HUNGER, END THE EXPLOITATION OF ETHIOPIA, and FREE MUJTABAA, STOP THE WALK. It was the group on the other side of the road that he found more surprising, and potentially more troublesome. It was solely made up of Africans, and they stood in silence, as if too shy to speak up in front of their more vociferous neighbours. They were holding up a few amateurish signs, hand-written on cardboard or, in one case, on what appeared to be an old sheet.

Some of those Adrian had called the dolphin- and tree-loving crowd blocked their path. 'Free Mujtabaa!' they shouted over and over again. Adrian stopped a few yards in front of them. He stood, legs apart, leaning slightly back, hands on hips, as if refreshing himself beneath the shower of shouted slogans. Anne held back, hesitant, looking like she would rather not be involved. Emma and Mujtabaa, still holding hands, stopped a couple of yards behind them.

'May I point out,' Adrian said pleasantly, holding up his hands, standing up straighter, ready to do battle, 'May I point out something that seems to have escaped your attention: Mujtabaa is already free.'

'No, he isn't,' one of the demonstrators – a lanky individual, sharp and angular, with curly hair to his shoulders – shouted back. 'He isn't free to return home. He's being exploited. You're exploiters.' The man was given to making short, abrupt movements as if he were barely able to contain his anger and it was in danger of erupting at any moment.

Adrian held up his hands against a further verbal barrage. 'He is not being exploited. Mujtabaa is free to return home at any time he wishes – and he will do so with the blessing of Africa Assist.'

'Bullshit!'

'If you don't believe me, ask him. Please ask him.'

The lanky fellow ignored the suggestion, instead taking a step towards Adrian. He lowered his voice, speaking urgently, but in a more private and persuasive manner. 'Man, you've got to stop this. This walk can't be allowed to continue.' He started to prod Adrian on the chest, his finger both raising the volume and emphasizing each word, his face almost touching Adrian's. 'You're parading this man through London like he's some kind of freak. Charity is about caring for people, treating them with dignity and love. But you're using Mujtabaa. The way you're treating him is immoral. It's unethical.'

Adrian brushed his hand aside, but continued to smile pleasantly. It was an act. He was breathing deeply, forcing himself to remain calm, not to be riled by these people. Yet he knew that his smile would further inflame the demonstrator in front of him – and it did. The demonstrator's voice again increased in volume as his finger relinquished the task of tapping out the message on Adrian's chest and replaced it with a couple of half-hearted jabs. 'It's disgusting, man! You're murderers!'

A journalist thrust a microphone in their direction, inveigling his way between them like a referee in a boxing match.

A middle-aged lady with straight grey hair and a colourful, hand-knitted cardigan over a black shirt and slacks put a restraining hand on the lanky fellow's arm. 'Rufus, calm down.' He threw her off, and she stepped back, wounded by her sudden dismissal, puffing out her already ample chest (which Adrian took to be full of righteous indignation). She glanced at her comrades for support and they renewed their chanting with added ferocity. 'Free Mujtabaa, free Mujtabaa, free Mujtabaa!' Their voices seemed to incite the lanky fellow to increase his efforts. 'You're stopping this walk right here, right now,' he shouted in Adrian's face.

Shaking his head: 'I don't think so.'

'We won't allow you to go any further.' And, quite suddenly, quite unexpectedly, he threw a punch that glanced off the PR consultant's cheek. Adrian was stocky, and the lanky fellow much slighter than him, so it caught both men by surprise when he stumbled, possibly even tripped, and fell backwards onto the road. He was shocked more than anything else to find himself suddenly sitting on the tarmac, holding his hand up to his face. He was still sufficiently aware of what was going on, however, to see a man holding a camera leap out of a Thames Television estate car that had drawn up immediately behind the demonstrators, and start filming the confrontation – the vanquished in the roadway and the victor standing over him. The latter looked more uncomfortable than victorious.

Adrian had the presence of mind to stay where he was, but also to build on his performance – for that is what it quickly became. He leant back on one elbow as if struggling to recover from some conscience-stealing Henry Cooper left hook, keeping his hand to his cheek. The demonstrators had stopped chanting. Everyone was frozen. Emma stood by Mujtabaa, one hand clutching his arm, the other to her mouth. Anne quickly crossed the road from where she'd been talking to the Africans. 'Are you all right, Adrian?'

'I'm fine,' he said in a low voice, so only she could hear him. He held out his hand and she helped him struggle off the tarmacked canvas. His assailant had retreated, somewhat shamefaced, to stand behind the middle-aged woman. Slowly, at first a little tentatively, the group took up their chant again. 'Free Mujtabaa, free Mujtabaa…' but the presence of the camera quickly encouraged the demonstrators to redouble their efforts.

Adrian was content to allow the chanting to proceed uninterrupted while he recovered his breath, as well as his dignity. He had to remain cool and keep his wits about him. He knew that impressions, surface emotions, were all-important in his world. You especially didn't allow yourself to show scorn for your customers.

Adrian held up his hands. It was a grand gesture, like that of a general about to address his troops. 'May I just say…' He was ignored. 'May I just say…' The chanting became louder. He shouted louder still: 'Whatever happened to freedom of speech?'

Faced by such a blatantly middle-class appeal to human rights, the predominantly middle-class demonstrators lapsed into a sulky silence. Everyone was aware of the camera. In less than a minute it had transformed them all into actors.

'May I point out to you,' he said pleasantly, standing up straighter, projecting his voice, enunciating his words for the benefit of his unseen audience of millions – 'May I just say, Mujtabaa came to this country of his own free will. He is doing this walk of his own free will. And he is free to return home to Ethiopia at any time he wishes.' He paused, his eyes roaming over the earnest, well-intentioned faces before him. 'He's doing this walk because he wants to help his people. Now, if you'll excuse us, we'll proceed. We shall continue our task of raising money for the victims of the famine in Ethiopia.'

At that moment, another demonstrator, a young man with decidedly bookish looks, and long, greasy hair tied back in a ponytail, stepped forward from amongst his friends, and approached Mujtabaa. Emma hung on to Moosh's hand, determined to offer him moral support. 'Hi,' the demonstrator said. He coughed, in an attempt to clear his throat. The Ethiopian, towering over the protester, watched impassively from hollowed eyes, his face a bony blank. He was leaning slightly on his staff, like Death listening to the supplications of someone who wished to stay in the world for a little while longer.

No one moved, except for the camera operator, who shuffled sideways for a better angle. Everyone waited. Emma looked at Mujtabaa. His right hand was resting on the hilt of his *jile*, and it flashed through her mind that he could cut off this young man's balls if he became too troublesome. She blushed at the thought, and had to stop herself smiling.

'He doesn't speak English,' she said.

Adrian called out. 'If you have a question for Mujtabaa, you'll have to put it in Ethiopian – Afar to be specific.'

The young man turned, his eyes watering, his mouth opening and closing like a fish. The camera continued recording. 'I don't speak Ethiopian.' He sounded like he was blaming Adrian personally for his lack of education.

Adrian looked at a loss, as if he'd like to help out, but couldn't. 'Do none of you speak *any* of the 80-odd languages they speak in Ethiopia?' There was an element of surprise in his voice as he addressed the group of demonstrators. 'One of you, surely, must speak one of their languages?' Then added for good measure, 'If you're so interested in his cause.'

The young man with the ponytail retreated hesitatingly towards his friends, defeated. The two parties gazed at each other in silence for a few seconds. It was like the aftermath of an inconclusive confrontation, with the combatants not knowing what to do next. Finally, Adrian said, 'Let's go,' and the walkers continued on their way, their departure filmed by Thames Television. A few yards further up the street, Adrian turned round to see what was happening. Some of the demonstrators were reaching into their pockets and giving money to his collectors, while others were talking to the media. He laughed. He turned to Anne: 'What were those Africans there for? They didn't say too much.'

'They were telling me they're not happy to see one of their own paraded through the streets like this. They see it as abuse. They said it was as bad as child abuse.'

Adrian raised his eyebrows. 'Really?'

'You're surprised?'

'I am.'

'They think you should help him now; give him money and send him home.'

'Where are they from?'

'All over. They're Muslims, rather than Africans, or that's the impression I got.'

'Again!' Adrian looked thoughtful, more concerned by the silent demonstrators than by the white, middle-class ones. 'They're a minority though, surely, and scarcely a vocal one? Their influence would be minimal, I imagine.' He picked up his pace, as if relieved of some worry. 'We can probably ignore them.'

'I got the impression, Adrian, that they simply want to be consulted. It's being excluded that they're objecting to. Maybe you could talk to them, and make them feel a part of this?'

He turned towards her, surprised. 'I'm sorry, Anne, I forget your sensitivities. I'll think about it, I promise.'

'Thank you.'

It struck him then, as they continued along the street, that Anne lived in a different world, and that she'd have little if any comprehension of the life he had inhabited for the best part of his career. She was a true innocent abroad. He looked at her walking – no, *marching* – beside him, and was suddenly aware that she was as much a stranger in this country as Mujtabaa. She no longer belonged among her own people. He wondered if she knew anything at all about the times they were living in, if she'd heard about Prince Andrew marrying Sarah Ferguson, the bombing of Libya by US forces, Terry Waite being taken hostage, or the surging stock market. Had she heard about the booming Japanese economy, the Challenger disaster, or about the war Russia was fighting in Afghanistan? He doubted that she knew of any of these events and, if she did, that she would even consider any of them to be important. Momentarily, he wondered if he felt scorn for such ignorance, or envy. He himself couldn't imagine not knowing about what was going on in the world, didn't think he could exist without devouring several newspapers every morning and watching the television news every evening. He lived by the media. Having a finger on the pulse anchored him in some way to life, to what he regarded as civilization.

'Are you happy to have left public relations temporarily for the charity business, Adrian?'

He was startled by the sudden question. He thought for a moment. 'Well, I'm not sure that I have left the public-relations field; I'm trying to make Africa Assist better known right now. This walk is a public-relations exercise, Anne. And, yes, it's also a wonderful opportunity to do something absolutely altruistic for a change – I'm enjoying that.'

He realized the nurse was one of those rare creatures in the charity business; someone who'd likely started out young and idealistic, yet had managed to remain idealistic. Most people changed, so far as he could tell, becoming cynical, disillusioned or bitter, either wondering what was in it for them or wondering how it might replace something that was lacking in themselves. Since working for Africa Assist, Adrian had puzzled over which group did the most harm – the bleeding hearts or those who tried to bleed the system dry. So far as he could see, Anne was like neither.

She was looking at him quizzically, half smiling. 'I myself think it comes naturally to you to try to help people.'

He laughed. 'I'm not so sure many people would agree with you there, Anne. I'm definitely no saint.'

''I think you're being too modest.'

'Well, thank you.' He was surprised to find himself genuinely moved by her comment. 'But I'd be lying if I didn't admit that this is also the opportunity to orchestrate a big media event, the chance to manipulate people's expectations and persuade them to part with their money.' He was earnest, as well as enthusiastic. 'And that's what I'm good at. If I hadn't come up with the idea of the walk when I was with you in Korem, I know I would have come up with something else – another big idea. I've always succeeded in the past, so why not now?'

'Have you always had such faith in your abilities?'

'To be honest, yes.'

156

'But this time it is for a worthy cause.'

'Exactly.' He scrutinized her. 'So please try not to look at me as the devil incarnate.' He was close to pleading.

'I would never do that, and never have.' She turned away, embarrassed, but with a faint smile on her lips.

Adrian understood the negative views about the charity business. People advocated that aid should be replaced by trade, that an open economy – or capitalism – was more likely to benefit an undeveloped country than any amount of foreign aid. He himself, unusually for him, believed in a middle way, a nebulous, scarcely thought-through path. Charity certainly had its faults, and significant ones. It had only taken the year his company had worked with Africa Assist to discover how nasty the charity business really was, in which respect the agencies were little different from the commercial clients he'd dealt with for most of his life. He'd quickly ascertained that the government agencies around the world were bungling, incompetent bureaucracies that ran their businesses as if their pockets were bottomless. They were both wasteful and inefficient, and the whole system cried out for reform. He'd heard all the horror stories about Arctic tents being airlifted to the tropics, fleets of trucks arriving at one disaster area without spark plugs, and purgatives and digestion remedies being flown into famine areas instead of maize and milk powder. He also knew all about the company kickbacks, the stolen food, the corruption, and the way a beneficiary country's elite almost always grew fat on the back of Western aid.

The voluntary agencies were only a little better. In the main they were staffed by individuals who had their own private reasons (usually neurotic) for dedicating their lives to other people. And in many instances, especially amongst those who worked overseas, they were forced to provide assistance on a shoestring. Although these non-governmental organizations willingly devoted their lives to helping the less fortunate, the scope of their influence was as individualistic and limited as they themselves were, and no matter how well-intentioned they were, without the necessary funds, they were amateurs who were often helpless to bring about any meaningful change.

Adrian's sympathies lay with neither group; not with the Anne Chaffeys of this world, and not with the other camp either. His sympathies possibly lay in the middle, neither one thing nor the other. Although he was determined to raise as much money as possible for the Ethiopian people and, more importantly, to make sure it reached those people instead of lining the pockets of administrators, he also understood that he was no bleeding heart. He saw himself as an excellent businessman, albeit a businessman with a conscience – most of the time – a pragmatist rather than an idealist.

He looked at Anne walking by his side and was surprised to feel this sudden, brief urge to protect her – from what, he had no idea, unless it was from life. He suspected she didn't need any help from him, that she was very much her own woman, yet that didn't stop him from wanting to save her. He could see her goodness. He could also see that, unlike most of the do-gooders in the business, she had no obvious personality defects. She wasn't suffering from any outrageous chip on the shoulder, or none that he could see.

He addressed the road ahead, not unlike a barrister putting a question to both a witness and to the court in general. 'Do you believe in God, Anne?'

It was her turn to be taken aback. 'Oh yes, Adrian, indeed I do.' Then, like many reserved people, quickly deflecting the question back onto the questioner: 'And how about you?'

'Definitely not.'

'That's a very confident answer, if I may say so. And why would that be?'

'I suppose the easy answer would be to say that an all-loving God wouldn't allow this suffering–'

She frowned. 'You mean...?'

'Yes. Mujtabaa, Ethiopia, almost anywhere you care to look in the world. But I'm aware I'm ignoring the complexities of the issue, also the fact that you'll say we have free will. It's more likely that I simply don't believe; I don't have faith. To be honest, I'm envious of people like you, those who do. It must be comforting.' He smiled at her. 'But you can't just conjure faith up out of nothing.'

She thought for a moment, taking his comments, as she always did, seriously. 'People with faith often have to work hard to hold onto it, you know.'

He stared at her, puzzled, the hint of a smile around his mouth, as if faintly amused by such a possibility. 'I don't wish to pry, but you don't strike me as someone who has doubts.'

She appeared to be flustered by this unexpected attention on what, to her, must be an intimate matter, and she quickened her pace, perhaps to escape further questioning.

There was little traffic on Barnes Common and, when cars did appear, the road was too narrow for them to be able to stop. Dave followed close behind the walkers in the mobile home. He shouted out of the window to Adrian that it didn't matter about there being no one around, it gave Mujtabaa a nice rest. And that was true. They could have been a group of friends taking a walk in the countryside. The sun was shining, the birds were singing and the crowds and traffic of London were seemingly many miles away. It struck Adrian at that moment that perhaps Dave was becoming a little less dogged in his devotion to Balcombe; maybe he was even beginning to see the merits of what they were doing.

When they reached Upper Richmond Road, the traffic situation became, in a perverse way, worse. Now there were many cars passing by but, with red lines down both sides of the road, it was impossible for them to stop. Fortunately, there were many pedestrians around, and they were extremely generous.

A bus, crawling past in nose-to-tail traffic, drew alongside the walkers, its passengers staring out from its dim interior. The conductress shouted from the platform, 'Want a lift, sweetheart?' and gave Mujtabaa the thumbs up and a big grin. 'You're going a treat, young man. Keep it up. We're all behind you.'

Putney High Street was jammed with shoppers and the Africa Assist group made even slower progress, often coming to a complete halt. No one was concerned. Volunteers worked both pavements, also diving amongst the almost stationary cars, as well as into every shop and restaurant. Many drivers sounded their horns in support. For the first time on the walk, police arrived to try to keep the traffic moving, and to attempt to break up the crowds blocking the pavements. But they were friendly and helpful, many putting money into the collecting tins themselves.

As usual, journalists tried to speak to Adrian, Anne or Emma (they'd quickly learnt it was a waste of their time to try to get anything out of Mujtabaa, so they simply photographed him), even though Adrian had let it be known he would only give interviews in the morning, before they set off, or in the evening, after they'd stopped walking. Sometimes he would now give an impromptu debrief in the middle of the day when they stopped for lunch. Both Anne and Emma had told Adrian that they didn't wish to speak to reporters, and he respected their decision. He let it be known they were off-limits, so it annoyed him now that they were being pestered.

On Putney Bridge, they were forced to stop so that Mujtabaa could again look down into the river. It was another photo opportunity, so Adrian didn't object. They pointed out the train bridge a hundred yards away, and the Ethiopian stared, wide-eyed, as a train rumbled across it. Anne explained to him, as best she could, what it was, but, as usual, he said nothing.

'You know what, Anne, I think Mujtabaa is looking healthier. Have you noticed that?'

'I think so too, Adrian. It's possible the supplements we're giving him are beginning to have an effect.'

'I hope so.'

They sat a short distance from the Winnebago, on an old stone bench in the shelter of a large oak tree. The All Saints' sacristy was at their backs. Over to their left, behind some trees, was Fulham Palace. Side by side in a shadowy bower, they stared solemnly at the sunlight dappled on lovingly tended lawn and gravelled drive. They watched a sparrow, in a nearby flowerbed, splash dust across its back, as if enjoying a refreshing evening dip. A few yards away, on the other side of the closed, wrought-iron gates, the traffic hummed on Putney Bridge. How green it all looked, luxuriant and peaceful, and Emma strained every fibre of her being to try to see it through the eyes of her immobile companion. He had possibly never sheltered under a tree in his entire life, certainly not an oak tree that was 200 or 300 years old; and never in his wildest dreams would he have imagined so much greenery. Even the sparrow must appear as strange to him, surely, as, say, a vulture would to her?

She turned and studied him. He was staring to the front, his eyes, dark and heavy, giving nothing away. He looked incongruous – not just out of place in a churchyard in central London, but as if he were unused to sitting. One hand was resting on his lap, the other held his staff. To Emma, he only ever looked what she would have described as 'right' when he was standing, legs crossed near the ankles, his left hand resting on top of his staff and placed under his right armpit, his right arm bent with the palm of his hand placed against his forehead as he stared into the distance. He looked out of place now, she told herself, because he was hemmed in by civilization. His normal state was to be free. He shouldn't be like her – it would be wrong for him. Her life was a prison. Every day she was at the beck and call of other people, of forces beyond her control. They ran her life, controlled every minute of her day. They told her when to go to bed and when to get up. They said this was good for her to eat and that was bad. They advised her on what to read if she was to broaden her mind and what to ignore because it was rubbish. They chose the school she went to and the uniform she wore. They even chose the subjects she had to study to get into university. (They'd already decided she was to go to university, too.) They insisted she pursue certain career paths because they'd prove more lucrative. They expected her to marry, to settle down and to have two point three children. These people had already mapped out her whole life for her. She hated that, having her whole life corralled, her soul imprisoned, her mind shackled. And why should Moosh end up like that? Why should he have his life run by strangers? Why couldn't he return to Ethiopia and be with his people, wild and free? That was the life he should be

161

living; crossing immense tracts of desert beneath the burning sun, living by his wits, fighting his enemies, answering to no one. And, just briefly, she pictured herself at his side, his companion, ally and lover, and it made her heart leap.

She turned to him, searching for his face beneath the mass of tousled hair. 'I wish you could understand me sometimes, Moosh. It's like talking to a deaf person, or talking to myself. I'm always doing that, you know – talking to myself. They say it's a sign of madness, but I think it's a way of stopping yourself going mad.'

She lowered her head, but carried straight on. 'I wish you'd kiss me. Do you understand what I'm saying to you? Surely you do; surely you can feel what I feel.' She whispered these words. She wanted him to turn and kiss her, wanted it more than anything else in the world. He wouldn't be like Robert, with his tongue always trying to force itself into her mouth – disgusting! – and his hands all over her body, and having to fight him off and try to keep breathing. It wouldn't be like that with Moosh. It would be a pure kiss, a mingling of souls, a union of two people who understood, loved and respected each other. And she'd feel faint in his arms, be enveloped by his strength and never ever want to be with anyone else.

Safia suddenly invaded her thoughts, but was brutally dismissed. She isn't here, she's probably dead. And if she isn't, she'd understand.

Emma looked up, willing him to turn his head, willing him to take her in his arms and kiss her. She was frowning with the effort. Turn... Turn... Turn... And then he did. She closed her eyes. She waited, her mouth slightly open, for the caress of his lips on hers. She was aware of the hammering of her heart. Kiss me, she thought. Go on, Moosh, kiss me... She thought she was going to faint.

A minute later she opened her eyes. He was sitting straight-backed beside her, looking across the lawn towards the gates. She took a deep breath and sighed. What was it with boys? The ones you liked never did anything, and the ones you wouldn't give the time of day to, they were all over you like a rash.

She could hear Anne talking to the parish priest in the vestry, but they were too far away to hear what was being said. Her father had gone off to be interviewed by David 'Hello, good evening and welcome' Frost. Emma had begged to go with him, desperate to meet the great man, but her father had insisted she stay with Anne and help look after Mujtabaa. She had lost it. She'd stormed out of the Winnebago, and refused to answer when he shouted goodbye. After the meeting with Frost, he was to see James Balcombe and a group of African Muslims. The idea was to get them to back the walk – or at least to drop their objections to it – and to include them in the organizational details over the next two or three days. That meeting didn't interest her at all.

Dave had gone to the pub. 'If you were a bit older, Emma, you could have come with me – with your Dad's permission, of course.' She was grateful that she wasn't a bit older, but forced herself to smile, for politeness' sake. She was beginning to think him creepy.

She looked at Mujtabaa. He was so serene. 'Cool,' she said out loud. 'You're really cool.' He smiled at her, and again she thought of the hurried, furtive fumblings of Robert on their way back from school, his greedy, grasping crudity as he fought to get a hand beneath her bra or into her pants. Mujtabaa wouldn't be like that. He would know how to love a woman. Loving would come naturally to him, because he was a real man... For a moment she fantasized, briefly allowing her imagination to paint a picture of two naked bodies, one black, the other white, locked together in some kind of spiritual, pure union, on a sand dune beneath the setting sun... Just as quickly, she dismissed the picture. She was not interested in sex, not like that. She wanted love.

Then he stood up and walked away from her, across the lawn. She watched him. 'What's up?' He stopped when he was at the gates. He stared through the bars for a moment, then pushed against them. She stood up. 'What are you doing, Moosh?' He ignored her, and lifted the latch. As the gates swung open, he turned briefly and grinned at her over his shoulder, before walking out onto the road. She ran after him. 'I'm not sure it's a

163

good idea wandering off like this, you know.' But she was more excited than worried, and didn't make any attempt to stop him.

They turned right onto the bridge. The traffic was heavy in both directions; the tail end of the rush hour. One or two cars already had their headlights on. The mobile home was now out of sight. The All Saints' church clock struck eight, but she could barely hear it over the sound of the traffic.

She was panting after her exertions. She took his hand briefly, perhaps a subconscious attempt to hold him back or not to lose him. 'Do you want to go back across the bridge, Moosh? Is that where you want to go?'

Halfway across, she turned to her friend and pulled his *shämma* tighter around him, trying to cover his body and make him less conspicuous, but she couldn't hide the amulets around his neck. She looked down at his dusty legs and dirty, sandalled feet and decided there was nothing she could do about those. 'We'll just go for a short walk together, just you and me.'

He was staring over the parapet at a barge passing beneath them, heading upstream, red light blinking astern. 'But you have to try and blend in with everyone else, Moosh.' He frowned, and she shook her head: 'Fat chance.' And she grinned. He grinned, too, a portcullis of brilliant white teeth shining at her out of the dusk. 'I almost think you understand me.' She felt so free.

And that was when she had her idea. On the far side of the bridge, at the lights, they crossed Lower Richmond Road into Putney High Street. 'Can you walk faster? We have to get back before they notice we're missing.' But his pace didn't change. They had spent days trying to make him walk more slowly, and now he didn't know any different.

It was a Thursday night, and there were many people around. Cars were full of couples out for the evening, and the pavements were crowded. Emma wondered if she and Mujtabaa would be taken for a couple going out together. She glanced at him and doubted it. They were an incongruous pair: the schoolgirl in jeans and T-shirt, and the ebony-black Ethiopian dressed in a *shämma*, carrying a walking staff. His dagger, fortunately, had been left behind in the Winnebago. Two couples walked towards them, staring, but Emma avoided eye contact. She heard one woman say to her friend: 'Wasn't that the African, the one doing the walk?' She hurried on, not looking back, suddenly aware of the inconvenience of being a celebrity.

They stopped at a pedestrian crossing, and she took his hand again, like a small adult accompanying a very tall child. He pointed to the green man when it flashed up, and said something. She smiled and nodded, 'Yes, we can cross now.' On the other side of the road, she stopped. She looked at him, but his face was once again its usual expressionless self. She nudged him in the ribs and pointed. He looked in the direction she was pointing, and then he nodded slightly, like he had an inkling of what the sign meant.

'McDonald's. That's where you want to go, isn't it?'

They walked towards the red and yellow logo. When they reached the door, she wanted to tell him to keep his head down, but didn't know how to. The thing was to be as quick as possible and hope no one noticed them. She went through the doors behind a group of kids about her own age. She pulled Mujtabaa behind her and, as soon as they were inside, pulled and pushed him away from the food counter towards the tables at the back of the restaurant. Unfortunately, he behaved like a tourist who has just arrived in central London for the first time, staring around him, open-mouthed like he'd never seen anything remotely as interesting before in his entire life. She tried to hurry him towards a quiet section, near the door to the toilets. One or two people looked up as they passed, but most ignored them. She pushed him into a seat, his back to the bulk of the restaurant, and sat next to him. She glanced apprehensively across at him. No one was looking, apart from a young boy of six or seven who was pointing at them and trying to get his mother to look. But she was intent on shutting him up. 'Don't point, Derek, it's rude to point. I don't care who it is, you don't point.' Eventually the young boy gave up and turned back to his table.

Emma stood up and indicated that Mujtabaa was not to move. He was barely looking at her, too intent on studying a Ronald McDonald cut-out, suspended from the ceiling, turning slowly, and promising a giant burger, chips and coke for just £1.99. He reminded her of a baby in its cot looking up at a mobile.

She walked away. After a few steps, she turned round to check what he was doing. He had twisted round in his seat and was watching her quizzically, not unlike a dog, unsure if it was allowed to follow its master or if it had to remain seated. She held up her hands to him to indicate that he shouldn't move.

When she reached the queues for food, she again glanced in his direction. He was engrossed in the mobile again. She reached the front of the queue and ordered two burgers, fries and cokes.

He leaned forward to look at the tray of food when she put it on the table, eyes almost popping out of his head. She couldn't stop grinning at him. It was like taking a toddler to McDonald's for the first time. 'I didn't get too much, Moosh. We have to be careful, you know, you won't be used to this kind of food.'

She gave him one of the burgers, some fries and a coke. 'I don't think a little will do you any harm, though. And you deserve it after all you've done. It'll build up your strength.' She couldn't stop talking. She was so happy, so pleased she could do something for him.

He was pushing the straw in his cup of coke with the tip of his index finger. 'That's a straw,' she said. '*Straw*. Look, it works like this.' She sipped some of her own coke through the straw. He stared at her, mesmerized. 'Go on, you try it.' She held up his coke, pushing the straw towards his mouth. He leant forward tentatively, putting his mouth over the tip of the straw. 'Go on, suck.'

He frowned at her, leaning forward over the cup, the straw protruding from his mouth. 'Suck!' She took a deep breath to show him how. Then he did suck. He leapt back in his seat as the bubbly liquid hit the back of his throat and went up his nose. His eyes watered. He blinked madly, wiping his nose with the back of his hand. 'You like it?' She was clutching his forearm. His answer was to lean forward and take another sip. He was very serious, very thoughtful. He prodded the ice with his straw.

'Hey, look.' She lifted a piece of ice out of the coke and placed it on the palm of her hand. She held out her hand to him and he watched the ice melting. She licked it with her tongue. She took another piece of ice out of her cup and, holding on to one of his hands, placed the ice on his palm. He stared at it wide-eyed. 'Lick it,' she said. 'Go on, lick it,' and she mimicked a licking motion on her own hand. Tentatively he touched the ice with the tip of his tongue. He said something.

'You're saying it's cold, right?'

Some youngsters at a nearby table were staring at them. She put Moosh's coke back on the table. 'You can do it yourself, but try some burger first.'

She picked her burger up and took a bite, just to show him. He picked up his burger in both hands and raised it to his mouth. His eyes were only just visible over the top of the burger. He took a tiny bite from the edge of the burger and chewed it thoughtfully, as if trying to work out how he felt about this new sensation. He nodded, and immediately took a bigger bite, then, having only chewed that two or three times, took another big bite, and another one. His cheeks bulged beneath his bulging eyes, and food was falling out of his mouth, but he still held his burger just an inch or two in front of his lips, as if he was scared it might run off and he wanted to make sure he could take another bite as soon as there was any possibility, any possibility at all, of squeezing some more into his mouth. Emma giggled. 'Moosh, Moosh, slow down. It's not going anywhere. Take it easy.' She pulled his hands away from his mouth.

At that moment one of the kids from the nearby table approached. Out of the corner of her eye, Emma could see his friends watching. He spoke to Emma even though he was staring at Mujtabaa. 'We was wondering if this is the bloke that's been on the telly, doing that walk. You know, the starving geezer.'

She looked as cold as she could. 'Maybe. What's it to you?'

'Only asked.'

Mujtabaa was still chewing away, like his jaws weren't used to having to work so hard. He didn't pay any attention to the boy.

'He sure behaves like he's starving.' The boy was fascinated. 'Unless his table manners are always this gross.'

On the spur of the moment Emma decided to trust him; he

was a pretty honest-looking kid. 'Look, don't tell anyone. I don't want people to recognize him.'

The kid nodded. 'Sure, that's cool.' He leant forward, lowering his voice. 'Can me and my friends join you?'

Emma thought quickly. Mujtabaa wouldn't stand out so much in a group, that was for sure. So she agreed. Three others, two girls and another young boy came over and sat with them, bringing their half-eaten meals with them. They sat in silence and stared at Mujtabaa.

'What's his name?'

'Mujtabaa.'

'That's it! I remember now.'

'Blimey, he certainly looks hungry.'

Mujtabaa stared at the kids, his cheeks still bulging with food. Now that he'd finished his own food, he was enjoying Emma's.

'He really is starving,' the other boy said. 'Here, he can have my fries. There's not much left, though.' He pushed a bag of fries across the table to Mujtabaa.

'Only if you eat them slowly, Moosh.'

'What did you call him?' It was one of the girls.

'Moosh. That's my nickname for him. It's short for Mujtabaa.'

They watched him attack his second burger with as much enthusiasm as his first. Emma pulled her tray away from him. His face fell. 'Slowly, Moosh, slowly! You'll only get it back if you eat slowly.' She tried to signal to him with her hands that he had to slow down, and all the kids chorused, 'Slowly, eat slowly.'

Mujtabaa looked puzzled. The tray of food was pushed back in front of him.

'Here, pal, you ain't got any ketchup on there.' One of the boys leant over and squeezed some ketchup all over Mujtabaa's fries. The kids laughed, chorusing, 'You got to have ketchup on your chips, that's the best part.' Mujtabaa stared at the red liquid, transfixed.

While he was eating, the kids spoke to Emma. 'Where's he from?'

'Ethiopia.'

'Yeah? That's in Africa somewhere, innit?'

'Yes.'

'How old is he?'

'No one's sure, but probably about 16.'

'Doesn't he know how old he is?'

'It's not important to his people how old you are. They don't care about age, not like we do.'

'That's cool, but how come you're looking after him?'

'Because it was my Dad who brought him to this country.'

'Is that your Dad, the bloke on the telly all the time?'

'Yes.' She grinned, proud of her father's fame. She looked at Mujtabaa. He was sitting back from the table now; only a little food was left in the containers. One of the girls said, 'He don't look so good now, your friend, does he?'

Emma frowned. Great beads of sweat stood out on his forehead and, if it was possible for a man the colour of ebony to look pale, then he looked pale. In fact, he looked green rather than pale, an awful greenish, smoky black. She held up his coke. 'Here, Moosh, have a drink. It'll cool you down.' But he pushed the drink aside with the back of his hand, and that small gesture alarmed Emma. 'He needs some fresh air,' she said. 'I should get him outside.' She looked around her helplessly. How was she to get him outside without attracting attention?

At that very moment, as she turned back to speak to Mujtabaa, he leant forward and threw up all over the table and the containers of food, splashing the clothes of two of the kids.

They leapt to their feet shouting, 'Yuk!' and 'Oh my God!' – unlike Mujtabaa and Emma who sat there in absolute silence, perfectly still, staring at the mass of vomit, stunned, as if someone had placed the meaning of life down on the table in front of them, and all it needed now was a little close examination.

Other people in the restaurant stood up and stared at the group in the corner. One or two edged closer for a better look, and the small boy who'd been pointing the Ethiopian out to his mother when they first entered the restaurant was again pointing at him, but now with added enthusiasm, his earlier interest now clearly vindicated. This time his mother made no attempt to stop him. The four kids who'd joined Emma and Mujtabaa at their table were now backing away, hands still half-raised in shock, as if unable to deal with this new turn of events.

Emma jumped to her feet. 'Sorry, sorry about that,' she said over and over again, trying to pull her friend to his feet, telling herself not to panic. She managed to get him to stand up, and dragged him towards the toilets. She hesitated momentarily between the men's toilet and the women's toilet, then decided men were less likely to make a fuss about a member of the opposite sex being in their toilets, and dragged him into their section. It was empty. She stood him at the sink, grabbed handfuls of paper towels and, soaking them under the tap, proceeded to wipe down the front of his *shämma*. Every few seconds she examined his face in the mirror, trying to gauge the likelihood of him throwing up again. She tried drying him with more paper towels. 'We have to get out of here, Moosh.' She dreaded going back through the restaurant, but knew they couldn't hide in the toilets all night. She wished she could discuss their options with Moosh.

As she moved towards the door, steeling herself to face the people outside, Mujtabaa spun away from her and crashed into one of the cubicles. He left the door open. He was groaning, and mumbling what sounded to Emma like some kind of prayer. She turned away. She was asking herself what she could do when she heard the unmistakable sound of a bowel evacuation. It sounded like water, like liquid. She groaned – and began to pray. Anne had told her how dangerous it would be for him if he ever had diarrhoea. The fear she felt overcame her embarrassment, and in sheer desperation she threw herself through the open toilet door. Thank God, she thought, he'd learnt enough in his few days in England to relieve himself in the bowl. He was slumped forward on the toilet seat, his head in his hands. His *sanafil*, the skirt-like cloth, lay crumpled at his feet. The stench was terrible. She flushed the toilet while he was still on it, and he never moved. She grabbed a handful of toilet paper and thrust it in his face, but was ignored. Trying to think what Anne would do in this situation, and battling her own instincts, she leant across his back and reached down to wipe him. She tried not to look, but couldn't help seeing the sharp edges of his hip bones. His spine stuck out like a ridge, running from beneath his *shämma* down to his coccyx. His buttocks were without any fatty tissue. She used half a roll of toilet paper, and again flushed. She pushed the door to behind her.

She crouched down in front of him, holding his arms. 'Moosh, we have to get you back to the mobile home. We have to get back to Anne. Do you understand?' She was frightened now, almost sobbing. She didn't want him to die, but that was all she could think of – him dying, and whether she had enough money to pay for a taxi back across Putney Bridge.

'Moosh, you have to come with me. We'll go back to Anne. To the lady in the straw hat, okay? She'll know what to do. Come on, Moosh, please!' But he didn't stir. Then in sheer panic: 'For God's sake, open your eyes! At least open your eyes for me. Can you hear me? Moosh! Please!'

Someone came into the toilet. Emma held her breath.

'Is there anyone there?'

She said nothing.

'It's the manager here. Can I be of assistance?'

She stood up and opened the door, thankful for an adult presence. But she was dismayed to find the manager wasn't much older than herself and looked just as frightened. He even had acne. He was staring over her shoulder, through the half-open toilet door, possibly thinking himself in the presence of a Hollywood film star, almost bowing before this unseen icon.

'My friend isn't well.' She vaguely indicated the toilet behind her.

'Would you like me to call an ambulance?'

Emma grabbed his arm. 'Oh no! No, please don't do that.'

'It's no trouble, honestly.'

'No, he's not that ill. He doesn't need an ambulance. But a taxi would be great.'

The automatic urinal cleansing system gushed noisily.

The two young people stared at the African. He was standing in the toilet doorway, holding on to the frame, bent almost double, the *sanafil* still around his feet. She stooped down to lift it back up beneath his *shämma*, half averting her eyes, horrified at the possibility she might glimpse *that* part of his body. She took his hand and placed it on the *sanafil*. 'Hold it, Moosh.' She glanced at him, but his eyes were quite dead, like those of a drugged person.

'He's the bloke doing the walk, isn't he? That's what they're saying in the front.'

She cursed the kids who'd joined them at their table. They must have told everyone. 'Yes,' she said, without turning round, 'but we don't want any publicity, thanks.' And she was aware of the irony of this statement. Now she wanted nothing more than to disappear with Moosh into the ground, vanish from sight, and be left alone.

'Oh,' said the manager, obviously at a loss as to what he should do next. He wanted to stay in the toilets as long as he could with this black bloke and the posh girl because he understood that the longer he stayed in there, the more kudos he'd gain with the kitchen staff. He might become a bit of a star himself, because surely some of their fame would rub off on him? To think this was happening in his restaurant. Wait until he told his mates – they'd be so jealous. He wished he could get a photo.

His thoughts were interrupted by the Ethiopian subsiding to the floor, groaning loudly and relieving himself as he did so – or that's what it sounded like to the horrified manager.

'Oh my God,' cried Emma. 'Look, you tidy him up, you wipe him. You're a man. Please.' And she grabbed a roll of toilet paper and thrust it in the manager's direction. The young man sprang back. 'I hardly think that's part of my job description. He's your friend. I don't even know the bloke.'

Emma groaned and leant over Mujtabaa again, struggling to reach under his *shämma* as best she could. The *sanafil* had again dropped to the floor. She managed to wrestle it from around his feet and throw it into the washbasin. A thin green liquid had run down the insides of his legs and onto the floor.

'Is helping one of your customers to his feet part of your job description?'

'I guess.'

Together they struggled to lift the Ethiopian. He continued to cling to the doorframe.

'Come on, Moosh, we have to go.'

'He don't look too good,' said the manager helpfully. 'Are you sure you don't want an ambulance?'

'That won't be necessary, thank you,' she said coldly.

Dad's going to kill me, she thought. She yanked Moosh roughly away from the door, desperation overcoming any feelings of pity. He stumbled forward, grabbing her round the shoulders. The manager leapt to her assistance. 'Here, let me help.' He went to Mujtabaa's other side, placing his arm round his shoulders. It was a tight squeeze, Emma having to let go of Moosh to get past the washbasin to the door leading into the restaurant. She was happy to do so, to leave the carrying to the manager. She lifted the *sanafil* out of the washbasin, folding it so the soiled parts were hidden.

The manager, with the young Ethiopian hanging off his neck, succeeded in opening the first door with one hand and then dragging the comatose figure the couple of yards to the second door. He managed to open that and, looking very much like a foot soldier carrying a wounded companion back to the safety of the trenches, or a good friend carrying a drunk towards a taxi stand, emerged into the restaurant. He looked as if he expected to be greeted by applause. He wasn't, although he was gratified to find a small crowd of customers, including the kids who'd joined Emma and Mujtabaa, standing in a semi-circle expectantly around the entrance to the toilets. Amongst them was a sprinkling of McDonald's staff, one of whom now jumped forward to say to the manager, 'Bobby, let me help.'

'No, I'm fine,' said the manager, clinging more tightly to his prize. He wasn't going to give him up now, even if the smell of vomit and diarrhoea was overwhelming. He turned, a little awkwardly because of the weight slumped over his shoulders, and said to Emma, 'You can sit down here and have a cup of tea if you want. It's on the house. It might make your friend feel better.' Surely a cuppa would have the same therapeutic effects on an African as it did on an Englishman?

'No, we really have to go, but thanks all the same.' She sounded like someone who was looking for an excuse to leave a boring party early.

'If you have to,' said the manager resignedly. He raised his voice: 'Excuse me, excuse me, stand back, please,' and the three of them made their way through the small crowd of gawpers towards the front door of the restaurant.

Outside, Putney High Street was busy and noisy. It was almost dark. Emma moved up beside Moosh, ready to take him off the manager, but the young man wasn't keen to hand over his prize quite yet, especially when they both, simultaneously, spotted a photographer jump out of a car that had just drawn up at the kerb. The manager clung to the black guy, as if knowing instinctively that it was extremely important they weren't separated at this point in time. This could be his 15 minutes of fame.

Emma, however, as soon as she spied the photographer, immediately started to pull Moosh in the opposite direction, trying to dislodge him from the manager's shoulders. And this was the photograph that appeared on the front page of the *Express* the next day: a proud, almost posed manager standing in front of his restaurant, supporting a sick, emaciated African, with a wild, obviously frightened, if not hysterical Emma Burles trying to wrest the skeletal figure off him.

But that was the next day. Right now Emma was struggling to hold on to the idea that she might get Moosh back to the mobile home, and quietly, calmly walk up the steps to say to her father, 'Here we are, Dad. We've just been sitting outside enjoying the evening air.' But she knew that the chances of that occurring were rapidly disappearing.

Everyone was staring, everybody whispering and pointing. Flashlights were suddenly exploding in every direction. The *Express* reporter was shouting: 'Look over here, luv! Over this way!' And at that very moment a police car came speeding down the High Street, blue light flashing, siren whooping. It stopped in front of McDonald's, and a police officer leapt out. He pushed his way through the crowd.

'Emma Burles?' he asked. Her heart sank. She nodded.

'Your Dad phoned us, Emma.' Such chatty familiarity, she thought. 'He's worried about you and... and...' He struggled to remember Mujtabaa's name, finally choosing simply to nod in the direction of the Ethiopian and add, 'your friend.'

'We're okay,' she said. 'Thanks.'

'Would you like us to take you back to your father?'

'Thanks. That would be great.' She turned to Moosh, saying to the policeman, 'Would you give us a hand?'

The McDonald's manager, with obvious reluctance, surrendered the African into the arms of the Law, but, having noted out of the corner of his eye, with the publicity seeker's unfailing instinct, that the *Express* photographer was still firing off shots, he succeeded in dragging this action out for an interminable length of time. The policeman, who'd had more than his share of dealing with vomit-stained, incontinent people, took Mujtabaa's arm with obvious reluctance, averting his face as he did so. He pushed him into the back of the police car, and let Emma in beside him from the other side. He closed the door and climbed into the front passenger seat. 'We're taking them back to All Saints church,' he said to his colleague, and the car pulled away from the crowd, and the waving manager. The siren had been turned off, but the blue light continued to flash. Emma wished they'd turn that off, too. It would simply add to the melodrama of her reunion with her father.

A few minutes later they drew up in the church's driveway. Adrian came running down the steps of the Winnebago, followed by Dave and Anne.

'We were worried sick about you,' he said to his daughter as she got out of the car. 'Is he all right?' He bent down to peer into the back of the police car. 'Where did you find them?' he asked one of the policemen.

'They were coming out of the local McDonald's, Mr Burles. We got a tip-off.' He then added, possibly to try to make things easier for Emma, 'I believe they were on their way back here.'

'We were, Dad. We were on our way back.'

'Is he all right?' he asked his daughter.

'He's fine. And so am I,' she added, giving him a withering

look. 'In case you're interested.'

'I don't care about you right now, young lady,' and he bent down to look into the back of the police car again. 'My God, it stinks of vomit in here. Has Mujtabaa been sick?' he asked over his shoulder.

'Oh dear,' said Anne pushing her way past Emma. Adrian stood aside and let Anne lean into the car. She said something to Mujtabaa. A few seconds later she straightened up and turned to Emma. 'How sick was he?'

Emma shrugged. 'He was just sick. You know...'

'This is important, Emma. If he's been sick, it could be dangerous. He can't afford to lose too much fluid.'

'He was quite sick...'

Anne pursed her lips. 'We have to get him to hospital, Adrian. He's not well.'

'Let's get him inside first.' He turned to the policeman: 'Officer, will you help us?'

At that moment, more cars drove through the gates into the church grounds. They were television crew and newspaper reporters, led by the man from the *Express*. Flashbulbs erupted like fireworks in the darkness around them, and shouts of 'Is he all right? Is Mujtabaa ill? Tell us what's happening.' They jostled for better angles, pushing and elbowing, thrusting cameras into faces.

Adrian started swearing. 'Dave, get them out of here.'

'How am I supposed to do that? Anyway, I thought you said all publicity was good publicity.'

Adrian was tempted to kill him, but it would have to be later.

Anne and one of the police officers were manoeuvring Mujtabaa out of the back of the car. He looked a dead weight. His head lolled forward on his chest.

'Is he dead?' one of the reporters shouted. 'Has he died?'

Adrian was cursing under his breath. 'No, he has not died. For Christ's sake, give us a break!' He snapped at Emma, 'Get inside.' She retreated into the Winnebago. A few seconds later, the policeman and Anne together managed to push, pull and carry Mujtabaa into the mobile home and lay him on his bunk.

Adrian thanked the officer.

'Do you want us to call an ambulance, sir?'

'No, that won't be necessary. I have the name of a doctor if we need one. Thank you all the same.'

The officer was about to leave when Adrian said: 'You can't get rid of those reporters for us, can you?'

'I can try. This is church land, after all.'

Adrian thanked him, closing the door as he left. He turned to Anne: 'How is he?'

'He hasn't got a temperature.' She looked at Emma: 'Has he had diarrhoea, do you know?'

'He did have a bit, yes.'

She spoke to Adrian. 'I think he's lost a lot of fluid. I can give him some water and put electrolytes in it. That should help. But I think we should get him to hospital just in case.'

'We have to look after him here.'

'I don't think that's good enough, Adrian.'

'Why not? He's not in danger of dying, surely?'

'I don't know, but for my own peace of mind I'd like a doctor to look at him.'

'I'm paying you to take care of him.'

'And that's what I'm trying to do.' She put her hands on her hips, defiant, ready to do battle. 'It's an extra precaution, that's all.'

'I'm not happy for him to go to hospital. If the NHS gets its hands on him, we'll never see him again.' He threw his hands in the air. 'Show over.'

'But his life may be in danger.' The old nurse looked distressed. She was talking about a person, while it appeared that he was talking about an event.

'It's in danger anyway,' Adrian said. 'Mujtabaa could have died in the desert if we hadn't picked him up. And I'm sorry if it sounds callous, but he could die here, now. It's all relative.'

They stood inches apart, facing each other, one seeking out an opening that would allow him to make the winning thrust, the other a complete innocent – as well as unwilling participant – in the practice of aggressive encounters.

'That's a terrible thing you're saying, Adrian. I have to say I'm appalled!' Anne's hands were now crossed over her lap, and she was staring at him as if she couldn't quite believe what she was hearing. He leant forward, then seemed to think better of what he was about to say, and straightened up. He took a deep breath, possibly in an attempt to regain his composure. 'If I call Dr Somerville, will that make you happier? I could ask him to come and check Mujtabaa over.'

She nodded. Her opposition riled him. It made him want to get in the last word. 'One thing's for certain: Mujtabaa's not going to hospital. Over my dead body.'

'Well, let's hope it's not over his,' she snorted as she turned away.

He went outside, slamming the door behind him. The mobile phone was in the driver's cabin.

Anne turned to the young girl and said in a low voice, 'What came over you, Emma? That was totally irresponsible, taking Mujtabaa off like that.'

'I didn't mean any harm. I'm sorry, Anne.'

'You should know better at your age. That's the kind of behaviour one would expect from a child.'

Emma sat slumped in her seat, head down, looking the picture of misery.

Adrian finally returned from making his call. 'I want you to understand that I'm as worried about Mujtabaa as you are, Anne, but I also know that he has to finish this walk. There isn't an option. There's too much depending on that now. If he dies, well… Well, it doesn't bear thinking about.'

She nodded her head. It was almost imperceptible, as if her thoughts were elsewhere. Then Adrian turned to his daughter. 'Of all the stupid things to do. I can't believe my own daughter could behave like that. What on earth were you thinking of? What were you doing in McDonald's? Feeding him burgers and chips?'

She lowered her head.

'You weren't! You didn't give him a hamburger, did you? Surely not?'

Anne shook her head in disbelief.

'You could have killed him,' he said.

'Well, it's not as cruel as killing him by starving him!' she shouted, blinking through her tears, hating his righteousness, suddenly defiant. 'So what's the big deal?' She slipped her fingers beneath her spectacles and hurriedly wiped her eyes.

'We're doing everything that's humanly possible to keep him alive. And he's a damn sight better off here than where he was. You know that.' He took a step towards his daughter, head down, almost as if he was going to attempt to gore her. 'He's here for a purpose, Emma. It's what he has to do. The whole country's falling in love with this man, and you take it on yourself to... to...' He struggled for the right words. 'You had absolutely no right to do something like that, no right at all. I'm furious with you.'

She refused to look at him, but muttered, 'You haven't any right either.'

'What did you say?' he shouted, moving another step forward. 'What did you say?'

She ignored his question, saying: 'Anyway, he was the one who wanted to go. He just walked off. I had to follow him. What else could I do?'

'I don't believe you.'

'I don't care if you don't believe me, it's true.'

'He does have a tendency to wander, Adrian. I told you that in Korem, remember?'

He ignored her. 'How could you be so stupid? Tomorrow morning you're off back to your mother. I don't trust you – I *can't* trust you to stay here with us any longer. I'd send you home in a cab right now if there weren't reporters still outside. But tomorrow morning, you're out of here. I'll not have this walk ambushed by you.' He partly opened the door, saw that there was now no one around, and stepped outside.

In silence, Emma climbed up onto her bunk. Tears were rolling down her cheek. She lay down, her back to Mujtabaa and Anne. The nurse went and stood by the bunk, reaching up to put a hand on the young girl's shoulder. Emma started to shake with sobs, silently but convulsively. Anne stroked her hair.

179

'Don't worry, dear. Your father will be all right. It will have blown over by the morning.'

'You don't know him,' she sobbed.

'I'll have a word with him.'

'I hate him!'

'You're being unfair to your father. He's a good man, you know. I believe he sees very clearly the unfairness and the suffering in this world, and he's trying to put things right. He's battling impossible odds, but doesn't give up. He needs your support, Emma.'

She was lying very still, obviously listening. Anne patted her on the head. 'I'm sure he'll allow you to stay. Now I have to go and clean up our friend.'

She sponged down Mujtabaa, but, with Adrian's words always in mind, didn't use soap. She also rinsed out his *sanafil*. While this was going on, the young man moaned softly, a low, continuous sound that resonated with misery.

Adrian brought the family GP into the Winnebago, explaining the situation as he did so. Dr Somerville, ever practical and with scarcely a word, checked Mujtabaa over. Finally he straightened up, struggling to catch his breath even after such minimal exertion, and said, as if a little disappointed with his prognosis, 'He'll survive.' Adrian visibly relaxed. Anne smiled with relief. 'Interesting case. Suggest you give him plenty of fluid, and let him have a good night's rest. We'll see how he is in the morning.' He gave the patient an injection before leaving.

There was an awkward silence in the mobile home. Neither Adrian nor Anne seemed to know what to say, so they stood for a minute or two staring at Mujtabaa as he lay, eyes closed, on his bunk. Eventually Adrian said, 'I'm going to have to speak to the reporters who snuck back into the grounds with Dr Somerville.' She nodded.

He went outside and announced that he expected Mujtabaa would be all right to continue his walk in the morning, and that the whole McDonald's incident had been most unfortunate, but would not have any adverse effects on their fundraising efforts. He told them his daughter, although well-intentioned, now understood that what she'd done had been both unfortunate and irresponsible, and that it wouldn't happen again. The reporters left to file their stories.

A few minutes later, as he climbed back into the mobile home, Adrian worried about what would appear in the morning's newspapers, but persuaded himself that anything would be better than nothing. Anne lay next to Emma, who'd cried herself to sleep, and prayed for Mujtabaa.

Friday

She made up her mind before even climbing out of her bunk. She dressed quickly behind the curtain, and threw her few things into a backpack. Pushing aside the curtain, she climbed down the small ladder. Her father and Dave were sitting at the table and, apart from their mugs of coffee, looked as if they hadn't moved all night. Anne sat like an acolyte next to Mujtabaa, waiting for him to finish drinking a glass of milk.

She swung her backpack over her shoulder. 'I'm off.' It came out awkwardly, abrupt and unnatural, possibly because her real intention had been to walk out without saying anything at all, in a disdainful, I'm-not-going-to-sink-to-your-level silence. She was annoyed she wasn't able to pull this off.

Her father frowned, but raised his head for only half a second. 'I want you to eat breakfast before you go anywhere.'

'I don't want anything.'

Anne moved across to the sink and started washing dishes. Dave picked up one of the newspapers on the table and pretended to read it. She glimpsed the front-page headline in *The Sun*: 'MUJTABURGER!'

She scowled at her father.

'Sit down.' He nodded to the space on the bench across the table from him, next to Dave. 'Anne, would you get Emma a cup of tea, please?'

'I can make my own if I want one.'

'I'm happy to get it for you, dear.'

'Sit down,' he said again.

It was like going back almost ten years. Entering his study. The Persian rug on the parquet floor. Some kind of floral pattern, with a white border. 'Feet off the border,' he would snap at the little girl in front of him, 'how many times do I have to tell you?' And obediently she'd step warily around the forbidden whiteness before approaching the columns of miniature soldiers lined up in the full-length glass display cabinet. She would study them carefully, her eyes roaming over the ranks, envying them their right to a place in this mysterious male world, where a stoical silence reigned supreme and death and glory were the ultimate prizes. They glinted beneath the blazing lights, motionless and perfect, frozen in time, waiting an eternity for the order to advance. She loved, too, the horses, perfect miniatures, with nostrils flared and muscles bulging; at the halt, or walking, trotting, cantering and galloping, a few rearing in the air. She wanted to reach out and move them, just a few inches forward, to bring them to life, but she was never allowed to do so. Only her father was allowed to move them, and he rarely did. What she really wanted was an excuse to touch the miniatures, to feel the heaviness of the lead and the gloss of the paint, but that was forbidden, too. Even the act of looking was frowned upon. So she would stand in silence and stare, sensing all the while, but never able to put into words, that her father loved these tiny, perfect figures more than he loved her. She felt they were together, her father and his soldiers, allies in some conflict she barely comprehended, and that she was separate and alone, out on the flank, forbidden to take part. Looking up through the glass, eyes wide beneath her fringe, she became slowly and dimly aware of feelings of jealousy, as well as an inability to compete.

Yet she could remember other occasions when, if her father was in a good mood, she would sit on his lap, lying against him, breathing in the reassuring smell of cigarettes and aftershave and the crisp freshness of ironed cotton, an ear pressed against his chest as she listened to him talk. 'And those are the Black Watch Highlanders in their red doublets and dark green kilts. See how steadfast they stand, firing at their enemies.' And she asked him what steadfast meant, and he explained the word to her. 'The officer who commands them, I call him Hamish McDuff.'

'Is that his real name, Daddy?'

'I believe so,' he answered with a smile.

Then he'd tell her about the Somerset Light Infantry with their spiked, dark-green helmets, and the Argyll and Sutherland Highlanders, and the South Australian Lancers, and the 27th Light Cavalry, until they all swirled in her head, wheeling, turning and marching beneath the bright lights, and she could almost hear the drums and bugles and clashing cymbals. And then there were the ones she loved best of all – six Arabs on dromedaries (another new word!).

'I know what you like about those,' her father said. 'It's their red, green and blue swirling robes, and those white burnooses. That's what protects them from the burning desert sun, you know.'

But now, as she stood before him in the Winnebago, if there had been a Persian rug with a white border on the floor, then doubtless he would have snapped at her, 'Feet off the border'. She still obeyed him, although, now that she was older, she refused to allow herself to be intimidated by his temper. She threw herself with what she hoped was an air of indifferent nonchalance onto the seat, and ignored him. She studied the newspapers spread out on the table.

It appeared they'd made the front page of every newspaper in the land. Most of them carried a photograph of Moosh being supported by the manager outside McDonald's, with Emma trying to pull him away. In the main, the tabloids treated the story with a degree of levity, a harmless escapade by two young people stealing away for a night out on the town, whereas the broadsheets took a more serious approach, concerned about what could have happened to Mujtabaa, and discussing the nutritional benefits of American fast food for a starving African native. The McDonald's Company had issued a press statement in which they claimed there was no evidence there had been anything wrong with the food the young Ethiopian had eaten, it was simply that the meal was too rich and nutritious for a seriously malnourished person. The spokesperson also said the company was looking at its legal position.

She turned one of the tabloids towards herself. It carried the headline: 'HUNGRY FOR A TAKE-AWAY!' Out of the corner of her eye she started to read the story.

Her father put down the *Telegraph* and studied his daughter in silence. She sat sullen and heavy across the table from him, saying nothing, now only pretending to read. She was distracted by the flickering, silent images of the TV above her head. She glimpsed a reporter interviewing the young manager of the McDonald's outlet. The story was receiving a lot of air time, too, it seemed.

'Proud of yourself?'

She didn't answer. Dave stirred sugar into his coffee noisily, as if to show he had more important things on his mind than to get involved in a family argument.

'It's in all of the US papers, too – and on their TV stations.'

'Well, that's good, isn't it?' She wasn't quite sure herself.

'But you could have killed him! Of all the damn silly things to do.'

'You've said that already. Anyway, I didn't kill him, did I?'

Her studied, defiant indifference was intended to defend herself rather than inflame him, but seemed to have the opposite effect.

'That could have been the end of the walk yesterday. Do you understand that? You could have ruined everything. All the work we've put into this, all the money could have disappeared without trace.'

'He was starving, I wanted to give him a bit of a treat, that's all.'

Anne put a mug of tea down in front of her, and her father said, 'She'd better have some toast as well.'

Emma looked up, but avoided contact with her father's eyes, addressing the caravan in general. 'Doesn't anyone listen to me? I don't want anything. Are you all deaf? I can't be any clearer: I don't want anything.'

'You have to eat. We have a long day ahead of us.'

"I don't have to eat. Moosh doesn't eat, so why should I?' Then, barely audible, 'Anyway, I don't have a long day ahead of me.' She closed the newspaper emphatically, drowning half of her last sentence, and picked up another. Every movement was angry, hurried, unintentionally mimicking her father.

185

No one spoke. All that could be heard inside the mobile home was the clink of cutlery and china in the sink as Anne started washing up, and the sound of Dave noisily sipping his coffee. Moosh was watching her from his bunk, a silent presence. She gave him a quick smile, wanting him to know they were still friends. He was holding the TV remote control, turning it over and over in his hands, but no longer changing channels.

'I'm not letting you get away with this, Emma. You can't do something as irresponsible as this and then expect to just get up and walk away.'

'For God's sake, Dad, stop going on about it. He's fine now, isn't he? Look at him.'

'It's a miracle if he is, and no thanks to you.'

'It's no thanks to you either, if it comes to that.'

'And what's that supposed to mean?'

Dave stood up. 'Think I'll nip outside for a bit of fresh air!' He squeezed past her, and clambered down the steps of the mobile home. Anne hurriedly dried her hands on the tea towel and followed him, obviously deciding she, too, suddenly needed fresh air. She closed the door behind her.

Father and daughter sat across the table from each other, enveloped in an oppressive silence. He stared at her, frowning, obviously unable to work her out. Eventually: 'Do you want some toast?'

She didn't, but took a mouthful of tea. She put the mug down, but kept both hands on it, either to stop them shaking or to anchor herself, it was hard to tell. Her heart was pounding. She didn't look at him; she couldn't. But she knew he wouldn't have missed the fact she was having something, even if only a mouthful of tea, after having said she wouldn't.

'I'm leaving.' She was pleased with herself: that was how an adult would say it, although they probably wouldn't have looked at the table when they did so.

He didn't seem to understand or, if he did, didn't seem to want to understand. 'What?'

'I'm leaving! You told me last night I had to go home, so I am.' For the briefest of moments her eyes looked into his, and they were full of aggression and defiance. 'I'm going home.'

'I'm willing to forget about last night,' he said. 'You don't have to go home.' A second later, as an afterthought, possibly to demonstrate his authority: 'So long as you promise not to carry out any more foolish escapades.'

'I'm going, anyway.'

He shook his head, as if trying to clear it so he could take in what she was saying. He turned and looked across at Mujtabaa, who had now begun to flick from channel to channel with the remote control. Fortunately, the TV was still on mute and he hadn't yet worked out why there was no sound. But every time the channel changed, when a new image presented itself to him on the screen – from some people talking in a studio to a car driving along a country road to cowboys riding horses or to children playing in the street – he gave a little start of surprise, and his hands would lift from his lap and half open in astonishment. Adrian wasn't amused by such innocent actions, and his eyes continued their sweep of the mobile home, finally settling back on his daughter.

She felt she was winning.

'You're not going anywhere, young lady. I need you here.' He said it emphatically, as if to say that was the end of the matter, and punctuated his order by looking back down at the newspapers spread across the table. 'You asked to come on this walk, and you can't leave now just because it happens to suit you.'

God, she hated the way he could dismiss her so thoroughly. She hated the way he could be so condescending. I'm not even a person in his eyes, she thought, just a kid. 'You don't need me,' she said, annoyed that her voice sounded too loud and too forced.

'Don't argue with me, Emma. I have enough on my plate right now to waste time arguing with you. I need you here, and that's the end of the matter.'

She thought: They're all such clichés. He speaks in clichés all the time. What are his real feelings? Why can't he speak like a normal person?

'You don't need anybody here, except for Mujtabaa. He's the only person you need here.'

'And what's that supposed to mean?'

'The only reason the rest of us are here is to be bossed around by you. That's all we're good for.' It had been like that for as long as she could remember.

'I don't know what's got into your head suddenly, but I value the contribution you're making. Mujtabaa's very fond of you, I can see that. You're closest to him in age, and that's important. So if you won't stay for my sake, stay for his.'

She stood up. Turning towards him, body tight and flushed, trying to blink back the tears, aware of Moosh behind her, almost certainly watching, listening to all these words he couldn't understand. 'I think it's immoral the way you're using Moosh. It stinks. It's got nothing to do with helping people. Mum's right, you're just exploiting him for your own good. You're using us, too, all of us – me and Anne and Dave. It's horrible what you're doing.' It came pouring out, in a rush, perhaps more than she intended. And, like a small wave running onto the sand and dying, she finished with, 'I don't want to have anything more to do with it.'

He also stood up, squashed awkwardly between the bench and table. 'If you leave now, you're not coming back. And I mean that. I'm not having people swanning in and out of this expedition whenever it takes their fancy. This isn't some kind of game, you know.'

And she thought, Mum's right, he doesn't listen. He's so busy listening to himself, he has no time to hear what other people are saying.

'Do I make myself clear?' Talking down to her, treating her as a child. She hated that. But she could feel his anger just below the surface and it frightened her. She knew how it could burst out suddenly. He was leaning down on the table, resting on his fists, and it went through her head that he looked like a gorilla.

Moosh was changing channels faster and faster.

She picked up her backpack, threw in her hairbrush and a couple of articles of clothing lying on the seats. She wanted to hug herself. She was pleased that she'd ignored what he'd just asked, dismissed it as thoroughly as he would dismiss something she said.

'Do you understand what I'm saying? Answer me.'

'Yes.'

He was still behind the table. She wanted him to stay there. She didn't want him to come out and touch her or attempt to hold her. She couldn't bear that.

'I'll be extremely angry if you leave now, Emma.'

'So you'll just have to be angry.'

'Jesus!' He banged the top of the table with his fist. He scowled at her, and sat down heavily. Mujtabaa was watching him, looking both puzzled and wary.

'You're too young to know what you want... You haven't the maturity...'

'I do know what I want. I want to leave.'

He closed his eyes in exasperation. 'Can I say anything to make you change your mind?'

'No.'

And the tables had turned right around. He was almost begging her to stay, only he couldn't bring himself to do so, not outright.

'How will you get home?'

'The Underground.'

Sinking to such banalities. It was all so unimportant, except for Moosh. He was all that counted here, and yet he sat on a bench just across from them, quiet and still, like someone in the audience, not an actor on stage. The remote control lay on his lap, as if he had no need for it now that she and her father had stopped fighting. She wondered if he knew their argument had been about him. She wished she could talk to him, confide in him, tell him that it wasn't his fault. She knew he'd take her side.

It was upsetting to leave Moosh. Almost certainly he'd think she was deserting him; why else would she suddenly disappear? She was angry with herself for letting him down, but what else could she do?

She opened the door of the mobile home. 'Anne, will you tell Moosh that I was happy to meet him. And tell him that I hope it works out well for him – and his people too.'

'Are you leaving us, dear?'

She nodded, and the nurse said, looking meaningfully at Adrian, 'That's a great shame, a very great shame.'

The old nurse chose to ignore the tears in Emma's eyes. 'I'll try to tell him,' she said, stepping up into the mobile home. 'He won't be happy.' Emma stood in front of Moosh, half listening, her thoughts all over the place. She wanted to apologize to her friend – for dragging him down to this, a sordid caravan in the middle of a vast foreign city, a place that was dirty, corrupt and greedy, the complete opposite of everything he stood for and the beautiful place he came from. She wanted to explain to him how upset she was by all that they'd asked him to do, that she felt it was against Nature, against everything that was decent and noble. That was what she wanted to say to him, but she couldn't. She didn't have the words – even in English she didn't have the words. She couldn't ask Anne to say it for her because she couldn't say it herself, so she held out her hand instead. And when Anne had finished translating (which seemed to take a long time, but maybe she was explaining what was going on as well), Moosh, without raising his head, held out his hand and limply held hers. He didn't look at her. He was like a toddler who has just understood his parents are about to leave him alone at kindergarten for the first time, and the feelings are too overwhelming to absorb.

She wanted to cry, but she knew she mustn't, not now, not in front of her father. She held out her hand to the nurse. 'It was lovely meeting you, too, Anne.'

But the nurse ignored the young girl's outstretched hand, and hugged her. 'Take care of yourself, dear. I hope we'll see you before we go back.' She held Emma's hands in hers, and said, possibly a little louder, as if she wanted to make sure Adrian heard her: 'You're a lovely person. I shall keep you in my prayers.'

Emma turned towards the door and, without looking at her father, left the Winnebago. The door banged shut behind her of its own accord.

A second later, Dave came back into the mobile home, grinning and oblivious. 'Where's young Emma off to, then?'

'Home.' Adrian stood up, unwilling to expand. 'We'd better

get going. We can't hang around here all day.' But instead of moving, he fell back onto the seat. 'Dave, will you make us another coffee before we leave?'

'Sure.'

'We have to wait for the doctor. We'll leave after he's been.' And his head fell forward onto his chest and his eyes closed.

His daughter had deserted him, that's what really hurt. He'd been aware, if only vaguely, of it happening for a while now, of the knowledge that she was slipping away from him. He sensed a shift in their relationship. In the past she'd supported him, even admired him for everything he did, no matter what. Dad could do no wrong; Dad was perfect; Dad was god. Lately, however, she'd been acting more her own woman – growing independent, or rebellious, depending on how you looked at it, he supposed. No doubt it was puberty. His little girl was becoming a woman, and he wasn't so sure he liked that. Isn't that what everyone warned you about: the emotional rollercoaster, the tumultuous upheavals, the tantrums and impenetrable sulks? He supposed he'd been naïve to believe that he and Emma were different, that they'd avoid all that nonsense and their relationship would remain unaffected. They were special, he had told himself; they'd always be there for each other. Sure, in some far-off, distant time, there might be a man, a husband, but he would never totally displace Adrian. As her father, he'd always have an unassailable place in her heart. But now there was a subtle repositioning between them; signs of her casting off on her own, of breaking away from him – although it was probably more of a drifting apart than a breaking away. There were the arguments about homework, about staying out late, about inappropriate clothes – probably nothing that was different from what every father in the land had to cope with, yet in his eyes it was far more devastating. There hadn't been any arguments about young men so far, but their presence was always in the background, lurking, priapic, hormone-saturated and acne-ridden, waiting for the chance to do unspeakable things to his precious girl. And their influence was growing on her, while his was diminishing. That's how it was, and that's what he couldn't bear. He wanted his child back, he wanted things to stay as they had always been.

He wasn't even sure she appreciated that he was doing all of this for her. He persuaded himself that she was the reason he'd become involved with Africa Assist in the first place. Not entirely, but she'd definitely influenced his decision. Although she'd never come out and said anything against public relations, he'd sensed, if not her disapproval, then her lack of enthusiasm for his chosen profession – influenced by her mother, no doubt. It wasn't hard for him to understand how his world must appear in her eyes: he wasn't doing anything that contributed to society or benefited humankind. Typical teenager angst probably, yet her lack of support – more, her lack of enthusiasm – had still affected him. Once, he'd attempted to justify himself to her – and Judith also – by explaining how PR kept the wheels of industry turning, which benefited everyone through increased profits and full employment, but he knew his justifications had persuaded neither of them. Emma had definitely been keen for him to work for Africa Assist (far more so than Judith, who now tended to regard everything he did, charitable or otherwise, with a jaundiced eye). And yes, he agreed with his daughter that what he was doing now was more obviously *good*. Faith, hope and charity, and the greatest of these is charity; you can't say fairer than that.

Yet now she was leaving him on his own at the most important time in his career. That's what really hurt. Of course, there was still Anne, but she was little more than an old-fashioned do-gooder; well-meaning no doubt, but scarcely the kind of person you could confide in or rely on in a crisis. There was also the small matter of her lack of enthusiasm for the walk, or, if that was too strong a claim, her over-zealous regard for Mujtabaa's welfare and her perpetual concern about the distance he had to walk. (For a person who seemingly marched everywhere, she was very good at dragging her feet.) As for Dave, he was no more than a follower, someone who simply obeyed orders. In Adrian's mind he was dismissed almost without a moment's thought. The truth was, he couldn't expect much support from either Anne or

Dave, and this made him feel both alone and exposed. He was used to having support – and not just from Emma. In his own company, there was a team of people he could rely on – talented, dedicated staff who listened to what he said, offered advice, but always, most importantly, unfailingly carried out his wishes. Now he felt increasingly like a general without an army.

But sitting at the table in the mobile home – Anne reading a book, Dave filling in bank deposit slips, and Mujtabaa on his bunk, as always silent, unmoving and utterly self-contained; each of them waiting to be put into motion by him – there and then he promised himself that he wasn't going to allow his daughter to wreck the walk. He'd manage without her. They were almost at their destination. Although Emma had left, everything would still work out. It was going to be a success, he just had to hold things together for a couple more days. He'd never had to cope with failure, and he had no intention of learning to do so now. He wasn't about to let everything slip through his fingers at this late stage. And why should it do that, anyway? He was the ideal person to run a show like this. He was the perfect organization man, the publicity magician, the puppeteer – that had long been his reputation. Those were his strengths: planning, organizing, strategy. He was the one who pulled the strings, he was the one who could make everyone dance to his tune.

'Is Mujtabaa up to walking this morning, Anne?'

'As far as I can tell he's suffered no ill-effects from last night. It might be sensible to let him rest a little, however. Perhaps we can wait to see what the doctor says.'

Two hours later, after Dr Somerville had visited and given Mujtabaa the all-clear, they were back on the road. Adrian now walked ahead, and Anne, with the goatskin waterbag, walked just a few steps behind the Ethiopian in what had once been Emma's place. Television crews and several journalists accompanied them, one of whom told Adrian that the level of debate in society had reached fever pitch. 'Everywhere you go, there are people arguing about the walk – for and against. In pubs, workplaces, on public transport – you can't get away from it. You're also getting a lot of coverage on the Continent. And I'm sure you know about the Panorama special tomorrow night with David Dimbleby.'

It was impossible to keep to the pavement now; it was left for the public. The Africa Assist group lay claim to at least half of the road. The inside lane was marked off with traffic cones, restricting cars to the outside lane, where they crawled past the walkers, an endless, slow-moving stream, faces peering out through side windows. Sometimes windows were lowered and passengers shouted encouragement as they went past. Many cars sounded their horns. Adrian waved back – more like raised an arm, with just a hint of a victorious general entering a city – but Anne never waved; possibly she felt it wasn't her place to do so. Mujtabaa didn't acknowledge anyone either, neither those in cars nor on the pavement, and Adrian didn't ask him to. To Adrian it seemed – and, unusually for him, he wasn't sure of the right words to describe what he thought about this – more noble, sincere, even meaningful if Mujtabaa didn't acknowledge the people who'd come to cheer him on his way. If he'd done so, it might have begun to look like a publicity stunt, or as if he was a politician seeking votes. Adrian wanted it to have the appearance of a pilgrimage, a Gandhi-like happening, something the young man had to do whether people were around to witness it or not. So he was happy that Mujtabaa kept his eyes on the road ahead, looking neither to left nor right, and sometimes only staring at the ground right before him.

Generally, he appeared unaware of the city around him, as if the daily lives of its inhabitants left him completely untouched. The car crashes and road rage; the domestic crises and disasters; the robberies, rapes and drug deals; the film stars chased by paparazzi and the glitzy new restaurant openings; the unemployment and inflation figures; the storms and posturings in both Houses of Parliament; the battle between the unions and Thatcher; the stock market's dizzying rise… The Ethiopian walked through it all and comprehended none of it, in fact knew nothing about any of it. Londoners and their lives were as alien to him as he was to them. But then, quite abruptly, the outside world seemingly imposed itself on the young man's consciousness. It was as if his deep reverie had been interrupted, and he'd been compelled to halt. He said something to Anne, who then called out to Adrian. He turned, as if he also had been many miles away. 'What is it?'

'He's still saying he wants to ride in a car – or a "small truck".'

Adrian looked taken aback. 'I've already told him, Anne, he can ride in a car when he gets to Trafalgar Square. I'm happy to hire a Ferrari if that's what makes him happy.'

The nurse spoke to Mujtabaa. He weighed up what she said, as if giving it polite consideration, then nodded gravely. She called to Adrian, 'He says he's happy with that.' Adrian rolled his eyes and muttered, 'That's big of him.' Then out loud, he asked: 'Does he want the Ferrari?'

'I suspect he'll be happy with any car, Adrian, but thank you for asking.' She smiled at him sweetly, as if amused by their interaction.

Before setting off again, Anne noticed that the young Ethiopian was holding something. She raised his arm. The television remote control lay on the cracked, greyish palm of his hand. She looked up at his face, but he kept his eyes averted, like a child having been caught out being naughty. She smiled, and closed his fingers over the control. 'You hold on to it, Mujtabaa. Just try not to lose it or you'll upset Adrian.'

It was the hottest day so far, and London had the stifling summer smell of dirty, damp, decaying cloth. The heat weighed on all of them, making every step an effort. Their minds and limbs were overcome by languor. They trudged northeast out of Fulham, towards Chelsea. Adrian now, for the first time, felt they had left the suburbs and were entering London proper. They passed the New King's Road antique shops. In windows, on both sides of the street, priceless furniture and ornaments were on display. The Africa Assist volunteers went into all of these shops, where the price of a Ming vase, Chippendale chair or Louis Quatorze desk would have fed Mujtabaa and his clan for months, if not years. Some shoppers emerged onto the pavement in time to watch the passing procession. They stared in disbelief at what to them was a foreign world, a different century, something totally alien to their structured, pampered lives. There was an uncanny silence as they scrutinized the African walker.

At World's End, the inhabitants of the faceless multi-storey blocks of flats on the right of the road came out in force and, true to the history of the city's poor, gave generously. 'He doesn't understand how we can live on top of each other like that,' Anne explained to Adrian. 'He sees flats as stacks of huts, and when he looks up high and sees people through the glass, walking around inside their homes, he thinks they must be spirits.'

In the King's Road, fashionably dressed young people (the women mini-skirted, with vividly coloured accessories and makeup, and big, heavily styled hair; the men power suited, with Hawaiian shirts and mullet hairstyles) applauded with enthusiasm, and ran around oohing and aahing to each other as if Mujtabaa were some kind of fashion statement or accessory. Perhaps he was an exciting new happening which was there to be experienced, absorbed and then, finally, inevitably, discarded.

It was even possible they considered him thin enough to be a model, fashionably anorexic, and suitable for the pages of *Vogue* or *Harpers*, or to be photographed by David Bailey or Richard Avedon. Despite their frivolous attitude, they were generous. Several rushed up to walk next to the young man while their friends took photographs. How wonderful, they cried. What a splendid idea. It's so *real*. A genuine happening! One young thing kissed Mujtabaa on the cheek after her photograph had been taken clutching his arm. 'You're so cute,' she whispered before floating away to join her friends. It was like a dare.

They passed a McDonald's restaurant. No one said anything.

Off to the left and right they caught glimpses of beautiful streets lined with mews houses, yet many of the people they met were not so beautiful. They treated the Africa Assist walk with arrogance, as if it had no right to be there, in their neighbourhood. It was too disruptive, there were too many people involved. Hadn't they moved into the area to avoid such unpleasant reminders of reality?

They stopped in Sloane Square for a couple of hours. Adrian spoke to reporters, while passers-by parted with their money carelessly, without effort, in much the same way that they'd acquired it. Generosity was not a part of the equation, it was more because they felt they *should*. 'Darling, it's perfectly dreadful. That poor young man,' they said to each other as they handed over their high-denomination notes and substantial cheques. A Brink's Mat van collected the tins of money that were deposited with Dave and took them to the bank. They were now compelled to make the run two or three times a day.

Adrian decided they should walk 200 yards back down the King's Road and turn right into Sloane Avenue. As a PR man, he knew this part of the world well – especially from his business lunches at various highly rated eateries. He also knew the streets were paved with gold – despite Anne telling him that Mujtabaa thought the people of England must be poor because he couldn't see their cows or goats or camels anywhere. Money almost dripped off the trees, washing along the gutters, oozing up from the footpaths – it was ubiquitous. In every shop window fashionably dressed mannequins posed; along every pavement fashionably dressed mannequins paraded. Yuppies, immaculate in sharply tailored dark suits and white shirts, strode confidently through their own territory, on the hunt for some deal, aloof but intent, like sharks. The small group passed Paul Smith and Kenzo. Luxury cars glided past, almost purring, the occupants hidden from pedestrians behind tinted glass. On the corner of Brompton Road and Sloane Avenue they stared up at the huge Michelin man outside Bibendum. Mujtabaa regarded him wide-eyed. 'Maybe he thinks it's one of our gods,' said Adrian, and, in a moment of affection, placed a hand on the young man's shoulder. 'You must think we're a very strange people, Mujtabaa.'

He was missing his daughter, but said nothing. Anne was missing Emma, but said nothing. Both of them were wondering if Mujtabaa was also missing Emma and saying nothing.

They stopped on the corner of Knightsbridge and Brompton Road. The Brompton Oratory shone a brilliant white in the afternoon sun, the statue of Our Lady at the very top of the dome looking down with apparent pity upon the people far below. The Jesuits had invited them to spend the night in the church's grounds. In fact they'd offered to put them up in the presbytery, but Adrian had refused – politely – saying he wanted to stay in the mobile home until the end. He was also determined that no religious denomination should become affiliated with the walk. Spiritual hunger was of no concern to him.

Later that afternoon, when Dave had gone off to the Africa Assist offices to debrief James – something Adrian was keen to avoid at all costs – he suddenly found himself confronted by the nurse.

'Adrian, I wish to speak to you.' He was startled. 'I don't believe you've given due consideration to your daughter's side of the story, and I'd like to try to remedy that.'

He was non-committal. 'Sure, if that's how you feel. Go ahead.'

She sat down opposite him. 'Mujtabaa said something to me yesterday, when we were crossing the Common, that has perhaps helped me understand better – or at least feel more sympathetic towards what Emma did.'

'And what was it he said?' There was a tone of condescension, or perhaps disbelief, in those few words.

'He believes that he and Safia and their child, as well as the Afar people, will only receive food if he continues to walk. Unfortunately, he doesn't understand how far or for how long he has to do this.'

Adrian shrugged. 'That's a bit of an exaggeration, surely? We've told him–'

She cut him short. 'It's the way he sees it, Adrian. He hasn't said this to me in so many words, but I think he also feels he isn't being given enough food. He won't ask for more because he's afraid of behaving like a beggar.'

'That's preposterous.'

She ignored his interruption. 'You have to realize that he sees us as being very different from his own people. They share everything, especially when times are hard, whereas we share nothing. He can see that we have so much food, and yet we don't give him any more. We keep it all for ourselves.'

'Jesus, Anne!' She censured him with her eyes. 'We're doing it for a reason. It's also only for a short time.'

'He doesn't understand that, Adrian. How can he? You know what he sees? He sees people passing him in the street, cramming food into their mouths. "Many of them are fat – like hippos", those were the words he used – "fat, like hippos". They have crumbs and scraps spilling from their lips, and often they're clutching bottles and cans of drink in their hands. That's how he sees us, always cramming food into our mouths, like wild animals at a waterhole after a long drought. He can see that we have so much food we can't eat it all, so we leave what's left over outside what he calls our huts, at the side of the road. He told me that once he saw huge round metal drums, as tall as himself, overflowing with scraps of food. The food was scattered over the ground and being picked at and fought over by screaming birds. Emma saw them too. It was outside a hotel, and your daughter was ashamed for us, for all of us.'

Adrian could feel her anger, and he didn't miss the insinuation that Emma, rather than her father, had been the one who'd been ashamed.

They sat in the Winnebago in silence. Adrian looked across at Mujtabaa, who was lying on his bunk, motionless. For once, he didn't know what to say. Even though he knew the truth of what Anne had said, or at least guessed as much, hearing it as if from the Ethiopian himself certainly gave it more strength.

'I think it's possible, at times, to forget the sheer misery of someone who doesn't have enough to eat. It's as simple as that: the sheer, unadulterated, agonizing misery.'

He sighed. 'And you think my daughter…?'

'Emma empathizes with how Mujtabaa feels far more than you or I ever could. And, if you don't mind me saying so, I think you should be proud of your child's sensitivities.'

Saturday

*I*t was a perfect summer morning: warm, with a few wisps of cloud drifting languidly towards the horizon and the gentlest of breezes stirring the leaves on the trees. As usual, Anne was up first, and then Mujtabaa, who always rose immediately after her, as if he'd been waiting for permission. She sat quiet and self-composed over a cup of tea, reading her book, determined perhaps to persuade herself that this day was much the same as any other. Adrian and Dave were up half an hour later. Over breakfast – for which the two men again stuck to toast and coffee – they discussed their plans, the distribution of volunteers and the best pick-up points for the Brink's Mat van. Adrian pushed every point, questioned every proposal, and agonized over every decision. He went into painstaking detail, and was most emphatic that everything had to be carried out so there was no risk of any mishap. Nothing could be allowed to go wrong.

Mujtabaa stood on one leg, leaning on his staff, alone outside the mobile home. Every now and again Adrian would half rise from his seat and look out of the window, possibly fearful the young man might once again take it into his head to go off to McDonald's. Overnight, an even larger pile of old clothing had been left at the main door of the Oratory. Every morning the pile grew in volume, and Adrian wondered out loud, a hint of exasperation in his voice, if the people who left the clothing expected Mujtabaa to eat it instead of food. Dave agreed wholeheartedly, and said he suspected they were simply clearing out their homes, making use of the opportunity to get rid of stuff they no longer wanted. 'Charity scarcely comes into it,' he said.

Anne frowned, but kept her peace. Her task now, for which she'd volunteered and which Adrian had agreed to with a

200

dismissive shrug, was to phone the St Vincent de Paul Society and tell them where the clothes were located so they could pick them up later in the day. She sat in the cabin of the Winnebago with Dave, and he helped her make the call. Like a young child, ramrod straight and wide-eyed, she held the brick-sized mobile to her ear with both hands and shouted her instructions into the mouthpiece.

Adrian confirmed their departure with the police before preparing to leave the grounds of the Brompton Oratory at 11 o'clock. Four Jesuit priests, pale and ascetic in their black suits, faint undertakers' smiles frozen on their faces, gathered to farewell them. One had spoken to Adrian earlier that morning.

'We are concerned for the spiritual welfare of your African friend, Mr Burles,' Father Anselm had said.

'I don't think there's any need to be, Father.'

The priest regarded him loftily, as if from another world, his hands clasped against his chest, half in a position of prayer, half in a pugilistic posture. He summoned up a quotation from what was obviously a bountiful supply in his head, and which he doubtless considered irrefutable. 'Peter said to them: do penance, and be baptized every one of you in the name of Jesus Christ, for the remission of your sins, and you shall receive the gift of the Holy Ghost.' The faintest of victorious smiles appeared at the corners of his mouth. 'To deprive a soul in your care of the chance of eternal happiness, Mr Burles, would be an unforgivable sin.'

'In my book, Father, it would be an unforgivable sin to force religion down Mujtabaa's throat – against his will.' He was reasonable, but also already regretting having placed themselves overnight in the position of guests of the Jesuits, even though it had only been in the grounds.

Father Anselm spoke quietly, almost whispering, his eyes an icy, piercing blue of conviction. 'The Church believes baptism is a necessary condition of salvation. It's necessary to turn away from everything that's evil and sinful in order to become a disciple of the Lord.'

'I'm sorry, Father, but I don't happen to believe that. And Mujtabaa has said nothing to me about wanting to receive the gift of the Holy Ghost. If he believes in a deity, I suspect it will be Allah, but in my honest opinion, he's more likely to see salvation in a plate of food right now than in any religion.'

The priest suggested that Mujtabaa could be baptized in a matter of minutes, and no one need ever know. Adrian felt compelled to speak more bluntly. 'As a matter of principle, I refuse to compel someone in my care to undergo *indoctrination* into something he knows nothing about. And, as I said before, he may be a Muslim, in which case, baptism would be an insult.' The priest's departure had been frosty.

Now, the four priests, with Father Anselm standing a little apart from the others, possibly in disgrace for having failed to safeguard the soul of the Ethiopian, raised their hands in the most restrained of farewell gestures – or possibly benedictions. Anne was the only one in the Africa Assist group to raise a hand in acknowledgement.

Two police motorbikes went ahead of the group along Knightsbridge, and close behind came the Winnebago bedecked with streamers and posters for Africa Assist, Walk against Want and Mujtabaa. About 20 or 30 yards behind came Adrian, and several yards behind him was the Ethiopian. He walked alone, his gait slow and loping, his body loose, his wrists resting over either end of the walking staff that lay across his shoulders. He looked very relaxed, and Adrian worried that he was too relaxed, too casual, too disrespectful. But then, how could he be disrespectful, he told himself; such a thing was surely not possible? A few yards behind the young man and a little to one side, in Emma's place, was Anne with the goatskin waterbag. Another 20 yards behind her came a police car and, from that day, at the insistence of the City of Westminster Council, an ambulance. A further two police motorbikes brought up the rear. Their procession had become stretched during the week towards the one-hundred-yard mark.

Adrian was everywhere, sometimes up with Dave in the mobile home, sometimes running back for a few minutes alongside Mujtabaa, or having a quick word with either Anne, one of the police escorts or a volunteer. The collectors operated on both sides of the road and were strung out for at least another hundred yards ahead and behind Mujtabaa, as well as alongside. People happily reached into their pockets, wallets and purses, handing over notes and coins, writing out cheques on the spot, even offering credit cards if they had nothing else. Everyone who saw Mujtabaa wanted to give. They wanted to alleviate his suffering and that of his people, but Adrian suspected that they also wanted to alleviate their own consciences. On this very theme, the cover story of the latest issue of *TIME* magazine, beneath a photograph of Mujtabaa, was headlined: OUR CONSCIENCE WALKS AMONGST US.

Harrods was busy with Saturday morning shoppers. Adrian stared across the road at the ornate sandstone façade, the terracotta monolith with its green awnings and small lights strung across its frontage, and thought what an affront it must be to Mujtabaa to have to see this shrine to Western consumerism. But of course he'd have no idea what the place was or what it stood for. Even if someone tried to explain to him that it was one of the world's greatest shops – *It's like a huge market stall, Mujtabaa* – he'd still have no comprehension of what it meant.

As they progressed along Knightsbridge, Adrian appreciated how big the walk had become. The crowds were mainly on the left of the road, because that was the side on which the traffic had been stopped and the side they were walking on, but there were also a lot of people on the far side, as well as crowding the many traffic islands. Cars approaching from Hyde Park Corner were sounding their horns, people on buses crowded the windows on both decks, and the few people working in offices over the weekend hung out of the windows. There was now a festive air about the procession, with people throwing streamers and confetti in their path, as well as flowers. In front of a beautiful old building that was now the Mandarin Oriental Hotel stood a small group of guests and staff. They were applauding politely, and Adrian immediately took note of their well-cut clothes and immaculate, expensive hair-dos. He ran up to a volunteer – a young student he suspected – and told her to be sure to approach this group outside the hotel. 'They've got more money than they know what to do with,' he shouted over the noise of the crowd. 'Squeeze every penny out of them. Be pushy!' She grinned, and dived through the lines of spectators to obey. A few moments later he saw the hotel guests delving into their handbags and wallets, looking a little shocked at having been so successfully held up.

When they reached Hyde Park Corner, Dave drove the Winnebago ahead into Constitution Row and waited there with the police motorcycle escort. Police on foot stopped the flow of traffic, while Mujtabaa, Adrian and Anne, along with about a dozen volunteers, stood before the Doric-pillared portico of St George's Hospital waiting to cross. Police accompanied them in a slow procession across the road to the central area. They rested for a short time near the Wellington Arch. Hundreds of people had set up base on the central reservation. Many looked as if they'd been there for hours. For the first time, Adrian noticed a sprinkling of Ethiopian flags in the crowd. In spite of all the publicity over the past few days, many people still offered Mujtabaa food. Anne, Adrian or Dave were continually stepping forward to prevent this, thanking the people, explaining why the young man's food intake had to be carefully regulated, and suggesting they contribute money instead.

'But he's hungry, pal,' said one young, hippie-looking individual who was particularly insistent. He was holding out what appeared to Dave to be a salad roll wrapped in cling film. They could have bought it especially for Mujtabaa. His girlfriend, all beads and bracelets and in a flowing, loose, tie-dyed dress, clung to the man's arm, listlessly nodding her agreement. They both looked stoned.

Dave said, 'I can assure you we're giving him plenty of food.'

'He doesn't exactly look over-fed to me.' Nodding mechanically, salad roll still in his outstretched hand, the hippie regarded Mujtabaa with intense interest, as if he might be a kindred soul.

'There are only certain foods he can eat,' Anne explained patiently. 'We have to be careful.'

The hippie ignored the old woman. 'Here, pal. Get it down

you,' thrusting the roll closer, perhaps hoping that its proximity might tempt him. There was something aggressive about the offer of charity. Like, *Eat this or I'll fucking clock you.*

Mujtabaa stood immobile, head slightly bowed, seemingly uninterested in the proceedings taking place directly in front of him.

'If there weren't so many pigs about, I'd offer you a smoke.'

His girlfriend laughed. 'Hey, man, why not? He'd love that.'

Eventually, the couple moved off, the man muttering something about *fucking do-gooders* as they did so.

On the far side of the central reservation, the traffic pouring down from Piccadilly and Park Lane was stopped by the police. The small party crossed into Constitution Row. They kept to the pavement running alongside St James's Park, next to the riding track. Two riders trotted past and Mujtabaa stared, open-mouthed at his first horses. He asked Anne if her people ate them.

Many families were out enjoying the sun, sitting on the grass, kicking balls around or feeding the ducks, but they all rushed across to the horse-riding path at the approach of the Ethiopian. No one needed to be told who he was. They cheered, whistled and clapped. Many women had tears in their eyes when they saw his emaciated body. Little children pointed, eyes wide with wonder, probably not because they saw him as being any different from them, but because he had almost no clothes on.

It was obvious that Mujtabaa was tired, so Anne asked Adrian to halt and give him time to sit on the grass. People wanted to meet him, but the police prevented the crowd pressing too close.

It was during this halt that Anne noticed Mujtabaa wasn't sitting quite as expected (even though he rarely sat). He wasn't slumped, with his shoulders bent or his head bowed, as an exhausted person might sit. Rather, he was sitting bolt upright, arms hanging by his side and staring straight ahead, away from the people around them. And she was astonished to see that his mouth was open and his teeth clenched as if he was angry. Most alarming of all, he was making short, staccato grunting sounds, each one escaping from his mouth, half strangled, as if it had been forced to fight its way out into the open. Tears were falling, not from the lower eyelids, but from the very corners of his eyes, as if they too, like the frightening sounds of despair, were attempting to slip out secretly and therefore, hopefully, go unobserved. She hesitated. His grief was private, she told herself, and she was loath to draw anyone else's attention to it. Among those standing around them, most of whom were listening to Adrian, no one seemed to have noticed. Very quietly she got off her camping chair and moved it closer to Mujtabaa. She put a hand on his arm, and left it there, but said nothing.

A few minutes later, Adrian came and stood over them. 'Is he all right?'

'I think he's a little down.' She sounded noncommittal. 'Apathy and depression are two of the main signs of malnutrition, of course, so it's scarcely surprising.'

'But he's getting more food now than he would in the desert.' He almost sounded indignant.

'That doesn't mean he isn't still hungry.' She took a deep breath and looked up at him: 'Maybe it's because he misses Emma. I believe her presence cheered him up.'

'There's nothing I can do about that.'

'Are you sure?' But he had already turned away.

Precisely one hour after they stopped, Adrian said, 'We should be on our way.'

Mujtabaa turned onto all fours before attempting to raise himself off the ground. Adrian stepped forward and reached down to take one of his hands. Slowly, like a frail octogenarian, he pulled himself to his feet. Adrian held on to his hand and looked into his eyes (which were now dry). It could have been the first time he'd really looked at him.

'Well done, Mujtabaa. You're doing so well.' He patted the young man on his upper arm, but his words of encouragement convinced neither of them. Mujtabaa stood, head bowed like the statue of a fallen soldier at the Cenotaph, motionless, overcome with grief. 'Keep it up. You haven't far to go now.' For a moment his hand rested on the young man's shoulder. He turned to Anne: 'Have you told him how close we are to the end?'

She nodded: 'I have, and I hope he understands. I explained it like you would to a child. Remember when your parents would say, Only two more sleeps until… Or, only one more sleep until…? I did that. I told Mujtabaa there was only one more sleep until the end of the walk.'

'Any reaction?'

'None at all.'

Across the road was the high wall surrounding the gardens of Buckingham Palace. The upper branches of ancient trees could be seen over the electrified barbed-wire fence running along the top of the wall. Adrian wondered if the Queen was at home, and whether she'd be tempted to emerge to take a look at the strange group walking past her front door.

When they walked into the area that surrounded the Queen Victoria Memorial between Buckingham Palace and The Mall, they were confronted by a medley of ice-cream vans and souvenir stalls. The stallholders were selling an assortment of small Ethiopian flags, photographs of Mujtabaa – supposedly signed – and miniature imitation *jile*s alongside plastic replicas of Buckingham Palace, portraits of the Queen and the Duke of Edinburgh and Union Jacks. Adrian regretted Africa Assist didn't have the rights to the merchandise. It was a slip-up. But then, he told himself, the walk had become bigger than even he could ever have imagined.

Through all the noise, colour and excitement, Mujtabaa walked. His walk was slow and measured, his face, if not solemn, was certainly melancholic. One hand rested on the hilt of his *jile*, the other held his hardwood staff. He looked neither to left nor to right, and on the rare occasion someone in the crowd managed to dodge the police and rush forward to touch him or offer him food, his step barely faltered. Adrian looked at him and wondered where he was; maybe by himself in the middle of the Danakil Desert. He was certainly not walking with them through central London. Adrian admired how he retained his air of dignity and calm despite being poor and malnourished, despite the horde of strangers around him, despite the ordeal they were putting him through.

As they walked past the gates of Buckingham Palace, Mujtabaa

207

stopped and stared up at the massive Portland stone building with its gold embellishments, high windows and guards standing to attention in the courtyard. The Royal Standard was flying from the top of the building, meaning the Queen was at home. Adrian scanned the windows, but could see no one. Anne told Mujtabaa that this was where the country's chief lived. She didn't tell him that the chief was a woman, believing, as she said to Adrian later that evening, that he wouldn't have been impressed.

'And what would he have said if you'd told him our other chief, our Prime Minister, is a woman too?' he asked.

'Heaven forbid!' said the nurse, clapping her hands together with glee. 'I think he might have packed his bags and gone home at that point.'

And the two of them had laughed, sharing a brief moment of intimacy, an appreciation of the absurdity of their situation.

Without a word, Mujtabaa set off again, Anne now worrying that he'd been insulted because the chief hadn't come out to greet him.

The sun was at its height and many in the crowd wore sunglasses and hats. Ladies were in summer frocks, men in T-shirts and shorts. A few people splashed in the water at the base of the Queen Victoria Memorial.

For the last night of the walk they stopped on the southern edge of the lake in Green Park. They were sitting in the mobile home. Adrian put the *Evening Standard* down. It was full of photographs of Mujtabaa at Buckingham Palace.

'Anne, will you ask Mujtabaa if he'd like to stay in London? Tell him he's famous now, and that he could make a lot of money here. Everyone loves him. If he wanted me to, I could be his manager.' The nurse's eyes widened, but it was scarcely perceptible. Adrian continued, but now in a more self-justifying tone of voice: 'Tell him we could bring his wife out here, too, that she could live here with him, and, of course, his child. I'm sure that could be arranged.'

She spoke to Mujtabaa. He sat before them, silent.

'What does he think?'

'I have no idea, Adrian. As you can see, he hasn't replied.'

'He could have anything he wants, anything at all. He's a celebrity. He has the world at his feet.' He appeared puzzled. How could Mujtabaa not understand what was at stake here? 'Maybe he needs a little time to think about it. Tell him I'll talk to him about it again on Monday, after the rally.'

A short while later, he stepped outside. He was bursting with energy. He was confident. The walk was going to be a huge success – was *already* a huge success. He chatted to some of the reporters still hanging around, and shared a beer with them. Then he climbed into the Winnebago's cabin and phoned home. After chatting briefly to Judith, he said, 'Put her on the phone, will you? Let me speak to her.'

'She says she doesn't want to.'

'I insist. I'm her father. Tell her she has to.'

'I'll tell her, but you know how stubborn she is.'

He tried to think of the best way to start the conversation, but then decided to say whatever felt right at the moment, whatever came into his head.

'Hello.'

He chose to ignore the flat, wary tone of her voice. 'Darling, I want to tell you how sorry I am about our argument yesterday. And I'd like you to come back. It's not the same without you. We all miss you.'

'Do you?' She might as well have said, no, you don't.

'All of us. Moosh in particular.'

'How do you know?'

'You can tell.' Searching around for the right words, a more convincing explanation. 'He's said as much to Anne.' There was a long silence. 'We're worried about him. He's scarcely eaten or drunk anything all day.'

'Great! Isn't that what you want – for him to starve himself to death?'

He could hear the sarcasm, although it was barely discernible beneath the venom. 'We're giving him enough to keep going, darling. You know we can't give him more than that at the moment.'

'Do I?'

She made it so hard. 'I'm not trying to be cruel, believe me. And I know some people are unhappy with Mujtabaa doing this walk – you amongst them. And maybe you're right. But if you or anyone else can tell me of a better way to raise money for Ethiopia, I'd genuinely like to hear it.'

There was a long silence.

'What will it take to get you to come back?'

'I'm not coming back.'

'There must be something I can do, darling. Be reasonable – please.'

'Why? I don't want to have anything to do with your walk. I think it's cruel.'

'Mujtabaa hasn't complained. He's told us he's doing it for his family and friends, so for all we know he could be happy doing the walk.'

'No, he isn't! Anyway, how can he complain when he can't speak English?'

'He could tell Anne. She understands what he says.' They were getting nowhere. 'Will you come back?' He didn't want to plead, but was aware that he was heading in that direction. 'I want you to come back.'

'You can't tell me what to do.'

'I'm not. I'm asking you.'

'I'm sick of being treated like a child. You always do that. I'm not a child, you know.'

'You're right. I apologize. I'm sorry.' He closed his eyes, virtually screwed them up, with the effort. 'It's the last day tomorrow. It would mean so much to Moosh – and to me, and to Anne – if you were here with us. For him, it's a really important day.'

'I don't think it's right what you're doing. I don't want to be part of it.'

'At least think about it – please.'

She made some kind of sound, possibly expelling air through her nose, possibly a snort – but whether of derision or acquiescence he couldn't tell – then she hung up.

She turned from the phone with a little gasp of irritation, shutting her eyes momentarily to accentuate her feelings. 'He's using Moosh, Mum.'

'Your father uses everyone, darling. He's always been like that. He can't help himself. It's best not to let it upset you.' Judith had been working in the garden, and was now sitting in an armchair, drinking a cold lemonade.

'But this is different. Moosh is...' Emma struggled to express what she was feeling. 'He's so innocent. He can't protect himself, not like other people.'

'That's true, darling. But for once maybe your father's using someone for a good reason. Look at the money that's being collected. Africa needs that money. The continent's been exploited for a long time, and now we have an opportunity to give something back to the natives.'

'But it's Moosh who's raising the money.'

'He is, darling, but he couldn't raise it by himself. He needs Africa Assist – and your father.'

Emma screwed up her face, unwilling to admit her mother could be right.

'Your father means well. He may be mistaken in his actions, but he means well.'

Her daughter threw herself onto the sofa, almost lying across the seat, her feet stretched out before her. 'What do you think I should do?'

'Do I think you should go back and join your father, is that what you're asking?'

'Is that what you think – that I should go back to the walk?' The young girl's eyes opened wide, questioning.

Her mother smiled. 'I'm not saying anything. You mustn't put words into my mouth.'

Her daughter's eyes returned to their normal size, and she gave a little 'Oh' that sounded very like disappointment. The two women regarded each other in silence.

'I think you should do what *you* want to do, darling.'

Her daughter was possibly expecting more substantial advice. 'But I don't think I know what I want to do!'

Judith, who had never been very good at discussing anything to do with emotional matters with her daughter, now seemed keen to discover such an intimacy. As likely as not, she expected this would entail little more than holding a conversation that raised itself for a few minutes above the level of the mundane or the commonplace.

'Darling, can I confess something to you?' Her daughter's affirmative response was no more than a look of boredom, possibly indifference; she almost, but not quite, rolled her eyes. Her mother persevered. 'I have never done what I wanted – ever. I have always done what other people wanted – and that includes your father. I don't want you to end up like me.' She took a deep breath, a replica of the one she had taken in the garden not half an hour ago, when she'd discovered and pruned a particularly nasty sucker on her *Hulthemia persica*. It was one of relief.

'Is it so bad being you?' The irony was blatant.

Her mother ignored the question. 'I tried to leave home once, when I was a little older than you – about 18, from memory. And do you know what my mother said to me? "There's nothing a nice girl can do away from home that she can't do at home." I shall never forget that.' She half laughed. 'So I stayed. Quite ridiculous, I know, but it has always been like that. I've never in my life done anything for me. I've never lived my own life, followed my own path...' She ran out of words then, of explanations, and seemingly fell silent at the enormity of her loss. She took a sip of lemonade – so thoughtfully it could have been a fine wine. It was hard to tell if she was trying to communicate her feelings to her daughter or whether she was simply raking through the past for her own sake. 'Do you remember when I wanted to go and stay with my friend Elizabeth in New York for a month – it must have been a couple of years ago now – and your father forbade me to go?'

'No.'

'He didn't forbid me to go, but he made it very obvious he couldn't manage on his own. He said he couldn't cope, that having to look after himself and you for a month was too much to expect.'

'I remember you talking about it.'

The pitying – or was it scornful? – look on her daughter's face wasn't hard to discern. To avoid seeing it for longer than she had to, Judith stood up. 'I'm going to have a drink, a real drink.' As she walked over to the drinks cabinet in the corner, she said: 'It was no different to the discussions we had over children.'

'What do you mean?'

'That's why you're an only child. I've told you before. Your father said he couldn't cope with more than one child. He said it was unfair of me to ask that of him.'

'That's pathetic.' After a second of silence: 'Isn't it?'

Judith poured herself a gin and tonic, ignoring the inevitable emanations of irritation from her daughter that were always aimed at her whenever she had a drink.

'You let him have his own way too much, Mum.'

'He's used to having his own way. He's an only child, too.'

'Are you saying that I'm like that? I'm like that because I'm an only child?'

'No, I wasn't, darling, most definitely not.' Then, as an afterthought: 'Although you can be just as stubborn.' She bent down and kissed her daughter on the forehead, possibly in an attempt to reassure her. Emma closed her eyes. There was a detectable hint of rejection, a shutting out. Her mother straightened up. 'Your father's used to getting his own way, that's all I'm saying.'

'Didn't you ever stand up to him, say no, just once or twice?'

Judith returned to her armchair, placing her drink on the small table next to her. 'In the little things, it was easier not to.' She looked around the room, as though seeking a topic to latch onto.

She then told her daughter how Adrian had always done whatever he wanted to do, just as she had always done whatever Adrian wanted to do. That's how it had been for as long as she could remember. If he wanted to go camping in the Lake District every summer, and she wanted to go to the French Riviera, they went to the Lake District. If he wanted to go to the cinema, and she wanted to go to the theatre, they went to the cinema. If he wanted to see *Top Gun*, and she wanted to see *Out of Africa*, they went and saw *Top Gun*. If he wanted to eat out at an Italian restaurant, and she fancied Lebanese for a change, they went to the Italian. If he wanted meat for supper, and she wanted fish, they ate meat. If he wanted a quiet evening in front of the television, and she wanted friends round for a meal, they had a quiet evening in front of the television. If he didn't want to visit her parents for Christmas, they didn't. If he didn't want her to spend anything on clothes in a particular month, she didn't. And so it went on. 'I told myself it was less painful that way, less trouble,' she concluded, 'and that I didn't honestly care too much about such things – about anything. I was too easy-going to bother battling with his obstinacy.'

Emma suspected it was more a case of her being too compliant.

Motes danced in the rays of the afternoon sun. They streamed through the French windows and settled neatly into rectangles on the polished floorboards. Mother and daughter sat, a little puzzled, a little unhappy, a little worn out, most probably like millions of other women around the world as they pondered the men who'd embedded themselves into their lives like parasitic cuckoos into the hosts' nest, cuckoos they were now expected to feed, nurture and – hardest of all – love.

Everything around them was distant, the faintest of hums that left them alone, together, in an uneasy space. The smell of new-mown grass entered the room from the garden, the fridge gurgled briefly in the kitchen, and the comfortably prosperous suburb outside their front door, tree-lined and litter-free, was empty of people. In its unreality, it was very much like a dream, almost impenetrable.

Her mother sat across from Emma in a skirt of chequered beiges and browns and a white shirt – even though she'd just come in from the garden. Her feet were bare, but there were doubtless, as always, practical flat, slip-on shoes handy nearby. Despite her work in the flowerbeds, not one strand of hair was out of place, and her make-up was still neatly applied. Emma wondered what had attracted her father to this woman all those years ago. She appeared so... well, straight.

'Perhaps I allow him to get his own way too often.'

'So why don't you stand up to him more?'

'You're right, I should. Maybe it's a generational thing. Anyway, it's too late now.'

'It's never too late.'

Her mother, infused with alcohol and melancholy, was beginning to settle in her armchair, like the specks of sunlit dust settling on the polished floorboards and Indian rugs, her wisps of memories drifting and fading across the years as the light drifted and faded across the room.

'The conversations between your father and me become more and more oblique. Sometimes I think that what isn't said says so much more than what is.'

Their daughter had listened to those silences throughout her childhood. They were the sound of her earliest years and, to her, they spoke volumes. If her mother did speak to her father, as often as not it was to make a snide comment or a cynical riposte. So despite her young age, Emma already knew that it was easier to criticize obliquely and to sprinkle sarcasm in your wake than to stand face to face and have a real argument. She swore to herself that she wouldn't end up in such a marriage, where the couple is held together, like glue, by a lack of love, mutual disrespect and selfish disregard, and where one partner always holds the whip hand.

Emma raised herself, then manoeuvred her feet beneath her bottom, into some kind of teenage lotus position. She stared at her mother as if she might be the one to blame for everything.

'Your father married me because I had money.'

This came out of the blue. It was a new angle, a *non sequitur* that a person of Emma's age, brought up on the fast and barely logical cuts of film and television, had little problem adjusting to. 'Right.'

'Money's important to your father – very important. You know that.'

'I suppose. But that doesn't explain why you married him.'

'I'm not sure, darling. To be frank, I have no idea. He certainly didn't ride up on a white stallion for me.'

'What do you mean?'

Her mother didn't answer for a minute. 'Your father was very persistent. He wouldn't take no for an answer. I think he wore me down in the end. He's like that in everything he does – you know that.'

Emma nodded, struggling to see these two old people she knew so well as people she hadn't known at all – young people. Her imagination was scarcely up to the task. They remained youthful strangers, both distant and foreign. 'So what happened to all that money he supposedly married you for?'

'It helped to set him up. Your father's good at business. I'm not saying he wasted it. But my money helped him to establish himself.'

The two women stared at each other. Only recently, the older woman had begun to understand that she might share her feelings with the younger, that perhaps now there was a maturity there that would allow them to talk about things – about life, about the man they shared their lives with. Sadly, the younger woman had almost simultaneously begun to understand that she wasn't interested in sharing intimacies with her mother.

Judith persevered. 'Success is everything to your father. He has never given up on wanting to be someone to reckon with. He likes to be at the top of the pile. That's why this walk is so important to him.'

'Is that why you don't want it to be a success?' She could hardly be bothered to ask the question.

'Did I say that, darling?'

'You've made it pretty obvious.'

Judith raised her eyebrows, then took a sip of her drink. 'Maybe that's how I do feel... But I wish your father well, really. He's a good man, and his heart is in the right place – at least it is for this walk.'

Emma was beginning to lose patience. 'If the walk's successful then you'll have nothing left to complain about.'

'Oh, darling, am I that dreadful?' Fishing for something positive from her 14-year-old, unwilling to have to admit to this portrait of herself as a complaisant complainer. But her daughter didn't answer. Already she was immersed in her own thoughts, trying to work out whether or not she should return to Moosh.

Her mother hadn't been any help at all.

Across London, on the edge of Green Park, amongst the gathering shadows, Adrian sat on the grass outside the mobile home. All around him, on the far side of the ancient amphitheatre of nature, were the lights and hum of the darkening city. The TV cameras and journalists had all departed. This was the calm before the storm, yes, but there was also the heavy weight of expectation hanging in the air.

He sat apart from everyone else, on his own. He was on the threshold of his crowning glory. It struck him that the walk would most likely be even bigger than when, a few years earlier, he'd succeeded in persuading the Prime Minister to speak on behalf of one of his major corporate clients. This would be the summit of his career, yet only now did it dawn on him that there was no one to share the moment with. Judith and he now communicated on only the most mundane and superficial of levels, rarely moving beyond an opinion on a book one of them had read or a movie one of them had seen. What each had done during their separately led days was left untouched, and anything of any meaning or importance, anything that involved the emotions, was never discussed. He found her both distant and withholding. As for his work, she never even attempted to pretend to any interest in it. She loathed the whole industry, and repeatedly told him so. Now, on top of everything, Emma had left him too. He nursed that indefinable pain every father feels when a child sets off into new worlds, leaving him behind, alone in the places they had once shared. It was the pain of knowing he was no longer the centre of her life, and would never be again. Emma was special, she'd believed in him – perhaps still did? That was the wonderful thing about children: they have such faith in their parents. In their eyes, you can do no wrong. But that is the awful thing about them, too: eventually they see the truth, they see you for what you are. And that was the problem with Emma: she now saw through him. And she wasn't yet 15.

Adrian had never had a talent for friendship. He told himself this was because he'd always been too busy building his career, but really it had been a lack of interest in those around him. He was too involved in himself, too narcissistic to be involved with others. Nor had he ever felt at ease in the world of beer-swilling jocularity, arguing about football or appraising passing female talent. His friendships, if that is what they could be called, had been superficial, mirroring the world of PR – all gloss and forced bonhomie, paid for with a drink and a few platitudes. He was unable to think of one ex-colleague who'd be able to stomach his present success, let alone be able to share it with him in any meaningful way. The truth was, although Adrian was a brilliant networker, he was also a bit of a loner. And now he was alone.

A little way off, Anne and Mujtabaa were near a group of young people, one of whom was playing a guitar and singing quietly. Their demeanour announced them to be idealists, seekers and optimists who were unhappy with the state of the world and were determined to do things differently. In Mujtabaa they saw someone of their own age, but they also saw someone who was trying to make a difference, to right a wrong, and to make life fairer. Once they'd greeted him, they kept their distance. They had no desire to impose; they acknowledged his need for space. And in Anne they recognized a kindred soul. They were scarcely aware of an age difference; they liked her too much for that.

The Ethiopian stood on one leg, near to Anne, motionless, facing the lake, his hands draped over his walking staff, which lay across the back of his shoulders. The music washed around him. Ducks moved in and out of the darkness, gliding across the inky waters of the lake behind little crescents of phosphorescence. Beneath a tree, a few yards away, a police officer stood guard, stiff and stolid, heavy on the ground compared to the African he was there to protect.

Sunday

*T*here is something magical about a city centre early on a Sunday morning. The streets and squares are deserted, except for a few parked cars. The traffic lights blink red, red and amber, green, then amber, then back to red, red and amber, green... endlessly, for no one. A lone dustcart may pass, or a food or newspaper delivery van, but there's little else to be seen. Office buildings are empty, with no lights in the windows, and no staff pouring in or out of the massive front doors. There's no clutter and clatter of deal making, financial trading or commercial buying or selling. There may be the modest smell of a bakery on one corner, or the sound of tables and chairs being placed outside a café on another, but almost every sign of life is small and isolated. Perhaps a cyclist will pass by, or an early-morning jogger, but these incidents are few and far between and have about them an air of peaceful relaxation. Even the pigeons seem to rise late on Sunday mornings and, when they do take off, the sharp *thwack, thwack, thwack* of their wings is all that can be heard in the perfect stillness.

The place is empty. The city is yours. It's a momentary flashback to one of the pleasures of childhood: finding yourself alone in a playground, and having the swings, slides, roundabouts and climbing frames all to yourself. No other child is around to spoil the fun. The feeling is purely selfish, and perhaps that is where the magic lies.

Outside the mobile home, it looks like the aftermath of a pop festival. People lie in sleeping bags on the grass or huddle in makeshift tents. Here and there a couple is still upright, having talked their way through the night. The lone guitarist plucks his strings forlornly, but no longer sings. He is surrounded by dozing fans. Rubbish is scattered everywhere, across the grass and around the overflowing dustbins. Ducks lie beside the pond, beaks tucked across their backs.

With the help of Inspector Davidson, Adrian calculated that it would take around two-and-a-half to three hours for Mujtabaa, walking slowly and with frequent stops, to travel the distance between Green Park and Trafalgar Square. He allowed 30 minutes for the length of Birdcage Walk and Great George Street, around an hour to circle Parliament Square and go along Parliament Street, and a final hour to walk up Whitehall to Charing Cross, and across that to Trafalgar Square.

Adrian was insistent they didn't rush this last day. 'We have to spin it out. We want everyone to see Mujtabaa. More importantly, we want them to have time to donate. Once he's passed them, there's the risk they won't reach into their pockets. He has to be there for them to do that. So if he starts speeding up, we have to hold him back. That will be my task. We all know exactly when we have to be at each point along the route, so if we get there early, we wait. This will give us more time to collect money, and give Mujtabaa the chance to rest. It may sound cynical, but the slower he walks, the more people will think he's suffering, and the more generous they'll be. If we start running late, it doesn't matter. People are going to be in Trafalgar Square all afternoon, and if they have to wait longer, it will help build up the feeling of excitement and expectation.'

Dave stood up. 'I don't know what we'll do when this is over,' he said, 'but one thing's for sure: Mujtabaa will be able to eat as much as he likes.' He put a hand on the young man's shoulder: 'A slap-up dinner for you tonight, my friend – whatever takes your fancy.'

Anne quietly suggested that maybe this wasn't such a good idea, and her translation was therefore a more medically correct version of what Dave had just said.

Inspector Davidson left almost at the same time as Emma arrived – soon after ten. Adrian leapt forward to hug her, but she remained stiff and unyielding in his arms. She lowered her voice:

'I want you to know, Dad, I only came back because of Moosh.'

'I understand that, darling. Thank you, anyway.'

When Anne hugged her, Emma hugged her warmly back. This wasn't lost on Adrian. Then she waved to Mujtabaa: 'Hi, Moosh.' He grinned and nodded his head enthusiastically for at least a minute. He even shuffled his feet a little, almost like he was performing an impromptu, celebratory dance.

'See how pleased he is to see you,' said Anne.

Dave said, 'Yes, your boyfriend's missed you.'

Emma ignored this comment – with obvious effort – and Anne, looking meaningfully at Adrian, filled in the awkward silence with, 'Everyone is back together again, and that is how it should be.'

All morning they fretted, wanting to leave the mobile home but being forced to wait, knowing that if they set off before midday they'd arrive at Trafalgar Square too early. Adrian decided it was better to give his daughter space, so he spent a considerable amount of time outside the mobile home talking to the media. There was a crowd of television crews and reporters a short distance from the mobile home, held at bay by the determination of half a dozen police. Despite their entreaties, Adrian refused to allow any of them near Mujtabaa. The young man stayed out of sight, inside the Winnebago.

When Adrian finally went back inside and gave the word, Anne rose slowly, almost reluctantly, to get her ward ready, as she did every morning. First, she removed Mujtabaa's *shämma*. Then she made sure his *jile* was hanging at the correct angle from his belt, and gave his walking stave a quick wipe. She could have been a mother preparing her son for his first formal dance, and it was likely she therefore wanted to scrub his face, hands and feet for such an important day, but she would also have known that Adrian wouldn't forgive her if she did such a thing at this late stage of the walk. 'It's the best I can do,' she said, half to herself, stepping back and giving Mujtabaa the once over. The amulets lay on his neck, flamboyantly decorative, as if intent on mocking the dull and wasted bleakness of their setting. She regarded his skeletal frame and said to him in English, almost under her breath: 'I don't know how you have the strength to keep going, young man.' He stared solemnly down at her.

It was then that Adrian, looking a little self-conscious, stepped forward and awkwardly embraced Mujtabaa. 'Your people will never forget you for what you've achieved for them. This walk will change their lives, possibly the lives of millions. And your own family, in particular, will thank you with all their hearts.'

Anne translated, and the Ethiopian bowed several times, smiling and nodding as he said something. 'He said, "I and my family and my people thank you, my friend".'

Adrian said, 'It's we who must thank you.' He stepped back. 'You've been magnificent.' He turned to his daughter. 'Darling, would you like to say anything to Mujtabaa before we set off?'

She looked embarrassed, but moved forward to stand in front of the young Ethiopian. He watched her, an inquisitive expression on his face, his eyes black and mysterious beneath his protruding forehead. There may have been the slightest of smiles on his lips; it was hard to tell. For a moment neither moved. The young girl, her head down, reached out, first with one hand, then with the other, and took one of Mujtabaa's hands in hers. Without looking up, she took a deep breath and said, so quietly it was difficult to hear her: 'I love you, Moosh, I really do.' No one stirred. 'That's all.' Anne translated, and still no one moved. The Ethiopian let go of Emma's hands and took a small step forward. He put his stick-like arms round her and hugged her. She lay her head on his chest, and they stood there, both with their eyes shut, as motionless and silent as statues. Anne was blinking back the tears, her head to one side. Dave turned away, saying, 'You'll have us all blubbing soon, Emma.' Adrian said nothing. In fact he looked, perhaps for the first time on the walk, like he had no idea what was happening around him.

When the teenagers stood apart, Dave, looking even more ill at ease than Adrian, shambled across to the Ethiopian and gave him a big hug. Still clasping the frail figure, he said: 'Mujtabaa, pal, I want you to know that I think you're a great kid. I had my doubts at the start of this walk, but not now. What you've achieved over the past few days has been nothing short of sensational. I'm proud to have known you.' Anne translated, and the young Ethiopian nodded thoughtfully. Only then did Dave release him, and step back.

Adrian said, 'It's time for us to leave.' And everyone stirred, as if embarrassed by those few minutes of emotion. Emma opened the door, then turned back and said, 'Wait, Anne hasn't had a chance to say anything to Moosh. Do you want to say something, Anne? You don't have to if you don't want to, you know.'

Anne hesitated, looking ill at ease suddenly to find herself the centre of attention. She turned to Mujtabaa and spoke hesitatingly, before reaching out and squeezing his hand. Emma left the mobile home, followed by her father and Dave. When Anne followed them, the young girl asked her what she'd said.

'I told him we would soon both be going home.'

Emma hugged her. 'Oh, that's so sad.'

'No, it isn't. It's what we both want.'

'I meant it's sad for me. I'll miss you both so much.'

As well as the media, there was a crowd of about 200 people outside the mobile home, and they all cheered and clapped when Mujtabaa appeared. He briefly looked up and half-raised an arm, and Adrian realized it was the biggest reaction he'd yet seen from the young Ethiopian.

Emma shouted to Anne: 'Do you know what Mujtabaa means, Anne?'

She shook her head. 'Do you?'

'I looked it up yesterday, at the library. It means "selected" or "chosen".'

'Well I never! That's most appropriate, don't you think?'

Along Birdcage Walk soldiers crowded behind the fence of Wellington Barracks. Members of the public lined the other side of the road, along the edge of the Park.

As Mujtabaa walked in front of where people were standing, they fell silent. Before he reached them, there was frequently a party-like atmosphere, and after he had passed by, the atmosphere once again became joyful, but at the moment he was before them, everyone was silent. People stared. A few clapped, but the applause was hesitant, as if they were overawed by the appearance of the young man from Africa and were unsure as to how they should behave. They didn't know what to say or do, whether to clap or be silent, whether to laugh or cry, be happy or sad. When she first noticed this behaviour, Emma was upset for Mujtabaa, afraid that he would take it personally and wonder why no one was waving. She worried that he'd think the people of England were unfriendly. But as she became used to the people lining the road in silence, and realized that Moosh seemed unaware of their silence, she relaxed. She came to see it as a sign of respect for him.

When they entered Parliament Square, the central area, directly in front of the soaring campanile of Westminster Cathedral, was black with people. Flags flew from every mast and the bells of both the Abbey and the Cathedral rang in competition with each other. The statues of Britain's greatest politicians looked down on the proceedings with varying degrees of interest and disdain, while the Houses of Parliament, half-covered in scaffolding and tarpaulins, squatted beside the sunlit Thames. Adrian thought how strange it was that Mujtabaa would know nothing about this being the seat of democracy in the Western world – in fact nothing about either democracy or the West.

In Whitehall, the crowds were thick on both sides of the grand thoroughfare. The procession passed Downing Street, the Queen's Life Guard building and the old War Office. The buildings had an air of sombre magnificence about them, superior and aloof, as if they had witnessed far more splendid sights than this casually dressed crowd of modern-day commoners amassed beneath their porticos to cheer on a native from some distant part of the Empire. Trafalgar Square and the surrounding streets had been blocked off, so there was no traffic. The Union Jack and the black, yellow and red flag of Ethiopia flew from countless public buildings. Dozens of new volunteer collectors had now joined the walk, and they were continually running across to the mobile home and handing full tins through the window to an Africa Assist employee in the front seat next to Dave. Empty tins were given back. At Trafalgar Square, the collection tins were to be picked up by an armoured truck and taken directly to the security company's warehouse, where the money would be stored until the banks opened on Monday. At one point, the Africa Assist employee, taking another tin from a collector, commented on the huge amount of money being collected.

'It's a fraction of what people have already pledged over the telephone or mailed into us,' said Dave, and let out an uncharacteristic whoop of joy.

There were so many people in Trafalgar Square that the pigeons had been forced to leave. People crowded round the bases of the statues, splashed in the fountains, even sat astride the Landseer lions. They also stood shoulder to shoulder around the foot of the giant platform that had been erected at the southern end of the Square, in front of Nelson's Column. Archbishop Runcie and Cardinal Hume had already addressed the crowds, and an event official was now speaking. 'Mujtabaa is just one hundred yards from his destination, one hundred yards from us here in Trafalgar Square. This young man, even though weak from starvation, has travelled all the way from his own country for his people. He has walked from Heathrow, through the streets of London, for his people. And he is now about to join us here. When he does, I ask you all to give him a big welcome.'

With those few words, a hush fell on the crowd. There was only the slightest of murmurs to betray the presence of so many thousands of people. Adrian, still in Whitehall, wondered what had happened. He was reassured by seeing the solid mass of people at the end of the street, all turned towards the approaching walkers, but why were they so silent?

As Mujtabaa walked past the statue of Charles I and entered Trafalgar Square, the voice again came over the loudspeaker: 'Ladies and gentlemen, please give your warmest, most heartfelt welcome to Mujtabaa Bin Qurban-Ali!' A roar exploded across the Square, stopping the Ethiopian in his tracks. He looked up, astonishment and fear on his face, a hand on his *jile*. Anne hurried to him and, on tiptoes, pulling him down towards her, spoke into his ear. Emma rushed forward, too, and squeezed his arm. She was proud of her friend.

The bells of St Martin-in-the Fields began to ring. The crowd was chanting, *Muj-ta-baa! Muj-ta-baa! Muj-ta-baa!* It was a rock star welcome; all that was missing was the strobe lighting. Pigeons took flight from every building around the Square, wheeling this way and that across the cloudless sky. In every direction, people were cheering and clapping. Reluctantly, Anne encouraged Mujtabaa to move forward, loath to be the person responsible for introducing him to the insanity ahead. Perhaps for the first time since leaving Heathrow, the Ethiopian now understood that he'd reached the end of his journey; this was the place the white ghosts had wanted him to walk to. Although it was surely, to him, just another foreign spot in a foreign country, it must also seem of a size and a magnificence that signified more than the other places he had visited. The crowd alone must tell him he had no further to go. This was his final destination.

Dave drove the Winnebago into The Mall, two police motorbikes forcing a way for him through the crowds. Police on foot could barely hold back the crowd as it closed in on either side of the tall black figure in his sandals and skirt-like *sanafil*, shadowed by Adrian, Anne and Emma. A path ebbed and flowed before them, expanding and contracting as they made their way through the good-natured crowd towards the platform.

Mujtabaa hesitated as he stepped from the road up onto the central area, then stumbled and fell. He landed on his hands and knees. Anne and Emma rushed to crouch down on either side of him. The young man remained motionless, his head bowed, his spine shockingly visible to those standing around him. Anne was speaking to him, but he neither moved nor spoke. Holding his arms, the two women encouraged him to rise. The people around them had fallen silent, while those in the distance, not knowing what was happening, continued to applaud and cheer. But slowly the silence rippled outwards from Mujtabaa and spread to the furthest corners of the Square.

'It's been too much for him,' Anne whispered. She wanted to magic the young man away from all of this madness, from the stares of the crowd, and from the uncomfortable feeling that everyone wanted something off him. She could sense their hunger. They wanted to devour him, even though he was no more than a skeleton.

Adrian walked back to where they were standing. 'Is he all right? He can't stop here, Anne. You have to get him to the platform. He can sit down there.'

'He needs to rest for a second. Try to be patient.'

Adrian groaned. The expectancy of the crowd hemmed them in on all sides, stifling, demanding and without respite. 'But he's almost there. He's so close.'

The voice on the platform, disembodied and distant, was speaking to the crowd, trying to fill in time, like a Dimbleby on some royal occasion. 'As I'm sure you all appreciate, ladies and gentlemen, Mujtabaa is very weak, and this walk over the past few days has really taken it out of him. Please be patient. He's just catching his breath, and then he'll join us on the platform. While we're waiting, I'd like to remind you once again of some of the startling statistics still coming out of Mujtabaa's country...'

Not more statistics! went through Adrian's head. Is there no escaping them? Then, almost immediately, Mujtabaa straightened up and, letting go of Emma and Anne – very much as a toddler will let go of his mother's hands to set off on unsteady feet across a room – once again started to walk, with faltering steps, in the direction of the platform. There was a collective sigh of relief from the people around them, and a few applauded. Then the whole Square once again fell silent. Everyone who was able to see Mujtabaa, watched his slow progress through the mass of people. A television reporter was walking backwards, a camera on his shoulder, the lens just a few feet from the young Ethiopian's face. As they neared the bottom of the steps that led up to the platform, Adrian moved ahead. He climbed a couple of steps and turned round to take Mujtabaa's hand. He took one step up, then paused.

'Come on, Mujtabaa. Come on, you're almost there.' Adrian, pleading, took another step, pulling the young man by the hand as he did so. Anne, who was close behind Mujtabaa, had one hand held up behind his back ready to support him should that be necessary. He looked like he was walking on stilts, stiff and awkward.

'Take it easy, Mujtabaa, you're doing great. That's it, well done.'

As the young man ascended to the platform, each step taken with painful slowness, he was watched by the hundreds of people around them and millions of people in front of their television sets at home. When, finally, he straightened up at the top, swaying slightly from the effort, the crowd renewed their shouting and clapping. He was ushered to a seat at the front of the platform, but Adrian told the official that Mujtabaa preferred to stand, even though he was weak. So the young man stood at the front of the platform in his habitual pose, legs crossed at the ankles, leaning sideways, his walking staff like a support beneath his armpit, that arm bent, his hand flat against his forehead.

Adrian felt it would be out of place for himself, Emma and Anne to sit when Mujtabaa was standing, so they also stood, a little behind him and to one side. But first he walked along the line of officials and celebrities, shaking hands with each of them. They all remained standing after he passed. Along with James Balcombe, who was managing to look both nervous and elated simultaneously, he rejoined Emma, Anne and Mujtabaa.

He stared down at the mass of humanity – a sea of faces, white and black, young and old, rich and poor, like open flowers stretching towards the sunlight from the platform. He felt proud, not that all these people had turned out for Mujtabaa, but that they had turned out because of him. It was his determination that had brought everyone to this spot. It's not a bad turnout for a PR exercise, he thought. This will make everyone in the business sit up. Adrian Burles hasn't lost his touch.

Dotted through the crowd he saw the scarlet vests of the Africa Assist collectors. A few people were waving the flag of Ethiopia above their heads, and for a brief moment he puzzled about what statement they were intent on making. At his feet, directly in front of the platform, were the media, the TV cameras and the press photographers. Then his eyes fell on a lady languidly waving a white cloth above her head, and he recognized 'Veronica' from what seemed like a long time ago. She was standing amongst a group of Africans, the only white face in the group, and he saw many of those he and James Balcombe had been talking to over the last few days. Then he was distracted by a tall man, with a chaos of red hair, standing still and expressionless to one side of the media. He was unshaven and looked unwashed. Adrian vaguely recalled him from somewhere, but before it came to him his attention was diverted to a father suddenly holding his young child aloft so that it could better see what was going on. The boy was obviously more interested in the people around him than what was going on above his head, on the platform. Then Adrian spotted the numerous faces framed by the windows of Canada House and South Africa House. The Square, and every building around it, was full of decent, well-meaning citizens who wanted to do their bit to right the wrongs of the world – at least, that was how he interpreted their presence. The vast crowd gave off an almost overpowering feeling of love. This was the very essence of charity: simple, straightforward concern for one's neighbour. It had nothing to do with money – that was too removed, too second-hand. It was more to do with deeds, with *being there* for someone and sharing their pain. People were crowded into the six-columned portico of St Martin-in-the-Fields, and there were others in front of the National Gallery, more than at any time in its history – including all the New Year's Eve celebrations.

One of the rally organizers asked Adrian to address the crowd. He was prepared. When he stepped forward to the microphone, he felt buoyed up by all of the people below him, as if he were surfing on a wave of emotion. He spoke quietly, measuring his words.

'When you go without food for a long time,' he said, 'you suffer severe hunger pangs.' The few pockets in the crowd still making a noise now fell silent. 'However, after a few days your body learns to adapt, and the pain goes away. Your body then starts to live off its stores of fat. If you are a very fat person, your reserves may keep you going for a few weeks. If you are not a very fat person, they will keep you going for a much shorter period of time. Those reserves of fat give you enough strength and enough energy to perform tasks that are not too strenuous, like going out to look for food, or walking down the street to beg for money. Eventually, however, you start to metabolize tissue protein. This is a fancy way of saying that your body starts to eat its own muscles: you start to cannibalize yourself. Not surprisingly, this soon results in feelings of listlessness and depression. You are too tired to do anything now, certainly you cannot be bothered to work, or to go out and beg. But your mind still works.' He paused dramatically. Not a sound could be heard.

'The fact that your mind still works is a shame, because it means it will be quite clear to you what is going on. You will have feelings of anger and irritability, possibly fits of impotent rage. You won't be bothered with sex. You'll have completely lost interest in sex because your body is telling you that reproduction is no longer a priority. Your survival is now the only priority. Even the future of your people or your family is no longer of any concern to you. Slowly your mind drifts. You can no longer concentrate. You become indifferent to what is going on around you. You become indifferent to everything, absolutely everything. Your husband or your wife, even your own child, can die beside you, and you will not care, you will not give a damn.' And for a split second his mind went back to the mother at the Korem clinic, whose dead baby had been removed from her side as he stood over her.

'The truth is,' he continued, 'you now no longer care about your own survival. Whether you live or die is of absolutely no concern to you. It doesn't matter one way or the other. At this stage an aid worker may come up and hand you a piece of bread, and you will let it fall to the ground. All you want to do is lie down. And that, eventually, is what you do: you lie down. You lie down... and you do not think... and you do not move...' His eyes swept slowly over the crowd. 'And then you die.'

He paused. There was no sound in the Square. Although everyone was listening to Adrian, all eyes were on Mujtabaa, standing there, solitary, like a burnt match sticking vertically out of a pile of grey ash. They were linking Adrian's words with the man from the Danakil, imagining him experience each of those different stages of malnutrition.

230

He started to speak again. He told the crowd about the terrible suffering still going on in Ethiopia, despite the success of Live Aid, and what Africa Assist was doing to try to alleviate the people's distress. 'We will never forget these people. We must never forget these people.' He told them about his pet projects, those that would eventually help people like Mujtabaa help themselves. And he told them about the considerable amount of money that had been raised on this walk, and where it would all go.

He also told the crowd about Mujtabaa; his courage, his perseverance and the hopes he had for his family and his people. 'This man is a saint. He is a soldier. And he is a man of enormous strength and courage. I thank him with all my heart for having agreed to undertake this walk.' The young man from the Danakil Desert, towering over the nurse at his side, stood as straight as a spear and almost as thin, his eyes, full of the known and the unknowable, looking somewhere distant, over the roof of the National Gallery. All the words that had been said about him, now and over the past few days, meant nothing to him. He heard them, but they were without meaning. Although wearing only the skirt around his waist, his *sanafil* and sandals, and carrying only his hardwood stave, although covered in dust and with his frizzled hair still encrusted with salt, it was the citizens of London – well fed, well clothed and well washed – who waited and listened at his feet.

Adrian finished by saying, 'I know that I speak for Mujtabaa as well as for everyone at Africa Assist when I thank you all, most sincerely, for your generosity, your support, your kindness, and for being here today.' This also was greeted by enthusiastic applause before he continued: 'I especially want to thank Anne Chaffey, the nurse who runs a health clinic in Korem, who has accompanied Mujtabaa and cared for him ever since we left Ethiopia.' As the crowd clapped and cheered, Anne's only reaction was a modest smile and to bow her head. To save her further discomfort, Adrian continued: 'Also my assistant at Africa Assist, Dave Parker, who has done a wonderful job organizing this walk, keeping us all in line and making sure everything ran smoothly. I also want to thank all of our volunteers who have worked tirelessly for this walk to be the success it has.' Followed by more applause. 'Finally my daughter, Emma, who is known as Moosh's shadow, who has done her very best to introduce him to the joys of pop music…' He missed just a beat before adding, 'as well as takeaway food.' There was a lot of laughter and clapping and Emma covered her face with embarrassment.

When the applause died down, James Balcombe stepped up to the microphone. Uncharacteristically, he spoke very briefly. 'To date – and we're still counting – this man standing before you has raised over £12 million.' The crowd understood that, it was a sum that could be easily grasped, and it was concrete evidence of how generous they had all been. There was a roar of appreciation from the crowd. He also pointed out that Africa Assist used less money to run their organization than any other charity in the UK. 'Over 95 per cent of what we receive goes directly to the people who need it. Less than five per cent goes on administration costs.' This also was followed by more cheers and applause. He then thanked Mujtabaa and Adrian, Anne Chaffey, Emma and David Parker. As he finished speaking, Mujtabaa whispered something to Anne. She had to stand on tiptoe and he had to lean his head towards her in order for her to hear. She turned and spoke to Adrian who again stepped up to the microphone. 'Mujtabaa has asked Anne to thank everyone for helping him, his family and his tribe. He says he will not forget the kindness of the white people.'

While everyone was cheering and clapping, Adrian went up to Mujtabaa and put an arm around his shoulders. Someone on the platform, a woman with a guitar trying to imitate Joan Baez, started to sing *We shall overcome* in a hoarse voice. Slowly the crowd picked up the tune and sang with her.

It was all over. They could now go. Adrian hugged Mujtabaa. 'You're a free man. Now you can return home.' It had already been arranged that Mujtabaa and Anne would go home with him and Emma, so they could stay and rest for a few days before flying back to Ethiopia. Anne would also take some time off to visit her sister in Sheffield. Adrian had dreams of getting

Mujtabaa invited onto a few chat shows, so gaining some more publicity and raising even more money. He considered it too great an opportunity to miss.

The executive director of Africa Assist was banging his PR consultant on the back. 'Excellent show, Adrian. Everything we'd hoped for. Why don't you all come back to my place? We're having a small celebration.'

'We have to get Mujtabaa home, James.'

'But he can come too, and Anne and your daughter.'

'I think we should forget about it for now. Mujtabaa's tired, he has to rest. We have to take care of his health.'

With more back slappings and several 'Jolly good shows', Balcombe said goodbye and dived off to talk to Vanessa Redgrave. Although she was a bit too left leaning for him, he obviously considered her worth cultivating.

They slowly descended the steps, Adrian and Emma first, followed closely by Mujtabaa and Anne. Adrian was shouting to them. At the bottom of the steps he turned and hugged Emma.

'Where's Dave?' she shouted in his ear.

'He's waiting for us on the corner of The Mall.'

They immersed themselves gradually in the swirling sea of friendly, singing faces beneath the platform. Everyone was smiling, and everyone wanted to shake Adrian's hand. It was as if, between them all, they'd solved the problems of the world, and everyone felt good. They were happy. Despite Anne's best efforts to prevent them, people reached out to touch Mujtabaa or to pat him on the back. Adrian could barely make headway through the crowd, and wondered at the lack of organization, but he was almost too relaxed to care. Inspector Davidson suddenly appeared with a couple of other officers, pushing their way through the crowd towards Adrian. 'We'll escort you to your van.'

Adrian turned to beckon the others. A couple with a young baby had fallen in immediately behind him, and behind them two teenagers were singing *We shall overcome* at the tops of their voices and doing an impromptu dance. Adrian felt hemmed in. He stood on tiptoe. He could see Anne holding on to Mujtabaa.

She was looking worried, but Emma, her back to her father, appeared to be heading in their direction to help. They'll be all right, he thought. As he raised an arm to wave to them, to direct them in the right direction, he saw the man with the wild red hair coming towards him, at an angle, from the left, and it suddenly struck him where he'd seen him before.

He looked like a man striding into the surf, his arms flailing to left and right, pulling himself through the waves of people, his long, dirty raincoat, like great splashes of grey water, flying up around him. Everyone was falling away from the crazy figure, leaping out of his path to avoid any contact. And Adrian, with absolute certainty, understood that he himself was the wild man's goal. At that moment, everything slowed down, almost jammed, as when the film gets caught in an old eight-millimetre projector and the negative starts to burn at the edges. Stand your ground, he told himself, and the words echoed in the empty chambers of his paralysed mind: *stand your ground.* But the wild man thumped him on the shoulder and sent Adrian reeling backwards against someone in the crowd. He had a problem staying on his feet. The red-haired homeless man, with his white sepulchral face, wild eyes and cruel babbling mouth, stood in front of him, waving his arms and shouting. He had created his own small arena in the throng, everyone shuffling outwards to form a circle around them. Adrian stood on the circumference, and he could have been a bystander too, a spectator, except that the wild, red-haired man was trying to drag him into the circle, towards the epicentre of everyone's attention. He was shouting at him, in fact he was screaming his head off, and Adrian was frowning and thinking, Why doesn't he shut up? What's he going on about? But he couldn't hear what was being said because of the roar of blood in his ears, a pounding, booming, interrupted sound that blocked out the crowd and brought an eerie, distant hush to everything around him. Adrian told himself to listen, to concentrate on the torrent of words pouring out of that babbling mouth, looking obscenely pink and wet amongst the tangle of red beard. He shook his head, trying to clear his ears. Concentrate, he told himself. He blinked, and looked up. And at that very instant the wild figure stopped shouting. Adrian thought, Damn, I've missed what he was saying, and wanted to laugh. But the wild figure had produced a knife from beneath his raincoat, and Adrian said to himself, He's only got a carving knife for heaven's sake, that's not so bad. But over the man's shoulder, coming towards them, he saw Mujtabaa, and suddenly, with great urgency, he thought, Stay away from this, stay right out of this, don't come near. I don't want you to get hurt. But by then it was too late to stop him, and the young Ethiopian stepped between Adrian and the red-haired man.

She saw her dad's eyes bulge and his mouth open. He looked like he was about to be sick. He was stepping back from Moosh as if her friend were contaminated, holding him at arm's length. Her dad was looking straight at her, into her eyes, over the heads of all those people, and he was pleading with her across the distance that separated them. She could see he was frightened. Frantic, desperate to reach him, she pushed past a couple with a baby. Some dancing teenagers swore at her as she elbowed her way past them, but she didn't apologize, so intent was she on getting to her father. What could be wrong? She noticed how badly the homeless man smelt as she pushed him to one side. Now she could see, right in front of her, Moosh leaning against her father, resting, like close friends sharing a quiet moment together. She thought, it's all been too much for him, he's exhausted. But she was more concerned for her father at that moment; the pain showing on his face was so unbearable.

'Dad, Dad, are you all right?' – her voice sounding distant, even to herself, almost distorted. But her father was no longer looking at her. He would only look down, staring at Moosh. She followed his gaze and, at first, was unable to see what could be of interest. Moosh had one hand on the hilt of his *jile* and the other resting against his midriff. He had dropped his staff. Then she saw the redness seeping through his black fingers, long globules of red ballooning out, before bursting and falling, splattering onto his *sanafil* and down onto his bare feet. And she thought, What's happening? Why doesn't he say anything? She moved to his side, puzzled, and put an arm round him. 'What's up, Moosh? Are you all right?' – forgetting that the Ethiopian couldn't understand her. He turned to face her, looking stern, saying nothing, and he too appeared puzzled. She was impatient. Did no one understand what was going on? Moosh smiled at her, but with eyes that were already cold and distant. He sagged against her. And at that same moment, the homeless man's voice penetrated her consciousness. Why doesn't he leave us alone, she thought; can't he see we have enough problems here without him going on like this? She briefly glanced towards him and saw that he was waving a bloody carving knife from side to side, his eyes a painful red from either tiredness, alcohol, drugs or craziness, and he was shouting at Moosh and her dad.

Reality came crashing back in, as if the film had once again engaged with the sprockets. People around Adrian started to move normally, and sound returned. Anne rushed up and, for the first time on the walk, she appeared flustered, overwhelmed by the situation, almost in a state of shock, and Adrian thought, she's a nurse, she should be able to cope with this. But it was obvious she couldn't. She was holding fast to Mujtabaa's arm and either trying to gulp in more oxygen or trying to say something. Emma had taken a handkerchief out of her backpack and was tentatively trying to push it beneath Mujtabaa's fingers and directly over the wound. At the same time, she was trying to stop him from falling to the ground. She was like a child attempting to prop up a giant. Her father could see the grim determination on his daughter's face, and he felt a sudden wave of love sweep over him. She said something, which he only just caught over the chaos around them. 'It's not fair. You didn't have a chance to draw your *jile.*'

Adrian eased himself between Anne and Mujtabaa, and gently lowered the young man to the ground. As he did so, he was half aware of Inspector Davidson coming up behind the red-haired homeless man and grabbing the hand that held the knife. He twisted it until the weapon fell to the ground, and immediately the man started to cry, shaking his head and shoulders as if unable to work out what to do next. 'He shouldn't have got everything. That's all I'm saying. He shouldn't have got everything.' Inspector Davidson had a hand on the man's shoulder, even though he didn't look like he was about to flee. Other police arrived. They handcuffed the man, and started to move the crowd back. Walkie-talkies crackled around them, and the television crews and photographers closed in like predators.

Adrian found himself surrendering Mujtabaa to Emma. She was sitting on the ground as she manoeuvred him onto her lap, nestling his head against her chest. 'Has someone called an ambulance, Dad?' He wondered at her coolness, at the clarity of her words. She was still holding the handkerchief over Mujtabaa's wound, but already it was saturated with blood. She was resting her cheek on the young man's chaos of curly hair and whispering to him. Then he said something to her. His eyes were closed, but his lips moved. She looked wildly around for Anne. The nurse bent down, supporting herself on Adrian's shoulder, trying to catch what the Ethiopian was saying. His voice was barely audible. She straightened up, clutching Adrian's arm. 'He says he wants to go for a ride in a small truck.'

Emma cried, 'Oh God, tell him yes, Anne, tell him yes.'

Mujtabaa opened his eyes and looked up at Emma, but there was no focus, no contact. She sobbed, and clutched him tighter. But he closed his eyes and it was no longer certain that he could hear her words. The photographers captured this image: the dying, skeletal, almost naked Ethiopian lying in the arms of an English schoolgirl, two teenagers from different sides of the world.

Both Adrian and Anne looked down at Emma and were amazed by her strength. Adrian, crouching, almost on his knees, fumbled for Mujtabaa's hand. 'Forgive me,' he said, but possibly only his daughter heard the words. 'I had no idea...' He, also, had tears in his eyes, and it was then that he became aware of everything slipping between his fingers, events moving beyond him, and he was unable to grasp any of it – it had all become too nebulous. For the first time in his life, he no longer had any control over what was happening around him. Like a person at the centre of an earthquake, he was unable to find anything to focus on; there was nothing around him that was stable enough to anchor him.

Two paramedics appeared from out of the crowd with a stretcher. They prised the Ethiopian away from Emma and laid him on the canvas, but she refused to let go of his hand. She continued to hold it as they carried Mujtabaa through the crowd to the waiting ambulance. The front of her denim jacket and T-shirt were stained with blood. Emma and Anne went in the ambulance to St George's Hospital, which they'd passed only the day before surrounded by cheering crowds. The police escorted Adrian to the Winnebago, where he broke the news to Dave. Then the two men drove in silence to the hospital. The media were there before them.

In Trafalgar Square, James Balcombe, as chairman of Africa Assist, told the crowd what had happened – or as much as anyone knew – and he asked them to pray for Mujtabaa's recovery. He asked them to disperse quietly and to keep the young Ethiopian in their thoughts. A woman in the crowd started to sing *Give Peace a Chance*, her voice tuneless and cracking with emotion. A few people joined in. Slowly the crowd dispersed, although small groups huddled together for many more hours, asking questions, stating theories, trying to understand how such a thing could happen in a civilized society.

Later, when the Square was almost empty and the pigeons had moved back in, the platform itself and the scattered piles of rubbish were the sole reminders of what had happened there that Sunday.

―――――――

After

*T*here are no roads to the village, only tracks. There is no signpost pointing to where it is, just barely discernible scars and scratches in the ground to indicate that some people have already been there. For those who do eventually reach this spot, unmarked on all but a handful of maps, there is little to be seen. In the overwhelming expanse of glistening white salt flats and – to the north and east – purplish black lava fields, there is nothing but a scattering of derelict sheds and huts, sheets of corrugated metal and discarded oil drums. They lie there – no, they've subsided there – in the middle of nowhere, deflated and stupefied by the heat.

Here and there are dotted the remnants of some traditional huts made from lengths of dom-palm fibre and shaped like upturned boats. As the last bastions against an encroaching civilization, they have seemingly fared better than the dilapidated – and incongruous – Western-style sheds that have moved into the area. These gape, flap and shrivel where they stand, the darkness of their windows and doorways mirrored in the eyes of the spectral figures that materialize briefly into the blinding light then disappear back into one of the rare patches of shade. It's an inhospitable, insubstantial place, clinging as perilously to the surface of the continent as it does to the cartographers' cognizance.

'It's unlikely Mujtabaa lived here.' Anne, who was driving the run-down Toyota four-wheel drive with a tarpaulin over the flatbed rear, had to raise her voice to be heard above the sound of the labouring engine.

'But I thought it was where he was from,' Emma said. 'He told you that, didn't he, Anne?'

'Not in so many words. He was a nomad, Emma – in fact a transhumant rather than a nomad.'

'What's that?'

Adrian interrupted. 'It's when a tribe wanders between several locations, but always leaving a small group of people permanently in one of them.'

'But couldn't this place have been one of those?'

'Possibly,' Anne said. 'Mujtabaa may have come from around here. He certainly came from this direction to reach Korem.'

'Where he came from,' her father added, 'is probably not even marked on the map – if he can be said to have come from anywhere at all.'

They had flown out of London three days earlier. Mujtabaa's body was held for over a week by the Coroner before an autopsy was done, and then embalmed for the journey back to Ethiopia. There was huge, worldwide publicity after the events in Trafalgar Square: long articles in the newspapers, programmes on television and even questions in the House of Commons. There was a lot of breast-beating and soul-searching, and the flood of money into the offices of Africa Assist became a tidal wave.

A few days before their departure from England, Anne was with Adrian in his study. He turned on all the lights for her with a flourish, like a magician performing the finale of a trick. Anne, momentarily taken aback by his enthusiasm, told herself she shouldn't have been. It was a part of his nature. He is like a child, she told herself, so eager and passionate. She admired him for that.

'I didn't know you collected toy soldiers,' she said.

'My father was a collector – in a small way. It was an interest I inherited. It was a while before it became a bit of an obsession for me.'

They stood by the display case and he pointed out, as well as named, all the pieces behind the glass. He wouldn't stop talking. And while he spoke, she wondered at adults who spend their days acquiring: forever on the hunt for something else that they can buy, possess, collect, lock away and call their own. On his deathbed, while reflecting on his life, would there be memories of his toy-soldier collection, or of Judith and Emma? Perhaps he'd think of the walk, Mujtabaa and the people he'd helped in Africa? She didn't wish to hazard a guess as to which way he'd lean.

'Did you know Churchill used to collect toy soldiers?' She wasn't surprised, but attempted to appear so. 'Also Steven Spielberg, and Princess Margaret – she had an amazing collection, most of them given to her by the Britains company when she was a child. But I expect she was never allowed to play with them.'

The longer they stayed in the study, the more morose he became. She sensed this, and tried to compensate by showing increased enthusiasm for his little figurines. She blamed herself for the fact that he was growing quieter and retreating back into himself, yet her exclamations of surprise and delight had slowly dried up, almost simultaneously with his explanations of regimental dress and history. The pauses in their conversation began to resemble an overstretched supply line.

After one particularly long silence, he said: 'I'm thinking of throwing it in, Anne.'

She was shocked. 'Now why would you do that? After all you've achieved.'

He looked at her blankly, before understanding. 'I'm talking about my collection, my toy soldiers.'

'I'm sorry. I thought...'

'It seems so...' He struggled to find the right word, eventually settling on, '*worthless*. Perhaps I should say, unimportant, that might be more accurate.' He half smiled, like he was too embarrassed to admit to the emotions he was feeling. 'Maybe James will let me work for Africa Assist full time – although I'd probably drive him crazy, or vice versa. Perhaps I should even come out to Africa, although I'm not sure Judith would be thrilled with that idea.

'I think what I'm saying is that it doesn't seem right somehow. You meet a person like Mujtabaa and suddenly all those things that once seemed so important to you now seem so unimportant.

It's like you see them in perspective for the first time.'

'That can happen.' She'd seen it happen many times before. In fact, wasn't that what had happened to her once?

'I heard a story once about an advertising man – a copywriter, I think – who wrote advertisements for Oxfam, and he was sent out to somewhere in Africa on a fact-finding mission – just as I did – and when he returned to the UK, he handed in his notice to the agency where he worked, sold his house and car, and went and lived in the Highlands of Scotland. He lived sustainably – went the whole hog, just dropped out. I'm ashamed to admit that I laughed when I heard the story, but I see exactly where he was coming from now.'

Then he was saying: 'I've known about famines in parts of Africa for a long time. Why wouldn't I know about them, especially in the last few years? Everyone does. But it's meeting and getting to know an individual that makes those famines real, something you can readily grasp.'

That was your reason for the walk, she thought. That's what you told me in Korem. To personalize the suffering. She nodded her head. She'd seen this transformation in so many people over the years, and yet it never ceased to amaze and delight her.

'It makes one re-evaluate things.'

'And do you believe giving up your work or your toy soldiers will help Mujtabaa?'

He appeared surprised by her question. 'It's possible, don't you think?'

She waited, wanting to give him the necessary time to work out the answer for himself.

'I'm not sure. To be honest, I don't even know now if one death is worth £16 million, or however much we've collected. Whereas a week ago I wouldn't have had any doubts.'

'I'm not able to judge that, Adrian, although I can say that it wasn't your fault Mujtabaa died. It wasn't because of any decision you made.'

'There was always the risk he'd die. I knew that, and I knowingly gambled with his life. I remember thinking, if 2,000 die, or 2,001 die, what's the difference? I thought that, Anne.

Isn't that terrible?' He seemed determined to prosecute the case against himself. 'Perhaps it would have been better if we'd left him in the desert – never brought him to London. Not better for his people of course, nor for everyone else. And that's what you thought, isn't it? Probably still do.'

'I've never said that, Adrian.'

'Not in so many words. But I'm pretty sure you thought it.'

It was true. She'd had her doubts about the walk, about the morality of such an event, but she'd let herself be won over by his enthusiasm. Despite Mujtabaa's death, she'd reached the conclusion that Adrian had been right all along. It had been a difficult decision to come to, and one that was very finely balanced, but the good, in her mind at least, probably outweighed the bad.

'Adrian, you have to think of the thousands of lives that will be saved because of that money.' She put a hand on his arm. 'You mustn't blame yourself. You did the right thing – and if you didn't, only God can decide that.'

'I wish I had your faith.'

As he turned out the lights and they left the room, she said: 'You had to try. You're not the kind of person who could do nothing. It's true, Mujtabaa died, but he'd have been happy with what he achieved. He found it hard, certainly, especially when sometimes he didn't understand what was happening. You know what he told me near the end of the walk – I've never told anyone up to now.'

'What was that?'

And she quickly recounted how Mujtabaa had begun to plan for his return to his people. He told her he wanted to fly back to Ethiopia. He wished to take all of the money to feed his people in a plane, and for Adrian, Anne and Emma to go with him. He was very excited when he told Anne that even Abherra – whom she guessed was the tribal chief, or *dardar* – would look at Mujtabaa with admiration, even astonishment, if he flew above their heads, round and round in a circle, waving to everyone out of a flying machine. He wanted to fly round the camp many times so that his friends would have the chance see him. When he landed near the camp, they'd rush over and would watch in amazement as Mujtabaa stepped out of the plane. They'd be even more astonished when the headman, and the lady in the straw hat and the girl with glass over her eyes appeared by his side.

'Why, it's Mujtabaa,' they'd say as all of this unfolded. 'Look, I cannot believe it, Mujtabaa has come back to us from the land of the spirits in a flying machine. How well he looks! And see, he's come back with some white ghosts. They're holding hands and talking together like the best of friends. And look at all the money he's holding. There's so much, he's barely able to carry it.'

Anne told Adrian that Mujtabaa had pictured his people all gathering round, talking excitedly, wanting to touch him, wanting to hold his hand, asking how he'd come by so much money. At first Mujtabaa had said to Anne that he'd clap his hands, slap his friends on the back and laugh and shout – but then, almost immediately, he'd had second thoughts. Maybe it would look better if he remained silent, a little solemn and distant, to show how much he'd learnt in the land of the white man. It might be better if he kept his face serious, his expression a little thoughtful, as if he had a lot on his mind and no time for unimportant things like the number of camels he now owned. That would surely impress his friends even more. They'd whisper amongst themselves, not daring to raise their voices in his presence. Even Safia would hang back, respectful and a little overawed. She'd appreciate that he could marry any woman in the clan now. No one would refuse him now that he'd been to the land of the white ghosts and seen what he'd seen.

'Yes,' Anne smiled at the memory, 'I think it all went a little to his head – but in the nicest possible way. You know, Adrian, he was such an innocent.'

Mujtabaa had told Anne that he was convinced he'd be the most popular man in the *mela*. They might even make him the new *dardar*. So many things could happen. But first, before anything else, he had to arrange for the new wells and livestock, and to fly lots of food to his people. None of his friends would be able to understand how he'd won all of these things by walking, so it would be necessary to take everything with him when he returned to the desert. His people had to see all of these good things for themselves, they couldn't just be told about them.

And there'd be a special gift for Safia. He would take a magic box back with him to put in the corner of their hut. And he'd show her how to point the stick at the box and press it in a special way, and then she'd see people appear inside the box. And he'd show her how to change what she saw, so that she could see different people doing different things.

Adrian was smiling as he listened to Anne. 'I like that. I like the way he could picture all of that. So there's no doubt he understood how much he'd achieved if he was imagining such a triumphant return to his people. That's good.'

They both sank into a brief reverie about their Ethiopian friend, sadness and fondness vying for the upper hand. Eventually, they left the study. At the top of the stairs, the nurse lowered her voice. 'How is Emma?' On her arrival at their home, after visiting her sister up in Yorkshire for a couple of days, Anne had been shocked to see the young girl, slumped in an armchair, red-eyed and pale-faced, speaking only in a colourless monotone.

'She's not good. She cries at the slightest thing. We go for walks together and talk about Mujtabaa. She cannot stop talking about him.'

'It's wonderful she can talk to you.'

'She talks to her mother more.' He turned to the nurse, one hand grasping the banisters, suddenly intimate. 'But you know what's good about this?' Briefly, she wondered at the confidences he was revealing. 'We've never been closer, as a family. This tragedy has drawn us together. Even my wife is involved.'

They went downstairs. In the sitting room Anne reached out and squeezed Emma's hand. 'I'm so pleased you're coming with us to Ethiopia.'

'I had to, Anne.' She spoke seriously. 'It's what Moosh would have wanted.'

Fearful of being accompanied by hordes of media people, Anne and Emma had begged Adrian to keep their travel arrangements secret. Against his own inclinations, he had agreed.

They drove the hundred miles from Korem, where they'd spent the night at Anne's health clinic, to Mek'ele, another town high up on the Ethiopian Plateau. Their local helper, Ahmed, rode in the back of the four-wheel drive with the food and the coffin.

The next day, on a pleasantly warm September afternoon, they left Mek'ele, and ten miles out of town found the dirt road that slalomed down the near-vertical face of the cliff to the desert. The temperature rose almost as rapidly as they descended. Adrian admired Anne's calm assurance behind the wheel, the quiet determination on her face in the shadow beneath her straw hat. She seemed more in her element than in London. When Emma commented on how dangerous the road was, Anne replied: 'One becomes fatalistic when living in Africa. We believe that when our time is up, it's up, and there's nothing we can do about it.'

'Let's hope our time isn't up now,' Adrian muttered, glancing into the void below.

'None of us has control over that.'

'But you do have a steering wheel in your hands, Anne.' Then, to his daughter squashed between the two of them: 'She is holding a steering wheel, isn't she?' And they all laughed.

The Danakil Desert lay at the base of the Plateau. It was grey and yellow, interspersed with ember-red and dark-brown volcanic stains. Overhead, the sky was an unblemished, blazing blue. Emma stared out of the window at the featureless landscape, and thought it the loneliest, most uninviting and hottest place she'd ever seen.

'I'm glad you came with us, Dad.'

'Why's that?'

'It wouldn't have been the same without you. I think it's great that you can say goodbye to Moosh. He was your friend, too.'

He squeezed her hand. 'I'm glad, too.' In fact he'd originally told Anne he wouldn't be able to accompany them to Ethiopia, insisting he'd be too busy organizing the distribution of the money that had been collected.

'It's important for Emma that you come, Adrian. And for Mujtabaa.' It had been said as if she just wished to pop the thought into his head, and it had worked. He had thought about it, and decided Anne was right.

The following day they reached their destination. They stared out through the dirty windscreen at the burnt and blackened landscape, dust-laden tracks leading off in every direction, and wondered where everyone could be. Around them was either blinding light or dark shadow, without any gradations in between.

'Is this the right place?' Emma asked, dabbing her forehead with a wet handkerchief.

'There isn't anywhere else.' Anne took a drink of water from a bottle she kept beneath the dashboard. She leant forward and looked across her young passenger to Adrian. 'Shall we see if there's anyone here?' He nodded.

She turned off the engine and they all climbed out of the truck. The silence surged in around them. After the incessant roar of the four-wheel drive, the silence was startling. No birds sang, no insects hummed, no leaves rustled. It was like suddenly finding oneself standing on Mars, with only the faintest, distant susurration of other orbiting heavenly bodies overhead.

Emma wished they'd remained inside the four-wheel drive. The heat was unbearable. She remembered the primitive facilities at Korem with feelings verging on affection, certainly with longing, like the town had been the very essence of civilization. There'd been the clinic, a store, a petrol station, a church and a Coke machine. Everything had been hopelessly out of date, but at least it had been there.

This village, however, was no more than a ghost town. A couple of goats, all skin and bone, wandered around like lost souls. There was no rubbish, no garbage, to be seen anywhere.

'There must be people here. They'd never leave those goats behind.'

They left Ahmed by the truck and set off between the huts. Peering up from beneath her wide-brimmed hat, Anne said, 'There would have been more people here before the famine. Either they've headed off for the refugee camps or they've been relocated.'

The ground was crisp, caked hard like the surface of a crème brûlée, except that this one was whiteish, salt-coloured, and burnt the eyes. Rounding the corner of a shed, they saw, in the open entrance beneath a makeshift awning, a group of Afar. There were three old people – although Anne later told Emma they were probably only around 50 years old – a man and two women squatting on the left, while on the right sat two young women, either side of 20 – it was impossible to tell which. One of these had a baby at her breast. Further away, in the shadows inside the hut, Emma could just make out another woman, older than the rest, with a hard, thin face.

These pale, undernourished ghosts watched the three people approach. They seemed too uninterested to be surprised by the presence of strangers. Their faces gave nothing away. Emma remembered Anne telling her how famine victims await death, while the dead await the hyenas, and she shivered despite the heat.

Anne crouched down on the baked ground, between the discarded stalks of *qat*, while Adrian and Emma stood nearby. The heat was suffocating, as if Nature hadn't allowed enough oxygen for this small group to share. The nurse spoke to the women for several minutes, quietly, seemingly intent on not waking them from their slumbers. The women's replies were rare and monosyllabic. They kept their heads down, only ever glancing at their questioner out of the corner of their eyes. When she showed them the photographs of Mujtabaa, they barely looked at them.

'I've told them we have some food for them.' Anne smiled wryly. 'They're only slightly more interested.'

Adrian asked, 'What about Mujtabaa?'

'They're not saying. As you know, they don't really understand photographs, so we'll have to show him to them.'

They walked back to the truck.

Emma said, 'They don't seem very pleased to see us.'

'They can't afford to be hospitable in these surroundings. They're close to death – resigned to it. They know we can do little for them, and they have long since given up doing anything for themselves.'

'I thought maybe one of the two younger women might be Safia.'

'The Danakil covers a huge area. It's most unlikely.' The nurse briefly placed a hand on the young girl's arm. 'Even showing Mujtabaa to them probably won't result in anything.'

Anne drove the truck at a crawl through the deserted village to where the group of locals huddled in the shade. She reversed up to the shack. Adrian untied the canvas at the back. The women sat and stared at him through clouded, unseeing eyes. Anne gestured to them to approach, but no one moved.

'We'll have to lift everything out.'

The locals watched the white man wrestle the sacks of grain and the boxes of food to the edge of the back of the truck one by one. Anne, Emma or Ahmed then took them and lowered them to the ground, before carrying everything into the shadow of the hut. No one tried to help.

'First we'll give them some food.' Anne opened one of the boxes and took out a packet of porridge. She mixed this with milk in a bowl and handed it to the silent locals. She said, 'This isn't the answer, of course,' not wanting the young girl to have the wrong idea. 'It sounds harsh, but why bother to plant crops when food is free?'

'You surprise me, Anne,' said Adrian.

His daughter ignored him. 'But what else could we do for them?'

'We could educate them – feed their brains, give them a reason for living. And stop their despair.' To Emma, it didn't sound a very tempting option. She watched the two younger women eat the porridge, but the older women simply left their bowls resting on the ground.

'I'm going to have to feed them.' While she was doing this, Anne tried to explain to the women, in the most general of terms, who Mujtabaa was, and where he'd been, 'but it's almost impossible'.

Emma watched the women eat, slowly, almost with indifference. She felt separate from them. It was like they were on stage and she was in the auditorium. There was an invisible wall between them, as between the living and the dead. She stared at the shrivelled, wrinkled breasts of the women and the monkey-like face of the tiny baby, and for the first time in her life she became aware of the presence of death. She saw that these people had already died and she, on behalf of the living, had been called on to bear witness. She reached out and took her father's hand.

The nurse said, 'Now we can show them.'

Adrian, with the help of Ahmed, dragged the coffin to the back of the Toyota and lowered it to the ground. It wasn't heavy. The natives didn't watch them directly, although Emma noticed they were observing what was going on out of the corner of their eyes. It was like the three of them, and Ahmed, were performing some rather embarrassing act and it would have been impolite to stare. The two men carried the coffin into the shade. Anne and Adrian started to undo the wing nuts on the lid, while Emma stood by, fighting the butterflies which had suddenly arisen in her stomach. The nurse looked at her. 'Why don't you stand back a little, Emma?' Grateful for the suggestion, she did so.

Adrian removed the lid of the coffin, and Anne lifted back the cotton shroud. A wave of formaldehyde hit them in the face. The native women looked down at the grey, set face in silence. One of the women whispered something.

Emma was startled. 'Do they know him?'

Anne spoke to the natives, but they said nothing more. 'This woman was asking us who he is.'

'Doesn't sound promising,' Adrian muttered.

Two of the younger women were still staring at the dead man and speaking in low voices.

'They're saying a group went through here a few days ago. They were heading for Korem, I think.' Anne listened to the women, then asked them a question, but they ignored her.

'Could Safia have been with them?' Emma, still standing back from the open coffin, didn't try to hide the sudden hope in her voice.

'It's unlikely. And they're not very clear.'

'But aren't they interested? Don't they care about Mujtabaa?'

The young girl flushed, indignant.

'I don't believe they know him, Emma. And if they do know him, then he's no longer of any concern to them. They're only interested in their own survival now – and probably that's not of much interest to them either.'

'But after all he did for them!'

'It means little to them. I wasn't even able to explain to them where he's been. They don't understand. If we put a plate of porridge in front of them and say, "This is from Mujtabaa," they'd possibly understand that, but no more.'

'It's so unfair.'

'All that Mujtabaa achieved will not be wasted. It will benefit hundreds of thousands of people. It's just that no one will say, "This is thanks to Mujtabaa" or, "This food was sent to us by Mujtabaa". But it doesn't lessen his achievement in any way.'

When the group of locals watched them drive away, Emma felt she was leaving them alone to die, deserting them. They could have been cattle in a slaughterhouse, their eyes passive, their bodies listless, watching indifferently from the shade of the shack. She made an effort to wave cheerily as they left, but the action seemed false and there was no response.

About a hundred miles away, to the west, lay the purple blue peaks of the plateau, like the tracing of an ECG recording against the sky. Between their vehicle and the mountains, sheets of water seemed to dazzle.

'Is that really water over there?' she asked.

'It's a mirage, Emma. The only water you'll find is the sea, in the opposite direction. It's more than a hundred miles away.'

Nature had split its canvas in two, the desert and the sky. Each reverberated in the heat, gleaming white where they met, then changing to a cobalt blue overhead and a drab yellow at their feet. Particles of salt had settled like snow on the sand ridges. Small whirlwinds raced across the surface, then faded as if exhausted by this modest display of activity.

They spent the night not far from the village. Adrian and the two women sat together by a small camp fire, Ahmed a few feet

251

away, too diffident to join them. They looked up at the clear, star-studded sky above their heads. 'It's so beautiful!'

Anne looked at Emma, surprised. 'You can see that?'

'It's magical.'

'I'm pleased. You know, there are people who visit a desert and see only emptiness, and there are people who visit a desert and see that it has everything.'

'I'm one of the former,' said Adrian.

'I'd like to come back.' The young girl was poking at the fire with a stick, sending showers of embers into the darkness. 'Can I come and work with you at the health clinic, Anne?'

'It's hard work, you know.'

'I don't mind, truly I don't.' She was so earnest. 'Can I, Dad?'

'If that's what you really want to do, darling, then, yes, I think it's a wonderful idea. Maybe when you're 16 or 17, if that's all right with Anne.'

Later, as the fire burned down and the darkness and cold crept in closer around them, Emma said, 'We must try and find Safia – and her son. We must tell them what happened. We must.' She lifted her glasses and rubbed away the tears with the back of her hand. Adrian put a comforting arm round her.

The older woman warned against the young girl's enthusiasm. 'It won't be easy.'

'Why not?'

'You remember the camp at Korem? Even if they were in that group, even if they got that far – and it's possible they didn't – it would still be difficult to track them down. And they could have gone to Mek'ele or Weldiya, we don't know.'

Emma could remember the camp: the thousands of people lying amongst the flaps of canvas and the old blankets, an indescribable ghetto of tents and huts in a mist of smoke, with the stink of human waste and the incessant buzzing of flies. In spite of the horror of their surroundings, the people had been dignified and calm, yet also lifeless. She thought the place reeked of death, even though she was too young to know anything about death. She understood it would be difficult to find anyone there, but surely it wouldn't be impossible?

'I think we have to try, Anne.' Adrian hugged his daughter to him as he said this.

'I'm only trying to warn her against disappointment.' It sounded like a mild rebuke.

They slept on the floor of the four-wheel drive, having lain the coffin on the ground next to it. In the morning, Anne said, 'We must bury Mujtabaa. No one else is going to.'

Suddenly Emma wanted to cry. The landscape perfectly matched the desolation she felt within her. The two women looked down at the coffin, while Ahmed stared quizzically at them, baffled by the trouble these three white people were taking over a dead person. Adrian was busy taking photographs. 'We have to take something back for the media.'

'We don't have any flowers for him.'

Anne hugged the young girl. 'He won't mind, dear. He wouldn't expect any.'

Adrian said, 'I'll have to help Ahmed.'

'We must make sure Mujtabaa faces towards Mecca, Adrian, even though his people aren't strict Muslims.'

The two men dug a shallow grave a short distance from the truck. It was difficult work because of all the rocks and hard-baked sand. It took a long time. The sweat poured off them. Eventually, they carried the coffin across to the grave and lowered it in. The hole was barely deep enough. They shovelled sand and rock onto the top.

Emma said, 'It doesn't seem right just leaving him like this. I want to build a cairn.' She looked around, but there were only slabs of lava to be seen. 'I want people to know where he's buried.' She blinked angrily, fighting back the tears, then took off her glasses to wipe her eyes.

Anne took her hand. 'It is right, Emma. It may not seem right to you, but to Mujtabaa it will be. This is his home, this is what his friends would have done if they'd been here and if they'd had the strength. It's all he would have wanted.'

Adrian, busy taking photographs, said, 'It's definitely more appropriate than burying him in an English churchyard – as some people wanted to do.'

His daughter nodded, only half convinced. She consoled herself with the thought that she'd walk through the refugee camps at Mek'ele, Korem and Weldiya and find Mujtabaa's wife and son, and she'd sit down and tell them everything he'd achieved for them, and how he'd died trying to save her father. She could picture the pride and the joy on Safia's face, and how the young woman would hug her baby and promise the strangers from another country that she'd bring her child up knowing what a great father he had. He won't be forgotten, Emma told herself, she and Safia would make sure of that.

She started to build a cairn. Anne and Adrian helped. The three of them toiled under the watchful, disbelieving gaze of Ahmed who sat in the cabin of the truck, smoking. Finally, the cairn was finished. The two women and the man stood and stared at it. Emma started to cry. 'It's so pathetic. It's not a memorial at all.'

Adrian clasped his daughter's hand, and she nestled up against him. 'Moosh will love it, darling.'

She looked up. 'You think so, Dad – really?'

'I'm certain of it,' and he kissed her on the forehead.

'Shall we say a prayer?' The nurse did not believe cairns could take the place of direct entreaties to the Almighty.

Emma nodded. Adrian removed his hat and stood, hands clasped before him, with the two women. In silence, they prayed for their dead friend.

The young girl turned away and went across to the truck. They saw her delve into her bag on the front seat. She walked back to the grave, blushing, and Adrian felt this sudden burst of love for her, for her glasses and braces, for her vulnerability and awkwardness, for her difference.

'You mustn't laugh, Dad.' And she bent down and, near the base of the cairn, placed a TV remote control. 'It's an old one, from the attic.'

'He'll love that, Emma. He will genuinely love that. It's a beautiful thought.'

She reached into the pockets of her shorts, 'And I've also got him this.' She held out a small model of a sports car, and then placed that also on the cairn.

'He'll be able to go for rides in his "small truck" for all eternity,' whispered Anne.

They surrounded the remote control and the model car with rocks to make them more secure, before climbing back up into the four-wheel drive. As they lumbered away over the rough track, Emma stole a quick glance in the wing mirror and saw the lone cairn rising above the sand, a speck against the vast, sun-blackened lava desert. Already it was disappearing into the distance.

Mujtabaa had returned home.

Acknowledgements

The Walk had a long gestation, and many people have given me help, advice, support and encouragement over those years. Here are just a few of the many.

Nebiyou M Gossaye of the Ethiopian Community Centre in Melbourne. Jennifer Compton, Steve Roberts, Nikita Lalwani, Wayne Burrows, Rosie Waitt and Michael Hughes. Robin Yates for giving so generously of his time with advice on toy soldiers. And Chris Brazier of *New Internationalist* for his professional, perceptive, as well as empathetic editing.

For her reading of countless drafts and timeless forbearance, but above all for her helpful and thoughtful comments, special thanks, and love, to Elizabeth.

When researching the background to my novel, I read a great number of books on famine, Ethiopia, the Afar and Western charities. I'm grateful to all of their authors, but it would be impossible to mention every single title here. However, I found the following especially enlightening: Linda Polman's *War Games* and *The Crisis Caravan,* Catherine Hamlin's *Hospital by the River,* Wilfrid Thesiger's *Danakil Diary,* Dawit Wolde Giorgis's *Red Tears,* and Michael Maren's *Road to Hell.*

About the author

Peter Barry is the author of two highly praised novels: *I Hate Martin Amis et al* and *We All Fall Down.* He was born in England, brought up in Scotland, and is now living in Australia. He is married and has three children.